To:
*La gloriosa donna
della mia mente* x

PENGUIN BOOKS

Spider

Michael Morley is a former television presenter, producer and director, and is currently a Senior Executive Director for an international TV company. He has produced a number of award-winning documentaries, including *Murder in Mind* about Denis Nilsen, which led to a high-profile High Court battle with the government over the right to broadcast it. For that same documentary Michael often visited the FBI's Behavioral Science Unit in Quantico, and followed FBI agents working in the field. He was also able to interview a number of notorious serial killers.

Michael divides his time between homes in Derbyshire and the Netherlands. He is married and has three sons.

All the characters and events in this book are entirely fictitious and no parallels should be drawn with any real-life detectives, criminals or cases.

'A terrifying read that will keep you hooked' Simon Kernick

'*Spider* chillingly captures the harsh realities of a deteriorated mind' Lynda La Plante

'A chillingly vivid thriller. Don't read it alone in the middle of the night' Steven Bochco

Spider

MICHAEL MORLEY

PENGUIN BOOKS

PENGUIN BOOKS

Published by the Penguin Group
Penguin Books Ltd, 80 Strand, London WC2R ORL, England
Penguin Group (USA) Inc., 375 Hudson Street, New York, New York 10014, USA
Penguin Group (Canada), 90 Eglinton Avenue East, Suite 700, Toronto, Ontario, Canada M4P 2Y3
(a division of Pearson Penguin Canada Inc.)
Penguin Ireland, 25 St Stephen's Green, Dublin 2, Ireland
(a division of Penguin Books Ltd)
Penguin Group (Australia), 250 Camberwell Road, Camberwell, Victoria 3124, Australia
(a division of Pearson Australia Group Pty Ltd)
Penguin Books India Pvt Ltd, 11 Community Centre, Panchsheel Park, New Delhi – 110 017, India
Penguin Group (NZ), 67 Apollo Drive, Rosedale, North Shore 0632, New Zealand
(a division of Pearson New Zealand Ltd)
Penguin Books (South Africa) (Pty) Ltd, 24 Sturdee Avenue, Rosebank, Johannesburg 2196, South Africa

Penguin Books Ltd, Registered Offices: 80 Strand, London WC2R ORL, England

www.penguin.com

First published 2008

1

Set in 11.75/14 pt Monotype Garamond
Typeset by Rowland Phototypesetting Ltd, Bury St Edmunds, Suffolk
Printed in England by Clays Ltd, St Ives plc

ISBN: 978-0-141-03121-7

Acknowledgements

My thanks to all the people who got *Spider* into print:

Massimo Del Frate, one of Italy's greatest and nicest drama producers, helped plant the seeds for this novel over lunch. He, his assistant Benedetta, and no doubt many unnamed others, were also kind enough to help me with the accuracy of the Italian police sections.

My wife and children gave up our precious times together to let me write, rewrite and rewrite again – thank you for your love, patience and support.

Stephanie Jackson at Dorling Kindersley was generous enough to introduce me to all the right people – Steph, thanks for going the extra mile when you didn't really need to.

Luigi Bonomi should wear a badge saying 'best agent in the world' – thanks for your inspiration, guidance and commercial skills – no one does it better.

Richenda Todd helped enormously with the blunt, brutal and brilliant advice she gave me early on.

Beverley Cousins at Penguin blessed me with an abundance of painstaking care, eagle eyes, great imagination and wonderful humour – Bev, it's a true joy learning from you! Thanks also to Alex Clarke, Rob Williams, Liz Smith, Claire Phillips and the rest of the team at Penguin – all your hard work and skills are hugely respected and appreciated.

Thanks also to Leonid Zagalsky in Moscow, for lending me his surname, advising me on the Russian sections and reminding me why you shouldn't play drinking games with Russians!

Nicki Kennedy and Sam Edenborough at ILA deserve special mention for all the international help they've given me, as does Jack Barclay at Everett, Baldwin, Barclay.

I've been inspired over the years by meetings with psychological profilers such as the FBI's Roy Hazelwood and Robert Ressler, and the UK's Paul Britton and Mike Berry. Similarly, I learned much from distinguished senior police officers in the UK such as Don Dovaston, who did much to pioneer profiling into serial child murders, and Dan Crompton, a police chief who dared to open his doors to the media when most other locked them shut.

I'd also like to extend my gratitude to the late, great Home Office pathologist, Professor Stephen Jones, who taught me much about death and dignity.

My final thanks go to all those real-life heroes who hunt the real-life monsters – thank God you're all there.

He who fights with monsters might take care,
lest he thereby become a monster.
Friedrich Nietzsche

PROLOGUE
Saturday, 30 June

Georgetown, South Carolina

At the cool, dusky end of a sizzling day, barbecues spit flames while party laughter rolls along the banks of South Carolina's winding Black River.

Across town, in the sombre silence of Georgetown cemetery a solitary figure searches for the grave of someone once dear to him. He's travelled for days to make this pilgrimage and is already physically and emotionally drained. In his arms he carries a bundle of flowers, her favourite Rocky Shoals Spider Lilies. The first time he'd spoken to her, she'd been in a local park surrounded by thousands of them, and the flower had taken on a special meaning for both of them.

The headstones of the crowded cemetery bear names almost as old as America itself. Locals have been burying people in these plots since the country's first Spanish settlers grew old and died here, way back in the mid sixteenth century.

The grave he's looking for belongs to no one famous; there's no towering statue, no ornate family tomb to mark her place. Her anonymity disappeared only when her mutilated young body turned up bloated and decomposing in the Tupelo Swamp offshoot from the Black River, a stretch of ancient tumbling water that was once the conduit of commercial colonialism and the main waterway of South Carolina's plantations.

Finally, he sees her gravestone. Simple black marble, paid for by the community out of special grants for the poor. Engraved in gold lettering is her name: Sarah Elizabeth Kearney. But that wasn't what he called her. To him she was only ever 'Sugar' and he knew that to her he was only ever 'Spider'. Barely twenty-two years old, she was, like the Spider Lilies that had brought them together, just blossoming, just realizing her beauty and planting the seeds of her dreams.

Spider pulls out some weeds growing among the pebbles on her grave and lays down the big flowers. His mind slips back to their wonderful meeting twenty years ago this very day.

Sugar was so special.

She was his first.

The first he kidnapped.

The first he murdered.

PART ONE
Sunday, 1 July

I

San Quirico D'Orcia, Tuscany

Jack King's nightmare catapulted him from his sleep.

He sat bolt upright in bed and, despite being dazed and disorientated, he instinctively grabbed for his holstered gun. Only there was no gun, and there hadn't been one since he quit his job as an FBI profiler more than three years ago.

'Wake up!' urged his wife. 'Wake up, Jack! You're okay; you're just dreaming again, it's only a dream.'

But Jack wasn't okay. He was far from okay.

He tried to slow his breathing, get his heartbeat down to normal, but his head still fizzed with images: bleached-white bloodless corpses floating in the Black River – the buzz of flies around dismembered young limbs – bold type headlines announcing the Black River Killer's latest kill. The horror show ran like some grainy speeded-up old movie that he'd seen far too many times.

Nancy got out of bed and switched the lights on. 'These nightmares of yours, they're scaring me to death. Jack, you've really got to go and see someone.'

Most days Jack looked as though he was living the dream, owning and running a small boutique hotel in a Tuscan village that time had barely altered and crime had hardly touched. But some nights – well, some nights he just couldn't keep up the pretence. And this sure as hell was one of them.

Jack squinted into the ugly brightness of the bedroom lights, sweat soaked his bare chest and ran down his back.

'Did you hear me? *Jack?*'

The visions had gone but now his head was filled with sounds: women screaming in pain, their desperate cries for help echoing out from the dark pits of his memory, and finally the unmistakable sound of razor-sharp steel slicing into human flesh.

Jack let out a hot, slow breath. 'I hear you, Nancy. Just give me a minute.'

It had been three years since his burnout, and despite a change of continents and lifestyles, the past and all its horrors were still haunting him.

Maybe his wife was right. Maybe he finally had to see someone.

2

Georgetown, South Carolina

Sometimes, late at night, when he's teetering on the edge of sleep, his mind soft with secret thoughts and emotions, Spider is able to turn the clock back and return to his favourite time.

The first time.

Right now, with so many exciting things happening to him, he's keen to go back, eager to revisit the moments that have made him what he is.

Lying on his bed, his special bed, the room is dark and his eyes lightly closed. Soon months, years and decades flash by, until it is twenty years ago.

He's in sunny Georgetown, down on the Harborwalk at the waterfront. A young woman strolls past, happy and carefree. She's slim bodied, dark-haired, respectable and simply dressed in a pink T-shirt, stylishly faded jeans and trainers. It's her week off work and she's chilling out, oblivious to the world, oblivious to the man she's just magnetised to her.

Spider watches her dine, alone.

Watches her go to her apartment above the baker's shop, alone.

And for days he watches her living there, alone.

Alone – and vulnerable. Just as he hoped.

Sarah Kearney never sees him, Spider's very careful about that, so careful he's almost invisible. But he's around. Always there. There, brushing by her in supermarkets, as she grocery shops for one. There, as she queues in the cinema for her solitary seat at the latest romcom. There, as she browses in the bookshop, and finally buys the cookery book, with its special recipes just for one.

The memories are delicious. Spider savours every second of his mental feast. My, oh my, remembering the old ones, especially the first one, is almost as good as planning the new ones, the next one.

But Sarah had been sweet. As sweet as Sugar.

Spider's heart races as he recalls how he followed her in his old Chevy as she caught a bus out to Landsford, a 400-acre state park off US-21 out towards Richburg. He had been his usual invisible self as she'd sauntered around the nineteenth century canals, sat a while near an old lock-keeper's cottage and finally headed out of the crowds to a solitary spot near the Catawba River.

Twenty years later he could still remember every word they'd spoken.

You never forget your first kill. Not a single second of it.

The air had been fresh with pine and grass, the sun hot and high, and Sugar, well Sugar had been sitting sweetly on a carpet of white flowers, cherishing one of the massive spiky blooms in the cup of her hand.

Pretty as a picture.

And then he'd shown himself. Confident and calm, polite and unthreatening. Just like he'd planned. Just like he'd dreamed.

'They're beautiful,' he said, walking confidently towards her. 'What are they?'

For a second she seemed startled, then she spoke up, just like her daddy had taught her. 'Lilies. Rocky Shoals Spider Lilies.' There was a warm drawl in her hesitant voice. A voice he'd craved to hear. A voice he knew he would soon be the last to listen to.

They sat and talked; he made her laugh, flattered her with compliments and even made her blush a little. It was a perfect afternoon. Just as he'd hoped.

They had coffee in the crowded café and he told her how he worked as a company auditor, a stuffy job that he hated. He had to come to the park for some space and air.

She knows just what he meant; she loved to be outside too.

When it got to the point where they should go, he'd told her that he'd had a lovely time, in fact he couldn't remember the last time he enjoyed himself so much. She blushed again and said she'd had fun too. It damn near broke his heart that he had to leave, had to deliver some boring accounts to some boring businessmen east of Georgetown.

She looked disappointed. He was sure of that. She'd *wanted* to spend more time with him, he could remember that clearly. In fact, looking back, it was almost as though she'd picked him, as much as he'd picked her.

Don't people always say that in the end it is always the women who do the choosing?

They'd been together for almost three hours when they finally passed through the park's gates and, looking back now, well it seems incredible, but if truth be known, for a moment he'd thought of not going through with it.

That made him smile.

Not gone through with it? How could he have thought that? My, how things would have been different if he'd simply said goodbye and gone his own way.

3

San Quirico D'Orcia, Tuscany

Neither Jack nor Nancy could get back to sleep. That had become routine too. His wife was the only person he could bring himself to talk to, the only one who could even begin to understand what had happened to him, and how it had left him.

The real nightmare had started long before the nocturnal ones. Overworking and over-caring had led to Jack's collapse at JFK, after a cold case conference in LA, right in the middle of the hunt for BRK and just days before the birth of their son.

Now, he and Nancy went over the ground again, searching for a way to find some peace: Jack's weeks in intensive care, unable to speak or walk properly, afraid that he'd die or be crippled for the rest of his life; Nancy's fears that he'd let his job ruin their marriage, her thoughts of leaving him, taking Zack to her parents' house and starting over again. As usual, they didn't leave a stone unturned. And as usual they didn't make any real progress.

Nancy King was tall, trim and tough. The daughter of a Marine, she knew how to deal with a crisis. Or at least she thought she did. After Jack's crash and burn, they'd seen La Casa Strada on an Internet auction and she'd just known that they had to buy that hotel and start over in a new country.

A new beginning. A new way of life.

That's what she'd said they'd needed, and that was what she'd been determined they'd have. Only now, well now, it seemed that new beginning was on hold.

And *on hold* was something Nancy wasn't going to settle for.

Dawn was filtering through the shuttered windows when she finally got back to the prickly suggestion that Jack seek some professional help. 'The Bureau gave you a number for a psychiatrist in Florence, a good one who said she'd see you at the drop of a hat. Ring her in the morning.'

'The female trickcyclist –,' Jack tried to joke his way out of it, '– you really think I need to see this shrink?'

His wife raised an eyebrow. 'Honey, we both know you need to see a shrink. Now please get it done, yeah?'

He gave in. 'Yeah, I'll get it done.' He sounded defeated, but even as he spoke, he felt slightly better at hearing himself admit that after all this time there might just be some help on its way. 'You want some breakfast?' he asked, standing in front of an open window in his boxers, patting his belly.

Behind him, Nancy could see the sun shimmering and rising across the velvet green valley. Below them, she could hear their chef, arriving in the kitchen, opening his giant fridges for supplies and starting his routine preparations before his staff arrived. She loved this place, loved her new beginning and she so wanted Jack to love it too. 'Paolo's in, he'll cook us eggs, maybe some pancetta as well.'

Jack leaned over his wife and kissed her. 'I'll get coffee too, I think we both need it.'

She watched him pull on tracksuit pants and a T-shirt. Despite his emotional vulnerability, he still looked every inch the college athlete she'd fallen in love with. 'Eleven years, Jack King. In a few days' time we'll have been married for eleven years. How did it all fly by so fast?'

Jack didn't have the answer. 'I guess the good times always seem to go the quickest and the bad times stick around too long.'

He kissed her again and she squeezed his hand reassuringly. 'Don't worry, honey, everything will be better soon.'

Jack smiled at her, and as he headed for the kitchen he tried hard not to dwell on the fact that July the eighth, the day of his wedding anniversary, was also the day the Black River Killer had claimed his sixth and youngest victim.

4

Georgetown, South Carolina

Much in the manner that old men remember their first love affair, Spider finds himself comforted and aroused by his recollections of his first kill. Eyes still shut, his mind almost slipping into sleep, he rolls back twenty years and remembers the last moments of his momentous meeting with Sarah Kearney.

The summer sun and sweet floral smells of the South Carolina parkland sting his senses once more; he and Sugar stand inches apart, a delicious awkwardness at the end of their first meeting.

'Looks like rain,' he'd said, glancing up at the battleship-grey cloud heading their way. 'You got a ride?'

Sugar had shaken her head. Her pretty black hair swished as she did. 'No, I came out by bus.'

Of course you did, my darling, of course you did.

'Where you going? Can I drop you somewhere?'

'Hey, would you mind givin' me a ride to Georgetown? It's not outta ya way or nothin'. In fact, you go right through it and I can show ya a short cut an' all.'

'Course not. Nothing would give me more pleasure.'

The walk back to his car had been so exciting. Anticipation had crackled through his veins like a broken electric cable in a thunderstorm. But he hadn't forgotten himself. Oh no, he'd been the perfect gentleman, right up to the end.

He'd opened the passenger door for her, and closed it carefully once she was safely inside.

'Why thanks, that's really nice of you.'

What happened next had been the best bit. He'd pictured it dozens of times, even acted it out in his garage to make sure it would work properly.

'First rule of the road, better safe than sorry, always buckle up.' He'd said it with a smile and pointed at her seat belt.

She'd laughed at him.

Fancy that, she'd actually laughed at him. 'You're a real gent, aren't ya,' she'd said, 'real kind to ladies, that's pretty unusual these days.'

Pretty unusual. He smiled again at the recollection, she'd certainly been right there.

Then she'd done as he asked. Good little Sugar had clunked the seat belt into place and started to sit right back to make herself comfortable with her new gentleman friend.

Poor Sugar.

She'd never made it to comfortable.

As she tossed back her hair, Spider had made his move. Two fingers, bent double at the knuckles,

driven deep into her throat, either side of the windpipe. An unbreakable choke-hold.

Just remembering it made him tingle. He flexed
his hand and relived the excitement of pressing harder
and harder, pushing her neck back against the head-
rest and blocking off her airway.

Sugar had struggled but the seat belt had pinned
her back – just as he'd figured it would. She clawed
at his arm, but he'd thought of that as well; the
sleeves of his wool jacket just snapped off her nasty
fingernails.

He'd thought of everything. He always did. Always
would.

And that final kiss? Wow! He'd never forget it.

His lips to hers at the very moment he choked the
final breath from her body and caught it in his mouth.
Like he was swallowing her soul.

He breathes out. Feels her warmth again, feels that
part of her, still inside him – maybe even attached to
his own soul.

God it had been exciting. The most exciting,
wonderful moment of his life.

And then she had been his. Truly his.

Was it really twenty years ago that all that happened? He could hardly believe it.

My, how time flies so fast.

It only seemed like yesterday that he'd looked
across at Sugar's dead body in the passenger seat and
realized that they were joined for ever, as surely as if
they were man and wife.

Spider opens his eyes in the dullness of the present day and smiles. Sugar had indeed been special. It was so good to have her back in his life.

5

Georgetown, South Carolina

Fifteen-year-old Gerry Blake and his younger cousin Tommy Heinz couldn't believe what they were seeing. Day or night, they regularly cut through the graveyard. The old tombstones and creepy church had never held any fears for them.

Until now.

Today, they were in a rush to get to their friend Chuck's and go fishing with his dad in his boat out on the Black River. They both skidded to a halt on the rough shale path halfway through the churchyard; Tommy stumbled to his knees.

'Muuutherfucker!' screeched Gerry, drawing out the obscenity as he'd heard rappers do on MTV.

Tommy was already on his feet, panting like a dog, ready to run for the hills. He'd be out of there just as soon as Gerry came to his senses and got his ass into gear. For a second though, both boys instinctively huddled shoulder-to-shoulder and simply stared. What they saw was already branded into their memories for the rest of their lives.

The grave in front of them had been dug up.

A cheap pine coffin was splintered open and the

skeleton of a young woman in a soil-stained dress was upright, resting against the headstone. Blackened bony arms and legs dangled from the filthy cloth. But the image that would haunt the teenagers until their own dying days was that of the head. Or rather, the space where the head should have been.

6

Florence, Tuscany

The psychiatrist in Florence had been as good as her word. Jack had rung her cell phone and, despite being surprised by the call, *Dottoressa* Elisabetta Fenella had agreed to see him later that very day. The power of the FBI really did cross continents. Jack suspected the big bucks that the Bureau had no doubt promised to pay probably also had some sway.

The ninety-minute rail journey to Florence went quickly, mainly because of the beauty of the country-side that rolled past the dusty window of the airless, rundown and overcrowded carriage. He found himself mesmerized by the vineyards and olive plantations that battled for the best terraces across steep hillsides, drawn to the sunlight but scratching for patches of precious shade. In some places, the sun had scorched the ploughed fields into slabs, making the earth look as if it had been fashioned out of hunks of grey stone. In wetter valleys, golden stone cottages rose from fertile fields like farmhouse bread baking in an oven.

And Tuscany certainly was an oven.

Jack found himself bathed in sweat as the train

started to slow down into Florence. He blamed the lack of air-con, but he knew it was something else. Second thoughts.

Second thoughts about facing up to whatever was inside him, whatever memories were powerful and dark enough to scare him even when he was asleep.

The facts, the cold hard facts, came tumbling into his head. The Black River Killings had broken him.

Those weren't just his words, it was what every crime reporter in America had written after his collapse at JFK.

He'd failed to catch a man who'd murdered at least sixteen young women, and who would murder more. He'd failed.

They'd written that too. Written it so many times that it had stopped hurting. Or so he told everyone.

Maybe it was best if he stayed broken. Broken didn't mean completely unworkable or totally destroyed, it just meant he wasn't as good as he once was. Maybe seeing a shrink would only make things worse.

His head filled with static, a sort of tinnitus, a hissing noise, and then it became clearer, not hissing, cutting. The noises were back; slashing noises. Steel on skin. He covered his ears and closed his eyes.

The sounds slowly slipped away. Had he heard them, or imagined them? Maybe the train pulling into the station, the wheels on the track?

He took his hands away and opened his eyes.

Silence.

The train had stopped and the carriages were empty.

It was decision time.

7

San Quirico D'Orcia, Tuscany

San Quirico D'Orcia nestles in a stunning valley east of Montalcino, a third of the way along the breathtakingly beautiful route most tourists take to Montepulciano. A kilometre in the opposite direction, on the rising, winding road from San Quirico to Pienza, is the dramatic cypress-lined hillside that Ridley Scott used for the poignant scenes of the wife and child waiting for the return of Maximus in the film *Gladiator*.

The town's historic walls are broken and have lost much of their beauty. Behind them though stand buildings made of a glorious golden stone, reminding Nancy of the rough chunks of sweet honeycomb that she craved when she was a kid.

La Casa Strada lies on the very edge of the town walls and was once an olive oil business. That was until the mid-seventies, when a blisteringly hot summer brought the locusts of bankruptcy to many farms in the valleys of Tuscany. The owners, Laura and Sylvio Martinelli, gave up and moved in with family in Cortona. Sixty-year-old Sylvio got a job driving taxis, while sixty-five-year-old Laura turned her hand to baking *Torta della Nonna* for a local shop. Since then, their former home and work buildings had been modernized and extended beyond recognition; only the magnificent view over the rolling hills of Val D'Orcia remained unaltered and unalterable.

Nancy was winding herself slowly into her working day. She'd dropped Zack at a friend's house for a play day and was about to go through her planning routines for the week and coming month. She was relieved that the three-year-old had finally settled into his daily routine. A year earlier she used to endure terrible scenes at the International nursery in Pienza with him refusing to be left. Zack would cry and scream, clutching on to her shoulders or dress to prevent her putting him down. Worst of all, when she walked outside, she would see his tear-streaked face pressed against the window, begging her not to leave him. Nowadays though, Zack was 'a big boy', a 'good boy', and he understood that mommy and daddy needed to work during the day.

Nancy stuck her head through the kitchen door where the chefs were finishing the last of the breakfasts and shouted 'Good morning, everyone!', then waited for the replying chorus of '*Buon giorno*' before letting the door flap shut again.

She noticed that their local handyman, Guido, was in there fixing a troublesome ventilator hood that served Paolo's gas-fired eight-burner oven. For some time, their temperamental chef had been pressing Nancy for a new range, like the one his second cousin in Rome had. But Paolo would have to wait, cash was tight at the moment and she'd told him that until the summer's takings were in, he'd have to make do with the 'bargains' they might pick up from local catering auctions. Nancy smiled to herself. In truth, Guido had now fixed so many of the appliances that neither she nor Jack could really regard them as bargains any more.

There were other things that needed fixing too. Months back, part of the far end of the garden terrace had dramatically slipped away and created a sharp fall on to the next terrace and an intriguing hole in the hillside. Carlo reckoned there could be an old water well in there, while Paolo conjured up more exotic possibilities by pointing out that the area used to be a fortified Medici stronghold. Whatever it was, it was an eyesore, a nuisance and maybe even a danger. Any day soon, one of Carlo's friends was coming to do what he promised would be an inexpensive job of landscaping over it.

'Morning, Maria,' said Nancy, as their twenty-year-old receptionist finally arrived at her desk.

'Good morning, Mrs King,' said Maria Fazing. Her grumpy American owner had banned her from using her native Italian. Nancy insisted that as foreign tourists were their main target customers, she should always begin conversations in English. Maria put up with it because one day she would enter Miss Italia, then Miss World, and would eventually be grateful to have been forced to learn English. Or at least that's what she told herself.

Nancy checked the computer, then the answer-phone, and updated the list of room bookings. She also added four more people to that evening's dinner reservations and then checked their own website for e-mail enquiries. There were some requests for menus, a couple of letters in Italian that Nancy printed off for Maria to reply to, and someone wanting a quote for a fifth-wedding-anniversary dinner.

Maria was on the phone to some potential guests so Nancy had to wait to hand over the e-mail print-offs. She glanced down at a copy of *La Nazione*. The front-page headline screamed '*Omicidio!*' and carried a photo of a pretty dark-haired young woman called Cristina Barbuggiani. Nancy had also seen the girl's picture on TV bulletins and had heard staff talking about how her body had been chopped up and thrown in the sea. She turned away, letting out a long sigh, sad to realize that even here, in the most beautiful place she had ever lived, there was no escape from murder.

8

Florence, Tuscany

Jack stepped from the silence of the empty train into the noise and swelter of midday Florence, a broiling city of bustling bodies and blaring traffic. His mind was still clogged with the dregs of his nightmare when he reached the office of *Dottoressa* Elisabetta Fenella. The building stood just off Piazza San Lorenzo in the city's most famous market district and was over-looked by the majestic stone presence of the Basilica di San Lorenzo, a frontless fourth-century church, rebuilt by the Medicis.

Jack slipped from the scorching sunlight of the street into the cool shade of the building's entrance-way. He took a cramped, old-fashioned, iron-gated lift to the third floor and was ushered by a demure receptionist into a marble-floored, high-ceilinged consultation room. Overhead, two fans that probably predated Florence itself spun gracefully but point-lessly, batting currents of hot air from one side of the room to the other but doing nothing to cool the place. An antique oak desk squatted in a far corner, overlooked by a crucifix on the far wall and weighed down by papers and silver-framed photographs of a large extended family. Jack picked one up and studied a glamorous dark-haired woman in her late thirties, shoulder to elegant shoulder with a much older man.

The door behind him opened and the woman in the picture frame looked startled to find him at her desk.

'*Signore* King?' she asked, her voice betraying her disapproval of his nosiness.

'Yes,' answered Jack, embarrassed at being caught snooping. 'Forgive me, old police habits die hard.'

'Please.' She gestured towards two creamy cotton settees arranged either side of a square glass-topped coffee table.

'Thanks for seeing me at such short notice, I appreciate it.' Jack offered his hand and as she shook it he noticed a gold and diamond wedding ring that would cost an FBI field officer three months' salary.

'You're welcome. I'm afraid it was either today, or I wouldn't have been able to fit you in for several months.' Elisabetta Fenella put a brown file down on the coffee table and Jack noticed his name. He was *on file*.

No doubt the FBI had shipped it to her, FedExed her all the gory details about his burnout, his failure to cope with the pressure of his workload, and she'd had it waiting there, gathering years of dust but ever ready for the moment he inevitably cracked up and came calling.

The thought slapped the wind out of him.

Dottoressa Fenella cut to the chase. 'Your office

called me, what – something like two years ago? So, why did you choose *now* to ask to see me?'

It was a good question. And he wanted to give a good answer, wanted to come right out and say that he needed her intervention, needed her skills to hold back the evil that drowned him every night. But he couldn't. The words simply wouldn't come.

'Let me help you, Jack.' She saw his eyes fall on the file again. 'Read it if you like.' She pushed it towards him. 'I'm sure there's nothing in there that you don't already know.'

Jack stared at the file but didn't touch it. It was a test of strength and trust. She would hold nothing back, providing he was strong enough to do the same.

But was he?

A white flash went off in his head, as white as the tiles of the morgue, as white as the drained skin of more than a dozen dead women.

'Okay,' said Jack. 'Let's get on with this. I've wasted enough of your time already.'

9

Days Inn Grand Strand, South Carolina

Once Spider had taken what he wanted from the cemetery, he'd headed straight back to his rented room at the Days Inn Grand Strand, only minutes from Myrtle Beach International.

The act of grave-robbing had not given him a sleepless night. Far from it. It had exhilarated and exhausted him as much as any imaginable sexual marathon, and afterwards he'd slipped effortlessly into a full night's sleep.

Spider stirs now in his hotel bed and looks around the room to get his bearings. He wonders how the crummy joint managed to get one star, let alone two. Outside he can hear kids shouting and laughing as they jump in the pool and he longs for them to be quiet. He needs food, drink and much more rest, but such comforts will have to wait. Escape is now the only priority.

Although he is more than thirty miles from the desecrated grave, for him it's still too close for comfort. Despite the incredible desire to stay around, to mix with the locals and listen to them talk about what has happened, he knows he must leave. By now the cops are certain to be crawling all over the cemetery, and that in turn means that the story might be on every radio and television station. He's been scrupulously careful, and he will be even more careful before leaving the room, but despite all his precautions he's aware that there's always a chance that someone will see him, even if he hasn't seen them.

Spider uses the toilet and then takes a long, hot shower. There are two white bath towels. He takes one, partly dries himself and sits on the bed, wrapping it around him.

He notices that he's breathing hard and his hands are shaking. Even after all these years, after all the killings, he still gets 'the day-after shakes'. He knows it is only anxiety, the start of a panic attack. This is the time when the fear of being caught is at its most extreme, and experience has taught him that the further away from the crime scene he gets, the quicker the anxiety disappears.

When he feels a little better he goes back to the bed and sits down, flicking through the TV stations with a remote, zapping channels for any news from Georgetown. WTMA is finishing a warning about tropical depressions and hurricanes and WCSC is in the middle of a report on a Mount Pleasant woman who drowned while boating off Sullivan's Island. He flicks over to WCBD and instantly recognizes the video footage of the cemetery. After a few seconds a Hispanic-looking reporter appears on screen, talking to a news anchor back in the main studio: 'Here in this close-knit community of Georgetown there is widespread shock and outrage today, at what most locals regard as not just an unholy act but one of monstrous repulsiveness. Camera crews and journalists have been kept outside the cemetery, but as you'll have seen from our pictures, shot from the public highway, the desecration seems to be frenzied and extreme. There's speculation here that it could be the work of sick trophy-hunters or else of a highly disturbed individual who has some kind of mental illness that draws him to the graves of murder victims. The office of Georgetown's chief of police has today categorically stated that at this stage they see no reason to connect the incident with the so-called Black River Killer, the serial murderer believed to have been responsible for the death of Sarah Elizabeth Kearney.'

Spider is both amused and irritated. Does the press really believe such nonsense? Don't they have the intelligence to realize what is really going on? He doubts that the police are so stupid. Surely they won't misunderstand the significance of what has been done?

He lies back on the bed, his hair wet on the pillow. Next to him is the other bath towel, wrapped delicately around the object of his affection. The decapitated skull of Sarah Kearney. Spider turns on his left side and with his right hand gently strokes his fingers backwards and forwards across the smooth bone. Has it really been twenty years? Twenty years since he shared the intimacy of her death, and the secret comforts of her cool body?

'We'll have to go soon, my little Sugarbaby,' he says softly, kissing her lightly in the middle of the forehead. 'Sleep just a little longer, but then you and I will have to go. There's still much for us both to do.'

10

San Quirico D'Orcia, Tuscany

Nancy King was relaxing on the shaded terrace with her first cappuccino of the morning. On her lap was Paolo's new summer menu. She was pleased to see most of her old favourites were still there, including a choice of classic *La Pasta Fatta in Casa*, with an amazingly simple tomato sauce to go with the fantastic home-made linguini or tagliatelli. How did the Italians squeeze so much flavour out of so few ingredients? She put the menu down, took a sip of her coffee and squinted out across the sun-hazed valleys. The Tuscan countryside undulated like a series of green waves crashing towards some out-of-sight shoreline. The powder-blue sky was cloudless. Nancy felt more relaxed and alive than she'd done for years. Tuscany had certainly been the right place to choose to start over again.

Jovanna, one of the two waitresses setting clean white linen on the tables for lunch, clacked her shoes across the paved patio and wooden outer decking, breaking Nancy's moment of meditation.

'*Scusi, Signora,*' she said respectfully. 'There is someone in reception for you. It is a police officer.'

Nancy held her breath. She pushed her bare feet into her backless shoes, and strode quickly from the sun-toasted terrace to the cool of the hotel reception. In those brief seconds every imaginable disaster flashed through her mind. Had Jack collapsed again? Had Zack been hurt? What had brought an Italian police officer, unannounced, to her doorstep?

Nancy had expected to see a policeman, a black-haired carabiniere with a five o'clock shadow and trademark white gloves. Instead, a beautiful young woman in an immaculately tailored charcoal-grey business suit stood waiting in the marbled floor reception area.

'*Buon giorno. Signora* King?'

'*Si.*' Nancy hesitated, her heart skipping a beat.

'*Buono. Sono Ispettore Orsetta Portinari. Ho bisogno . . .*'

'In English, tell me in English!' snapped Nancy, unable to hold back her fears.

'I'm sorry,' said the policewoman. She took a beat, and then effortlessly switched languages. 'I am Inspector Orsetta Portinari and I have been sent by my boss Massimo Albonetti in Rome. My boss and Mr King worked together some time ago and now *Direttore* Albonetti has sent me here to see if Mr King would help us.'

Nancy's fears came down a notch. 'You mean there's nothing wrong? Nothing's happened to Jack, or to my son?'

The young inspector looked confused. 'I am sorry. I am afraid I do not understand. Your son?'

Nancy brushed hair from her face. 'You haven't come here to tell me something bad about my husband, or my son Zack? They're both all right?'

Orsetta shook her head and smiled reassuringly. 'No. They are both all right.'

Nancy leant on the black granite counter of the reception desk and sighed with relief. She managed to compose herself before turning back to the detective. 'Strange how you always think the worst when you see a police officer – even if you've been married to one.'

'*Sì*,' said Orsetta.

'Jack's not here at the moment, he'll be gone all day. What exactly is this about?'

Orsetta's face gave away the fact that she wasn't going to offer Nancy a straight answer. 'With respect, Mrs King, it is police business and I would rather discuss it directly with your husband.'

Ten years of marriage to a cop had taught Nancy to know when she was being fobbed off. Similarly, she knew that cops ducked questions only when the case was important. Her mind flashed back to Maria's newspaper. 'Is it about that murdered girl?'

The detective frowned. 'I really need to speak directly to your husband. Perhaps you have a cell phone number for him?'

Nancy's eyes blazed. It seemed Italian cops were every bit as pushy and rude as American ones. 'I'd rather not do that. Police business is not our business any longer. Now, would you like to leave a message or not?'

Orsetta's face flushed. 'This is my card,' she said, slapping it down on the cold counter. 'It is an urgent police matter. Have him call me as soon as you see him.' She glared at Nancy. 'This is not a request, *Signora*, it is an instruction.'

For a second the two women locked eyes. Orsetta smiled as sweetly as she could, then elegantly turned on her immaculate heels and left.

I I

Days Inn Grand Strand, South Carolina

The lady who answers phones at UMail2Anywhere proves as good as her word. Within an hour of the call, Stan, the delivery boy, turns up with a length of bubble wrap, four cardboard boxes, three sheets of brown paper and a roll of sticky tape. Spider appears at the door seemingly with car oil all over his hands, gets the kid to dump the gear on his bed, then quickly washes and tips him for his trouble. He's just scrubbed the skull clean of prints and isn't about to add fresh ones to the parcel he intends to send Sugar home in.

Stan hangs around by the pool, drinking lime coke and checking out girls, while his big-tipping client takes his time wrapping some fragile cargo that has to be shipped air mail that afternoon. He seems a nice guy, not many customers give a tip these days, let alone ask his name and thank him. Waiting around for a real gent like that is no problem. The dude has even said he can find him some private work, running errands for a bit more than the basic he gets at UM2A. Says he might have something for him later that day, if he takes care of this package first, and does a real good job of looking after it.

Spider pulls on cotton gloves. Not long ago he'd read that cops could somehow pick up prints from inside rubber gloves. He isn't sure it's true, but doesn't intend taking any chances. When he's finished, he'll take the gloves with him. Meanwhile, he uses a Swiss Army penknife to cut off a length of the bubble wrap and forces it tight inside Sarah Kearney's skull. The plastic bulges through the eye sockets and jaw giving a grotesque illusion of membranes, muscles and even life. He wraps another sheet around the outside, holds it down with tape and places the whole thing inside one of the smaller boxes Stan brought him. He seals it with tape and wraps it in a sheet of brown paper. He cuts more bubble wrap, tapes it around the box and places it snugly inside one of the bigger boxes. He runs sticky tape around all the joints and carefully covers the outside with the remaining two sheets of brown paper. He takes a black felt-tip marker from his case and writes the delivery address in nondescript capital letters that contain no clue to his true handwriting. For a second he pauses and takes a slow, satisfying sniff of the pen. It smells of pear drops. Spider smiles at the irony of it all. Who would have thought that innocent reminders of childhood sweets could come to mind when you're handling the decapitated head of a woman you killed twenty years ago?

He flattens the spare boxes and puts them and the tape and bubble wrap inside his suitcase. Spider then carries the box out to the landing and places it at the foot of the front door. His room is on the second floor of the three-storey motel block and from the door he can clearly see Stan. The kid is checking out some teenagers in bikinis so tiny you could floss your teeth with them.

'Hey, Stan!' he shouts.

The delivery boy breaks from his adolescent day-dreaming and raises a hand to acknowledge the call. By the time Stan appears on the landing, Spider has removed his gloves, tucked a cell phone between his left ear and shoulder blade and is writing something on a motel notepad while seemingly talking to someone.

'Yeah, sure, I finished the work about an hour ago and I should be able to get the accounts faxed to you sometime this afternoon. Don't you worry about it.'

Stan can see the guy is real busy. He nods at the parcel on the floor and asks, 'It's ready to go?'

'Just a second,' says Spider to the party on the phone, covering the mouthpiece as he answers Stan. 'Yeah, you can take it. Thanks again for waiting. I'll call your number later for the other job.'

'Sure, no problem,' says Stan, picking up the box, smiling and walking away.

Spider carries on pretending to talk. He watches the boy until he is out of sight and then ducks back into the motel room. So far, so good, his plan is going well. He takes a bottle of ink from his suitcase and deliberately spills it over the bedsheets and pillows. Quickly, he uses the room towels to mop up the mess, then hauls the whole bundle into the shower and turns on the taps. Next, he calls room service and tells them he's tripped and spilt ink everywhere but is soaking the sheets to get the stain out. A Mexican maid is at his room quicker than a 100-metre sprinter on steroids. She shouts at him in Spanish but settles down when he gives her ten dollars and helps her squeeze out the soaking linen and put it into her cart. He feels better knowing that within ten minutes all the sheets, quilt cover, pillows and towels that may contain traces of his DNA will be in a boil wash in the laundry room.

Spider double-checks the bedroom to ensure he hasn't left anything behind. He grabs his belongings, locks the door and heads down to the twenty-four-hour reception desk to settle his bill. He pretends to be embarrassed about 'the accident' and is polite and apologetic. After a call is made to Housekeeping, he's told that everything is okay and there won't be any extra charge. He thanks the clerk, pays cash and leaves to collect his silver Chevy Metro hire car from the forecourt. He's only minutes away from the Thrifty Rent-a-Car depot on Jetport Road, where he'd used a false driver's ID to hire the eighty-dollars-a-day special and again had paid cash. Good old untraceable cash, the international currency of crime.

It takes an age for the attendant to get to him, then like everyone else, he objects furiously when he gets stung for the petrol surcharge. He's still complaining when he catches the shuttle over to the airport's main terminal. Spider's first stop is the Delta ticket desk, where he pays cash for his one-way trip out of South Carolina. He checks in his suitcase, collects his boarding pass and heads off for something to eat.

He has plenty of time before his flight.

There's one last call to make. One more piece of important business to take care of before he can catch his plane out of Myrtle.

12

Florence, Tuscany

Were the nightmares always the same? Was he frightened of going to sleep after them? During the waking hours did he have flashbacks of what happened in the dreams? The questions came thick and fast but Jack didn't duck any of them, not even when Elisabetta Fenella asked if he was depressed, tearful, overly emotional or even impotent.

Eventually, she managed to persuade him to take her through his childhood. Unlike that of those he had pursued in his professional life, his own past contained no trauma, no abuse or deprivation, just the solid love and support of two parents who had been teenage sweethearts. They stayed married for more than thirty years, inseparable until five years earlier when a hit-and-run driver killed his father soon after his retirement. Jack Snr had been a New York City cop all his working life and his mother, Brenda, had been a night sister at the Mount Sinai Medical Center near Central Park. His mother had died alone, in her sleep, just over three years ago of a heart attack. Jack still thought it was probably as much to do with being broken-hearted as with the high cholesterol that doctors believed had clogged her arteries.

'Would it be fair to say . . .' said Fenella, checking dates in her file, '. . . that just before your collapse, the stress was at its peak?'

'Stress comes with the job,' said Jack. 'I'm not sure I felt significantly pressured then.'

'But if we look at the timings, we see your mother dies, and then weeks later you collapse at an airport. You think they are entirely unconnected?'

Jack hated easy-fit psychology. Life was full of shitty coincidences and sometimes lots of good things happened all at once, sometimes you got dealt several crappy hands one after the other. 'I don't for one moment buy the idea that my mother's death in any way contributed to my illness,' he said, sounding slightly annoyed. 'Of course I loved her, of course it saddened me deeply, but I'd dealt with that. I'd understood that part of my life was over. Listen,' he continued, more sharply than he'd intended, 'every working day of my life, I was up close and personal to some form of death. I saw all variety of dead mothers, dead children and even dead babies. I met death in binders of crime scene photographs, on slabs down at the city morgue, under the buzz of a cranium bone saw in an autopsy and I saw death in the eyes and souls of all the evil bastards who had taken a life. Death and I are no strangers, we've been in close contact for a lot of my life.'

Fenella paused. She let the heat from his monologue cool in the air around them. She knew she needed to give him some space. In time he'd come to recognize that even he should have given himself the opportunity to grieve properly for his parents. She decided to move on and opened the file on the coffee table. She found herself swallowing hard and steadying herself for what lay ahead. The details of the Black River Killer's reign of terror made horrific reading, even for a hardened professional. 'This was the case you were working on when you were taken ill. Sixteen victims, maybe more, going back at least two decades?'

'Undoubtedly more,' said Jack. He glanced at the file papers and the gates to his memory burst open: victims' faces, glazed dead eyes, corpses mutilated as the killer hacked off the body part he always kept as a trophy; all the abominations rushed through again.

'Tell me about him,' urged Fenella.

There was so much Jack could say that he barely knew where to begin. 'BRK, that's what the press called him, started like so many of them do. His first prey, or at least what we think was his first, was a young woman living in an isolated area. Somehow he abducted, murdered and killed her, then he dumped her body in the Black River, hence his nickname. Once he realized he could kill and get away with it, he developed a taste for it. He grew more confident and started to experiment. His paraphilias probably widened, his fantasies grew deeper and we started to discover evidence that he tortured the women before he killed them.'

Fenella took a sip of water and made notes as Jack continued.

'It became part of BRK's MO to keep the corpses for as long as possible. Then, as soon as decomposition set in, he moved quickly to get rid of them, disposing of their bodies in the Black River. As time passed and he grew more experienced, he began dismembering the bodies and weighing down their severed limbs in plastic refuse sacks before scattering them miles apart. With every kill he'd become harder to catch.'

'How often do you think about the Black River Killer?'

'A lot. I still think of him a lot.'

Fenella glanced at some dates in her notes. 'It's more than three years since you worked on the case, what makes you still think about him so much?'

Jack shrugged.

'Is it when a new murder occurs, or do you find yourself just thinking about him without any reason?'

'He's not killed since I was working the investigation. His last victim was the one I was handling when I had the collapse.'

Fenella made more notes, then added, 'So it isn't news about him that triggers your thoughts and your nightmares?'

'No. He's always there at the back of my mind, I never lose his shadow, it's always around somewhere.'

'Tell me, during the day, when your mind turns to him, what are you thinking?'

'I wonder about what he's doing, who he might share his life with, how he manages to live with himself. How normal he may be, or appear to be.'

Fenella knew he was self-censoring, holding back the full force of what was filling his thoughts. 'And do you think about how he actually felt while committing those acts?'

'No, not as much as I used to,' he answered. 'When I was working on the case, I used to think about that a lot. We are trained to think like that, to put ourselves in the shoes of those we hunt. We have to think how they think, feel how they feel, and understand what it's like to do what they do.'

'And what do you think it's like?'

'For them? What do I think scum like BRK feel when they do these things?'

'Yes.'

Jack's face hardened. 'I think, for them, the experience is amazing. Godlike. They literally have the power of life and death. And that, for the BRKs of this world, killing is the ultimate thrill. Nothing on earth compares to it and, once they have experienced it, they are addicted as surely as if murder were a narcotic.'

The flashbacks came again: blood splatters, floaters in the river, fingertip searches. Jack mentally dammed the flood of images.

Fenella leant forward on the couch and lowered

her voice. 'You don't sound judgemental. How do you do that?'

'Do what?' He gave her a puzzled look.

'Suppress the disgust, the repulsion that you must feel?'

Jack was thrown for a minute. The honest answer was that he didn't feel anything any more. The endless diet of homicidal horror had bludgeoned his senses into dullness. But how could he say that out loud and not sound inhumane? How could he admit that victims and killers had ceased being people and had been reduced in his mind to objects and puzzles, a mere algebra of violence? 'It's a good question,' he conceded. 'To be judgemental would be to blinker myself as an investigator, and I can't afford to do that. I can't afford any killer or rapist I interview to see any sign of that. Whatever they've done, however they've taken a life, I have to show them that I'm there to understand why they did it, rather than condemn what they've done.'

Fenella noted that he still spoke, and to a large extent behaved, as though he were an FBI agent. It was something she'd come back to, perhaps at another session, if indeed there was one. 'I want to move on now to the exact content of your nightmares. Are you comfortable doing that?'

Jack shifted defensively in his seat. 'You going to go all Freudian and Jungian on me?'

'Maybe a little. Freud described dreaming as "the

royal road to the unconscious" and I think it's a route worth going down.'

'Then, let's go.' Jack was surprised to see that he'd clasped his hands and was bracing himself. He felt his temperature rise and his heartbeat quicken. He closed his eyes for a second and stared into the grey-black eggshell darkness of his mind. 'I'm at an autopsy. It's being held in the middle of a night, in some dead-end town I've never been to before. It's not my case; the cop in charge has asked me to step in at the last minute. We're all downstairs, in some kind of basement; looks more like a cellar in a house than an autopsy room. It's cold and has the sweet stink of old sump oil and running damp. The walls are brick and painted white, the floor is black and hard and your feet crunch when you move, as though you are walking on broken glass. Rusty pipes run along the ceiling and hiss and rumble in a way that makes you think they are going to break and burst at any minute.'

She noted the vividness and starkness of his language, how even in his dreams Jack had a sharpened sense of observation, was aware of sounds, smells and even things under his feet that he couldn't see.

'The ME's working like crazy, almost as though he's a surgeon trying to save a life, rather than a pathologist methodically opening up a body. He's moving so quickly around the slab I can't see who he is. Every time I reposition myself to try to say something, the guy shifts on to another part of the body. The girl on the slab is sixteen-year-old Lisa Maria Jenkins, BRK's last known victim. She'd been butchered like a piece of meat. Head, hands, legs, feet, all cut off. Her left hand was never discovered, BRK had kept it as a trophy. But in the dream, Lisa's intact; looking as beautiful as her last birthday picture, when her long brown hair was tied back in a pony-tail.'

Jack struggled to go on. Clearly the cognitive experience was troubling him, but Fenella did nothing to fill the silence or give him a way out. He pinched his eyes for a second, then continued. 'As I look at her face, I realize something's wrong. She's still breathing. I shout "Hey, look, look, she's alive!", but the ME ignores me and just carries on cutting her open, pulling intestines and organs out of a huge cavity in her stomach. Suddenly, the pipes break free from the wall and start pouring blood on to the floor, as if they're giant veins. I'm screaming now, "Stop! For Christ's sake, stop cutting her, she's alive!" But he blanks me. As I rush around the table to try to get hold of him he runs the buzz saw across her neck, decapitating her. I recognize him now. I realize why he's been dodging me, not letting me see his face.'

'You say you recognize him. Who is it, Jack?'

He raised his head and stared straight at her. 'It's me. The monster in my dreams is me.'

It was Fenella's turn to sit in silence, pen motionless on the notepaper.

'Tell me, please tell me; how can I control these nightmares?'

Fenella's heart went out to him. She understood his dilemma and it was a dark and dangerous one. 'Jack, you already have control. The level of lucidity you describe indicates that you deliberately trigger these thoughts. Subconsciously you *want* to see these things, you have a *need* to re-examine the case that you walked away from and, in the absence of new evidence, your imagination is inventing it.'

Jack was staring at the floor. He nodded slowly. He understood now, but what was the way out? 'What exactly do I have to do to stop them?'

The psychiatrist waited until he raised his eyes to look at her. 'You already know that, don't you?'

And he did.

Jack fully understood that he could choose to stop the nightmares any time he wanted. But he could only do so by admitting to himself that his personal hunt to catch the Black River Killer really was over.

13

FBI Field Office, New York

Special Agent Howie Baumguard sat at his desk, losing a messy hand-wrestling competition with a deli lunch. The bagel spewed salmon out of one side and low-fat cheese out of the other. He licked the cheese away but the salmon hit his paperwork before he could juggle it into his hungry mouth. He'd missed breakfast and had been forced to cancel a lunch appointment, so right now the bagel and a blisteringly hot Americano figured top of his list of life's priorities. Howie was carrying too much weight, not just for his own liking but also for that of Carrie, his size-zero, Botox-addicted wife, who'd pronounced that either the 'love handles' went or Howie could start learning how to cook for one on the few cents she'd leave him after she sued his fat ass for all the alimony she could get.

Not many people would have been able to even think about eating when faced with what was on Howie's desk, but the FBI man had seen much worse and eaten much more. The pictures had been sent in by the cops over in Georgetown and downloaded and printed up by Admin. The glossies were good

CSU shots, cold and brutal in their framing but hugely informative. Wide angles set the scene, first from out on the streets that surrounded the cemetery. Then there were 'aerials', high views, presumably from the nearby church, that showed the layout of the graves. Gradually the shots got closer to the desecration. They were framed wide-angle, then medium close-up, big close-up and finally damned near microscopic.

Howie's chubby fingers struggled to pick up the stray salmon. Finally, he caught it and then accidentally wiped the grease residue on a mid-shot of Sarah Elizabeth Kearney's decapitated corpse. Poor kid, thought Howie, dabbing away the grease, just twenty-two when she was butchered. If she'd lived, she would have been forty-two today, probably with a daughter of her own and maybe even grandkids. What kind of sick fuck would rob someone of their future like that? And more to the point, what even sicker fuck would dig her up two decades later and pull the skull off her skeletonized corpse? Howie shook his head in disbelief. To the best of his knowledge, twenty-first-century grave-robbing was damned unusual stuff. On the rare occasions that it happened, the perp was usually some whacked-out druggie, maybe a weird devil worshipper or, every now and then, an extremely disturbed husband who simply couldn't accept that his wife was gone for ever. Local cops always tried to hush up these kinds of cases and the newspapers usually played ball on the latter.

But there would be no chance of keeping this one

quiet. No siree, the press wires were already buzzing like a queen bee at mating time. Seemed a Georgetown hack had got lucky with some photographs of his own. The little weasel had no doubt got a tip-off from the cops or ambulance crews, or maybe had even been listening in to the 911 comm's traffic. Anyway, he'd netted himself an exclusive and the pictures were now J-pegging their way across the news world and banking him some big bucks.

Howie looked at one of the hack's shots, forwarded to him by Billy Blaine, a tame NYC journo who ran a press agency and often traded favours with the feds. The shot was certainly a good one. Howie wiped his fingers again and held up the print that had been faxed through to his office. Even though it was a telephoto 'snatch', it was rock steady, with no blur or shake. No doubt the guy had used one of those new-fangled stabilizers that cost more than most people's cameras. Howie was always teasing the CSU boys that hacks took better pictures and this was no exception. It had been shot low-angle between the headstones, so you could just see flashes of out-of-focus graves and a glint of sunshine from behind the photographer, but no sign of the cops and crime-scene tape that must have been making the shot incredibly difficult if not damn near impossible. Despite all the problems, everything that mattered was razor sharp, perfectly exposed and absolutely in focus. Smack, bang, centre of the frame was Sarah Kearney's headless skeleton, grotesquely propped against her headstone.

Howie shook his big head again. The picture had a truly shocking power. He held it out at arm's length, not because he had vision problems, but so he could imagine he was actually at the crime scene and had stepped back for a more considered look. Shit, thought Howie, if Steven Spielberg ever made horror movies then this was the kind of shot he'd take. It was out on its own, a real spine-tingler and too gruesome for the TV news channels. The Internet had no such scruples though; it was already top of the virals and had beaten the download record set after Saddam's hanging.

Howie took a hit of the Americano and turned his mind to Jack King. It had been nearly two months since they'd spoken, and even then it had only been small talk. Howie had been deliberately careful to avoid anything that might have scratched at old sores. 'How you doin'? How're Nancy and little Zack? Did you read about the Yankees star that got busted in Queens?' Guy stuff that kept their cop bonds and personal friendship alive. They'd been through hell together and Howie wasn't going to let the mere matter of a continent and six hours' time difference stand between him and his ex-boss. But now he was going to have to call Jack and tell him about the wacko shit going on at Kearney's grave. He needed to warn him that any minute all the stuff about him and his breakdown was likely to be back in the press again. Hell and damnation. Would this case never go away?

Howie Baumguard looked at the photographs again and knew what Jack would say. He knew it, just as sure as he knew that one day his stick-insect wife would leave him for a younger, fitter, more-at-home guy. No doubt about it, this was the work of one particular man, the work of BRK, the killer that he, Jack and all the rest of FBI's finest had never managed to catch.

14

Montepulciano, Tuscany

Ispettore Orsetta Portinari parked her car and, despite heels slightly too high and far too fashionable for most female detectives, walked elegantly up the steep cobbles and slabs of the Corso, the historic main street of Montepulciano.

Orsetta's friend Louisa had promised coffee, pictures of her sister's new baby and eighteen months' worth of unheard gossip. It seemed a good way to pass the time until the damned ex-FBI guy returned from wherever he was and called her. *Madonna porca!* His wife had been trouble; no wonder the man was spending time away from her. She must be hell to live with. Orsetta bought flowers and Tuscan cherries from a market stall and was within a hundred metres of her friend's home when her phone rang.

'*Pronto*,' she said, catching it just before the message system kicked in.

'Inspector Portinari?'

'*Sì*.'

'This is Jack King. My wife says you called to see me.'

She stepped out of the sun into a shaded doorway.

'Aah, *Signore* King, *grazie*. Thank you for calling me. My boss, Massimo Albonetti, he is in Belgium at the moment, at a Europol meeting, and he sent me to see you –'

'Massimo?' interrupted Jack, sounding surprised. 'What does that old goat want?'

'*Scusi?*'

Jack laughed. 'Apologies. Mass and I go back some. We spent a lot of time at the Academy, back when you guys were first interested in VICAP – the Violent Criminal Apprehension Program. You work for him?'

'*Sì,*' confirmed Orsetta, instantly picturing her sixteen-hours-a-day workaholic boss calling her into his dark office, rubbing his chubby bald head, chain-smoking and handing out files without even looking up. 'Yes, I work very hard for him.'

Jack imagined that was true. Massimo was a bulldog of a man. He was physically and mentally muscular, and when he got his teeth into something he didn't let go, even if he exhausted his teams in the process. 'Are you in CID, CSU, profiling or what?'

Orsetta looked down at her new shoes, dusty from the walk and in need of a loving shine. 'I work in a special department attached to our national Violent Crime Analysis Unit. Briefly, we are called behavioral analysts, but yes, I am what you call a psychological profiler.'

Jack understood. Police forces relabelled departments to suit the whim of whatever particular politician was pulling the purse strings at the time. 'I've heard worse names,' he said. 'But, Detective, as I'm sure you know, I'm not here on holiday. I've retired now, I help my wife – who, by the way, you seem to have upset – run a hotel out here. I'm no longer in the Job, so why the call?'

Orsetta mentally cursed the wife again. 'Massimo, I mean *Direttore* Albonetti, he said forget about that. Said you would never retire.'

Jack laughed again. 'He said that?'

'Well no, what he actually said was: "Jack King is no more retired than I am. Jack King cannot even spell the word retire."'

Jack fell silent. Massimo was right. He might no longer be putting in a twelve-hour day in New York or spending the night looking at crime-scene reports, but his brain was still clocking-on and doing the shifts. 'What does he want?'

A moped carrying two teenagers throttled its way uphill and drowned out the conversation. '*Scusi?*' shouted Orsetta, covering one ear.

'Massimo, what does he want?'

'I have a file here,' explained Orsetta, shouting above the scooter. 'A murder of a young woman that he thinks you can help us with. Are you back at your hotel, Mr King? I can drive over and show you.'

Jack looked at his watch. It was five p.m. and he still had to get across Florence to catch the train back to Siena. 'No, I'm not. I won't be back in San Quirico until very late tonight. I'm in Florence, so I'm still a few hours away from you.'

Orsetta was keen not to let him slip through her fingers. 'Mr King, the case we want you to look at, it is west of Florence, not too far. If you stay there, I can come and meet you. Please book into a hotel for the night, my office will be happy to pay any costs you incur.'

Jack paused and wondered how he could break the news to Nancy. She would go ape. He decided to do it anyway. The prospect of being involved in an active criminal case was simply too hard to resist.

'Okay,' he said. 'You've got twenty-four hours of my time. I'll call you when I've booked in some-where.'

Orsetta punched the air. '*Grazie*,' she said.

As Jack said goodbye, she clicked the phone off and gave one rueful glance towards the house of the friend whom she hadn't seen for eighteen months, and now probably wouldn't see again for another year and a half. Still, Orsetta had got her man. As she walked carefully back down Montepulciano's steep and winding road, she spotted an old woman asleep on a hard-backed chair by an open front door, a red shawl around her neck. Orsetta gently placed the flowers and cherries at her feet and walked away. As she did so, she wondered whether Jack King looked anything near as sexy as he sounded.

15

Sofitel Hotel, Florence, Tuscany

Jack always got Nancy three specific things on anniversaries – something to wear, something to eat and something to read. The three choices were designed to play on her senses of sight, touch and taste, and Jack liked to think he had the imagination to make some pretty interesting purchases. *Something to wear* was once a pink winter anorak, not too romantic until she put her hand in the pocket and discovered the plane tickets to Sweden and the booking at the Ice Palace where they were to spend the following week. This year *Something to wear* was red and lacy and he hoped it would awaken the magic of years gone by. *Something to eat* had traditionally been a visit to a new restaurant, except for the year when the local amateur players were putting on *Romeo and Juliet*. A flash of his gold shield in the right places had enabled him to hire the set for the afternoon, ship in violinists and pizza and have the two leading cast members perform extracts between the courses. True, it had been more comic than romantic, but it still rated as memorable. This year, well, he was leaving the food side up to Paolo, who had promised to do something gastronomically pornographic with white truffles and Italian brandy. *Something to read* had always been the easiest. Sometimes it had been a book that summed up their relationship. *Men are from Mars, Women are from Venus* had started the trend and occasionally Nancy had been cheeky enough to put in her own specific orders, asking for works by foreign poets with names he'd never heard of, like Szymborska and Saint-John Perse. This year, Jack had just hurriedly completed his trinity of gifts and was heading into the Sofitel on Via de Cerratani with an English translation of Dante's *Divine Comedy*. He hadn't really looked inside, but knew Dante was Tuscan and a medieval poet, so he reckoned his lucky find was relevant enough to prove popular.

The Sofitel was located inside a converted seventeenth-century palace and, most importantly, close to the railway station from where Jack hoped to catch an early-morning train back to his wife. There was a chance that she would have calmed down by then.

He fought his way through a swarm of German tourists who were buzzing phrases of mangled Italian at the front-desk staff. Finally he managed to secure a second-floor room looking out towards Piazza del Duomo. Best of all though, it had the kind of deep-freeze air-conditioning that he was used to back home. He clicked the fan on high and raided the mini-bar to make Bloody Marys. The session with the shrink had unsettled him. It had not been the gibberish he had anticipated; it had made sense.

Fenella was right. He was frightened. He was anxious, and he had to do something about it.

And even though he'd promised himself he would go back and see the sessions out, right now he was going to banish all those awful home truths with a good dose of trusty Russian vodka.

The first drink didn't touch the sides.

He ran his finger along the inside of the glass and licked tomato juice off it. Minutes later he took the second to the bed, where he flopped down, kicked off his shoes and called Portinari to find out where she was and decide whether to hold off eating or not. Her phone tripped to a recorded message in Italian which he guessed meant he should leave his name and number. After sinking the second vodka and tomato juice he flicked on CNN and decided to kill time by checking out Nancy's new book. It contained both the original Italian, on the left side of the page, and a translation on the right. He ploughed past the blurb on Dante, stuff describing him as the founder of the Italian language for the common people, a brief story about his exile from a house not far from Jack's hotel, and some remarks about the two writers who'd carried out the translation. Eventually he got to the first Canto and read it out loud in an atrocious Italian accent: '*Nel mezzo del cammin di nostra vita, mi ritrovai per una selva oscura, ché la diritta via era smarrita.*' Jack couldn't understand a word of it, but that didn't stop him enjoying every syllable as the melody of the words swirled as richly around his mouth as a fine

Italian brandy. He glanced over to the translation and found it had a personal resonance: 'Midway upon the journey of our life, I found myself within a forest dark, for the straightforward pathway had been lost.' Right now, he sure felt that way. He wondered just how his life in the FBI's elite psychological profiling unit had so quickly changed into a life in Italy helping run a small hotel. Was he here by choice, or because he had been unable to face up to the darkness that had overwhelmed him back in the US?

Another drink chased off his melancholia and the alcohol and the warmth of the room soon lured him into an unplanned doze. He dreamt something nice for once. He was somewhere with Nancy, far off on an undulating Tuscan hillside, the sun shining as brightly as it always did. Zack was running in front of them with a birthday balloon tied to his wrist. As Jack's eyes fixed on the balloon it exploded, with a bang so loud it made his blood race. He sat upright in bed and realized the noise was someone knocking on his door. He checked his watch and saw he'd been asleep for nearly three hours. 'Just a minute. Hang on!' he shouted, rubbing his eyes and giving himself a once-over in a wardrobe mirror, as he walked to the door. Instinctively, he slid back the spy hole cover and checked out the caller. Through his squinted view, he guessed someone from the front desk had a message for him. '*Signore* King?' asked a dark-haired girl as he opened up. Sure enough, she was carrying an official-looking document case.

'Hi there,' he said sleepily, patting his pocket. 'Hold on one minute, I'll get a pen.' He left her hanging, the spring-loaded door virtually banging shut in her face, while he searched for a pen and a few loose euros for a tip.

'Sorry,' said Jack, opening up again, the coins clinking in his palm.

The girl seemed bewildered. He took a closer look at her. She reminded him of an Italian Keira Knightley, only larger and with maybe a little more muscle than the featherweight film star. 'You have something for me?' he said, nodding towards the case. 'Do I need to sign first?'

'*Signore*, I don't want you to sign anything,' she announced, holding out her hand. 'I am Detective Inspector Portinari.'

'Shit! I'm so sorry,' said Jack, deftly pocketing the euros he had been about to tip her and shaking her outstretched hand. 'Please come in. It's been a long day and I'd almost given up on you coming tonight.'

He held the door this time. As she squeezed past him, she decided that his looks did indeed match up to the strong voice she'd heard on the phone. He was certainly much taller and broader than she'd imagined.

'I'm sorry I'm so late,' she said. 'Italian traffic is always bad, and then I had some trouble booking in downstairs.'

'Too many guests and not enough staff,' said Jack. 'You want a drink?'

'Is that cold?' she asked, pointing towards an unopened bottle of Orvieto that Jack had taken out of the mini-bar in order to reach the vodka.

'Sort of.' Jack checked the temperature of the bottle. 'You want to risk it?'

'Yes, please,' she answered, settling into a chair beside the bed and weighing up the room.

He uncorked the wine and poured two glasses.

'*Salute*,' she said, clinking her glass against his.

'*Salute*,' replied Jack, thinking how different Italian policewomen looked in comparison to some of the gun-slinging, 200-pound dames he'd worked with back in the States.

As Orsetta sipped her drink she looked across the top of the glass at the man she'd heard and read so much about. In profiling circles Jack King's published theories, lectures and criminal case studies were as legendary as his burnout. His specialism had been serial sexual offences and she'd read that during his career he'd been directly involved in the investigation and conviction of fifteen serial rapists and five serial child molesters. His hit rate on serial murder cases was even more impressive: twenty-nine successful clear-ups out of thirty cases that he'd worked. Only one had defeated him, and it was in connection with that single case that she now sat opposite him.

'We have a murder,' she began, gently placing the wine glass down on a nearby coffee table stacked with magazines about Florence, 'which has some disturbing similarities to the Black River case.'

Nothing registered on Jack's face but he felt his heart jump. He swirled the wine in his glass and asked, 'How similar?'

'Very,' said Orsetta. 'I have a case outline here.' She tapped the document bag at her side. 'There is also a confidential briefing that Massimo Albonetti has prepared for you.' She went to draw out the file but he held up his hand.

'No, please, not tonight. I've had a long day, and to be honest, I'm really in no state to dive into that kind of stuff right now.'

His hesitancy made Orsetta wonder if it really was just the lateness of the hour, or whether Jack simply wasn't yet over the burnout and all the emotional baggage that no doubt came with it. 'Breakfast in the morning?' she suggested, shooting a smile while studying his face for signs of stress. 'We could do it then.'

'Fine by me,' said Jack topping their glasses up. 'You want some olives? I've got a jar in the fridge.'

The smile vanished. 'Really, Mr King, you should know better than to offer an Italian lady olives from some hotel-room jar.'

If looks could kill, Jack was already having earth dropped on his coffin. He tossed a room service menu on to the bed next to her. 'You want to choose some food, and help me finish off this wine? I'm going to grab a steak sandwich and some salad, then crash out. We could eat and talk for a while.'

One half of Orsetta just wanted to go to her

69

own room, fall in a bath, and then catch an earlyish night. But her less responsible half always won. 'That sounds fine to me,' she said, handing back the menu. 'I need my steak medium-rare, please.'

Orsetta watched him dial in the order. His hair was jet black and cut fashionably short, but not so short that she couldn't run her fingers through it and hang on to a good handful if the need arose. He had strong cheekbones but looked as though he could do with a shave to banish an end-of-day shadow that some women would find rugged but she regarded as scruffy. He was plainly dressed in a white shirt and black trousers. The white showed off a healthy, light tan, the type picked up naturally, rather than one baked on through lounging around on some blanket on a beach. From the outline of his shoulders she could tell he was muscular, and she also liked that he wasn't showing off his physique. His shirt was a loose fit and was fastened all the way up, except for the collar button.

'Twenty minutes,' said Jack, putting the phone down and turning towards her. Orsetta looked away, a little embarrassed at the thought that he might notice she'd been sizing him up.

Jack seemed oblivious to her attentions, but had missed nothing. He picked up his wine glass again, settled into a chair opposite her, and went on: 'I guess Massimo sent you for three reasons. Firstly, you're no doubt a very good police officer and he respects your judgement. Secondly, he wants you to find out whether I'm up to the job that you need help on, or whether I'm really just a cabbage and it would be a waste of time asking me.'

Orsetta looked confused. 'How could you be a cabbage? This is a vegetable, no?'

Jack laughed. 'Yes, it is. It's a figure of speech, an expression we use. Not a very kind one actually; it means someone's mentally no more use than a vegetable.'

'Aaah,' said Orsetta, deciding to use the humour of the moment to be honest. 'Then yes, I suspect you are right. But I think my boss has also your best interests at heart. He wanted me to make sure that a case like this wouldn't be too unpleasant for you. He knows what you've been through, and he has only the greatest of respect for you.'

Jack gave her a thin smile of acknowledgement. He knew Massimo had to be careful about asking for his help, and guessed he would have been similarly cautious if their roles had been reversed. 'And I suspect the third reason is that, if you think I'm up to it, then he knows you will have to persuade me to help out, because let's face it, I need this kind of gig about as much as a reformed alcoholic needs a free crate of bourbon.'

'And are you persuadable?' asked Orsetta.

Jack didn't reply. He took another hit of wine and felt himself unwinding. He was glad to have company tonight, even if it was dangerously charming company.

'Maybe not?' continued Orsetta. 'That pause tells me you're a think first, reflect a while and then speak kind of person. Text-book introvert, with detached objective reasoning and logic. Am I right?'

Jack nearly spat out his drink. He couldn't believe it; the damn woman was profiling him. 'You running a Myers Briggs on me?' he asked, smiling playfully.

She sipped her wine and felt her pulse quicken. 'I bet an MBTI would place you more in the Perceiving category than the Judging one.'

'How so?' He sat down on the bed deliberately close to her, close enough to make most women shuffle back and claim some space. Orsetta didn't budge an inch.

'You switched your plans at the last minute, decided to stay in town. Perceivers are – let me remember – "comfortable moving into action, able to plan on the go." Am I right?'

This was home turf for Jack and he effortlessly took control of the conversation. 'Personality tests are never entirely accurate. Rorschach can help in some cases, Holland Codes has a value, as do the Minnesota Multiphasic Personality Inventory and all the rest of them, but they're not much fun and don't really open up the secrets of your imagination.'

'Imagination,' Orsetta echoed flirtatiously. 'Now I'm fascinated. Tell me what you believe goes on in my imagination.'

Jack put his glass down. 'Indulge me for a moment. Close your eyes and clear your head. You're walking somewhere nice, in some woods somewhere, on your own –'

'I wouldn't be,' she interrupted. 'I've worked too many cases to walk in woods on my own.'

'These are safe woods. Trust me, you can go there.' He waited for her to close her eyes. 'Now, picture yourself walking through them. Look around you, what season of the year do you think it is?'

'I can see tall trees,' she said, her never still hands shaping them in the space in front of her. 'It's summer, they're big evergreens stretching to the sky. There's light shining through the leaves and branches, a strong smell of pine. I can hear animals scurrying around and there's a small bird flying in and out of the trees. It feels lovely, I like it here.'

Jack studied her; he noticed the way she relaxed, happy to escape from the horrors of the case files that he was sure had gradually hardened her. 'Are you following a path or is the wood too dense for paths?'

She answered quickly, 'There is a path, it's a public walkway, but I'm not following it, I'm wandering away. I'm drawn to something, I think I hear a waterfall, but I can't see it. Yes, I can hear running water. As I'm searching, I see red-spotted mushrooms near some small logs that have been cut up; they're those fairy-tale mushrooms.'

'Forget the mushrooms, they're probably poisonous or at least hallucinogenic. Let's move on. Imagine something spooks you. You look around and there's an animal there, just a few paces away from you. What is it?'

'*Orso!*' she said quickly, then screwed up her eyes and struggled to find the right English word.'

'*Orso* grizzly, not *orsacchiotto*, not a teddy bear. It's a big slow black bear, its arms are open wide and it has a shiny snout and bright white teeth.'

'What do you do?' After his ordeal at the psychiatrist's earlier that day Jack found himself comforted by being back in control and on the right side of a Q and A session.

Orsetta licked her lips and concentrated. 'I move slowly. Very slowly. My eyes never leave the bear. If it takes a step nearer, then I'm going to pick up one of those small logs near the mushrooms and smash its leg, or maybe its face. Then I will run.' The thought of violence made her open her eyes. She blinked as she adjusted to the ugly lighting in the bedroom.

Jack started to regret what he was doing. He was only a fraction of the way through a mental scenario that had already told him more than he now felt he had a right to know.

'So?' said Orsetta, sensing his discomfort. 'What has the great Perceiver learned from his strange questions about woods and animals?'

If the wine hadn't clouded his judgement, he would have made small talk while they waited for their steak, but now he was too relaxed to censor himself. He went with the flow. 'You're an optimist and a romantic,' he said. It was a statement of fact, not a compliment.

She tilted her head quizzically in an attractive way. 'Why? How do you come to that conclusion?'

'Your trees were green – evergreen – you saw sunlight. If you'd described the forest as black and wintry, then it would have been more indicative of pessimism. Colours are often keys to our moods. And never forget, Mother Nature is a great undercover spy. Deploy her like I just did, send her on a mission deep into another person's imaginings and fantasies, and she will always return with their secrets.'

'Go on,' urged Orsetta, finding herself surprisingly excited by the revelations. It was almost as though he was a voyeur in her imagination, a secret traveller in her private inner world.

'You're very sensual,' Jack said, carefully and almost clinically. 'I suspect you're also intensely passionate –'

Orsetta reddened a little. '*Scusi?*'

'I'm only telling you what I deduced from the descriptions you gave, the language you used.'

Orsetta still looked puzzled.

'Let me explain. I asked you what season it was, and you didn't just say "summer", you also told me what you saw, how you felt and what you heard. You described the effect on almost all of your senses. You mentioned how you could smell – the pines in the forest – what you could hear – the birds and the animals – and how you felt about the place – that it was lovely.'

He saw so much and yet I told him so little, Orsetta

thought as he topped their glasses up. It felt as though with one flash of his profiling skills he'd x-rayed her entire personality. 'What did the water mean? I heard water but couldn't see it, what did that mean?'

Jack cleared his throat. 'Okay. The water you mentioned – well, water often represents our interest in sex. At the moment I don't think you're in a relationship as the water you talked of was out of sight. But you're seeking it, and it was loud enough to be heard even though you couldn't see it – that's indicative of the need for powerful, intense sexual closeness.'

Orsetta swallowed hard. She wished she hadn't asked. Her mind was picturing waterfalls and the pair of them having sex in the water. She tried to clear her head and stop herself from blushing. 'This isn't a standard test, no?' she joked. 'I'm sure you don't do it with most suspects.'

'No, not too standard,' said Jack. 'It's just something I do sometimes to open people up. Actually, it works well on suspects, throws them off guard and gives you an insight into them before you start asking offence-related questions.'

'Was there anything else?' asked Orsetta, waving a hand across her face to mask the redness. 'Or can I relax now?'

'Well,' said Jack, unable to stop himself, 'based on what you've told me, I'd guess you're also obstinate, headstrong, self-centred, adventurous and very driven.'

'I am *what*?'

'You mentioned that there was a path in the woods – that path represents the route of your life, the one your parents, your upbringing and your education have laid out for you. But you deliberately chose not to take it – you said you were "wandering away". This means you want things on your own terms, or not at all.'

Orsetta felt completely exposed. Her Myers Briggs game had been meant as an ice-breaker, a bit of flirtatious fun, but this was something else. Her eyes fell on the book that Jack had bought and she saw it as a chance to gain respite from his scrutiny. 'Aah, Dante,' she said. '*The Divine Comedy* is one of my favourites.'

'For my wife,' he said, quickly and deliberately.

Orsetta found herself blushing again. For a second she'd forgotten he was married.

'It's a good choice, I hope she likes it,' she said, as pleasantly as she could manage.

There was silence, agonizingly awkward for Orsetta if not for Jack, who found silences every bit as informative as most people's conversations. Finally Orsetta cracked. 'Okay, let's finish it, she said; bravely. 'Tell me, Jack, you have to tell me the rest of your analysis.'

He looked across at her. The smart policewoman with the movie-star looks now seemed like a lost schoolgirl. All the sexual chemistry had drained from the room and the air was as unexcitingly stale as a deserted bar-room on a Monday morning.

'Commitment,' he said softly. 'The bear in your story represents the man who hurt you, the problem that creeps up on you when you're happy and you least expect it.'

Orsetta looked down at her hands. So there it was, out in the open. She'd hidden it away, piled all kinds of stuff on top of it, and this stranger, this brilliant stranger, had found it without breaking sweat. 'And I have to find another way of dealing with this, other than simply hitting it with a log?' She looked up and managed a smile but Jack could see that the gesture alone had taken all her courage.

'No. Using the log is fine. Beat away all you like; give the bear your best body-blows. But you've gotta learn not to run away afterwards. Staying there, looking the bear in the eyes and sorting out your terms of peace, that's what commitment's all about.'

She nodded, and without even realizing it found herself squeezing his hand, comforting herself with his strength and his closeness.

The knock on the door surprised both of them and broke the silence, a silence that this time felt far more intriguing than awkward.

'Food!' said Jack. 'Great, I'm starving.'

16

Not since he'd discovered that his sister was a lesbian had Special Agent Howie Baumguard been so stunned and speechless.

The air-con in his office had broken down – again – and it was now steam-room hot. He rubbed sweat from his creased brow with the thumb and forefinger of his left hand while he tried to work out what to do next.

Howie clicked the mouse on his desk pad and dragged the image that had just been sent through to his flat screen. 'God damn it! God damn it!' he shouted to an empty office.

He flipped the picture 180 degrees one way, and then rotated it back the other way. He changed the colour several times, examined it upside down and back to front. 'Jesus H. Christ!' he swore again at the empty room.

Howie quarter-framed the image and docked it in the top left-hand corner of his screen, then maximized another two shrunken frames and started to examine them through a similar process of flipping, rotating and decolouring. The new 360-degree

79

imaging kit he was using was so sharp and realistic that he felt he could almost pick objects up off the screen and toss them around in his hands like a baseball.

'God damn it!' he shouted, finally reaching the limit of his patience.

Howie stood up and headed to the Men's room. Not only because he'd drunk so much coffee that he desperately needed a leak, but also because he needed to buy himself a little more thinking time.

He freshened up and returned painfully slowly to his desk, almost as though he was afraid of getting back there. Instead of sitting down, he chose to stand behind his swivel chair, his sausage-fingered hands drumming on the top curve of the seat, his eyes locked on his desk monitor.

'God damn!' Nothing had changed. It was still as disturbing as it had been the first time he'd seen it.

The computer showed three clear shots.

Shot one was of a cardboard box.

Shot two was of Sarah Kearney's decapitated skull.

But it was shot three that was making Howie curse out loud in an empty room. Full frame on the flat screen was the address on the box, the very thing that had made airport security scan the package and alert Howie's office. In black felt pen were the words 'Fragile. For the attention of Jack King, c/o the FBI.'

PART TWO
Monday, 2 July

17

Cops always say that when it comes to hookers, a year on the street puts ten on the face. By that score, Ludmila Zagalsky is twenty-five going on one hundred and thirty. In truth, Lu's bearing up slightly better than the maths predict; though two abortions and a drug problem that would shame even the wildest of rock stars don't bode well for the future.

Lu's been out on the streets since she was fifteen. Her latest pimp is a Russian called Oleg, who has pretty much most of the Beach Avenue business to himself. Oleg's a brute of a man, a mountain of lard with tattooed forearms the size of a bull's back legs and a big round shaven head that's as attractive as an overripe pumpkin. But he doesn't beat her, not like her drunken mother used to, a grizzled Muscovite jealous of her daughter's beauty. And he doesn't come into her bed 'to be close' like her stepfather used to. It's true that running away from Moscow and working for Oleg wasn't the brightest move she ever made, but it sure as hell was better than the alternative. Lu had turned tricks to save for the airfare out of Russia and she'd been turning them ever since.

She breakfasts every day on a couple of 'E's; chugging them back like most people do coffee and pastries. They keep her sane as she sets about the soul-destroying work of being violated and abused in return for rent money and little more. She starts around lunch and finishes whenever her last *mudak* – some sick, dumb asshole – has paid his cash, hauled himself off her and got out of her sorry life. Her first shift is Coney Island Avenue, down to 6th and 7th. At the end of that she meets up with Oleg around six p.m. and 'cashes out'. Sometimes, if she's earned more than her daily target take, he buys her a burger and beer before slapping her ass and sending her back to the street. Second shift sees her strutting her stuff down Beach Avenue, usually in red stilettos and not much else. If the cops from the 60th Precinct move her on, then she hits Riglemann Boardwalk down on the east side, heading out to Chambers Square.

Right now, at just gone one a.m., she's feeling blasted. Minutes after emptying her purse for Oleg and heading home, she gets a pull from some City dude cruising in a gold Lexus. She ends up jerking him off and keeping the cash for herself – *man, it will cost the perv a fortune to clean that leather.* Anyway, she's got two fifties tucked away for just ten minutes' trade and that's damn near a record for Lu. Most of the working girls say she's cheap, a *shluha vokzalnaja* – a train station whore – but lately Lu's been rolling in the big tricks and feels she's on the way up again.

Lexus-man had told her how he liked to come back to the 'hood' that he'd been brought up in and bragged how he'd got out and made his fortune in Manhattan. What an asshole, what a *swoloch*! Lu had soaked up his bullshit and taken him to a spot she favoured at the back of the Brighton Fish Market and had left him there as stinky as smoked mackerel when they were done. He didn't look such a high-and-mighty tycoon with his pants down and his cum all over his stomach and that fancy leather interior. She was still smiling at the sweet nothings she'd whispered in his big waxy ear and how she'd turned him on. '*U tebia ochen malenki hui, tolko pyat pat centimetrov?*' she'd purred as she'd started unzipping him. He might not have been so excited if he'd known she'd told him, 'You have a very small dick, how big is it . . . only five centimetres?' And there certainly wouldn't have been a tip if he'd known that '*U tebya rozha, kak obezyanya zhopa*' was not 'Thank you very much' but 'Your mug looks like a monkey's ass.' She laughs and says '*Mudak, mudak!*' as she strolls past Primorski's restaurant, pausing to look through the window as cleaners stack chairs on tables and sweep floors. She'd rather sell her ass any day of the week than sweep someone's floor.

She catches sight of a young waiter she knows called Ramzan and he waves at her but is too busy helping clear up to come to the door. Just last week he caught her eye down at a new bar off Ocean Parkway but by the time she'd shaken off the attention of an unwelcome punter he'd vanished. Her friend Grazyna says she should stay away from Ramzan, says he's a Chechen and she'd do well to remember how much Oleg hates Chechens. But Lu doesn't give a shit; Oleg can go fuck himself. Ramzan is tall, thin and handsome with kind eyes. He looks like the type of guy who would take care of her, maybe change her life for ever and get her out of this hellhole. Nose pressed to the glass, she watches Ramzan help one of the cleaning women move a table so that she can wipe beneath it and she feels a stab of jealousy. Fuck him, then. Lu Zagalsky waits for no one. She fishes in her purse and pulls out some crystal amphet; it'll help take the pain away. As she gears up, her punter-radar alerts her to a guy about to use the ATM next to Primorski's.

'It's broken,' she calls to him.

'Excuse me?'

'It's broken,' she repeats, with no trace of her native Russian. 'It's always broken.'

'Oh damn!' He takes off his glasses and returns a gold credit card to his wallet. 'Do you know where the next one is?'

'Yeah, sure. East end of the Avenue, 'bout three blocks down,' says Lu, scenting an easy final trick of the night. She puts her hands on her hips. 'I can show you if you promise to spend some of it on me.'

The man seems shocked and embarrassed. He glances up and down the street, looking as though he wants to, but doesn't really know what to say or do. 'Well – errm – I don't know. I mean, I-I've never done anything like that before. I'm not certain, I m-mean . . .'

Lu moves closer to him. First-timers are always an easy hit. Get them over the initial flushes of nerves and later on they'll show their gratitude with a big handout – in more ways than one. 'Don't worry, mister, I'll look after you,' she says, moving closer to him. 'You got a car?'

He takes a step back and answers nervously, 'Yes, yes I have. There.' He points vaguely to some boring four-door Hyundai that no one under ninety would be seen dead in. Poor schmuck probably hasn't had exciting sex with his wife in twenty years. Lu almost feels sorry for him. 'Twenty dollars hand relief, fifty dollars oral, a hundred dollars for the lot,' she says, as though waitressing in a diner and reading out the specials.

'But, but . . .' he stammers, 'I don't have any money. I j-just told you that.'

'Hey, don't sweat. I know that,' she says, running her fingers down the lapel of his old blue suit jacket. 'Look, you give me a ride and I'll show you to the ATM, then you can give me another ride – you get my meaning?'

'Y-yes. I understand,' he says, fumbling for his car keys, almost dropping them. They walk in silence to the car and he pops the doors open with the automatic zapper. They climb in. He fires up the engine, pulls on his seat belt and turns to her. 'I'm a l-little afraid of accidents. Would you please put on your seat belt, miss?' he says, leaning over and pulling the strap out for her. 'First rule of the road, better safe than sorry, always buckle up.'

18

Sofitel Hotel, Florence, Tuscany

From the moment Jack awoke, he was chasing time.

He stumbled to the bathroom, nursing the mother of all hangovers. He'd badly overslept and had less than two hours in which to meet Orsetta, find out about the case she wanted help with and then catch a train back to Siena. It was going to be tight.

Showering and shaving took fifteen minutes and he arrived in the restaurant with his skin still stinging from aftershave. Orsetta was sitting in a corner, sipping a cappuccino and reading a newspaper.

'Morning. Anything good in there?' he said, taking a seat opposite her.

'*Buon giorno,*' she replied, without looking up. 'Unfortunately there is never anything good in Italian newspapers.'

Jack knew what she meant. He used to read the crime-packed American papers solely as a means of keeping track of 'the enemy'.

A waiter appeared and he ordered black coffee, juice and some chopped fruit and yoghurt. It wasn't what he wanted, but he knew that he'd reached the age when he could no longer eat a cooked breakfast and not expect it to show up somewhere on his waistline.

Orsetta folded her newspaper and was putting it down when she noticed printing ink on her fingers. 'Looks like I'm being processed,' she joked, holding up her hands.

'Always good to have a set of dabs on file,' said Jack.

Orsetta rubbed her hands on a napkin, then dipped into a black calfskin document bag at her feet. She produced a weighty A4-sized Jiffy bag and then folded her arms over the top of it and looked intently across the table.

'What?' asked Jack, sensing her hesitation.

'Yesterday, you said you might need persuading to help us. Do you still feel that way?'

Jack was dry-mouthed and when he spoke his voice was as rough as gravel. The booze had left him dehydrated and he hoped the juice and coffee would come quickly. 'And yesterday you admitted you were checking me out to see that I wasn't a "cabbage case". Do you still think I might be?'

The word 'cabbage' made her laugh again. '*Touché*,' she said and slid the package across the white linen tablecloth.

'Heavy,' he said, weighing it in one hand. 'Okay if I read this on the train and call you later?'

'You need to call Massimo,' she answered. 'He's put a personal letter in there for you. As I said last night, he really wanted to come in person, but is out of the country.'

Jack's coffee, juice, fruit and yoghurt arrived. Within seconds he'd drained half the orange, letting the waiter move away before picking up the conversation. 'BRK's victims are always women on their own. Their typical age is mid-twenties and his MO is always to be "subtle" rather than "snatch". Believe me, this guy probably has charm. We've never had sightings of him abducting his victims, or trying to abduct them. We presume he grooms the women, maybe even seduces them. We suspect he lures them into an area where they feel safe with him, and then he strikes.'

'Premeditated and organized.'

Precisely. He's an organized killer, a planner, never taking unnecessary risks, never making foolish mistakes. He's the kind of guy that measures twice before cutting wood. Probably measures three times before cutting flesh.'

Orsetta drank her cappuccino, noting the seamless way he'd lapsed into the lexicon of murder, while mundanely mixing plain yoghurt into his chopped fruit. 'We only have one victim, a young woman from Livorno, a town on the western shoreline of the Tyrrhenian Sea. In this case there is also no evidence of the victim being forcefully abducted. We also believe our offender falls into the organized category, but it is too early in the investigation for us to say that he has not made mistakes or left clues. I hope in this respect our offender is different from yours.'

Jack finished chewing, then added, 'BRK dismembered all his later victims and scattered pieces of them in the sea, like a kid throwing bread to gulls. By the time we'd discovered what the fish hadn't eaten there was nothing for Forensics to go over, they couldn't come up with anything other than rock salt and barnacles.'

'I'm really glad I've already eaten,' said Orsetta, grimacing. She glanced at her wristwatch. 'I am afraid I am due back in Rome. In fact, I am overdue back in Rome. I hadn't planned on staying last night so I really must go.'

Jack wasn't buying her need to rush off. He suspected she was anxious to avoid any potential awkwardness between them.

'Hey, if last night I opened up doors to places you didn't want to go, then I'm sorry. Maybe we both should have known better than to play such games, eh?'

Orsetta managed a thin smile. 'Indeed we should. You know, what you said – well, it was right. I am avoiding commitment. But right now, I need to.'

Jack put his hands up to let her know that she didn't need to explain herself, but he could tell that she wanted to anyway.

'I was in a relationship for four years. I thought I was in heaven. I thought he was the great love of my life. Well, it turns out that he was the love of another woman's life as well, and had been for nearly ten years. Probably more than one other woman, if truth be told.'

'I'm sorry. Please forgive me for bringing all that up; I'm sure it was painful.'

'Of course,' said Orsetta. 'You're completely forgiven, providing, that is, that you are going to agree to help us.'

'I am,' said Jack. He tapped his hand on the case notes she'd passed to him. 'I'll read these this morning and I'll call Mass and tell him he'll have my preliminary profile within a few days.'

Orsetta folded a ten-euro tip in with the money she'd left to settle the breakfast bill. 'You have to promise me one thing, then,' she said, standing up and gathering her things.

'Sure,' Jack said, dropping his napkin and rising to say goodbye. 'What's that?'

Orsetta smiled. 'If you come to Rome to see us, then next time dinner is on me, and we stay away from the mind-games, yes?'

'I'll look forward to it,' said Jack. He gently took hold of her shoulders as she leant towards him and they kissed each other on both cheeks.

'*Ciao*,' she said, and left him with a smile that could light up New York, and a waft of peach perfume that could jump-start a dying heart. After she'd gone, he couldn't help but put his hand to his cheek where her lips had been.

19

Brighton Beach, Brooklyn, New York

Lu Zagalsky glances over at the frightened punter in the driver's seat and wonders if she's wasting her time. First off, the loser can't get money out of the ATM machine, now he wants her to buckle up to travel less than a mile on a damned nearly deserted road in the middle of the goddamn night. Chances are that the sucker won't even be able to get it up and will then refuse to pay. 'Whatever,' she says, deciding to give it a go and clunking the belt into place. She slides some gum into her mouth and chews noisily as he cruises east down Beach Avenue.

'*Vy goyoreeteh po rusky?*' she asks, keen to check if he knows any Russian before she starts hurling any serious insults his way.

'I'm sorry. Say that again?' the driver says politely, his hands never leaving the wheel, his eyes fixed safely on the road.

'Just wanted to know if you spoke Russian,' says Lu. 'Lots of guys round here do, it's pretty much a Russian neighbourhood, you know?'

'Okay, I see,' says the guy, checking his speedo, making sure he doesn't break the thirty miles an hour

94

barrier. Jeez, it's been a while since Lu has seen anyone as strung up and hung up as this punter.

'No, no, I don't speak any Russian,' he adds. 'I'm an accountant, just working down here at the moment, that's why I'm a bit lost.'

Suddenly the punter gets a whole lot more interesting. I mean, Lu tells herself, whoever heard of a poor accountant? Let him pull a ton of paper out of the ATM, get him somewhere he can take his pants off and then do a runner with the cash and maybe his wallet too? The plan sounds a good one. Hardly original, hookers have been working it for years. Nevertheless, it's still surprisingly effective, especially on a dumb ass *ebanat* like this one.

'Next left,' says Lu, pointing through the windshield. 'See the electronics store on the corner?'

'Yes, yes, I see it,' he says, leaning forward and squinting.

'Left there, then the next ATM's 'bout a hundred yards down on the right.'

Ebanat! she says to herself as he indicates way too early, slows almost to a stop in order to round the corner and then takes an eternity to park at the kerb. She's seen grandmas drive faster than this jerk.

'I'll only be a minute,' he tells her, flapping the door shut as he heads to the cash machine.

Within seconds, Lu has the glove locker open and is scanning it for anything stealable. Shit, man, the guy doesn't even have a CD worth taking! Just car documents and a squeegee for the windows. Lu clicks the compartment shut as she watches him turn around from the machine, put his wallet away in his jacket and return to the car. 'Thank you,' he says, politely. Very boringly, he puts his seat belt on again, checks the handbrake and starts the engine.

'Okay, mister,' says Lu, her patience about to snap. 'Now you're all cashed-up, let's go some place and spend some of it on me. You got a hotel nearby?'

'N-no,' he says, his nerves showing again. 'I've got a rental, off Fillmore, other side of the Marine Park. Maybe you c-could come back there?'

'Maybe I c-could,' she says cheekily. 'You know the way?' she adds, not certain this guy knows the route to his own shoelaces, let alone how to get home.

'I th-think so,' he stutters.

'Good, then let's get rollin'!' she says, trying to whip up some urgency. 'It's not too late to give you a night you'll never forget.' She shoots him her sexiest smile, the one that melts even Oleg, but she doesn't detect even a flicker of warmth on his face as he coldly clunks the column gear-shift into Drive and pulls away.

Lu stares out of the side window and neither of them speaks much as the bright lights of the Beach fade behind them. After about ten minutes she sees signs for Fillmore and Gerritsen and in the yellow headlight beams she spots houseboats tottering on stilts and dozens of shabby moorings in need of paint and varnish. Somewhere between Gerritsen and East 38th her last punter of the night turns the car into a rundown driveway cut through overgrown bushes and overhanging trees and comes to a stop.

'We here?' Lu says, surprised that he's completed the task without any further checks, delays or complications.

'Yes, please wait a minute,' says the driver, pressing some automatic key fob that opens a big up-and-over metal door to a double garage. He slips the car into Drive again, nudges it slowly in and automatically lowers the door.

Lu's out of her seat and out of the car before the garage door's even come down. She wants to get this over with as quickly as possible and then catch a cab out of here. More than anything though, right now she wants the washroom. He flicks on a light and she blinks at the brightness.

'I have a key, I just have to find it,' he says, slowly inspecting several brass and steel keys on some kind of ring.

'Here it is,' he finally announces, then negotiates a route around the front of the car to a connecting door from the garage to the kitchen of the old house.

More lights come on and Lu looks around. Not much to the place: a tacky old kitchen dog-legs into a crummy living area with an old three-piece suite, a fireplace and dirty white rug but no TV. Lu has never been in a house that doesn't have a TV; in fact, she didn't think such places existed. 'Hey, can I use your john?' she shouts to him as he locks the back door linking to the garage.

'By the front entrance, or there's one upstairs,' he says, nodding to the open wooden stairs that climb from the far corner of the lounge.

Lu goes for the downstairs john. While she's in there, she tries to work out how much he's good for. The house is a disappointment, there's no sign of a wife around, and that means no jewellery. The guy had to stop for cash, so there's probably nothing more than loose change on his bedside table; maybe, if she's lucky, a watch or some gold ring or neck chain, though he didn't look like the type to wear anything that expensive. She makes up her mind that the best bet is to sting him for a special 'overnight' rate, on account that she agreed to come back to his place. Five hundred bucks for the rest of the night, that's what she is going to ask him for. Or at least that will be her starting price. She guesses that if he's an accountant, then probably the only thing he's good at is figures, and that means he may want to bargain her down a bit. Yep, start around five hundred dollars, Lu; if you're smart, you might end up with two fifty to three hundred.

She finishes off, flushes the toilet and runs water in the sink. Staring into a mirror over a dirty glass shelf, she sees her eye-shadow and liner are smudged and the whites of her eyes are starting to look blood-shot. Hardly a picture of beauty, but what the fuck, this ain't no Hollywood audition, and the weak-spined *mudak* out there with a hard on ain't goin' to be saying no to what she's offering. Maybe, if all goes well here, then tomorrow she'll give herself some time off, rest up a bit and cut Oleg a slice of tonight's extra cash as though she'd been out on her early shift as usual.

Lu powders some shine off the bridge of her nose, kisses her newly lipsticked lips together and opens the door, ready to demand her five hundred bucks and put up with anything the useless little creep wants in return. 'Okay, mister, it's playtime!' she shouts, heading back into the lounge.

From behind her, a rope noose is slipped over her head and jerked viciously back. Ludmila Zagalsky is swept from her feet and crashes head first to the ground, her fingers clawing as the rope bites and burns into her neck, choking off all air from her lungs.

'Welcome to Spider's web,' says a cold and stutter-free voice from above her.

20

Florence, Tuscany

The railway station in Florence was a cauldron of heat, cooking a human minestrone of travellers from all over Europe. Tempers boiled as tourists bumped and banged into each other, searching for directions to their trains. Finally, streams of people surged, spilled and dribbled down their chosen platforms, squeezing into the baking-hot carriages.

Jack was fortunate enough to find an empty one at the far end of the Siena train but it was still unpleasantly hot and stank of a thousand strangers' bodies. He chugged back half a bottle of lukewarm water he'd taken from the fridge at the Sofitel and shook his shirt from his sticky body.

He tried to open a window but it was jammed. As he sat back on the broken springs of the dusty seat, he could see that outside a couple of members of the transport police, the Polizia Stradale, were sharing a cigarette in the shade after making what had currently become a routine check for terrorist bombs. Above their heads robot CCTV cameras scanned the tracks. Jack recognized them as state-of-the-art IMAS cameras. Even here, in historic Florence, Bill

Gates was present. The Microsoft-based Integrated Multimedia Archive System powered more than three thousand cameras on Italian tracks and had become the global standard-setter for video capture and information analysis.

On the sticky table in front of Jack was the still unopened envelope given to him by Orsetta, on behalf of Massimo Albonetti. He and Mass had become friends a long time ago, during an Interpol exchange held in Rome. A year later, Massimo had helped Jack crack a paedophile ring in Little Italy when New York's Italian underworld had closed its doors to local cops and sought to settle the problem the traditional Mafia way using torture and murder. Albonetti was a no-nonsense cop, who, like Jack, had a degree in psychology and saw profiling merely as a powerful tool to help investigators focus on behavioural clues, not as a crystal ball that would magically produce the name of a killer.

Jack finished his bottled water and slit open the envelope with his finger. He pulled out a piece of expensive cream paper covered in Massimo's handwriting.

Dear Jack,
I am pleased you are reading this. It means that the things I have heard about you retiring are simply not true and that a policeman's heart and brain still beat vigorously inside of you. I am very glad that this is so!
I hope you will excuse me, old friend, but I was unable

*to get away from this awful Europol meeting in Brussels, so
I sent Detective Portinari to visit you instead and persuade
you to give us your expert assistance on a very disturbing
homicide. Jack, if after reading the documentation you feel it
is too difficult a case for you to be involved in, then I fully
respect your right to decline.*

*Like many of your friends, I have been praying for
you to make a full and fast recovery from your illness and
if I didn't think that only you could really help us with
this particular case, then honestly, I would never have
troubled you.*

*Inside this package are some brief confidential documents
which will give you a quick insight into the investigation,
and why I have been forced by events to ask for your help.*

*Perhaps when you have come to your decision you will
call me, either on my office number or my cell phone?*

I remain, your friend,

Massimo

Jack let out a slow sigh. He hadn't heard from
Massimo since his breakdown, but this was an entirely
different note from the kind and supportive one his
friend had sent back then. Did he really want to
immerse himself in a case that had such a distinct
echo of BRK about it? Was he ready for that kind
of test? Could he honestly convince Nancy that him
going back to police work was for the best? The
questions flooded into his mind, but the answers
stayed elusively out of reach.

Jack pulled the envelope open again and emptied

out another sealed envelope, marked confidential, with his name on it. He'd received many such documents in the past, summaries that reduced to stark facts and figures the death of some innocent victim and the lifelong anguish of their family.

Down the platform, a long, shrill whistle cut through the stifling air. The train doors thudded shut and the metal snake slowly stirred itself, slithering lazily out of the shade of the engine shed and into the blistering brightness of the mid-day sunshine. Jack felt a wave of sadness hit him. It had been a long time since he'd journeyed into the lonely, stressful world of murder and deep down he wasn't quite certain he was truly ready to go there again.

Marine Park, Brooklyn, New York

For a second, Ludmila Zagalsky thinks she is dead, then as soon as she opens her eyes, she wishes she was. Now, despite being totally disorientated, she instantly remembers the full severity of the dilemma she's in. That useless *mudak*, that creep who was so boring that he wouldn't even drive above the speed limit, had jumped her and nearly choked her to death with his own handmade hangman's noose. Fuck, Lu, she thinks to herself, how many times have you told people never to trust anyone? Now you let this happen. Remember, girl, life is full of fucking surprises, and they always bite you on the ass.

Slowly, consciousness and awareness return to her traumatized mind. She's flat out on her back, looking up at the ceiling, but, she realizes, she's no longer in the lounge, she's somewhere else.

Where?

There's a light on, shining painfully into her eyes, but somehow the room looks black. Lu tries to move her head to one side to take in more information but she feels that the noose is still there, pulling across her windpipe.

A noose? What the fuck is happening here?

The pressure is from below her though, not from above. She realizes too that her wrists and ankles are cuffed with leather restraints. She tugs at them and alarm spreads through her body when she hears what sounds like the rustle of chains beneath her.

The pieces of the jigsaw slowly slot into place. She feels cold. Cold all over. She's naked, spreadeagled on some kind of bondage table. The rope is tied underneath it, so that when she tries to raise her head she starts to choke. She would scream, scream for all she's worth, except that she can barely breathe.

I'm choking! Oh my God, I'm choking!

Some form of cloth is jammed in her mouth and held in place by sticky parcel tape wound around her face.

Panic grips her. Her heart is racing dangerously and she knows that unless she calms down she will suffocate.

Come on girl, get your shit together. Get it together or you are one dead bitch.

She concentrates hard on breathing slowly through her nose and gradually manages to dip her pulse rate and control herself.

And then, as she lies there, staring at the strangely black ceiling, she sees him again. Leaning over her.

His face is so big and so close to her that she can see the pores on his skin. She can see the hairs in his nose and feel the heat of his breath.

Not so fucking harmless now, is he, girl?

'Hello, my little Sugar,' he says softly, smelling her skin, rubbing his face against hers like a pet dog sniffing out a new visitor. 'Don't worry, my little darling, Spider's here. Spider's right beside you.'

She isn't as pretty as the other Sugars, Spider thinks to himself, but he can tell she is just the same as them. They all thought that they were strong and didn't need anyone, could play the game by their rules, could come and go in people's lives as and when they wished. Well, they were wrong. All wrong. No one leaves Spider. No one. Ever.

He pulls over a leather-topped, wooden stool so he can sit facing her. 'How long you stay – alive – depends upon how well you listen,' he says.

Spider has a stack of digitally printed photographs in his left hand.

'Poor Sugar. I know you live in a world of lies,' he says pityingly, 'but don't worry, I'm not going to deceive you. I think relationships should be based on honesty between couples, and I promise you now, right at the beginning of our relationship, that I will always be honest with you.'

He pauses for a moment and then almost tenderly brushes away some strands of black hair that are plastered to her sweating brow and streaked across her eyes. 'I'm going to show you some photographs, some family snaps,' he says, 'so you know that everything I am about to say to you is the truth. Would you like that? Would you like to see my pictures?'

Lu thinks she's going crazy. She's naked and tied up and now some perverted wacko wants to show her his family album. Man, they get weirder by the fucking day.

'Oh, I'm sorry,' says Spider sarcastically, laying the photographs face down on her chest. 'I should loosen your noose; that rope must be really cutting into you.'

Lu hears him fumbling with the rope and feels the tension ease around her neck. Man, that feels good. She never realized that one of the sweetest feelings in life was that of simply not being choked to death by a rope.

'Better?' asks Spider.

Lu manages a small nod.

He lifts the photographs off her prostrate body and rearranges them in some kind of order, almost as though he's just drawn a hand of cards. 'The photographs that I'm about to show you are of other women, women who've been in the same position as you. If you read the newspapers, then you may well even recognize one or two of them.'

He leans closer to her. 'Do you read the papers, Sugar? You sure don't look like you do. Well, maybe the funnies, but I guess that's about it.'

Lu visualizes spitting in his arrogant face, kicking him in the balls for being a mouthy *swoloch*, leaving him rolling in agony on the sidewalk to watch her cute Russian butt wiggle off in the distance.

'Let's play a little game of "Before and After",' says

Spider, shuffling the photographs and then holding one out in front of Lu's face. 'This is "Before",' he says.

Lu focuses on a red-headed girl with sunglasses; she's wearing a flowing floral green dress and strappy sandals. It's taken in a shopping mall; the girl's on a cell phone and in the background people are riding an elevator to an upper floor.

'And "After",' says Spider, replacing it with another shot.

This time the woman's naked – and dead. She's lying on her back, hands across her chest and her hair looks unnaturally red against her shockingly white skin.

Lu notices something else.

The dead girl is lying on the same type of table that she is tied to. Maybe the very same table!

Spider takes the photographs away and smiles. 'Don't be nervous, Sugar. I know what you're thinking and you're wrong, oh so very wrong. You're not naked because I'm going to do anything sexual to you. There may be a time for intimacy. But not now. Not in this life.'

The words don't compute in Lu Zagalsky's brain. *Not now* – what did he mean? *Not in this life*. She's heard every kind of wacko talk about every kind of crazy shit that turns them on. Piss on me, dress me in rubber, drag me around on a dog lead, but never anything like this. This shit just doesn't happen.

Spider moves behind her. He combs his fingers through her tangled hair as it dangles off the edge of the bondage table. The moment reminds him of when he was a young boy waiting in the hairdresser's salon while his mom had her hair washed leaning backwards over a sink, a strange man laughing all the time and soaping her hair so vigorously. More than anything he had wanted to play with the magical clouds of bubbles that tumbled on to the floor. But the strange man wouldn't let him and kept brushing him away, telling him to sit down and let mommy have some time without being pestered by him.

Spider rubs the tips of his fingers into her hair, just like he'd seen the man do with his mom, then he smoothes the palms of his hands over her face and forehead to wipe away the bubbles. 'You have nice hair, Sugar, but you should take better care of it. Maybe not use so many sprays, and get a slightly classier cut; I'm sure you can afford to indulge yourself every once in a while.' He gently massages her temples and forehead and then moves back to the stool, so he can sit facing her once more. Dark thoughts cross his mind. Thoughts of how he would like to explore her body when she's dead; relieve himself in the cool of her orifices and then hold her freshly limp corpse until all her energy has flowed into him.

He touches her face again. 'Do you like flowers?' he asks.

What the fuck? Do I like flowers?

He stares down on her again, his wild eyes boring into her, his crazy voice croaking out crazy words.

'Have you ever seen Spider Lilies?' he continues. 'They're so beautiful, so white and fragile.'

Lu's never even seen normal lilies let alone these Spider things that Mr Crazy is babbling on about.

'One day, I will lay them all over your body. I will cover you in them. And when others have forgotten you, I will always bring Spider Lilies to you.'

Spider spins around and walks away from her. He feels the urge rising within him, stimulating him, arousing him.

He wants her now.

He wants to feel the magic of owning her.

Possessing her.

Consuming her.

Killing her.

But Spider knows he mustn't let the want over-whelm him, he mustn't let the fire within him wreck all his plans.

He won't give in to it.

He's learned not to.

Spider knows how to control the current that's surging through his veins and prevent it over-powering him in just one moment of blind, bloody passion.

Lu Zagalsky is in a cold sweat. With her head freed of the neck noose, she manages to turn her face for the first time, craning sideways towards the sick *mudak* who's in the corner of the room, looking away from her. What she sees sends another ripple of panic through her. And, despite the futility of it all, she starts kicking, and straining at the ropes around her wrists.

It isn't just the ceiling that's covered in black plastic. Every inch of the whole room, all the walls and even the floor are covered in the stuff.

It's as though she's inside a giant bodybag.

And it's about to be zipped up.

22

Florence, Tuscany

Jack waited until the train guard had checked his ticket and left the carriage before he settled down to work on Massimo Albonetti's file.

One glance at the documents was enough to put him on edge.

There were two thick documents, the first in Italian, the second, he presumed, its English translation. He put the Italian version to one side and focused on the English one. It kicked off with a well-written executive summary, which he suspected had been penned by Massimo himself. It stated what Orsetta had already told him, that the Italian police believed they were investigating a serial killer who posed a seriously high risk to the public.

Jack scanned back to the top of the document and saw it was dated the last week of June; the case was certainly a live one. He realized he was reading a translation of a confidential memo that had been sent to the Italian Prime Minister's private office. From this first page, Jack was aware that he was probably one of maybe only half a dozen people privileged enough to see the report.

A photograph of a victim was paper-clipped to the file. She was a beautiful young woman in her twenties with long, dark brown hair and even darker eyes. She was wearing inexpensive, slightly owlish glasses, but they suited her. The text named her as Cristina Barbuggiani, a 26-year-old librarian from Livorno, who kept herself to herself and was described as bright, shy and academic. Her age fitted BRK's profile to a T. Cristina had been a history graduate and had spent much of her spare time travelling to Montelupo Fiorentino just outside Florence, to help on the archaeological excavation of some Roman ruins. Farms, villas and even early factories set up to produce wine, olive oil and corn had been unearthed in the area.

Jack wondered why serial killers always seemed randomly to select the most undeserving of victims. Why were international drug-runners, paedophiles and rapists never their victims?

The report's top-line executive summary described another of the similarities with the BRK case that Orsetta had outlined to him over breakfast. Dismembered pieces of Cristina's body had been found spread across kilometres of the western coastline. Each piece, and apparently there had been thirteen in total, had been found wrapped in black plastic bags and weighted down. This too fitted with BRK's chosen method of disposal. Jack read on and learned that from where the body parts were recovered, it was deduced that they had been thrown in from the shore – from a beach, cliff or nearby rocks. No boat had been used. The feet, shins, thighs, trunk, lower and upper arms of the victim had been disposed of and found in entirely different places. Jack turned a page and the air in his lungs froze. All the body parts had been recovered, bagged and tagged, and had autopsy reference numbers. All, that is, except for the left hand. Jack understood the significance immediately. In his entire career, he'd only ever come across one offender who'd kept such a trophy. The Black River Killer. After four years, the silence was over, and BRK had returned.

23

Marine Park, Brooklyn, New York

Spider checks the gag and restraints, locks the basement door and heads upstairs to rest.

As he walks into his bedroom he glances up at the mirrored tiles that cover the ceiling. They're there so that he can see himself perfectly as he lies on his specially adapted bed. He thinks of them as his 'Window to Heaven'.

He empties his pockets on to the bedside table, opens up his clam-shell cell phone and thumbs through the Menu. Under Media Gallery he chooses View and flicks through the digital shots made by the phone's two-mega-pixel lens. For two nights he'd covertly snapped Lu Zagalsky plying her trade across the streets of Brooklyn Beach, high-heeling her way alongside the cars that cruised Little Odessa. He'd got to know and photograph her every move as she grafted punter after punter, leaving them with empty balls and empty wallets. She was typical of all women: they took your money and left. Only difference was, this girl did it in twenty minutes rather than in twenty years. But the outcome was the same, in the end they all left.

Except in your world, Spider, isn't that right? In Spider's World, no one leaves. What is it you tell them? Even when your mortal flesh is gone, you will still live inside of me; you will still be part of me. Your soul and my soul will be together for ever.

Spider looks at the small digital picture of her and thinks how, like all the rest, there's something about her that reminds him of his dead mother. The hair colour is almost identical, and the shape and colour of her eyes too. But that's where the similarities end. This girl is a whore and a slut; someone almost unworthy of what he has in mind for her. For this will be no ordinary kill. This will be a unique murder, a killing that will make her more famous than any of his previous victims. Spider feels an ache of passion, a lustful gnawing inside him, as he thinks of how she'll die and what her cool, dead body will be like when he's finished with her. He strips off his clothes and goes to the en-suite bathroom to use the toilet, wash and clean his teeth. He brushes them three times a day, not twice. It's something his mom used to make him do. Cleanliness is next to godliness. That was back in the happy days, the days before she *left* him.

Left without even saying goodbye.

He'd come home from school and had been told that his mom had gone, that she was dead, but he shouldn't worry or be sad because she was now in a 'Better Place', she was in heaven with the angels.

How could that be? How could Mom have

gone somewhere so much better, and not taken him with her?

He was only nine years old when it happened. And while he was already smart enough not to trust everyone about everything, he did trust his mom and dad; as they had said, they were the only people in the world you really could rely on, the only people who would always tell you the truth and would always look after you.

Always. For ever and ever.

But it was all a lie, wasn't it?

For weeks she'd been in hospital and he'd missed her. Missed her every day that he was away from her.

'I can't get to sleep, Daddy. When's she coming home? When will Momma be back?'

They'd taken him to visit her in hospital during all those weeks, and every day she looked sadder, thinner and somehow paler. They said she was fighting what they called cancer and it looked to him like this cancer thing was winning but, oh no, they said, your momma's a fighter, she'll be okay, she'll be fine in the end.

Liars. All of them, goddamn liars.

Even when there were those tubes sticking out all over her, his dad had hugged him and told him that he shouldn't be frightened, that they were only there to help his momma get well again.

Well again! How he'd longed for that day.

Sometimes he'd climb on to the hard hospital bed because she was too weak to even sit up and put her arms around him. He'd lie down next to her and cry on her pillow. She'd lift her hand, now all bony and thin, with plasters and tubes sticking out of bruised veins, and stroke his face. Her voice was thin and weak, not the one that used to shout down the garden for him to come inside right now and get his dinner, and it was hard to hear her, but the words were always the same: 'Don't cry, baby, I'll be better soon. Wipe away those tears, Momma will be home very soon now.'

And then, all of a sudden, she was gone. Gone to heaven. Gone to the Better Place without him.

Where are you, Momma? I'm waiting. Still waiting.

Given time, Spider might have recovered from the traumatic loss of his mother, but sometimes fate can be cruel, and sometimes that cruelty can have lifelong consequences. Within only weeks of his mother's death, his father, Spider's emotional anchor during this critical period of grieving, was knocked down and killed by a police patrol car turning out on a fake 911 call made by local kids who just wanted to see the cruisers zip by with their blues and reds flashing.

Spider's pine bed is high-sided, like the one he had as a child. Only this one is coffin-shaped. He built it himself, using the tools of his dead father. The bottom of the bed contains a deep, space-saving, slide-out drawer. Inside, Spider keeps pictures of his parents, newspaper clippings about his father's death and some other precious mementos – his trophies. Stripped of flesh and muscle, boiled and scrubbed squeaky-clean are the bony joints of victims' fingers lying like a stack of stumpy chopsticks. He had no desire to retain their hands. He cut them off solely because it made it quicker and easier for him to get to the finger he wanted, the wedding finger. And when he did, he took care to slice off his precious trophy without damaging it. At the back of the drawer, wrapped in a handkerchief, is also a collection of cheap and expensive engagement and wedding rings.

Spider sits naked on the bed's padded red mattress and out of habit plays with the gold chain around his neck. On it are his dead mother's wedding and engagement rings. He raises them to his mouth and kisses them. He thinks of her for a moment and then lets go of the chain. From the side of the bed he picks up a plastic canister, twists the top and shakes its contents into the palm of a hand. Slowly, he spreads white talcum powder all over his body, until he's white, entirely white.

White as a corpse.

As white as Momma's face in the Chapel of Rest.

Spider lies down and looks up at his Window to Heaven. On the other side, he's sure, really sure, he can see Momma in the Better Place, her dead white arms stretching out to embrace him.

24

West Village, SoHo, New York

There were two reasons Howie Baumguard couldn't sleep – one was food and the other was homicide. Right now, he reckoned his plate was filled with far too much of one and far too little of the other. Bare-chested and bare-footed, with his grumbling stomach rolling over some string-tied blue cotton pyjama bottoms, he tiptoed downstairs, trying not to wake the rest of the family. For some time he'd managed to fool himself that he resembled Tony Soprano. Maybe thinning too much up top and certainly thickening too much around the middle, but still a force to be reckoned with. A good shave, a splash of cologne and a jazzy shirt and he always felt great. Great, that was, until his stick-insect wife told him he looked more like the Doughboy monster in *Ghostbusters* than James Gandolfini, who even she conceded was so big he was as sexy as hell. So last night, at the end of a gruelling day, he'd come home to a shrink-wrapped shrimp salad and zero-fat milk for his dinner. Man, is there no fun left in life? Well, screw her and screw the calories, now is munch time.

'Look out, Fridge, Howie's coming in!' he said as he pulled open the double doors of the larder. His face lit up as brightly as the interior light. He grabbed a foil-wrapped cold chicken and waltzed it to the kitchen table, along with a jar of cranberry jelly. The rollover stainless-steel bread bin yielded more treasure: great slabs of white bread and a jelly-doughnut (left by Howie Jnr, who already seemed to have eaten three out of the four-pack).

For good measure Howie popped a can of beer and took a long slug before settling down in the cool of the kitchen. He ripped off a leg of chicken and gnawed away at the delicious meat. A heavy sprinkle of bad-for-your-heart salt turned it from good into fantastic. He knew he was eating for comfort – and, boy, it was working. Another deep hit of beer and he felt a thousand times better than he had done for the last two sleepless hours, sloped on his side feeling hungry and worrying about the call that he was about to make.

Howie unplugged his cell phone from the charger on the kitchen worktop and hit the speed dial for Jack King. It took an age to connect. Finally an Italian ring tone kicked in and a woman's voice answered.

'*Buon giorno*, hello, La Casa Strada. I am Maria, how may I help you?'

Howie immediately thought of a couple of ways in which a girl with a voice as sexy as hers could help him, both of which would instantly get him on the path to divorce, so instead he stuck to his main reason for calling. 'Hi there, I'm ringing from America and I'm trying to get hold of Jack King. Could you please put me through to him?'

He felt bad because good old Jack was no doubt enjoying a fine Tuscan morning and now his old buddy Howie was about to turn all that into a ball of elephant crap.

'I am sorry, *Signore* King he is not here at the moment. Would you like to be speaking with *Signora* King?'

Given the option, Howie would rather shave his own eyeballs than risk a dressing-down from Nitric Nancy.

'Yeah, put me through please,' he said, wincing while he waited. Man, Nancy had really scorched him a few times in the past. Fact was, she and Howie had never really hit it off. In the early days, he was sure she'd resented how much time he and Jack had spent together. Then at the end, well, even though she'd never said it, he knew she partly blamed him for Jack's breakdown.

'Hello, Howie?' said Nancy, a hint of incredulity in her voice. 'What are you doing calling at this time?'

Hell, that kind of put him on the spot. What could he say now? Well, Nancy, someone's mailed the severed head of the victim of a twenty-year-old murder to your husband and I was just wondering when he could swing by and pick it up? Nope, that didn't seem a runner.

Howie went for a safer option. 'Hi, Nancy, I'm up

out of bed raiding the fridge, but I need to speak to Jack, we need to chat about some stuff.'

'What stuff?' said Nancy, quicker than a New Jersey switchblade.

'Just an old case. Some new evidence has kinda cropped up. Any idea when I can get him?'

Nancy knew she was being blanked, knew it as surely as when that female Italian detective refused to tell her why she'd called. And she also knew there was no point asking Jack's old buddy if there was any connection or not.

'Howie, is this going to hurt us? Right now Jack is still on the mend, and, you know, we really could do without any extra stress.' She found herself scratching at her neck, a nervous habit that she thought she had under control. 'Tell me honestly, is this going to set him back?'

Howie needed to drain the last of the beer can before he could answer her. 'Truth is, Nancy, we're going to have to reopen the BRK files, and there's a good chance the press are going to be dragging up lots of old stuff on Jack.'

'Oh my God!'

'I'm real sorry,' said Howie, hearing her catching her breath on the other end of the line. 'Are you okay?'

She breathed out hard. 'No, I'm not, Howie. I'm really not okay.'

The good feeling that the beer and chicken had given him vanished. Howie knew it'd take more than a food-high to stop him feeling bad about this one. 'Nancy, can you at least see that it's best that I talk to Jack first? Best that I fill him in before he starts catching things on the news or in the papers?'

'Howie, I don't know. I can't even think straight at the moment. Jack is in Florence, I'll have him call you when he gets back.'

'Thanks,' said Howie, pushing the plate of chicken away.

'Sure,' said Nancy, her voice tinged with bitterness. 'By the way, Carrie's right – you are a fat selfish pig who thinks more about the FBI than about anything that should really matter to you.'

The line was dead before Howie could even think of a reply. It was just gone four a.m. but there was only one thing to do now, and that was open another can of beer.

25

Florence – Siena, Tuscany

Jack read the case documentation twice. He turned back to the handwritten covering letter and dialled the cell phone number of Massimo Albonetti. The outskirts of Florence faded behind him as the train rattled and rumbled towards Siena.

'*Pronto*,' said a strong, male Italian voice, the 'r' sounding as richly deep as if it had rolled out of the mouth of an opera-trained baritone.

'Massimo, it's Jack – Jack King.'

'Aaah, Jack,' Massimo responded warmly, hoping his former FBI colleague had not been too disturbed by his request for help. 'My friend, how are you?'

'I'm fine, Mass,' said Jack, picturing 'the old goat' at his desk in Rome, no doubt with an espresso on one side and a cigarette burning in an ashtray on the other. 'I'm sure your young inspector has reported back to you.'

Massimo cleared his voice, coughing politely into his hand. 'Forgive me, please. I am so sorry I couldn't be there to ask you in person. Jack, you've seen the file, so you know why I needed you to see it so urgently.'

'Yeah, I understand, Mass. No hard feelings, we

go back too far for that.' Jack recalled one of the many long nights they'd spent together, Italian reds to start with, American bourbon to finish. 'I'd have probably done the same thing myself.'

Massimo could hear Jack was on a train, knew he was returning to a family he was now being asked to turn his back on. 'Jack, I wouldn't have asked this of you if I thought we could solve this case without you. This man, this killer, no one knows him like you do.'

Jack frowned. He was under no illusions about what joining the investigation could cost him. 'It's hardcore, Massimo. Hunting this creep nearly robbed me of everything.'

Massimo felt awful. '*Sì*. I know this. If I was not a policeman, then I would advise you not to get involved. As a friend, I would urge you to stay away and think only of yourself and your family. But Jack, I am a policeman, and so are you. And I know that only you can make a big difference. I know your skills, and with your assistance we have every chance of catching this man.'

Sunlight blazed across an outspreading quilt of patterned green countryside. Jack stared towards the tree-lined horizon. Had BRK really been here? Had he brought his madness across the continents and poisoned this beautiful land with his bloodshed and barbarism?

'The Barbuggiani case, there can be no mistaking any of the critical details?'

'No,' said Massimo unhesitatingly. 'There is no

mistake,' he added, draining the last thick dregs of the inevitable espresso. 'You are thinking about the hand, Jack, aren't you?'

Dozens of images flickered through Jack's mind: the faces of women, the white morgue sheets being whipped back to reveal skeleton remains, the stumps of young girls' arms from which the monster had hacked away his prize, the left hand – always the left hand – the hand of marriage.

Massimo pulled on his cigarette. He wished he were face to face with his friend, glasses of something strong on a table between them, something to numb the shock he was sure Jack was feeling, something to remind them of old times. He blew out the smoke and tried not to make his words sound too hard. 'There is no mistake. This man, he severed the hand in the same way as your other cases.'

'Where?' pressed Jack. 'In the notes it's not clear exactly where he made the cut.'

'The incision was around the lower carpals.' Massimo picked a speck of tobacco from his tongue. 'It was a diagonal cut, slicing between the carpals and the ulna and radius bones.'

Jack started to sweat. His mind filled with more flashbacks, this time of the killer, not his victims. He saw the man at work, moving slowly and carefully, preparing meticulously for what he was about to do. The monster manoeuvring his victim's arm into position – was she alive at the time? Amputation attempts on the first victims were crude and sickeningly experimental; there were chisel marks and hesitant saw lines, chipping and gouging on bone, signs that maybe a hammer had been used to try to smash off his trophies. But that quickly became a thing of the past; soon BRK got himself the right tools for the job, no doubt read up on where to make the most effective cuts.

'Are you still there, Jack?' said Massimo. 'I can't hear you.'

'A bad line,' said Jack. 'Tell me, Mass – what had your guy used to cut with?' He steadied himself for the answer.

'Some kind of professional hacksaw. By the look of the teeth marks it's a bone saw, maybe an autopsy saw, most probably a butcher's bone saw.'

'Shit!' said Jack. 'Were the teeth on the saw clean, or were any of them broken?'

'Not clean,' confirmed Massimo. 'It was an old saw. It had been used before. Forensics say they think it's most likely a 35- or 40-centimetre blade with two sets of damaged teeth.'

'Thirty-five to 40, what's that, 15, 16 inches?'

Massimo confirmed the conversion. 'That's about right.'

'Let me guess,' said Jack. 'The first breaks come in a cluster of three. Then there's an undamaged stretch of teeth running for about 7 inches, that's roughly 17 centimetres, and then one more damaged tooth, slanting to the left.'

'Hard to say,' said Massimo. 'There's certainly evidence of some broken teeth. Jack, I'm afraid it's the same man. There can be no doubt about it.'

Jack couldn't speak. It was all still sinking in. Just over twenty-four hours ago he'd travelled to Florence seeking what Nancy called 'closure'. Now everything was very much open again. Wide open, like an infected wound that refuses to heal up.

Massimo waited patiently. Down the line he could hear silence and then the sound of a passing train. He knew his friend was struggling to come to terms with it all.

'Okay. I'm in,' said Jack decisively. 'I'll help you. There's no choice really. I have to give this another shot. I'll call you on a better line when I'm at home in San Quirico and we can work out the logistics from there.'

'*Va bene. Molto bene, grazie,*' said Massimo gently. He was going to add something else but the line went dead; Jack had already hung up.

Massimo held the phone in one hand and tapped it thoughtfully into the palm of the other, before returning it to the cradle. There were still some things he hadn't told Jack about Cristina Barbuggiani's murder; disturbing facts he could now only tell him when he saw him in person.

26

West Village, SoHo, New York

The first strokes of a watercolour dawn were being painted across New York as Howie settled down at the desk by a window in his den. Sometimes he worked better in the early hours, when his mind was clear of the clutter that came cascading in as soon as he set foot in the office.

The Bigwigs back in Virginia had now officially asked him to reopen the BRK case and he needed every waking second of the day to start ramping up the enquiry. They'd tasked him with putting together a small team (nothing over budget) to re-examine evidence and work with the cops in Georgetown to see whether the desecration of Sarah Kearney's grave gave them anything new.

Howie nursed a mug of black coffee and began to wade through a forest of background paperwork he'd hauled home from the office. He started with the computerized statistical and psychological profiles that had been produced by PROFILER and VICAP, the FBI's two main serial-killer computer systems. BRK took up a zillion gigs of data, and the depth of the study was making things tougher not easier. The stats were hard to stomach at any time of day, but pre-breakfast, they were totally unpalatable. More than thirty thousand witness statements spread across forty cities, spanning twenty years. More than eighty thousand vehicle-check entries, more than two thousand previous offender study cases. Howie felt his will to live draining from him. Man, the fingerprint checking alone was enough to reduce you to tears. IAFIS, the FBI's own Integrated Automated Fingerprint Identification System, had run more than seven thousand sets of prints through its database, making comparisons with more than forty million cases on its Criminal Master File, and had generated more than ten thousand latent fingerprint reports. On top of that, they'd used cutting-edge science to lift dozens of DNA traces out of the prints themselves. The boffins behind CODIS, the Bureau's Combined DNA Index System, had pumped their databases but the genetic profiles that they extracted hadn't matched any known offenders. In the old days, the problem had been that science hadn't been good enough to retrieve vital evidence; these days the difficulty was reversed. There was so much evidence; it was exhausting to work out what had come from the victim, the attacker or just innocent people whose paths had crossed a criminal crossroads. So how much closer had all the technology and science brought them to finding their man?

Not an inch.

Sure, there were prints, genetic profiles, statistical

profiles, suggested car sightings, and suchlike. But nothing that could lead them to a prime suspect. And without a suspect, they had jack shit. Data was great if your perp was already a convicted felon, but if he'd never been written up, then it wasn't worth a dime.

With all that in mind, Howie decided to go back to basics. He was determined to take a helicopter view, to try to avoid the forest of information and concentrate on the big chunky black trees that stood out like storm-blasted oaks at the centre of it all. To do that, he knew he had to start all over again, look at the mass of evidence as though it was the first time he'd seen it.

Some things were obvious. The twenty-year time span between the first accredited murder and his last killing meant the guy was at least middle-aged by now. More interestingly, that span meant that he'd killed throughout his most sexually active years and had carried on. A sure sign that he was more than a sexually motivated murderer and that he would never stop. There would be an end to it only when he was caught, or when he died.

All the murder victims were white women, and statistics showed that this meant he was probably also white. The spread of bodies was vast and covered more areas of the United States than the press had ever been told. BRK got his tag from the cluster of killings around the Black River in South Carolina, but the truth was that this guy had been killing all along the Atlantic coastline. Body parts had washed up in Jacksonville, Swan Quarter, Hertford and even Hampton. There had been discoveries as far north as the Canadian border, down to the Miami coast, and even out towards Mexico. There had been such a spread of abduction and disposal sites that detectives reasoned that BRK was the sole master of his own life, a single man, either unemployed or wealthy, who was able to go freely wherever and whenever he wanted, without being accountable to anyone.

Howie put down the basics:

White
Middle-aged
No criminal record
Driver's licence
Good geographic knowledge
Unemployed/Self-sufficient
Free to travel around
Single
No dependants

'Great!' he said, throwing his arms open with mock enthusiasm. 'Guess that narrows things down to a mere sixty million white American males.'

Howie knew the crime stats backwards, and remembering them never made him feel better. About seventeen thousand people are murdered each year in America, fewer than six killings per hundred thousand of the population. But most murders are easy-solves, domestics that go wrong, drug grudges, gang warfare fought out in the streets with more spectators than a ball game. Most homicides were the work of 'amateurs', first-timers who panicked after the kill and ran for cover, desperate to dump the victim and get as far away as possible, as quickly as possible. They weren't like BRK.

This perp, or 'this fucking weird sicko fruitcake' as Howie called him, wanted to hold on to the bodies as long as he could. There could be several reasons why. Profilers believed BRK was highly intelligent and knew that by moving the body away from the abduction scene he made things doubly difficult for any investigation. First off, no enquiry really starts until the body is found. A missing person's hunt attracts only a fraction of the police resources and press coverage of a murder hunt. When the corpse is removed from the abduction site, this critical crime scene gets rained on, trampled on by people and pissed on by dogs. In short, crucial evidence is destroyed. The next complication is jurisdiction. A well-placed body can have the FBI, the city cops and the sheriff's office rolling up their sleeves to slug it out for the right to run the investigation (or, in some cases that Howie's known, to avoid running it). Finally, the big humdinger. If a serial killer can lure his prey away, and kill in a closed and controlled environment in which he won't make evidential mistakes and can clean up after himself, then the CSI teams don't even have a death scene to investigate.

Most of the profilers reckoned this last factor was

the real reason BRK kept his bodies. But not Jack. Jack had often gone against the wisdom of the crowd. He reckoned there were other, much simpler reasons. As Howie picked up his coffee again, his old buddy's words came rolling back to him: 'He just can't bear to let his victims go. He wants to keep them for ever. Dead bodies can't run out on you. He's killing for companionship.'

Howie swallowed the bitter black coffee and considered how much better it would taste with another doughnut, especially a chocolate one. Right now he could do with food to aid his troubled thoughts.

The only real clue this guy gives us is how he disposes of the bodies.

He chops them up and spreads them all over the place.

He drives to rivers, swamps, estuaries, wherever there's deep water, and tosses the body parts in.

What does all that tell us?

Jack had asked the question many times and they'd come up with dozens of theories. He was drawn to water; he was a fisherman; he was brought up by a river; or maybe he saw his father use the river as a garbage chute. Maybe he was a sailor, perhaps he knew the local ports and used them to come and go, before and after the killings. The FBI had checked it all out, even double-checked some of it. Perhaps Jack's simple explanation had been right all along.

'I'll tell you what it is, Howie; next to fire, water is the best way to get rid of a corpse. Three-quarters of our planet is covered in water; that's a big place to hide bodies. Bury a corpse and you can almost always see the soil's been disturbed; people walk by, animals dig it up, before you know it there's a 911 being rung in. But weigh down body parts, then drop them in deep water and for a long time no one but Davy Jones will find out what you've done. When something eventually does come to the surface, it's stripped barer than a KFC drumstick during a Superbowl. Trust me, Howie, the only fixation this guy has with water is that it's a tool to help him. If he can find a better tool, then he'll switch from water in a shot.'

Howie went back to his profile and added:

Organized
Careful
Intelligent
Ruthless
Meticulous

He almost also wrote down 'pancakes, ham and fresh coffee'; because they were on his mind as he fought back another pre-breakfast grumble around his bulging belt-line.

If he had to describe the killer right now, he'd say he was looking at a white male, of above average intelligence, aged about forty-five, with no previous criminal record, who was financially independent, drove an unexceptional vehicle and probably didn't even have a parking ticket to his name. He wasn't a risk-taker; he was a grey type of fella who blended in with whatever was going on and never stood out from the crowd. He was single, most likely never married and was – was what? Howie paused as he considered his sexuality. Was he homosexual? Were they homosexual attacks on pretty heterosexual women? He didn't think so. Why should they be? Howie crossed it off his mental list. Were they heterosexual lust murders? Maybe. Perhaps the dismemberment was disguising something that he did to the corpse, something so depraved that he didn't want another living soul to discover what he'd done. It was a possibility. But there was no real trace evidence to support it. No semen on the bodies, or in body wounds, no sign of anything being rammed, jammed or slammed into any orifice. There had been some markings on the wrist and shin bones, possibly fetishist restraints, but more likely just the work of a methodical jailer making sure his prisoner didn't escape. He wished again that Jack was there to help him. Serial sex crimes had been his buddy's speciality. There had been no one better in the business.

'Remember, Howie, the primary sexual organ of the male and the female is not the genitals, it's the brain. Fantasy and planning happen in your head, not in your pants. Whatever these goons physically act out is merely a manifestation of what they mentally crave.'

Howie still didn't know whether to write homosexual or heterosexual. He just couldn't figure out what turned this weirdo on. And then he found the word he was searching for. Underneath Intelligent, Ruthless and Meticulous, he wrote a word he'd never written before:

Necrophile

Death was just the *start* of the killer's turn-on.

27

Siena, Tuscany

Jack's heart sank as his train arrived in Siena. The station was swarming with tourists and he suddenly remembered why: it was *Palio* day.

Jack and Nancy had never been to the famous *Palio alla Tonda* horse race through the streets of the city, but they'd heard all about it. Paolo had urged them to go, but Carlo, their quiet and far more conservative hotel manager, had begged them not to. The differing opinions pretty much coincided with how most of Italy viewed the controversial and highly dangerous spectacle. Some people loved the sense of tradition. It dated back to the mid seventeenth century and had historic echoes of the traditional Roman games of archery, fighting and racing. Others simply hated the fact that the horses often got badly injured and sometimes even had to be destroyed. Carlo had told them that years earlier one of the ten competing horses, each representing a local ward, fell and was trampled to death while the race was allowed to carry on. After that, he vowed he would never let his family watch the *Palio* again.

Outside the station, Jack could already hear the

clop of horses' hooves as several members of the carabinieri trotted past. He guessed they were heading off for a rehearsal of the dramatic sword-wielding charge that they would stage in the pageant at the Piazza del Campo. Jack could also spot bookmakers on the pavements, pocketing fistfuls of euros as the betting built up for the big event.

With traffic virtually banned from the entire city, getting a taxi was even more difficult and pricey than usual. Finally, Jack collapsed into the back of an old Renault Megane that seemed to be missing certain luxuries, such as rear suspension or a window that would roll down. Somewhere on the outskirts of Siena he fell asleep and was pleasantly surprised to wake as the taxi pulled up noisily on the gravel outside La Casa Strada in San Quirico.

As they rounded the side of the hotel, his heart lifted when little Zack clambered off his pedal trike and dashed towards him with open arms, shouting, 'Daddy, Daddy!'

'Hello, tiger, come here and give your old man a kiss,' said Jack, sweeping the toddler up into his arms and kissing his beautifully smooth face. 'You been good for Mommy?' he asked, walking towards Nancy, who was sitting on the patio with paperwork spread out over a metal garden table.

'Hi there, stranger,' she called from her chair, holding down some papers as a surprise gust of wind threatened to blow them away.

'Hi, hon,' said Jack, bending down to kiss her,

Zack still tucked under his right arm, as though he were a football.

'Down, Daddy, down!' urged the youngster.

'How was the train?' asked Nancy, slipping off her sunglasses to take a closer look at him.

Jack swung his son down and felt a warm glow as he watched the youngster dash back to his trike. He sat on the chair opposite his wife, tucking the plastic bags containing her presents surreptitiously beneath his seat. '*Palio* day in Siena. It was *so* crazy there; I had to walk miles to get a cab.' He pinched an olive from a round, white dish on the table. 'I know what Carlo said, but I think I'd like to go see it some day.'

'Maybe,' said Nancy cautiously. Her mind was on other things. 'What about the case? You done with it? Everything finished? Or is that too much to hope for?'

Jack let out a noise somewhere between a laugh and a sigh. 'Sheeesh, Nancy, am I that easy to read?'

She nodded.

'They've got something they really want me to look at.'

Nancy frowned. 'That girl, Olivetta, or whatever her name is?'

'Orsetta,' he said, noting her sensitivity. 'No, not her, Massimo.'

Nancy's eyes lit up a little. 'You spoke to Mass? He say how Benny and the kids are?'

'No, we didn't have time to talk about that,' said Jack, remembering how well Nancy and Mass's wife

Benedetta had got on when they'd met in Rome. Benny had shown her all the tourist sites, while he and Mass worked long hours together. 'I'm going to call him back in a minute, when I've freshened up and maybe grabbed a coffee.'

'I'll get the kitchen to send one up for you. You want anything to eat?'

'Yeah, could they do a panini of some kind?' he said, gathering the bags and getting ready to walk away.

'They're chefs, honey; they could do you a six-course lunch if you want.'

'Mozzarella and some salad would be just fine.' Jack pushed his chair back under the table and was about to leave when he caught the expression on his wife's face. 'You look like you're fit to burst, Nancy. You want to tell me what's eating you?'

Nancy took a deep breath. She'd have preferred to have this conversation later, in the cool of the evening when she could control their moods and there was nothing else to distract them. 'I don't want you to do this. I know it's probably connected to the murder of that young woman that's been in the news, and you feel that you should get involved, but you shouldn't, it's not going to be good for you.'

'Say all that again,' said Jack, a little crisper than he intended.

'It's all starting up again, isn't it?' said Nancy, knowing the day was about to be ruined.

Jack twisted his shoulders away from her, as he

always did when he tried to show her he was exasperated and she'd got everything out of proportion. 'Honey, I'm going to look at some papers and photographs, see some maps and reports, and give some advice, that's all.'

She looked at him distrustfully and rolled her tongue over the front of her teeth, one of the traits Jack always recognized as a sign that she was holding out on him. 'What else?' he said in the tone he usually reserved for suspects in an interview room.

'Howie called from New York.' She studied his face for a reaction, before adding with a sigh of resignation, 'Something's happened over there. He wouldn't tell me much but he mentioned BRK, said they were reopening the case.'

'He say why?' asked Jack, his pulse quickening.

'Like I said, he wouldn't tell me much. Just that the press were going to be all over it again, probably all over you too.' She took hold of his hand. 'Honey, we don't need this.' Her voice hardened. 'Actually, this is the very stuff that we came all the way here to get away from.' She looked to her left and then to her right, taking in the peace of the garden and the beauty of the view across the hills. 'Please don't put it all at risk, Jack, don't get drawn in again.'

Jack leant across the table, trying to make a connection. His face was uncompromising, but to the trained eye of his wife it betrayed vulnerability as well. 'Nancy, this man might be killing again. He may already have taken at least one young woman's life, right here in Italy, maybe the girl you referred to, and from the sound of what you've just said, he could well be active again back home.' Jack reached across and took hold of her other hand as well. 'I can't keep running away. The impotency of doing nothing is driving me crazy. I have to try to stop him.'

'Even if it hurts you?' said Nancy, feeling that this was a conversation she'd had over and over again. 'Even if it hurts us?'

Jack said nothing but Nancy could read the answer on his face. She pulled her hands free of his. 'I've got to see Paolo in the kitchen. I'll have him send some food over to you.'

Jack stood motionless as she pushed her chair away from the table so hard that it clattered on to the patio. He bent over and picked it up, then watched her walk quickly towards the restaurant. He knew from the shape of her back that her arms were up at her face and she was crying. And he knew that there was nothing in the world he could do to stop it.

28

Marine Park, Brooklyn, New York

Lu Zagalsky is in a shallow, fitful sleep when Spider slips off the gag and slams the needle of undiluted bleach directly into her voice box. The chemical will burn out her vocal cords and render her incapable of a squeak, let alone a scream. Keeping the gag on would be to run the risk of her choking on her own vomit, and he doesn't want her to die. At least, not just yet.

'Shh, shh, don't struggle,' says Spider, dropping the needle and holding down her shoulders.

The wrist-chain has worked a notch loose on her right-hand side and Lu instinctively tries to punch him. The metal links snap tight and nearly dislocate her arm.

'Stop it! Stop it now!' he shouts, quickly putting his right hand around her neck. His fingers are steely strong and they stab like knives into her throat. Spider feels enraged and aroused. His vice-like grip tightens around the tender tissue where the bleach is already eating through her larynx.

Lu thinks she's going to die. It's now! He's going to kill you right now! There'll be no Ramzan, no life outside the Beach, nothing more than this.

Despite the agonizing pain she manages to bend her neck and snake her mouth round his hand just enough to bite him.

Spider feels her teeth snap shut and sink deep into his left hand.

Her mouth locks closed on his flesh like the savage bite of a wild street dog. He tries to stay calm but this woman's jaw-power is extraordinary. Her bony canines are cutting their way into him, grinding through skin, slicing into the bones around his thumb. He frees his right hand from around her neck and punches her.

Lu barely feels the blow. Her mother brought her up on a daily diet of beatings a hundred times more brutal than the one this *ebanat*'s trying to dish out. She ignores the dull throb on her left cheekbone and chews down hard on the flesh in her mouth. She can feel his skin bursting around her teeth, his stinking *vonuchaya* blood seeping into her mouth.

'Fuuuuck!' Spider screams.

He punches her again, but he can't get any uplift to deliver a proper blow. The little bitch's teeth have bitten into nerves and tendons and the pain's so intense it sparks a bolt of agonizing electricity up his elbow. Spider falls on top of her and uses the momentum and his body weight to try to suffocate her, to try to jam his hand deep into her evil little mouth. Little bitch will either let go or choke to death, he thinks, as he pushes through the pain and bears down on her.

Lu doesn't lose her grip. Even as his weight collapses on her, she grinds her back teeth.

She can't see now and is struggling to breathe. His body heat and weight are overwhelming, there's no air to suck in.

Everything begins to go black and fuzzy for Lu, as once more he rams the palm of his right hand across her face and again leans all his weight upon it.

She starts to retch as he forces his left thumb deeper into her mouth, deeper into her bite.

She knows what he's doing; knows that he can't pull his hand free without severe damage, so he's trying to choke her. Well, you give it your best shot, mister, it's gonna take a lot to choke Lu Zagalsky; there have been bigger things in this mouth and heavier people on top of this body than a creep like you.

Lu drills deep into her childhood memory; the nightmares of abuse flood into her brain, the anger boils up and over. She bites so hard she feels one of her teeth crack and splinter away. The latest wave of pain is so severe that Spider falls off her and crashes to the floor.

Lu spits out his blood and her broken tooth. It feels good, it feels wonderful! She feels like Rocky when he beat Apollo Creed. Bloody, battered but victorious. Only she knows that this victory is going to be horribly costly. Her mind flashes back again to her bedroom in Moscow and the last time she bit a man like this.

You don't have to take this shit.

Whatever happens, you don't take this kind of shit.

Fight for your life, Lu, fight for every second you can draw breath. Whatever happens he can't take your spirit away from you.

Spider cradles his left hand in the palm of his right one. Jesus Christ, how did she do that? The flesh is open and he can see inside his own hand. He can see bones and veins, blood and tissue oozing from the crescent-shaped wound caused by her vicious teeth.

He wipes sweat off his head with his right forearm and looks across the basement for something with which to make a tourniquet. His eyes settle on a sink in the far corner and some cotton rags that will be okay if he washes them first.

He turns on the single mixer tap and lets cold water pour over his damaged hand into the deep ceramic trough. The water is red with his blood but it is cool and helps ease the pain that is roaring through him. He soaks one of the rags, the type he usually uses for gags and facial bindings, and squeezes it out as best he can. Spider wraps the sodden cotton around the bite wound, makes a loop and then grips one end of the rag in his teeth so he can pull tight. Further up his forearm he ties a second tourniquet across the veins he suspects may feed blood into the wound.

Lu watches helplessly from the bondage table. She's thinking of when she was a small child watching snowflakes for the first time from the window of her parents' tenement building, thinking of when she was free and innocent, running in the meadows of Gorky Park.

She's thinking of what life with Ramzan might have been like.

She's thinking of anything other than what might happen to her next.

Spider dries his left hand on his trousers and looks straight at her.

'Bad Sugar,' he says, shaking his head from side to side. 'Bad, bad Sugar.'

Lu's eyes are fixed on his hand. Not the hand she's bitten, but his good right hand. In it, gripped tight, is what looks like a large bone saw.

29

San Quirico D'Orcia, Tuscany

From a green-shuttered bedroom window of La Casa Strada, Jack looked down on a garden filled with apple, plum and pear trees. The row with Nancy had drained him and made him reflect, but deep down he knew he'd crossed the point of no return. Whatever his wife said, or did, he was going to help Massimo. And if necessary, he was going to help Howie too. Being truthful to himself, he now accepted that he'd never really managed to get BRK out of his system. In fact, because he was so totally removed from the case, it had preyed on his mind more than ever. Now, at least, by getting involved, by trying to do something, the mental anguish would be worthwhile, instead of just pointless.

Jack stared again out of the window. The only guests walking around the garden were an elderly couple; probably about the same age his mother and father would have been if they'd still been alive. They wandered along the stone pathway, holding hands and pausing every now and again to point out various fruits and plants to each other. Jack tried to recall their name: Giggs, or Griggs, something like that.

Anyway, Nancy had said that they were here to cele-
brate his seventieth birthday and her sixtieth, which
fell within five days of each other. How beautiful to
have reached that age and still be so in love. Jack
looked closer at the man, his sunburned face smiling
from beneath an ivory-coloured Panama hat. The
old guy seemed perfectly happy with his life, content
to be slowly pacing it out, hand in hand with his
soulmate. The couple stopped beneath the shade
of a cherry tree and admired Zack's pet rabbit as
it bounded around their legs, before darting off to
the far side of the orchard. The old man brushed
leaves off a nearby steamer chair and helped his wife
into it, before settling in another one alongside her.
No sooner was he comfortable than he stretched out
his gnarled old arm so they could hold hands again.

Jack would have loved to have brought his parents
here, to have had them stay for a month or two each
summer and watch their grandchild growing up. He
would have given almost anything to be looking down
from that very window on his own mother and father.
They'd seldom travelled out of New York State, let
alone America, but Italy was on their 'To Do' list
and deep down he was certain they'd have loved the
place. It was sad and ironic that it was the money
they'd left him that had enabled him and Nancy to
buy La Casa Strada, mortgage-free. For a moment
he pictured all three generations of Kings walking
together, down to the centre of town, to the Piazza
della Libertà, where they could sit on long stone

steps, while Zack and the grandfather that he had never got to know could choose ice cream from the nearby *gelateria*. Afterwards, they'd walk through the Renaissance gardens of Horti Leonini and Nancy and his mother would wait while Zack played hide and seek in the miniature maze. Somehow the argument with Nancy and the prospect of distance opening up again between them made him ache once more for his own mother and father.

Jack stepped back from the window, and from all his musings on what might have been. It was time to put Tuscany, and any thoughts of his parents, his wife or his child firmly to the back of his mind.

There was work to do.

He dialled the number of Massimo Albonetti.

30

Marine Park, Brooklyn, New York

Spider holds the bone saw in his hand and looks along the blade towards Lu Zagalsky as she thrashes about on the bondage table, desperately trying to break free of her chains. In his hand he holds sixteen inches of brutal steel that had once belonged to his father and for years had been used to butcher sides of beef and pork that the family bought wholesale. In later years, Spider had found more dramatic uses for it. And right now, he's thinking how fitting it would be to repay Lu's violence towards him, by cutting her up, limb by limb – while she's still alive.

But that's not the plan, Spider. Stick to the plan. You have great things in mind for her; don't ruin the bigger picture all because of one small setback.

Spider looks down at his bandaged hand, blood still weeping from where she'd sunk her teeth into the soft flesh. The bones around the thumb still throbbing painfully.

Lu Zagalsky can't hide the fear in her eyes. She tries to mouth words at him, to plead for her life, but nothing comes.

Her vocal cords have been bleached into silence.

'Whorebitch!' he shrieks and smashes the butt of the hardwood saw handle on to the bridge of her nose. 'You think you can hurt me, and get away with it?' he snarls. 'You fucking, arrogant little whorebitch!'

He hits her again with the butt of the saw and the pain from the second blow is so excruciating that she's sure he's broken her nose. Tears sting her eyes but her focus never leaves the blade.

'Look at you!' says Spider disgustedly. 'Look at how filthy and unworthy you are.' He stands back and laughs at her.

It's a spiteful, bullying, degrading laugh and in that split second Lu Zagalsky realizes that she's soiled herself. Something she would never, not even in her darkest nightmares, have dreamt could happen to her. He's right. This fucking crazy lunatic is right, sometime in the last five minutes, at the height of their struggle, she had failed to control herself.

Spider sneers at her. 'You're disgusting. You're no better than the others.'

Lu tries to look away from him and bury her illogical feelings of shame by reminding herself of what this animal has done to her, and to the other tortured and murdered women who have preceded her.

Spider's lips flatten into a thin smile. 'They've all done that. Sooner or later, all you dirty bitches shit and piss yourselves like that. Why did you think I stripped you naked?'

Lu feels like sobbing. Was even *this* planned? Is

everything now so hopeless. She turns her head away from him and tries again to tell herself that it is stupid to feel so childishly humiliated. Forget your stupid pride and dignity – this man is going to gut you like a fish; that saw in his hand is not there for fun, any second now he's going to cut your throat and go slash-crazy over all your sorry little ass.

Spider is feeling calm now. Everything is under control again. Nothing bad is going to happen. It feels good to have restored the balance of power.

He walks behind her tethered body, kneels down and tightens the loose chain around her right wrist.

Lu's heart starts to pound hard. He's doing something – he's tightening the chains – why? Is he now going to kill me?

Spider seems to read her fear. 'I *am* going to kill you, Sugar.' He holds the bone saw blade against her throat, the jagged teeth pressing painfully into her flesh. 'But not with this, and not right now.' He drags the saw blade lightly across her throat, enough to scrape the skin but not cut it. 'Oh no, I'm going to kill you with something much more amusing than this.'

31

Rome

Benedetta Albonetti was by no means the only love in Massimo's life. As well as his wife, he had another great passion: a very sexy young model.

His blue '97 Maserati Ghibli coupé had been a surprise gift. It had been left to him in the will of a Roman banker whom, almost two decades earlier, Massimo had saved during an armed robbery that ended in a very public and bloody shoot-out. Mass had picked up the classic car just six days after his fiftieth birthday and he intended to keep it until his dying day; which, Benedetta joked, would be sooner rather than later, judging by the way he drove it.

Today, despite leaving the office early, it had taken him almost an hour to get out of the centre of Rome and another twenty minutes before he had a chance to ease the manual gearbox into sixth and open up the twin turbo. While Massimo could clearly see the irony of enduring a two-hour journey in a car that could hit 100 kph in less than six seconds, instead of catching a sluggish metro train that would have got him home in less than thirty minutes, he couldn't care less. He loved every minute he spent in the Maserati, and, for him, the daily drive home to the seaside village of Ostia wasn't an ordeal, it was 'therapy'. It was his way of leaving work behind, both geographically and mentally. Usually, by the time he pulled up outside his modest three-bedroomed house, he was a completely different person from the police *Direttore* who immersed himself in a world of blood spatters, body swabs and bullet entry wounds.

Fifteen minutes from Ostia, his in-car telephone rang. When he answered, the voice of Jack King immediately made him slow down.

'Where are you?' asked Jack, acutely aware of the engine noise as the Maserati growled its reluctance to be shifted from sixth into fourth.

'On my way home,' shouted Mass, fiddling with the awkward blue-tooth ear attachment that he hated wearing. 'Benedetta and the children are flying to Nice, to be with her sister and some friends of hers. I have promised to take them to the airport, so I left the office early.'

'I hope they're well,' said Jack. 'Nancy was asking after them.'

'*Grazie*,' said Massimo. 'So, do I understand then that you have told your charming wife everything about our conversation?'

'Most of it,' answered Jack. 'Though of course I spared her some of the details. There's no need for her to know too much, you understand how they all worry.'

'Indeed,' said Massimo. 'And after talking with her, you are still willing to help?'

'Would I be calling if I wasn't? Where and when do you need me?'

'Rome. As soon as you can make it.'

'Okay. Fine.'

'When will that be, Jack?'

He thought for a moment. 'Not tomorrow. I need a day at home to sort things out, make sure Nancy is going to be okay running the hotel without me. How long do you think you'll need me?'

Massimo swore in Italian and sounded his horn at a big old Ford that seemed to extract great delight from undertaking and then cutting in front of the Maserati. '*Scusi*, some idiots on the road here,' he explained, then added, 'It's hard to imagine you as an hotelier, Jack. You should think of being away a week. Maybe a couple of days here in Rome, then I'm sure you'll want to go to the scene in Livorno.'

Jack ran the dates through his head. 'Sounds about right, but I don't have much leeway, I have to be back for the eighth, it's our wedding anniversary. I'm dead as Parma ham if I don't make that.'

'*Non c'è problema*,' said Massimo, fighting an urge to chase the old Ford, fill its bonnet with his exhaust fumes, then pull the guy over and show him his badge.

'You got a translator for me? You know my Italian is non-existent.'

'Orsetta will go with you. Her English is good enough, no?'

Jack hesitated. Really, he would rather she wasn't there, but it would be impossible to explain why. 'Sure, her English is just fine.'

'She is *bellissima*, no?' said Massimo, mischievously. '*Una bella donna*.'

'Leave it out, Mass, you know me better than that. I'm a one-woman man, always have been, hope I always will be.'

'*Perfetto*,' answered Massimo. 'Me too, but Orsetta, she would drive even the Holy Father to sin.'

'Well, it's not a complication I need in my life,' said Jack. 'The documents she gave me were useful, but I could do with more details.'

'We will prepare a full brief for you when you arrive.'

'Great, but I need the complete autopsy report as well. No disrespect, but your Medical Examiners are not US standard. Maybe we should have whoever did Cristina Barbuggiani's examination on standby for interview? Will you please check he isn't on holiday, and can see me sometime soon?'

'The pathologist you ask for is a she,' answered Mass. 'I will make sure she is available for interview while you are here.' Hesitantly, he added, 'There are – how should we say – some other post-mortem details that were not in the report that I sent you.'

Jack remembered that the papers he'd seen had

been a top-level report, sent to the Prime Minister's private office. 'Mass, the documents I saw had gone to the Prime Minister himself. Are you saying there's something you are keeping from him, or is it something that you are keeping just from me?'

Massimo Albonetti screwed up his face. 'I'm afraid it's something I have had to keep from both of you. Only a few people know what I refer to, and I am sorry but I cannot go into it on a phone line like this one. I promise though, I will tell you the very minute you get here.'

Massimo said '*Ciao*' and hung up before Jack could press the subject. And in that split second, Jack was sure he heard the Maserati growl down a gear and then let out a loud roar of hard acceleration.

32

Marine Park, Brooklyn, New York

Spider leaves the basement and returns to his bedroom to fix his damaged hand. Beneath the sink in the bathroom he unlocks a medical cabinet that would be the envy of many a drugstore.

He looks through his stock of local anaesthetics – Procaine, Lidocaine, Novocaine and Prilocaine. He'd obtained them via a fake medical trading firm that he'd set up, enabling him to deal with an array of online liquidation companies that regularly auctioned off surplus drugs and medical equipment. He'd found more than enough salesmen happy to take his order online and ship the supplies without ever asking for any medical licence checks.

He settles on 50ml of Lidocaine, his favourite anaesthetic. He discards the rags he used in the basement to patch himself up, throwing them into the shower tray, not to wash but to take away and burn. The cloths had been in contact with the victim and he'd eventually get rid of them, along with the clothes he was wearing. Spider swabs the bitten area with a sterile wipe and injects the drug into the tissue surrounding the bite. As the nerves and muscles start to relax he checks out the wound. The bitch's teeth have opened up quite a cut, deep enough for it not to heal on its own.

Spider dips into the cabinet again and finds a box of wound closure Steri-strips. It's difficult with one hand, but he takes his time and soon does a decent job of closing the cut with the adhesive strip. He finishes it off with a wraparound elastic bandage and strips of Band-Aid.

After relocking the medicine cabinet he returns to the bedroom and sits on the edge of his coffin-like bed. He nurses the hand and checks the bandage, then turns on a small portable television beside him. The set crackles into life but there's no picture on the screen, just a fog of sizzling grey static.

The first channel he tunes to throws up a black-and-white picture of the road outside his house. The screen is split into four. The top two shots show wide-angle views of all approach roads to the house, coming from east and west. The lower two pictures feature tighter shots of the outside of the garage and the front door. The framing has been precisely calculated to capture the head and shoulders of any callers and the cameras have fully remote tilt, pan and zoom facilities to track any movements. Spider presses the remote control again, and once more, four quarter-frame black-and-white pictures fill the screen. Camera One shows the basement in an extra-wide shot. The black plastic on the walls, ceiling and floor have lowered the light level so much that it's impossible to see where one surface ends and another begins. The result is that the prostrate body of Lu Zagalsky appears to be floating in the middle of space. Of all the camera shots, it's this one that Spider loves most. He imagines her in the total, never-ending darkness of afterlife, suspended there for ever – eternally his. The next shot comes from an overhead camera, fixed to a 'hothead', a special device that allows the lens to rotate 360 degrees as well as zoom in and out. The third and fourth cameras are set at much lower angles. Camera Three is fixed behind Lu's head and looks down her body. Camera Four is a reverse angle, positioned at the same height as Camera Three but looking up her body from a line along her left foot. From his remote control, Spider is able to direct his own deathly video show, pulling in every imaginable combination of wide shots, close-ups, zooms, pans and tilts of his victim.

He creeps in on Lu's face.

The picture goes soft as the auto-focus kicks in and takes a second to get the correct focal length and exposure rates. The remote-control box also has a digi-pic facility which allows him to freeze-frame shots and download them to store or make digital printouts.

Spider watches her for a minute or two, his eyes locked on hers. He tries to get inside her mind, tries to imagine what is going on in her head as she lies there, naked and vulnerable in almost virtual darkness. He notices that she doesn't blink, that her body is no longer riddled with fear. He suspects that mentally she is removing herself from the scene, using some form of crude meditation to block out the reality of what is happening to her.

Or what is going to happen to her.

Spider fires off a couple of digi-pics that he thinks will at a later date be both pleasurable and useful for him, and then he switches the screen view to his favourite shot on Camera One.

The Lidocaine is making him feel groggy. He knows it'll last two to three hours before wearing off. He cradles his injured hand and lies down on his side in the coffin bed. The bed feels good, he is ready to rest. He reaches out his undamaged hand and strokes the glass of the TV screen next to him.

She looks so beautiful down there.

So wonderfully peaceful.

So nearly dead.

33

West Village, SoHo, New York

Howie Baumguard's all-time favourite movie scene was in *Pulp Fiction*: the part when Vincent goes to the toilet during a stakeout at the apartment of runaway boxer Butch and then Butch unexpectedly appears in the doorway with a Mac-10 and blows the hitman away while his pants are still around his ankles. Like most boys, even those in their mid-thirties, Howie is hooked on toilet humour. But what he told people killed him most about this scene was the sheer realism of it. As a cop who had found people dead on the pan (one heavy drug-user and one geriatric Mafioso with a heart condition), he loved the fact that Tarantino 'has the balls to tell it how it is'. Fittingly, Howie was taking his regular-as-clockwork morning dump, just as his cell phone rang. Now usually Howie would take one peek at the user display and forget about it until a more opportune moment. But as this call showed an Italian prefix, he automatically jammed the phone to his ear.

'Baumguard residence, how the fuck can I help you?'

Jack's laugh rolled down the line before he answered.

'Well, Mr B, glad to find you're up bright and early. How're you doing?'

'Early bird gets to bite the head off the friggin' worm, you know me, boss.'

Jack let the 'boss' remark slide. He guessed the big guy had been saying it for so long that he still hadn't managed to kick the habit. 'Well, when you've finished your bowl of worms and Cheerios, maybe you can let me in on why you've been calling my beloved wife? You and she got some kind of thing going? Maybe she found a way into your heart at last?'

'Right through my ribcage, that's the only way your wife would like to get into my heart.'

They both laughed. Then Jack hit a more sombre tone. 'Seriously, buddy. I got told a bit about your call. Nancy said it was serious.'

Howie swallowed his last chuckle. 'Yeah, it is. Man, we've been through some weird stuff together, but what I'm about to pitch is going to stump even you.'

'Hang on,' said Jack, as Nancy entered the bedroom with a silver tray of food covered with a crisp cotton napkin. Jack looked up and instinctively put a hand over the mouthpiece. 'Thanks,' he said, and his mind flashed back to their row.

Nancy said nothing, but as she put the tray on the bed she managed a half-smile before leaving.

'Jack, you still there?' shouted Howie, from thousands of miles away.

'Yeah,' said Jack. 'I'm sorry about that; Nancy's just brought me some food. Where were we?'

'Remember Sarah Kearney, the BRK victim buried back in Georgetown?'

'Yeah, sure do,' said Jack, pulling off the napkin and looking at the salad bowl of rocket, sliced tomatoes and succulent mozzarella *fior di latte* that Paolo had probably made only a few hours ago. 'She was a local girl, wasn't she? No kin, but I think I read that the local community took care of her service and buried her?'

'That's right, they did,' said Howie. 'And now it damned well looks like they could have saved their money. Some sick fuck, maybe BRK, has been back and dug her up.'

The blood froze in Jack's veins. 'You sure? You don't think it's vandals, some local crackheads?'

'No. You can't take enough crack to make you do what this sicko did. He dug up the coffin, got out the poor kid's bones and then sat her up against the headstone.'

'Posed it?' asked Jack, wondering whether BRK was taunting the FBI by the way he had left the skeleton, knowing the press would soon be around to take photographs.

'Looks that way. Some kids going fishing found her.'

Jack pushed a cherry tomato around the bowl with his fork but he was already losing his appetite. 'What the fuck would he want to do that for?'

Howie shrugged. He'd asked himself the same question. 'Beats me. We know these fucks get off by revisiting their crime scenes, sitting by their victims' graves and stuff, but digging up bones, well, that's in a different league to the one I'm used to.'

Jack wasn't convinced that it had been done for sexual kicks. 'Maybe he's trying to attract our attention?'

'Then he's doing a fucking good job,' Howie scoffed.

'You remember Massimo Albonetti?' asked Jack, deciding he should introduce the Italian case he'd been asked to help with.

Howie had to think for a second. 'Yeah. Cop from Rome, went on to head up their profiling unit. Weren't you and he tight for a while?'

'We were. I like him, he's a good guy, and he's just asked for some help on a case that has much more than a passing similarity to BRK's handiwork.'

'I hope you're kidding me,' said Howie.

'I wish I was. A woman's body parts have turned up all over the western coastline, and from the briefing notes I've seen there are certainly enough similarities to put BRK into the reckoning.'

'The hand?'

'The hand,' confirmed Jack. 'The left hand is missing and the bone cuts are the same. But there's more. Victim description also fits our series – dark hair, mid-twenties, slightly smaller than average height, all the usual stuff is in there.'

Howie grimaced as he tried to weigh up the impact of BRK killing on another continent. 'Why the hell would BRK be killing in Italy, and at the same time messing around in the US with the body of an earlier victim?'

'You thinking the Italian job is a copycat?' asked Jack, looking down at his salad bowl and deciding to try the mozzarella, then in the same second remembering the verb *mozzare* means 'to cut'.

'That's hard to buy,' said Howie. 'You'd have to believe that the graveyard incident in South Carolina and your case in Italy are both unconnected coincidences happening at almost exactly the same time.'

'Or conversely,' said Jack, 'you have to accept BRK is now working on two continents.'

Suddenly, there was the sound of heavy-fisted banging on Howie's bathroom door. 'Howie, you gonna stay in there all day?' shouted Carrie. 'I have to go before my Pilates class.'

'You in the bathroom?' asked Jack. 'Tell me you're not doing what I think you might be doing.'

'Right in the middle of it when you rang.'

'Oh, man, too much detail!' said Jack in the most disgusted tone he could manage.

'Hey, you asked. And you know I can never lie to you.'

'Believe me, Howie, at times like this, it's okay to lie.'

'Are you gonna let me in there?' shouted Carrie again.

'Just a minute, Jack,' said Howie. He turned from the cell phone. 'Carrie, will you please shut the fuck up for just one friggin' minute? I'm on the phone to Jack in Italy and I'm on the pan as well.'

'Un-fucking-believable!' came the reply, and she banged once more on the door before storming off.

Howie cleared his head and focused again. 'I'm sorry, buddy, a bit of a domestic waging here. Where were we?'

'Connections,' said Jack. 'We were discussing whether there's a connection between the Kearney incident, BRK and the Italian killing.'

'I'm sure it's BRK who visited Kearney's grave,' said Howie forcefully.

'Sure as in gut sure, or sure as in forensics sure?'

'Bit of both,' said Howie. 'He cut Kearney's head off her corpse and took it away.'

'Say what?'

'Sawed the skull clean off. And before you ask, we don't have anything back yet on exactly what he used to do that, but it was a saw cut, not brute force or blunt instrument.'

Jack pictured Sarah Kearney's desecrated body and felt a bolt of anger shoot through him. 'Heads aren't BRK's style. Okay, he's decapitated bodies before. Christ, he's severed every limb and mutilated every body part known to man, but that's functional not emotional; he did it to dispose of victims, not to take trophies. The hand has always been his thing, his one thing. I'm still not sure this is connected.'

'It's connected, Jack, trust me.'

'Go on,' said Jack, sensing he didn't yet have the full picture.

'We have the head. He mailed it directly to us.'

'To the FBI?' asked Jack.

'He mailed it to our New York office. Airport boys at International in Myrtle pulled the package as a matter of routine and scanned it.'

'He would have known that they would do that,' added Jack. 'No prints I suppose, nothing from AFIS?'

'It's cleaner than the Pope's underpants.'

'It's still not a clincher,' said Jack, continuing the role of devil's advocate. 'I accept that Sarah Kearney's grave has a special link to BRK. But exhuming the corpse is not in his MO, severing heads is not part of his offender profile and direct contact with the FBI is certainly not his style.'

Howie knew not to argue with Jack when he was on an analytical roll. 'You might be right,' he conceded, 'but there's one more thing, something that might alter your view. Whoever did this – BRK or no BRK – they mailed Sarah Kearney's decapitated skull to you. They put it in a box and addressed it to Jack King, care of the FBI in New York. So you tell me, Jack, why would some random whacko send you the severed head of one of BRK's victims?'

34

Marine Park, Brooklyn, New York

Lu Zagalsky's fears rise as she hears the thump of his footsteps coming down the wooden basement stairs, then the click of the key in the lock of the heavy door at the bottom.

It's been six hours since she's seen him, but without being able to look at her watch, it's seemed even longer. Pain and exhaustion eventually helped her slip into a fitful sleep, which has done little to numb the agony of her broken nose, her scorched throat and aching body. Her sense of night and day is already starting to fade.

'Hello, Sugar,' he says cheerily, almost as though he were greeting an old friend.

Lu notices the bandage on his hand, blood staining the side. In his other hand he holds what looks like a drink and a newspaper that she recognizes as a copy of *USA Today*.

Spider sees her eyes darting all over him. 'I've been out,' he explains. 'I needed a breath of fresh air to calm myself down after what happened between us. I brought you back a vanilla milkshake; I thought you might like something cool and soothing for your throat.'

He lays the newspaper on the floor, as though covering a damp spot, and sets the shake down on the edge of the bondage table. 'I'm going to slacken the chains a little so you can sit up again and you can have the drink,' says Spider, adding with a touch of black humour, 'but not as much as last time, eh? Old Spider has learned his lesson, and I'm afraid you won't be free enough to bite the hand that feeds you.'

Lu's head roars with pain as he manoeuvres her into an upright position and blood pumps back through her body.

'Sip it slowly,' he says, angling the straw her way and putting it to her lips.

She sucks hard and the ice-cool liquid slips comfortingly down her raw throat. Her shrunken belly growls and rumbles its surprise at finally having something to digest.

'Good, good,' says Spider, taking the shake off her. 'Now, let's lie you down again.' He pushes her forehead back and dips below the bondage table to re-tighten the restraining chains.

Lu feels better for the drink, and allows herself a moment of brief optimism. He just fed you, Lu. If he's feeding you, he plans to keep you alive, at least for the time being.

Spider leans over her again, pulling at the chains, checking their tautness. 'That shake should make you feel a little better. It will help you settle down for a while now – while I'm gone.'

Gone? The word sizzled, as though he'd branded her with it.

'That's right,' he says, noticing the change in her eyes. 'I'm going to have to leave you now.'

Leave me? For where? For how long? Why?

Spider bends close to her face and points a finger upwards. 'Look closely at the ceiling and you'll see a camera.'

Lu stares at the blackness above her and finally spots the camera lens. A red light is blinking near it, like the eye of a rodent staring down at her.

Spider twists her head to one side. 'And over there, there's another little camera eye watching you.' He lets go of her. 'In fact, there are cameras all over the room, watching you all the time. And guess what? Wherever I am, I'll be watching you too. Isn't technology a wonderful thing?' He takes a small black device, about a quarter of the size of a cell phone, out of his pocket.

Lu can see that there's a blue light flashing on it and that it has three different coloured buttons, like the red, green and blue ones on a TV remote.

'This is a blue-toothed trigger device. As I leave here, I will activate several pressure pads on the outside of this basement. Should you try to escape, or should anyone try to get in while I'm gone, the devices will explode and this whole house will become a fireball. Even better than that, no matter where I am, I can dial in a number and press this little red button here and *kaboomb!* No more Sugar.'

Lu feels her face drain of what little colour she had left.

'I hope that milkshake was good, Sugar, because it is the last thing you will ever taste. You're going to get hungry soon. Then you're going to experience what starvation feels like. And then, after a certain period of time, your body will literally start to eat itself to death. And all the time, I'll be watching, right up until your last breath.'

PART THREE

Tuesday, 3 July

35

Rome

None of the offices smelled more of stale tobacco than that of Massimo Albonetti, head of the Ufficio Investigativo Centrale di Psicologia Criminale, an elite offshoot of the Unità di Analisi del Crimine Violento, modelled on the FBI's famed National Center for the Analysis of Violent Crime in Quantico. Crammed inside Massimo's nicotine den, in preparation for Jack King's visit, were Orsetta, case coordinator Benito Patrizio and assistant analyst Roberto Barcucci. In readiness for working with Jack, they were instructed to speak English, not Italian, though they all knew Massimo would be the first to lapse into their native tongue.

The Director's desk was cleared of all unrelated papers and files, leaving only a dark green leather-framed ink-blotter, a hard-backed faintly lined note-book, a cheap police-issue ballpoint pen, and a black-and-white photograph of Cristina Barbuggiani's face that seemed to stare right up at him. Massimo pressed a buzzer on his desk and spoke to Claudia, his secretary, who patrolled the other side of his office like a pit-bull guarding a sirloin steak.

'Claudia, please bring some water, juices, sodas and a double espresso for me. *Grazie*.'

He flicked off the buzzer and gently touched Cristina's picture before addressing his team. 'Orsetta, Jack will be staying at the Grand Plaza on Via del Corso. He's booked in for two nights, please authorize Admin to reserve a third. Have an unmarked car waiting to pick him up from the train station and take him straight there. He should be arriving around ten p.m.' Massimo thought once more about the transportation for Jack. 'Don't let them send an owl, make it a VIP sedan with a driver, I want him fully refreshed by the time he has got through our blessed traffic. The following morning have the same car and the same driver bring him to my office. I'll probably drop him back at the Plaza myself at the end of the day.'

'I head home that way, *Direttore*,' said Orsetta. 'I don't mind dropping him off myself.'

Massimo studied her face and thought about teasing her. It was only natural that she'd be intrigued by someone as well thought of as Jack King; come to think of it, he'd probably planted the seeds himself by quoting Jack's theories during many of his case conferences. 'Very kind of you, Orsetta. I'll keep it in mind and call you should I need you,' he said playfully.

Orsetta, dressed simply in figure-hugging black trousers and a long-collared white cotton blouse, felt herself blush as Massimo's brown eyes appeared to x-ray her mind. What the hell, she had decided that

Jack King was special and she hoped something special was going to happen when they met again.

'Roberto, have all the translations been finished? My old friend Jack is American; he can barely speak English let alone Italian.'

'*Sì, Direttore*,' laughed the assistant. He was so young and fresh-faced that Massimo didn't think the kid had even started shaving. A blessing he should enjoy while it lasted. 'We have done overviews of the main witness statements, a summary report on the major actions carried out and their results, also a forensics overview, with a run-down on soil and substance analysis. We're still running traces on the black plastic bags that the body parts were found in. It all takes time and right now we are short-handed.'

'Chase it, Roberto. You need more men, ask now, not in two weeks, when it is too late.' Massimo fixed his eyes on him, making sure the lesson was being learned.

'I need two more people,' replied Roberto quickly. 'Maybe three shifts each?'

'Then you'll have them, my young colleague,' said Massimo with a generous smile. 'What else?'

Roberto cleared his throat. 'We have translations of the summaries on fingerprints and DNA, but we have no known matches to any offenders.'

'Then, for the moment, keep looking,' instructed Massimo, silently cursing the fact that, unlike the FBI, the Italian Forensic Science Service did not have a fully integrated DNA database on which to carry out searches. It had established CODIS, its own highly efficient Combined DNA Index System as far back as 1999 but the national police, the carabinieri and many other public and private bodies continued to have separate databases that were not connected to CODIS. Moreover, the databases were so zealously guarded that often Massimo's unit had to apply to prosecutors or judges to instruct the owners to release information.

Massimo tried to put the DNA tangle out of his thoughts and pressed on. 'We're all presuming that this BRK is American, and that he is the FBI's problem and will stay the FBI's problem. But a murder here in Italy changes all that. It makes it our problem. My problem, your problem, our problem.' His eyes roamed over them, picking them out one at a time. 'You all understand me?'

'*Sì, Direttore*,' they managed, apologetically and not in unison.

'So why Italy?' continued Massimo, rubbing his big bald head while looking at his team for answers. 'Come on; give me some of your thoughts.'

Roberto went first, 'He's moved here, this is now his home. His job has brought him to Italy.'

'Possibly,' said Massimo. 'Next.'

'Holiday,' suggested Benito, the case coordinator. 'Even serial killers have holidays. Perhaps he just had the opportunity to kill while he was here.'

'Next,' said Massimo.

'Perhaps Cristina Barbuggiani had been on holiday

in America and he came over to visit her,' offered Orsetta.

'Check it,' said Massimo. 'Ask her family where she'd recently been on vacation, and whether there were any foreign friends that she spoke of.'

'What if this serial killer turns out to be Italian?' suggested Roberto. 'Maybe he came from Rome originally, then moved to America like many Italians do, and now, after a long and illustrious career killing Americans, he has decided to come back home and settle here.'

'Then why kill here?' questioned Massimo. 'I could understand a killer, perhaps of Italian blood, coming back to his native home to give it all up, to turn his back on the murders and live out the last of his days in the sunshine, a long and happy way from anyone investigating his crimes. But not to kill here. A dog does not shit in his own basket.'

'I have a dog that shits everywhere, including his own basket,' argued Benito, stroking a straggly black goatee that Massimo desperately wanted to cut off.

'Good point,' said Massimo. 'We should not close our minds to the fact that this man is an exception to all the rules we know, and that he will never stop killing. He is not a burned-out businessman looking for a place in the sun to retire to and rest his old bones in. He is a predator, looking for new prey, thirsting for fresh blood, and perhaps he has decided that Italy is a new hunting ground for him.'

'Perhaps it's not BRK,' suggested Orsetta. 'Perhaps it's a copycat.'

'I don't buy that,' interjected Benito. 'Two killers on two different continents with the same MO, targeting the same type of victims. It's a big ask.'

'No bigger than imagining he's come all the way here just to kill,' replied Orsetta, her voice rising in defence of her theory. 'I mean, it's not like he's short of choice in America, is it? He's got three hundred million people to choose from, so why on earth would he give up such a rich hunting ground to operate in a country that is alien to him?'

'Okay, we'll chalk that up as a maybe,' said Massimo. 'But, back to my point. Why here? What's the link?'

They sat silently, dredging their minds for inspiration. 'King,' suggested Orsetta. 'If it is BRK and not a copycat, then the only link I can think of is Jack King.'

Massimo frowned. 'Jack King?'

Orsetta struggled to build on her suggestion. 'I'm not saying King is the reason BRK may be killing in Italy, I'm just saying that he appears to be the only link.'

Benito curled his beard between his fingers. 'I agree. It's the only link that I can see as well.'

Massimo thought they were getting nowhere. 'Then we are in trouble. If the only connection we can come up with is Jack King, the man I invited to help us, then indeed we have nothing to go on. I want a bottom-up evaluation of all our statements, and I mean all of them. I want every last second of Cristina Barbuggiani's life accounted for. And let me make this very clear to you. I do *not* want this sociopath slaughtering dozens of young girls here in Italy. I do not want a second person to die. Do you understand me?' The looks on their faces told him that they did. 'Good. First killings in new areas are never perfect. This may be our best chance to catch him. No, let me correct myself. This may be our *only* chance to catch him. And that is the reason I have asked Jack King to put his own health at risk in order to help us try to catch this monster – this –' Massimo was stuck for the English words to express the full venom of his hatred for Cristina Barbuggiani's killer. As he resorted to his native tongue, he respectfully covered the dead girl's picture with his big hand. '*Uno che va in culo a sua madre!*'

'Motherfucker,' said Orsetta coolly. 'The word you're looking for, *Direttore*, is motherfucker.'

36

Marine Park, Brooklyn, New York

The house stands alone on the corner of a quiet cul-de-sac, heavily shaded from view by large maple trees and thick hawthorn hedges that dominate the front garden and small driveway. In the pre-dawn darkness, Spider walks around it, checking his security system, testing the sensors on the lights, the angles of the surveillance cameras and the electricity feeds that he's put into a variety of other hidden security devices that will do much more than just deter any unwanted intruders.

In the back yard he sits on the edge of a heavily weathered wooden table and gets to thinking about the old days; the time he lived here with his parents, the time before they went to the Better Place and he was taken away to the orphanage. Fifteen years ago he'd bought the house back, paying cash out of the inheritance left in a trust fund for him. The rest of the money he'd invested wisely, managing a strong portfolio of stocks, shares and bonds over the Internet. His father would have been proud of him. Dad had always said 'never take any unnecessary risks' and that had been the key to his success, in whatever he did.

He remembers life in the orphanage: the bullying, the squabbling, the shortage of food, the fetid warm smell of overcrowded and unclean dormitories and, more than anything, the endless noise. It wasn't until he'd moved out that he appreciated just how golden silence can be. Spider knows those years were formative for him. For better or worse, they shaped him into what he is today. He knows that the reason he still eats his food too quickly is because if he hadn't wolfed down his meals as a kid, the bigger boys in the orphanage would simply have taken whatever they wanted from his plate. He understands his comfort with violence stems from the day he could no longer take the ritual abuse and beatings that all new boys endured, and exploded into a rage that led to him fracturing the skull of one of his attackers by repeatedly banging his head on a toilet wall.

The orphanage had been packed with kids from the wrong side of the tracks and it served as a university of crime, teaching him a dozen ways to establish false identities, obtain bogus documents and set up fake companies. Crime was literally child's play for him.

In the cool of his back yard he fires up a dual-core Dell laptop and, through a false identity web account, goes online. He accesses Webmail and finds his way to his own security-coded intranet system. A few seconds later, he's able to pull up picture feeds from any of the cameras inside or outside the house. He toggles between the external views, then shrinks the screen to compress the pixels and increase the night-view quality. Satisfied with the settings, he punches up the internal camera feeds. In the dark of the yard Sugar's prostrate body shows up as an intense, white shape, almost like a white-hot crucifix. Spider ponders the picture. There is something about the girl that unsettles him. He'd felt it the other night, when he'd approached her, and he feels it again now. He somehow senses that, even spreadeagled and dying, she represents a danger to him. He dismisses his feelings as illogical. His planning has been good, and apart from that one bloody moment when she'd bitten him, he'd experienced no real difficulties with her.

Spider switches angles, choosing a close-up of her face. Her eyes are shut and the camera shot is so tight it almost looks as though she's in a peaceful sleep. He knows the truth is far from that. He imagines that by now the woman is in constant mental agony. He feels no compassion or concern for her. In fact, he feels nothing for her. Hookers are not his usual prey, but then this isn't going to be a usual kill. This kill wasn't planned solely for pleasure; this kill has a much bigger prize attached to it.

37

Mount Amiata, Tuscany

There were days when Tuscany looked so beautiful that Nancy imagined God must have made Italy himself, but then, for some reason known only to him, he subcontracted work on the rest of the world to some Poles who had promised to get it done cheaply and be finished by the end of the week.

Today was one of those days. With Zack in nursery, and Carlo and Paolo briefed on pending jobs at the hotel and restaurant, Jack and Nancy decided to make the most of their time together before he headed off to meet Massimo in Rome.

They spent the morning walking on Mount Amiata. Jack puffed and wheezed far more than he ever thought he would as they climbed the former volcano's great slabs of yellowish-brown rock.

The view from the top across the Val D'Orcia was as stunning as any they had ever seen. They stood side by side on the summit, a warm and gentle wind buffeting them, as they tried to pick out the more notable landmarks of Pienza, Montalcino, Radicofani and of course their own San Quirico.

'Do you know where San Quirico got its name

from?' asked Nancy, as Jack pointed a finger towards its distinctive ancient walls.

'No, I don't,' he conceded, 'but I've got a sneaky feeling that I know someone who does.'

The wind sprayed Nancy's hair across her face as she turned in the breeze. 'It's not nice. Seems the town takes its name from the child martyr Saint Quiricus.'

'Who was he?' asked Jack, eager for her to get to the point.

'Be patient. I'm getting there,' said his wife, well used to his ways. 'Back in the year 304, when Quiricus, or Cyricus as he was sometimes called, was only three years old, the same age as Zack, his mother Julietta was sentenced to death for being a Christian. When she appeared before the local governor in Tarsus and sentence was passed, she had her young son with her. The boy made a fuss, insisting that he wouldn't leave his mother, no matter what happened to him. The officials told him, rather brutally, that his mother was to be killed because she was a Christian. At which point, Quiricus declared that he was also a Christian and wished to die with her. This "stand" apparently maddened the governor so much that he grabbed the boy by his legs and smashed his head on some stone steps. Now here's the amazing bit: Julietta didn't weep; instead, she openly showed that she was happy.'

'Come again?' interrupted Jack. 'Happy?'

'Yes, happy. Apparently she was honoured that her son had been chosen to earn the crown of martyrdom.' It made Nancy wonder if history was repeating itself in the modern world. 'Maybe that's how the parents of suicide bombers feel these days, perhaps their mothers feel honoured.'

'Enough now,' said Jack, keen not to start such a debate. 'You're beginning to sound like my old grandmother.'

'That's no bad thing from what I remember. You liked her, didn't you?'

'Adored her,' corrected Jack, fondly remembering the old woman. 'She was a Bible-bashing nutcase, but I loved her to bits.'

'Anyway, Saint Quiricus is the patron saint of family happiness. And that, allegedly, is where our town got its name.'

'You love it here, don't you?' Jack asked, as a prelude to the conversation he'd been avoiding for as long as possible.

She wiped more hair from her face. 'I do. Don't you?'

He half turned away from her and gazed across the heat-hazed countryside. 'I know this will sound crazy, but I'm not, I'm not happy.' Jack waved his hand across the valley. 'All this is beautiful, but it's not helping me. In fact, even out here on this incredible mountain top, I feel trapped.'

'Trapped?' queried Nancy, conscious that her husband was feeling awkward and was avoiding looking directly at her.

'You said Tuscany would help me recover,' he

turned back to her, 'but what you really meant was that it would help you. All this, it's what you wanted, what you needed.'

'That's unfair!' she snapped. 'When you came out of hospital, you were completely wiped out, you were finished with it all, Jack.'

He shook his head and bit down on his lip. 'No, Nancy, *you* were finished with it. I was sick. I should have stayed in New York. I should have taken some time off, got myself strong again, and then gone back to work and finished the job.'

'Huh!' she exclaimed, and wheeled away from him.

He took a quick pace forward and grabbed her by the arm. 'Listen to me.'

She was startled that he'd been so rough.

He took his hand away. 'I love you. I love you and our little boy to bits, but this exile, this remoteness that's being enforced on me, it's killing me.'

Nancy was stung by the remark, and felt her eyes filling up.

'I'm a policeman, I chase bad guys and lock them up,' he went on, 'that's what I am, and that's what I do. It's all I've ever done, and it's all I know how to do. Bringing me all the way out here, and having me do nothing but help you move chairs and clean plates, isn't helping me, Nancy, it's making me sick.'

'Oh, Jack, how can you say that? You were so ill in New York that you could barely walk when I took you home from the hospital. Look at you now, you're fitter and healthier-looking than ever.'

Jack slapped his stomach and managed a half-smile. 'Physically, you're right. Tuscany helped build my strength. But mentally, well . . .'

She frowned at him. 'Well, what?'

'Mentally, it's destroying me. I feel useless, weak, impotent and . . .' he struggled for words, then added, 'cowardly.'

'Oh, honey.' Nancy wrapped her arms around him and for half a second she thought she felt him try to pull away. She stood with her head against his chest, just as she'd done the first night they'd gone out together. She didn't want him to get involved in criminal work again, but she didn't want to see him like this either. Nancy felt him squeeze her tight and kiss the top of her head. Finally, she broke from his arms and looked up at him. 'You're probably right. I did need to come here. I needed to have a life as far away from murder and morgues as possible. And I needed to have you as well. Not you for only two hours a night, slipping into bed next to me at two a.m. and then slipping out again before daybreak, but a full-time you.'

'I'm sorry,' he began.

Nancy cut him off. 'Shush, let me finish. You scared me so much when you collapsed. I can't imagine – I don't want to imagine – bringing Zack up on my own because you've worked yourself to death. Is that so selfish?'

'No, no it's not,' he conceded, knowing she had him on the back foot.

'I want to grow old with you, be it here, or be it anywhere else in the world. I just want us to live a long and happy life together.' She looked around, just as Jack had done moments ago. 'You're right. I do love it here, and I hope you'll learn to love it too. But more than anything I love you.' She forced a smile for him. 'I understand that you have to get involved again. I guess deep down I always knew you would. Unfinished business and all that.' She let out a sigh, then took his hand. 'But promise me that you're going to be careful.'

'I promise,' he said, just as he had done a hundred times before.

'And you've got to keep going to that psychiatrist. You'll do that?'

'I will.'

'Then do it. Do whatever you have to.' Nancy tried to smile again, but this time she couldn't, and the tears came.

Jack wrapped his arms around her and held her. From the top of Amiata they looked out towards the place where they'd built their new home and privately both wondered what the future held for them. Nancy turned to her husband and kissed him passionately.

38

Rome

There were two important facts that Massimo Albonetti had not yet shared with Jack King. The first was that the severed head of Cristina Barbuggiani had not been recovered at sea, like the other body parts, but had been boxed up by her killer and delivered to their headquarters in Rome, seemingly by a courier company in Milan. The second was even more shocking.

Both omissions were on Massimo's mind and were making him short-tempered as he passed out cold drinks and continued briefing his team for Jack's arrival.

'Roberto has completed the victimology report and had it translated,' said Orsetta, popping the tab on a can of Cola Lite.

'*Va bene*,' said Massimo, glad to be distracted from his thoughts. 'And what does it tell us, Roberto? Why did this man pick out Cristina Barbuggiani? What made her the unlucky one?'

'More than anything, she seemed simply to be in the wrong place at the wrong time –' began the young researcher.

'Bullshit!' exploded Massimo, his hand again sheltering Cristina's photograph from his more 'colourful' language. '*Che cazzo stai dicendo!*'

'In English, *Direttore*,' said Orsetta, with a smile.

Massimo glared at her and turned back to the researcher. 'Roberto, do not even think of telling that to Jack King. BRK is not an opportunist; he's not a common, spur-of-the-moment criminal. This man chose Cristina. He picked her out of the crowd. When Jack King asks you that question, do not shame this unit by telling him she was in the wrong place at the wrong time.' Massimo turned to Orsetta, holding Cristina's picture between his thumb and forefinger. 'Find me a lookalike. Go to the film casting agencies and find me an actress who looks like our Cristina and can behave like Cristina did.'

'I will fix it,' said Orsetta.

'And, Orsetta,' continued Massimo. 'What about *Patologia*, what did they have to say about the limbs?'

'The limbs, or the head?' she asked, opening her notebook.

'The limbs first,' answered Massimo, still not sure how he was going to break the news of the head to Jack. 'They were dumped in various places in the sea, while, as we know, the head was sent here. So, I guess he got rid of the body parts first, and hung on to the girl's head until the last moment?'

'Most likely,' said Orsetta, flicking to the relevant page of notes. 'As you request, I will start with the limbs first. Dismemberment and then dispersal of the body parts in sea water made setting the time of death very difficult. The labs said it was also made harder by the fact that they had no body fluids to test . . .'

'*Madonna porca!*' swore Massimo. 'How easy do these so-called scientists want their lives? How about we pass a law that all killers have to tag the bodies with the exact time of death before they dispose of them? Orsetta, save me from the excuses. Just tell me the facts that can help us.'

Orsetta, well used to his emotional flare-ups, continued unshaken. 'Decomposition was pretty uniform across the body parts, give or take a few hours. All the flesh had begun softening and liquefying. He'd tied the severed limbs in the plastic bags before dumping them at sea, so they went through a fairly normal putrefaction cycle. There had been discoloration, marbling and some blistering.'

'How long, Orsetta?' asked Massimo impatiently. 'How long had he kept her body?'

'They couldn't predict that accurately from the body parts, but —'

'*Affanculo!*' swore Massimo, slamming a meaty hand on his desk top. '*Non mi rompere le palle!*'

Orsetta reddened, not with embarrassment, but with anger. 'With the greatest respect, *Direttore*, I am not breaking your balls; these are the path lab reports, not mine. The body parts don't help us a lot because the decomposition rate is skewed by the fact that they were dumped in sea water.'

'*Mi dispiace*,' said Massimo, clasping his hands together as though in prayer. 'Please continue.' He reached out and once more gently touched the photograph of Cristina on his desk.

Orsetta picked up where she'd been stopped. 'Pathology says it looks like Cristina had been dead for about six to eight days before her body was dismembered and then exposed to the sea water.'

'Anything in the stomach or lungs that helps us?' asked Massimo, hopefully.

Orsetta frowned. 'Fortunately, Cristina's torso had been wrapped quickly and tightly in the plastic sacks, presumably to avoid a lot of spillage at the crime scene, and this went a long way to preserving parts of the vital organs. Lung tissue analysis was difficult, but from what they could work out, no diatoms were found in the body organs. They checked bone marrow too, and that came back clear of the diatoms as well.'

'Diatoms are microscopic organisms usually found in lakes, rivers or seas?' checked Roberto.

'That's right,' said Orsetta. 'Even bathwater in some places can contain them. Anyway, evidence that they were not absorbed while she was alive means she was not killed by drowning nor was she dismembered in the sea water, or any other water for that matter.'

'Surely that would have been unlikely anyway?' suggested Benito.

'You're right,' Massimo agreed. 'Unlikely, but not impossible. It has been known for a murderer to drown a victim in bathwater and then dismember the body in the same water, the logic being that there is only one crime scene for the killer to clean up, rather than a death site and a separate dismemberment site. We should always look for the unusual. If you can find it, then you have a sat nav guide to your murderer.'

Orsetta took a long drink of the cold cola. Massimo waited until she finished before he urged her to continue. 'Now her head,' said the *Direttore*. 'What does *Patologia* say about the head of Cristina Barbuggiani?'

Orsetta flicked over a page of her notes. 'The head . . .'

'Her head, Cristina's head,' snapped Massimo. 'It is not an object. We are dealing with a person here. Let's remember that.'

'Cristina's head,' Orsetta began again, 'we can treat as a pure sample, in that it had not been exposed to any sea water. So fixing the time and date of death is more possible here.' Her eyes dipped down to her notes, to find the pathologist's exact wording. '"The skin was easy enough to peel from the skull and the hair could be gently pulled out." From this, they fixed the rate of decomposition at about two weeks.'

Roberto was pondering something. 'How differently does a body decompose on land, compared to in water?'

'Very differently,' said Massimo. 'Bodies decompose in air twice as quickly as they do in water, and eight times as quickly as they do in soil.'

'And young people decay faster than old people,' added Benito.

'Why's that?' asked Roberto.

'Because of the fat levels,' explained Benito. 'Fluid and fat accelerate decomposition. So if you want to hang around in life, or death, stay off the burgers and beer.'

'Thank you, Benito,' said Massimo, cutting off the start of his case coordinator's stream of black humour. 'Maggots, Orsetta. Jack will want to know about infestation. Were all the usual suspects present?'

'Yes, they were,' confirmed Orsetta. 'Analysis revealed the presence of multiple fully formed Calliphora.'

'Blue-bottle fly,' explained Benito to Roberto.

Orsetta raised her eyebrows at him, making sure he'd finished with his interruptions, then carried on. 'The larvae were mature, elderly, fat, indolent, third-stage maggots, not in pupa cases. The estimate was that they had been laid about nine or ten days earlier. The lab said we should allow an extra day or two for the original flies to have found the head. Sorry, Cristina's head. So we're back with the fourteen-day estimate.'

Massimo looked up from his desk top. 'None of the progeny of the flies had themselves reached the breeding stage?'

'No,' she answered. 'I asked the same question. Apparently that would have taken about a month.'

'So again the timing coincides?' checked Roberto.

'Yes,' Orsetta confirmed. 'In the summary, the notes concur again that the head was probably kept in a lukewarm place for between ten and fourteen days.'

Massimo scribbled some words on his pad and the team waited silently until he had finished. 'We need to have a stab at a timeline. Let's look . . .'

Roberto interrupted him. '*Direttore*, I think I have a rough one.'

'Go on,' said Massimo, pleased to see the youngster had been thinking ahead.

'Cristina was last seen alive on the ninth of June and was reported missing on the tenth. From what we've been told by the pathology reports, it's likely that she was killed somewhere around the twelfth to the fourteenth. We're told the corpse was kept for six days before it was dismembered and disposed of. This takes us to the twentieth of June as probably the earliest that he started disposing of the limbs. We have our first public finding of remains two days later, on the twenty-second.'

Massimo held up a hand. 'That's good, but let's stop for a moment and back up a little. It looks as if this man held Cristina alive for between a minimum of two and a maximum of four days.' He looked up at his team, and continued, 'Then, when he killed her, he kept her body, or parts of it, for another six to eight days. Why? Why did he wait so long? What was he doing?' He let the dates and questions sink in, swallowed hard and added, 'Our killer then kept Cristina's severed head for another four or five days, before it was delivered to us. Again, why?'

Orsetta made the sign of the cross and bowed her head; she could not begin to imagine what agonies Cristina had endured, or what kind of man they were hunting.

'He has left us with many questions to answer, but let's concentrate on the main ones,' said Massimo, preparing to tick them off on his fingers. 'How did he manage to abduct Cristina? Where did he hold her for those two to four days that she was alive? Did he keep her corpse in the same place, for up to six days, or did he move her somewhere else? Why did he wait so long before sending Cristina's head to us?'

Massimo let his hand fall to his desk and glanced across at the framed picture of Cristina. She seemed not to have a worry in the world. Her face was unlined, radiant and full of promise. Her smile was so wide that the photographer had probably caught her just as a laugh was about to escape her lips. Massimo looked up again, and moved the conversation on to something he'd so far kept secret from Jack. 'And the other big question is: what exactly did the killer mean to tell us by the note that he sealed in a plastic bag and left inside Christina's skull?'

PART FOUR
Wednesday, 4 July

39

Rome

'Jack King, you look magnificent!' exclaimed Massimo Albonetti, throwing his arms around the former FBI agent as he entered his office.

'And you – my smooth Italian friend – you still look like a polished cue ball,' said Jack, playfully rubbing the top of Massimo's bald head.

Massimo slapped his hand away and shut the door behind them. 'They told me you were ill, but look at you. You're heavier and healthier than I've ever seen you.'

'Good food and a good wife, that's the secret,' said Jack, patting his stomach.

'Jack, please, I am Italian – these things you do not need to tell me.' He waved a hand towards a chair on the other side of his desk. 'Please, please sit down. Can I get you a drink? Coffee, water?'

'Just some water, please. I'm trying to fight the caffeine.'

'Me too,' said Massimo, 'but the caffeine is always winning.' He pressed his desk intercom. 'Claudia, two double espressos and some water, please.'

Jack shot him a disapproving glance.

Massimo shrugged his shoulders. 'If you don't want it when it comes, then I will have yours as well.'

Jack took the seat and leant on the desk. 'Benedetta and the kids good? Did they get away on holiday okay?'

'Yes, fine, thank you,' said Massimo. 'Though there was another terrorist scare at the airport and the children were disappointed at not being able to take certain toys on the plane. No toy guns, no water pistols – how does a young child cope these days without them?'

'Air travel will never be the same again,' said Jack. 'Pretty soon you're going to have to empty your body fluids, then zip yourself up in a clear plastic bag before they'll let you board. The boys and girls in the anti-terrorist units certainly have their work cut out for them.'

'*Sì*,' said Massimo, smiling. 'I thank God every night that I managed to avoid being drafted into that particular war.'

The small talk had come to an end, so Jack asked the question that had been preying on his mind ever since they'd last spoken. 'So, Mass, are you going to tell me what you couldn't tell me on the phone?'

The Italian sat back and his old chair creaked so loudly it sounded as though the joints might break. The question was far from unexpected, and the answer was simple, but he still hesitated to break the news. 'Jack, you know how much I respect you and treasure our friendship, so forgive me for this. Before

I tell you everything, I have to look you in the eye, man to man, friend to friend, and ask you: are you really all right now? Are you really strong enough mentally and physically to face up to what we are asking of you?'

It was the same question that Orsetta had alluded to, and one which Jack had been repeatedly asking himself over the last few days. 'I am,' he said forcefully, though deep down he still had his doubts. 'From what you've said, your murder, if it is not a copycat killing, may be the work of a man who killed at least sixteen young women in America. Now, I've tracked this bastard for close on half a decade, and the effort and strain damned near killed me. But I'll tell you this, Mass, watching him kill again and again, and being unable to try to stop him, well, that would be the worst thing in the world for me. For the sake of my own sanity, I have to be involved in this with you. I must, one more time, try to do everything I possibly can to get this guy off the streets.'

'Bravo, my friend,' said Massimo, relieved that he'd got the answer he'd been hoping for. 'I'm very proud that you have decided to work with us.'

'Okay, cut the gushy stuff,' said Jack light-heartedly. 'What is it you haven't been telling me?'

Massimo leant forward on his elbows and let Jack read the serious look on his face. This wasn't going to be easy. 'The report I sent you mentioned that Cristina's body had been dismembered, but some things were left out.'

Jack said nothing; his eyes asked the question for him.

'Cristina had been decapitated. He dismembered her body and severed her head. After he disposed of the other parts, he sent her head to our offices, here in Rome.'

There were a dozen questions Jack wanted to ask, but he started with the most obvious one. 'Why wasn't this in the confidential briefing notes? If I remember correctly, they'd gone to your Prime Minister's office.'

Massimo smiled. 'There is nothing confidential in Italian politics, especially in the Prime Minister's office. Send something confidential to the highest level and you merely push up the price at which an aide or civil servant will sell the document to the press.'

Massimo opened a long drawer that ran the full width of his desk. 'There's something more,' he said, determined to address all the outstanding issues with Jack as quickly as possible. He pulled out a thin file marked 'Barbuggiani/Confidential'. He handed it across the desk, adding, 'This is a copy of a note found inside the mouth of Cristina Barbuggiani. Forensics have the original.'

'Inside her skull?' checked Jack.

Massimo nodded. Jack slowly opened the file, his mind trying to put the various angles together. A pattern was clearly starting to emerge in both the US and Italian cases and he suspected he was about to see more links and similarities. Jack looked down at the photocopy. It was of a handwritten note. Black felt-tip ink, in capitals on plain white paper. The message was short, but devastating:

BUON GIORNO ITALIAN POLICE!
HERE IS A GIFT FOR YOU, WITH LOVE FROM BRK.
CALL IT A 'HEADS-UP' OF WHAT I'VE GOT IN STORE FOR YOU!
HA! HA! HA!

☺

BRK

A cold wave of emotion seeped down Jack's shoulders and spine, his eyes locked on the three letters that had ruined his life.

BRK.

The Black River Killer.

Jack read the note again and noticed that the three letters came up twice. It was almost as though the writer was trying too hard to convince the police that it was his handiwork.

'Are you okay, Jack?' asked Massimo.

'I've been better,' he said, rubbing a hand across his forehead. Something wasn't right, but he couldn't put his finger on it. Maybe it was the sick humour – *a heads-up* – or maybe once more he was just grasping for a reason, any reason, to convince himself that this wasn't proof that BRK was killing again. He took a long breath and cleared his head. 'I spoke to my old office in New York and it turns out that the corpse of an early BRK victim had been exhumed and the skull posted there, care of yours truly.'

Massimo screwed up his face. He felt for Jack. All this was a lot of pressure to pour on the guy at once. 'I saw a Bureau note on this, and heard some details had leaked to the press, but nothing was said about it being addressed to you.'

'Well, it was. Howie Baumguard, my old number two, is convinced it's BRK.'

'The Bureau note said nothing of that,' remarked Massimo.

'Same confidentiality problem as your Prime Minister's office,' said Jack, forcing a smile. 'Put that kind of information on the closed wires and it's sure to get out in the open.'

Massimo was wondering whether it was really possible for BRK to be almost simultaneously active in both Italy and the USA. 'Do you think this Black River Killer really is responsible for the incident back in America?'

Jack let out the breath he'd been holding. 'I really don't know. The issue is clouded now because of what you've just told me.'

Massimo scratched at a patch of stubble just below his left ear. 'Two decapitations. Two heads, both mailed by the killer . . .'

Jack cut him off. 'BRK has a thing about left hands, not heads. But you're right; it seems too much of a coincidence to believe that two separate killers send dead women's heads to law enforcement organizations at roughly the same time.'

'I agree,' said Massimo, 'and I really hope I'm wrong. I would much rather believe we're dealing with a first-time psycho, than entertain the thought that your infamous serial killer has decided to make Italy his new playground.'

Jack searched his mind for the name of the Italian victim, and felt bad that it didn't come. 'Cristina Bar–Bar –'

Massimo helped him. 'Barbuggiani.'

'Barbuggiani,' continued Jack. 'How was her head delivered to you?'

Massimo raised his eyes in exasperation. 'Not yet fully clear. Our goods bay took possession of a cardboard box. It was passed to the mail room and then one of the clerks, a young woman, opened it.'

'What can your bay tell us?'

'It wasn't signed in, and we can't find anyone to say that they took possession,' answered Massimo, looking embarrassed. 'It's possible that it was just left with other mail in one of the "In" crates. We security-scan all the mail and packages, but not until they are being sorted into the different departments.'

'Do I feel a security review and tightening of procedures coming on?' asked Jack.

'Already under way,' confirmed Massimo. 'There was a courier company stamp on the box, but we've not got anything on them yet.'

'Forensics find anything on either the box or your note?' asked Jack.

'No prints. ESDA testing also came back blank. We're running a trace on the notepaper and the ink.'

Jack shook his head. 'Not much point. It'll be the commonest possible.'

Massimo hoped he was wrong. 'Don't despair too early, my friend. Even the best of criminals make mistakes.'

'Not this guy,' said Jack. 'Let me tell you how he works. Before this son of a bitch does anything, he researches the backside off it. I bet you your life savings that the pen he used to write this pornography is the most commonly used felt-tip pen in America.'

'Or Italy.'

'I bet you a hundred euros it's American. The paper too. Your researchers will draw a blank on all your Italian manufacturers, I promise you, Mass.'

Massimo shrugged. 'Then maybe we discover the paper is a particular batch, issued to a particular region, on a particular date. Your colleagues in the FBI will be able to help us with this.'

'You betcha, they've got whole databases on ink and paper,' said Jack dismissively. 'But I'll guarantee you this as well: BRK knows we'll run those traces, he knows that eventually we will find the factory that produced the ink, the very tree the damned wood came from to make the paper.'

'What are you saying, Jack?'

'I'm saying this. He will have bought the most

common paper he could get his hands on, months and months, maybe even years, ago. He'll have bought it for cash, from a giant store, in a city that he no longer has anything to do with, and in the first place was probably only passing through. Even if we trace the day, the date, the time that he purchased it, the information will lead us nowhere.'

Massimo's door opened and Claudia, his PA, came in with the espressos and some small tumblers of water.

'*Grazie*,' said Massimo. Claudia smiled and left as quietly as a burglar.

'You want this?' Mass held out a cup of coffee to Jack.

'Yeah, I sure do,' said Jack, craving anything that would jolt him out of his moment of pessimism. 'Anyway, the pen and paper aren't the biggest clues.'

'You mean the text?' said Massimo, pulling his chair alongside Jack on the other side of his desk.

'Yeah. He thought long and hard about these words, Mass. What were your first impressions when you read it?'

Massimo turned the paper towards him and read silently. 'Shocking. Cold-blooded. Brutal. How you say in America, "straight to the point", is that right?'

'Yeah, that's right. What else?'

Mass puzzled for a moment. 'Clear – threatening – dangerous.' He started to struggle to add to his list. 'And you? What do you make of it?'

Jack scanned the paper again. 'He's begging for

attention. The bold capital letters, the brevity of the note, the use of exclamation marks, the fact that he mentions his own name twice – it all shows that he's craving, almost demanding our attention. As you know, when killers do this, it's usually a sign that they are full of pent-up anger and are bursting to release it. I'd say he's either about to kill again, or maybe has even killed since writing this letter.'

It wasn't a thought that Massimo wanted to consider. His resources were stretched to the limit and another murder would cause mayhem, not just on the Barbuggiani case, but on three other, unrelated ones that he was overseeing. He took out a cigarette, tapped the end of it repeatedly on his desk and asked, 'Will he have found the process of writing the letter arousing?'

'Undoubtedly,' said Jack. 'Not only arousing, but empowering. He'd also be particularly turned on by the waiting process, the anticipation that we would read it.'

Massimo looked down at the letter again. 'I noticed that he spelt *buon giorno* correctly. Not many foreigners would do that. I think maybe he is an educated man.'

'He's certainly no fool. Check the letter again and you'll see that the grammar, spelling and punctuation are all correct,' said Jack. 'But I think there are two reasons why he is precise and so correct. Firstly, like I've said before, it's not that he's hugely intelligent, it's that he's hugely careful. BRK researches everything he does, meticulously. This guy probably looked up the spelling of *buon giorno* to make sure he didn't make a mistake. His whole attitude to life is to be careful, to plan, to avoid making that one slip-up that could end his freedom, and that's mirrored in this letter as well.'

'And the second reason?' asked Mass.

'His ego. This is a murderer with the biggest ego on the planet. If you could see egos, then we'd just hire a plane, fly around a bit and pull him in. It would be as easy as that.'

'Why so egotistical?'

'BRK would be mortified if he'd done something wrong and thought we were laughing at him, rather than him laughing at us.' Jack moved the paper closer to Mass. 'Here, look at this.' He pointed out the smiley face. 'Kids use these on e-mails, they draw them as symbols to express that they're happy in an uncomplicated, pure, childish way. The smiley is pretty much the first face a kid gets to draw. By using it, he's showing us that he has no respect for any of our values, and is happy to be seen as a threat to the most precious thing we have, our children. He's using the smiley as a form of intimidation. And now look at this.' Jack ran his finger under the line 'HA! HA! HA!' 'He's going to great lengths to mock us. Note the bold capitals again, and three exclamation marks. That's his way of saying, "I see you all as a joke, don't you get it?" And then there's this, the sickest of lines.' Jack's finger pointed to 'CALL IT A "HEADS-UP" OF WHAT I'VE GOT IN STORE FOR YOU!'

The former FBI profiler leant back in his chair. 'He's warning us that he's going to kill again. Why?'

Massimo lit the cigarette, blew out smoke and considered his answer. 'It's a game. Maybe this whole thing is just one giant game for him.'

Jack blinked from the smoke wafting his way. 'You're right, and he wants to make certain that we'll play. I think he's here in Italy, and I'm a hundred per cent sure that he's going to kill again.'

San Quirico D'Orcia, Tuscany

At the same time that Jack was meeting Massimo in Rome, American tourist Terry McLeod paid the taxi driver, moved his baggage off the dusty road and snapped the first of his holiday pictures, the outside of La Casa Strada.

'Sure is a pretty place,' he told Maria, as he bowled into the cool reception area and announced his arrival.

'We have you staying with us for just five days. Is that correct, Meester McLeod?' she said in the English that she hoped one day would be good enough to see her compete internationally as a beauty queen.

'That's right. Wish it could be longer. Never been to Tuscany before, it looks really fantastic.' He peered at her name badge. 'Tell me, Maria, are the owners of this place around? What're their names again?'

'Mr and Mrs King,' said the receptionist, struggling

to understand him because he spoke so quickly. 'Mrs King is here, but not Mr King. Would you like me to call her for you?' She picked up the desk phone. 'Are you a friend from America?'

'No, no, don't do that,' he said. 'I'm sure I'll bump into them while I'm here. Lots of time to catch them, let it ride for now.'

Maria looked him over. He was about the same age as Mr King but nowhere near as tall or good-looking. He had a little fat belly that billowed beneath a pink Ralph Lauren polo shirt, like the one she'd hoped to buy her boyfriend Sergio. On closer examination, she noticed it had a thin brown stain running down the front of it, as though coffee or ice cream had dribbled from his machine-gun mouth and caught on his big stomach. 'May I have your passport, please?' she asked. 'And the credit card you wish to use to settle your bill? Breakfast is available until ten thirty and is included in your daily rate.'

McLeod handed over his passport and sized up the receptionist as she photocopied it. She was beautiful. He'd pay good money to have her sent up to his room along with a stack of beer and some decent air-conditioning. Man, Italy may be great on historic buildings but it sure sucked when it came to keeping things cool.

'Thank you,' said Maria.

McLeod smiled at her. 'How do you say that in Italian? Is it the same as in Spanish, *gracias*?'

'No,' said Maria sweetly, 'not quite. We say *grazie*.'

217

'Grat-sea,' he tried.

'*Perfetto*,' said Maria, deciding it would be rude to correct his slight mispronunciation. 'You are in the Scorpio suite,' she told him, taking a key from a set of hooks on the wall behind her. 'Please go straight down the corridor, here to the right of me, then first left and up some stairs, that's Scorpio.'

'Scorpio,' he repeated. 'Are all the rooms named after star signs?'

'Yes. Yes, they are,' said Maria, now growing tired of him and wishing he would go, so she could return to the magazine under her desk.

'How many are there? In total, how many rooms?'

Maria had to think for a moment. 'Six. No, eight. There are eight rooms in all.'

'Eight,' repeated McLeod, thinking for a minute of how he might be able to persuade the beautiful Maria to spend some time with him in one of them. Later. There would be time for that later. First though, he had a lot of planning to do. Business first – pleasure later.

40

Rome

The Cristina Barbuggiani case conference was due to start at two p.m., but Massimo had insisted they took a leisurely 'catch-up' lunch at a restaurant around the corner, explaining that in Italy two p.m. meant any time before four.

The conference was being staged in a dedicated Incident Room and people were chattering loudly and pointing at whiteboards as Jack and Massimo entered. The *Direttore* introduced Benito, Roberto and the pathologist, *Dottoressa* Annelies van der Splunder. 'Orsetta Portinari I think you already know,' he said, suppressing the start of a smile.

'Very pleased to see you again, Mr King,' said Orsetta warmly.

'And you, Inspector,' said Jack, a little less enthusiastically. 'Forgive me,' he went on, turning to the pathologist, a tall, plumpish woman in her late thirties with straw-like short blonde hair. 'Your name doesn't sound particularly Italian.'

'You really are a detective,' joked the *Dottoressa*. 'I'm Dutch. Had the good fortune to fall in love with an Italian and moved here about seven years ago. I worship Rome; this is home for me now.'

'Jack and his wife are also Italophiles,' added Massimo. 'They have a small, but I'm told very exclusive, hotel in Tuscany.'

'Sounds gorgeous,' said the pathologist. 'You must give me details. My partner Lunetta and I are always looking for places for a long weekend away.'

'Lunetta?' interjected Orsetta. 'Lunetta della Rossellina, the fashion model?'

'Yes,' said the pathologist, pleased the name had been recognized. 'Lunetta's love is clothes, and mine is food and wine – as I think you can see.'

'Then Italy is perfect for both of you,' said Massimo diplomatically. '*Dottoressa*, Jack has read your report, but I'm wondering if you'd be kind enough to update him on the conversation you and I had last night about Cristina's blood type.'

'Of course,' the pathologist said. 'Do you mind if we sit down? I need to get my glasses to go through some notes.'

The team gathered around a long, plain conference table made of beech and Annelies van der Splunder put on some round wire-framed glasses that Orsetta thought made her look half-headmistress, half-owl.

'The examinations I carried out were on the dismembered limbs, torso, stomach contents and head of a young white, Italian woman in her mid-twenties, who I now know was Cristina Barbuggiani, a citizen of Livorno. The dismembered body parts were delivered to me over a period of about a week, the poor woman's head being the last to arrive for my attention. The decapitated head gave me the most information, and from this I was able to ascertain that Cristina was AB Rhesus negative.'

'That's quite rare, isn't it?' asked Jack.

'Yes, it is. And even though blood typing is my pet subject, I'm afraid it's hard to say exactly how rare in Italy; probably less than nine per cent of the population are of the AB grouping. AB is the rarest and incidentally the newest of discovered blood groups. O is the oldest, it goes back to the Stone Age. A is the next oldest, and has its roots in the farming settlements of Norway, Denmark, Austria, Armenia and Japan. AB, however, dates back less than a thousand years and came about as all the blood groups began to mix in Europe.'

'And the Rhesus factoring?' asked Jack.

Annelies removed her glasses for a moment. 'As I'm sure you know, the D antigen is the most common. If it is present, we describe the grouping as positive. In Cristina, it was missing, therefore she is Rhesus negative. Probably only about three per cent of the population share her blood type.'

'This really helps us,' said Jack, turning to Massimo, 'but only if you can find it on him, or find the scene where BRK cut up Cristina's body. Evidentially, tying her blood to a suspect would be a very powerful argument in court.'

'Yes, but finding the scene?' said Benito, shrugging his shoulders. 'So far it has not been possible.'

'Where have you tried?' asked Jack, non-judgementally.

'We've had to focus mainly on Livorno and the big cities that have strong links with the town and province,' said Benito, 'so we're working out towards Pisa, which is twenty kilometres away, Lucca, forty kilometres, Florence, about eighty and finally Siena, which is about a hundred, maybe a hundred and twenty kilometres away. We're looking at hire car businesses, hotels and guesthouses and even long-distance trucking companies. We are asking them all if they have had to clean any blood from any of the vehicles or property used by recent clients. So far nothing.'

Jack doubted the search would provide anything to build a case on but he understood that they had to go through the motions. Often it was the routine checks, rather than brilliant detective work, that provided critical breakthroughs.

'Let me get this right,' he said, addressing the pathologist again. 'According to your report, you believe the killer kept the head for maybe up to two weeks before he sent it here?'

'Approximately,' said van der Splunder, cautiously. 'Please be careful not to mix up death and decapitation. Death was on, or about, the fourteenth; decapitation and dismemberment were most likely on or around the twentieth.'

'You mean death wasn't through decapitation – he killed her, kept her corpse, then beheaded her?'

'Exactly.'

'How did she die?' asked Jack.

The pathologist flinched. 'I found some evidence of pre-mortem focal bruising on the larynx.'

'She was strangled, or choked somehow?' asked Jack.

'I believe so,' said van der Splunder. 'There was no evidence of ligature strangulation, so I imagine it was done manually. Indeed, some of the marks on the throat are consistent with continuous deep pressure, possibly from a man's knuckles.'

Jack knew what it meant, and why she had flinched. It would have taken about four minutes to strangle Cristina in this way. He hoped that she'd blacked out after about thirty seconds when her brain became starved of oxygen, but he was sure it would still have been a horribly slow death. Perhaps the most horrible imaginable, with the killer using his hands to choke her to the point of death, then easing up and letting her recover, before choking her again. Jack knew many stranglers who had turned the act of murder into a sexual marathon, indulging their violence in small ebbs and flows, before brutally climaxing with the final fatal pressure of their fingers.

'Care to share your thoughts with us?' said Massimo casually.

Jack shook himself out of the death scene, and returned to the more functional business of the timeline. 'Let's presume BRK was responsible for Cristina's murder and also for the desecration of Sarah Kearney's grave in Georgetown. Given the approximate time of Cristina's death and the recorded time that some kids discovered Sarah's disturbed grave, we should be able to work out the window when he had to fly out of Italy and into America.'

Massimo nodded. 'We are already doing border patrol passport checks on all male US citizens over thirty years of age who entered and left Italy in the last three months. You will be amazed at how many come and go!'

Jack ploughed on. 'Well, if we get this timeline right, we should be able to narrow the focus considerably.' He moved to a whiteboard, picked up a black marker and wrote the key points as he talked. 'Cristina is last seen alive by friends on the night of June the ninth. The day after, the tenth, she's reported missing. She's killed around the fourteenth, but he hangs on to the corpse, keeping it intact for six days, which takes us to the twentieth.' He glanced over to the pathologist and she signalled her agreement with his account. 'On the twentieth he started disposing of the limbs. We have our first public finding of remains two days later, on the twenty-second, and the next significant date is the arrival of Cristina's head at police HQ in Rome on the twenty-fifth, which is examined by the good professor here on the twenty-sixth.' Jack paused to make sure he hadn't made any mistakes. No one corrected him, so he slotted in the last pieces of the jigsaw. 'The FBI thinks he was in the cemetery at Georgetown, South Carolina on the night of June the thirtieth, morning of July the first, so it's reasonable to presume that he may have left Italy on the evening of June the twenty-fifth, or morning of the twenty-sixth, which would have got him into America on the twenty-sixth or twenty-seventh, just a couple of days before the desecration of Sarah's grave.'

'Is there a direct flight from Italy to Georgetown?' asked Massimo.

Jack frowned. 'Don't know. Myrtle is quite a big international airport, maybe there are flights from Rome or Milan.'

'We'll re-focus on these tighter dates,' promised Benito, adding to his ever-lengthening list.

They stared at the board again, then Massimo asked, 'Why do you think he picked Livorno?'

'Good question,' replied Jack. 'In the past, BRK has always killed near a major coastline. A tidal sea is a very handy way to dispose of a body, so it might be as simple as that. Or there may be a bigger significance that we are yet to discover. We can't rule out a connection to a port – it could be that he is a sailor of some kind – although I have to say that we've done extensive checks with the American navy and haven't come up with any possible suspects.'

'Livorno has a very active port,' said Orsetta. 'Unless I'm mistaken, I think there's a naval academy there.'

'There is,' said Benito, 'it's the training school for officers. The Italian navy has been in Livorno since the late eighteen hundreds.'

'How do you know that?' asked Orsetta with a wry smile.

Benito held up his hands in mock surrender. 'Okay, so I once dreamt of being a sailor, and ended up as a policeman instead. It's nothing to be ashamed of.'

Once the laughter had died down Jack picked up the thread. 'We don't really know why BRK was in Livorno, but we're going to presume that he was there and that somehow he singled out Cristina. Were there any witness reports of her being seen with any strangers over the last few days before she disappeared?'

Massimo shook his head.

'Didn't think so,' continued Jack, 'so it's possible that BRK persuaded her to get into a vehicle and travel voluntarily with him to a secluded place that he'd set up beforehand.'

'Hang on,' said Massimo. 'Orsetta, wasn't Cristina into helping out at some architectural dig near Florence?'

'Yes, she was,' confirmed Orsetta. 'Friends said she was regularly at Montelupo Fiorentino; there was some talk about uncovering a frescoed burial chamber.'

'Our girl was a tomb raider?' asked Jack.

Orsetta corrected him. 'Not at all. In fact, just the opposite. She was very much on the official side of archaeology, she was said to be extremely community-minded and passionate about preserving Italian culture.'

'A sad loss,' said Massimo, considering for a second what kind of woman Cristina had been and how she no doubt would have had the makings of a good mother as well as a good citizen, if only she'd had the chance to realize her potential. He scratched his chin, then went on, 'Let's concentrate on that route from Livorno to Montelupo Fiorentino. Maybe BRK met her on the way there, or on the way back. Remember a few years ago we had an offender who used to target women he saw pictured in newspapers? Well, let's see if Cristina was recently in any papers, magazines, tourist handouts or even on any Internet sites.'

'Will do,' confirmed Benito.

Jack abandoned his whiteboard and turned once more to the pathologist. '*Dottoressa*, I know from your report that there were no traces of the offender's flesh, blood or semen on any of Cristina's limbs. But did toxicology test for any traces of lubrication or prophylactics, especially in the orifices of the skull?'

Annelies screwed up her face, not at the thought of how disgusting such an act was, but at recalling how badly decomposed the head had been. 'They haven't, but I wouldn't hold out much hope of success. Most tissue and organs had liquefied. There were some tiny markings in the mouth, but these were consistent with the plastic bag that held the note being jammed in there. Why do you ask?'

Jack slowly rubbed his face with his hands, as if washing off his tiredness. 'We know from case studies that killers who amputate heads very often use those skulls for sexual purposes, either penetrating the oral or ocular cavities or ejaculating over the skull itself. Similarly, we've had some success tracing forensically aware sexual offenders from the type of lubrication used on the condom they wore in the hope they wouldn't leave any tell-tale DNA at the scene.'

'I'll ask the lab to do their best,' said the pathologist, 'but as I said, I wouldn't hold out too much hope.'

'Thank you,' said Jack.

'I have a question,' said Massimo, Cristina's photograph neon-bright in his mind. 'This doesn't seem to be a killing purely for sexual gratification. So, why did he do it? Why did he take the life of this young woman?'

The question hung in a cloud of thoughtful silence, before Jack finally spoke. 'He desired her. The length of time that he spent with her before he killed her, and with her corpse afterwards, indicates that he was somehow attracted to her. Whatever the purpose of his kill, whether it was to relieve a violent tension inside him, to satisfy a deep sexual fantasy or to feed some dark psychological need, he was attracted to her. And once he had her, he wanted to keep her. You know as well as I do that maybe he was just trawling for a victim and her physical appearance was enough to set off some subliminal trigger in him that focused on her as a victim. Or it could be that there's a more substantial link, a previous meeting at which he became attracted to her. Somehow I don't think so. BRK stalks, kills and then –' Jack's voice trailed off as he tried to imagine what inner cravings drove the killer. 'Bearing in mind how long he seems to have kept her body post mortem, it seems an extra wave of desire came crashing in on him once she was dead. It's as though death feeds some psychological and possibly sexual need, fills some primal absence in his life.' Jack looked off into the distance, remembering the past cases, more than a dozen women who'd met their end in similar circumstances to Cristina. He turned back to Massimo. 'I guess we won't really be able to answer your question on why he kills until we actually catch him, and even then we might never find out the true reasons.'

'I agree,' said Massimo. 'In which case, the next big question we have to answer is: where will he kill again? Will it be here, in Italy, or back in the United States, where we believe he has returned to?'

Jack grimaced; not because of the seriousness of the questions, but because of a sharp pain inside his head, flying fast and low like a tornado and then fireballing to an explosive stop in his right temple. He felt a twitch erupt in the corner of his right eye, the same twitch he'd developed just weeks before collapsing at JFK.

'I don't know where,' said Jack, catching his breath and rubbing his face, hoping to massage away the twitch. Old wounds had reopened and the mental scars he hoped had healed were gaping painfully again.

41

FBI Field Office, New York

Howie Baumguard and his new partner, Angelita Fernandez, sat in the conference room waiting for the IT guy to fix the video link to Rome. Howie had brought along a cappuccino with a dense topping of chocolate.

'You going to share that?' asked Fernandez, a slightly chubby 39-year-old with shoulder-length dark hair that Howie noticed she sometimes pulled back and pinned up in a bagel-shaped plait.

'You mean I should have got you one?' he asked, almost regretting making Fernandez the first recruit to his BRK task force.

'Would have been nice,' she teased. 'It's okay though, I can improvise.' She wandered away from the conference table and came back with two plastic cups from the water cooler. She popped one inside the other, grabbed Howie's cappuccino and tipped herself a share. 'Thanks,' she said, sliding back his cup.

'Man, how I hate shy women. When are you girls going to get your shit together and start sticking up for yourselves?' he asked wryly.

230

'Got a picture,' announced the IT guy.

All eyes flicked to the pull-down screen at the front of the room. Jack appeared, sitting next to Massimo Albonetti, chatting intently about something that was so far still inaudible.

'Good-looking guy,' said Fernandez. 'Wouldn't mind sharing some of that too.'

'What? You like little bald Italians?' asked Howie.

'Not what I meant,' said Fernandez, 'but now you mention it, yeah, I think there are some I could give some bed space to.'

Howie smiled at her. Fernandez was eighteen months out from a painful divorce. By painful, it should be made clear that it was far more painful for her ex than for her. She'd returned home after a fourteen-hour shift to find him naked in their bed with a neighbouring housewife. After kicking the floozy's skinny butt all the way down the stairs and out on to the porch, she'd almost pounded her ex unconscious with her bare hands.

'Got sound,' announced the IT man. In fact, not only had the tech got sound, but it came through so loud, it almost tore the FBI agents' heads off.

'Down! Turn the friggin' thing down!' shouted Howie, jabbing fingers in his ears.

'Greetings from beautiful Rome,' announced Jack at the level of a jet plane taking off.

'*Ciao!*' said Massimo, who then turned to someone off-screen, covered his hand with his mouth and said something in Italian.

'We can't see you yet,' explained Jack. 'Massimo's just giving one of their IT whiz-kids a tough time. Are you on your own, Howie?'

'No,' replied the FBI man. 'I'm here with Special Agent Angelita Fernandez. She joined the task force yesterday.'

'Hi there, Mr King. Pleased to be working with you,' said Fernandez respectfully.

'Now we see you,' announced Massimo. 'I am sorry, Italian telecommunications have not been the same since Marconi died.'

They all laughed politely and waited for the rooms in Rome and New York to clear of geeks before they got down to business.

Jack stayed silent and let Massimo run the show.

'I want to discuss several major things during this video conference call,' he said, looking down at a checklist. 'Number one, Jack's involvement at our request. Number two, the mutual need to share information. Number three, the delivery of a package to Italian police here in Rome, containing the head of Cristina Barbuggiani. And number four, the attempted delivery of a package to the FBI, containing the head of . . .' Massimo's voice trailed away, as he looked to his side to check his notes again, '. . . the head of Sarah Kearney, an old victim, maybe the first victim, of the Black River Killer. Is there anything else anyone would like to add to this list?'

Howie leant towards his microphone, 'We need to discuss cross-operational issues, involvement of the authorities in South Carolina, mutual database access and such like, but we can take those discussions offline, if you prefer to.'

'Let's do that, please,' agreed Massimo. 'Maybe you can brief Jack and we'll supply him with a liaison officer at this end?'

'Sure,' said Howie.

'As you know,' continued Mass, diving into the agenda, 'my team here at the Ufficio Investigativo Centrale di Psicologia Criminale has contracted Jack to join us as a consultant in the case of Cristina Barbuggiani. We have done that because we believe there are disturbing similarities to your BRK cases in the United States. To be clear, Jack does not have any police powers and is solely here as an expert civilian. His role is to give us executive input: analysis and profiling work on present and emerging case details, plus, if we make an arrest, psychological input on interview strategy. The last factor will of course be very important if the killer turns out to be a non-Italian and purely American offender.'

'You couldn't have made a better choice,' said Howie, warmly. 'Nothing pleases me more than to see the old bull back in the ring.'

'Indeed,' said Massimo, not quite sure what the American compliment actually meant. 'We are sending this evening, by secure line, copies of photographs, translated reports and photographic evidence related to the case of the young woman I mentioned to you, Cristina Barbuggiani.'

Fernandez cupped her hand and whispered in Howie's ear, 'I've already pulled some background from Italian news reports and there's an Interpol bulletin too, though no mention of BRK.'

'The press in Italy,' continued Massimo, 'especially in Cristina's home town of Livorno, is treating this as an isolated local murder. They are unaware of any possible link to a serial killer. And we would very much like to keep it that way. Even talk of Italian serial killers is enough to drive Mr Berlusconi's media mad, and then they make our job all the more difficult. Any mention of an American serial murderer, or a former FBI profiler working with us, would result in our investigation being overrun by the *scarafaggi* – the cockroaches – of international news agencies. And this we can do without.'

'Don't worry, Mr Albonetti,' said Howie. 'We're good at keeping the scarafaggots, or whatever you called them, out. If the Italian link were known, it would make our life hell as well.'

Massimo nodded, approvingly. 'So that has cleared items one and two from our agenda.' Another thought hit him. 'I should just add, once we have liaison officers in place, we will adopt the standard practice of routine twice-a-day report exchanges, morning and night, other communication between designated senior investigating officers coming as and when needed.' He ticked the top two items on his list. 'Now let us turn to item three, the head of Cristina Barbuggiani, delivered, anonymously, to us here in Rome, in a package marked simply "To Whom It May Concern".'

'You say anonymously,' interjected Howie. 'Does that mean you don't know the name of the courier company, or the name of the delivery person from the courier company?'

'At the moment both,' conceded Massimo. 'We do not have a name for the person who delivered the package, and while we do have a name for the courier company we cannot at present make contact with them.'

'Why is that?' pushed Howie.

Massimo gave a small sigh. The Americans always wanted to dig another level, or rush things. 'You need to have a little patience with us on this matter. The address of the courier company isn't listed; we cannot find a telephone number or any business registrations with our authorities. This may mean the company doesn't exist. Or it may mean someone is operating a company illegally and is trying to avoid paying taxes. We think it most likely that it does not exist, but please trust us that we will find out all the information first and then share our report on this.'

Howie could sense the frustration of his Italian counterpart. 'No problem. I'm sure you guys will get to the bottom of it. I just wanted to check out what similarities or differences there were between the way your package was delivered in Italy and the way we got ours over here.'

Massimo nodded at the giant Howie on the

conference screen. 'I understand your point. More significant though, I think, is a note we discovered in our package. It was left for us inside the head of the victim. Jack and I have spent much time discussing this note, and he already sees great importance in its content.'

'There's a copy coming over to you,' said Jack, taking his cue. 'In brief, here's what it says: "*Buon giorno Italian police!*" Folks, please note that he spells *buon giorno* correctly and ends the sentence with an exclamation mark.'

Both Howie and Fernandez made notes.

'"*Here is a gift for you, with love from BRK,*"' continued Jack. 'He makes the clear claim that he is BRK and then ends the sentence with a point and again there are no spelling or grammar mistakes. The next line is a sizzler, get yourselves ready for this. He says "*Call it a 'heads-up' of what I've got in store for you!*" Heads-up hyphenated and again the exclamation mark. The language is simple, literate and there is a huge emphasis on trying to impress and engage us.'

'And is this all handwritten, or typed?' asked Howie.

'Handwritten,' answered Jack, 'but in block capitals, so the experts won't get much from his style.'

'We'll throw it over Manny Lieberman's desk when we get the copy in,' said Howie. 'He'll pick something up, he always does.'

'Any sign-off, a PS, or anything like that?' asked Fernandez unemotionally.

'*Ha, ha, ha,*' said Jack.

'I'm sorry, say again?' queried Fernandez, not sure if Jack was mocking her.

'The letters *H* and *A* – *HA* – he wrote them three times, and in capitals, and with an exclamation mark after each,' said Jack.

'Sure loves those exclamation marks,' said Howie. 'It's like he got a box of them for Christmas.'

'Then, he finished off with a smiley face and the letters BRK,' said Jack. 'So that's the second time in this short note that he's tried to tell us that this is all BRK's work.'

'You mean he's trying too hard?' asked Fernandez. 'Do you think this is a BRK copycat, Jack, rather than the real McCoy?'

'Mass and I have talked quite a bit about this, and we can't rule out that possibility,' said Jack. 'Though to be honest, I'm not sure it matters. Either way, we have a deadly psycho on our hands.'

Massimo raised a hand, 'Or two deadly psychopaths.'

'You're right,' said Jack, fixing his eyes on Howie on the screen. 'There are certainly similarities between the BRK's files and the new Italian case, but we can't lose track of the fact that there are big differences too.' Jack turned to Massimo. 'Okay if I give some bullet points on this?'

Mass nodded his consent, so Jack continued. 'Victimology looks right for BRK. Cristina was a slim woman who appeared to be in her mid-twenties. As

237

we know, he likes long, dark hair. He never goes for short-haired victims, so he has an image fixation here, meaning the victim represents a real person in his life. We're thinking usual suspects – ex-girlfriend, former wife, first love, mother, grandmother; some woman out there is the model for the victims he selects.'

'It's the old love–hate see-saw again, eh?' said Howie.

'Exactly,' confirmed Jack. 'Some offenders pick certain victims to kill because they represent people they hate but for some reason, usually psychological, they are powerless to harm that actual person. It's Kemper-like.' Everyone nodded, remembering the classic case of American serial killer Ed Kemper who was mentally bullied by his oppressive mother. Instead of killing his parent, he murdered his grandmother and grandfather, then a long list of co-eds at the school where his mother worked, even burying some of their heads in land beneath his mom's bedroom window and then making private fun of her, by telling her how all the girls at school really looked up to her.

'The big difference for me,' continued Jack, 'is the head thing. We're pretty certain BRK took trophies from his victims and we're fairly sure these amounted only to the left hand of the women he murdered.'

Fernandez looked down and wriggled the fingers of her left hand, grateful to see all the joints working and intact, including the one where her wedding ring had almost refused to come off despite her yanking at it like a cowboy on the back of a bronco.

Jack held up his own hand, as he finished his point. 'We can't prove the significance of this, but maybe it's because the left hand is somehow more representative of female fidelity; after all, it's the wedding-ring hand.' He fingered the gold band that encircled his own finger and for a fleeting second thought of Nancy, falling confetti and the day they had married almost eleven years earlier. 'Then again, it may be something not so romantic. The left hand may play a part in his life because he or a woman he once loved had a disfigured left hand. We just don't know, so we shouldn't jump to conclusions. That said, heads are something entirely new. He's removed heads from victims before, but never kept them for any reason, not even as trophies.'

'But these are not really trophies,' said Massimo, thoughtfully. 'He had no intention of keeping these body parts. Surely it was more an egotistical action, in keeping with the note he sent? It seems more like a show of strength to me, like he was looking to make sure he got our attention.'

Jack wasn't so sure. 'There's a lot of psychological debate about what a trophy actually is. Some experts say that just taking anything away from the crime scene, even a button or tiny piece of jewellery, makes it a trophy. It's a prize, something the killer has won in their own emotional and sexual battle to take a life and they keep it as a reminder of the elation they felt.

There's now widespread evidence of serial killers taking stuff from their victims and not keeping it for very long. Often, they "gift" it elsewhere; they pass stuff on to charity shops or give it to a family friend or neighbour. It's a repulsive thought, but they clearly get a kick out of putting part of a brutal crime scene into the hands of innocents.'

'Also, they grow bored with it,' added Howie. 'Some of them are like teenagers buying their first pornographic magazine. The first time, they're afraid and excited and it takes all their courage to go shop for it. Then they buy regularly and amass a collection; eventually they start throwing old mags out and need much harder stuff to light their fire.'

'Your line of expertise?' whispered Fernandez, a little too loudly for only Howie to hear.

'Back to the point,' said Jack, rescuing his buddy. 'I buy the egotist angles, that's certainly all over the note, but not the idea that this guy is after publicity. He's not a headline hunter. That theory would stand up if he'd sent the heads to the press, but he didn't, he deliberately sent them to law enforcement offices, so it's much more like he's throwing down a challenge to us.'

'We all need to spend a lot more time on the note,' added Massimo. 'As Jack said, we will be sending a copy over to you, and I'm sure we'll be having a much longer discussion about this.' He turned his left wrist to check his watch and couldn't help thinking of the saw cut across the same joint on Cristina

Barbuggiani. 'As time is moving on, let's briefly discuss item number four, the package that contained the head that I am told is of Sarah Kearney, one of BRK's earliest – maybe even first – victims.'

'Okay,' said Howie, unfastening his shirt cuffs and rolling up his sleeves in a businesslike manner. 'I don't want to get everyone too excited, but we've got some good news. We've got a healthy trail on the delivery of the package. It was shipped through Myrtle International by a company called UMail2 Anywhere. Turns out they're a very small courier company, just local to Myrtle Beach, and we've found who the pick-up boy was.'

'Did he get a good look at the customer?' asked Massimo, trying to hold back a surge of hope. A description of the killer would be a real breakthrough.

'We think so,' said Howie. 'It's a guy called Stan Mossman. Not at work today, seems he's got a pile of time off, days worked in-lieu, that sort of thing. He's thought to be partying out of state with friends. We don't know where, or we'd already have pulled him in. We've got someone from the local office out on his patch and hot on his heels, so hopefully we'll interview him tomorrow when he's due back.'

'Where was the pick-up?' asked Jack.

'Out at the Days Inn,' answered Fernandez. 'The Grand Strand on South Ocean Boulevard. Cheap and cheerful, just a spit from the airport.'

'That figures,' said Jack. 'I put my money on our killer catching a flight from Myrtle within as short a time as possible from the moment that he handed over that package to Mossman.'

'*Va bene*,' said Massimo, enthusiastically. 'This could be the most valuable thing we have. If you get a photo-fit together then we must talk quickly about issuing it in both our countries. Dealing with the *scarafaggi* will be bearable if they can help save the life of his next potential victim.'

Jack was the only one not looking optimistic. Something just wasn't right. It's such a loose end; BRK would never leave such a loose end.

And then he realized what it was.

'Howie, are you one hundred per cent sure your witness – this Stan guy – is out of state having fun, and he's not already dead and buried somewhere?'

'Shit!' said Howie, suddenly seeing the grim possibility. 'You're thinking BRK whacked him before he caught his plane?'

'That's absolutely what I'm thinking,' confirmed Jack. 'When was our man Stan's last day at work?'

Fernandez looked down at her notes. 'July first. The date we got the package posted to us. No one's seen him since then.'

42

San Quirico D'Orcia, Tuscany

The warm house lights and the dinner-table laughter from La Casa Strada spilled across the dark and silent hills of the Val D'Orcia as Nancy King carried out her final duties of the day. The restaurant had been full for the evening but now there were only a few guests still at their white-linen tables, drinking coffee and sipping brandy. For Nancy, this was one of the magical moments of running the restaurant. She loved to see a room full of happy guests, relaxing at her beautifully laid tables, bursting from the satisfaction of her food. The room hummed with conversations about which part of Europe someone planned to go to next, and whether or not Florence was really worth a day visit out of their schedule.

Paolo had let the rest of the kitchen staff go home and only Giuseppe remained, stacking pudding plates in the giant dishwasher that Jack joked was large enough to wash an average car. Paolo told him that when he had washed down the floors, he could go as well.

'Mrs King, would you care to join me for a glass of wine outside on the terrace, for our little talk?'

asked Paolo, with over-dramatic graciousness. He said the same words every night and Nancy always replied with the same pat answer and a theatrical nod of her head. 'That would be most delightful, *Signore* Balze, thank you for asking me.'

'Take a table, please, I'll be out in a moment,' said Paolo.

Nancy left him and walked through the kitchen door into the private garden outside. The night was alive with the pungent smell of roses and the incessant chirp of crickets. She'd heard somewhere that the insects could be roasted, or even baked into brownies, but she'd never managed to catch one, let alone pondered what to do with it gastronomically.

Suddenly, the door to the kitchen burst open. 'Surprise!' shouted Paolo, standing shoulder to shoulder with Giuseppe, who was holding a small cake with a plastic Statue of Liberty stuck in its middle and a lit birthday candle taped to Liberty's torch.

'Born in the USA,' they sang together, badly.

'Happy American Independence Day, Mrs King,' said Giuseppe. 'Please to blow out the candle and make the wish.'

'We didn't know the words to your national anthem,' explained Paolo, 'but we do know some Bruce Springsteen, yes, Giuseppe?'

Nancy applauded them both and blew out the candle. 'Thank you. Thank you so much,' she said, feeling genuinely touched by what they'd done.

'Get a knife,' Paolo instructed the kitchen boy.

'We will have a small piece with our drink, and you too, Giuseppe.'

'Wait a minute,' said Nancy. 'Before you cut it, let me get my camera from upstairs. I have to take a picture to show Jack what you made.'

'Actually, it is what Gio made,' corrected Paolo, referring to their pastry chef, as she hurried back to the house for her Sony Cybershot. 'He is sorry he could not stay, but his baby, it is sick back home.'

Nancy was still smiling as she bounded up the stairs. She slowed down to a quiet stride as she stepped past Zack's door, and then flicked on a light and entered her own bedroom.

What she saw next sucked the breath from her lungs.

Standing by her dressing table, a flashlight in one hand, and something heavy, square and black in the other, was a large masked man.

43

Marine Park, Brooklyn, New York

The digital clocks in Spider's empty bedroom set off a series of technological events of greater and lesser importance. Lights downstairs in the lounge and kitchen turn off. Softer lighting upstairs in the en-suite bathroom comes on, security lights outside continue to shine brightly, and downstairs the sound-proofed basement is plunged into absolute darkness.

Lu Zagalsky had been terrified the first time the lights had gone out. Her heart had tried to crack through her ribcage and make a run for it. The darkness seemed alive with some slithering, satanic shape that somehow felt out her face and tried to smother her, tried to suck and swallow her into the endless blackness. Now, though, she's almost grateful for the dark. The pain from her broken nose is nearly bearable, but her eyes feel as though they've had acid poured in them. Lu's thirst is ferocious. There isn't anything on earth she wouldn't do for a single glass of water. She'd heard somewhere that you could survive a long time without food, but you still had to have water. What she didn't know of course was that one day she would get to find out first hand exactly how long that survival would be. Lu is comforted by the fact that she's almost completely got over the hunger pains that were so severe for the first day after he left her. Now, she isn't hungry at all. Sadly, it's nothing she should be pleased with. After two days without food, sensors in either the gastrointestinal tract or in the mesenteric veins that drain the gut, send signals to the brain killing off the hunger pains and shutting down the digestive system. Lu's body is starting to do what will probably be irreparable damage to itself. It is starting to eat itself.

The lights in the basement come on again and her eyes burn with pain as she blinks into the brightness above her head. Upstairs, another digital clock triggers another device. A recording machine is activated.

The cameras around her start to pan, zoom and focus.

A digital hard drive whirrs into action to capture what Spider is sure will be the last hours of Lu Zagalsky's life.

44

San Quirico D'Orcia, Tuscany

Nancy King ducked as the stranger threw the flashlight at her. It missed, shattering into several pieces as it crashed into the wall behind her head. She screamed as he pushed his way past her and thundered down the stairs and out into the dimly lit garden.

'Paolo! Giuseppe, help!' she shouted from the bedroom window. 'Stop him! Stop him!'

Paolo whirled around from the table where he was slicing up the cake, just in time to see the heavy-set figure dressed in black burst into the garden area.

The intruder spotted the two men, and saw the knife in Paolo's hand. He stopped so quickly that he slipped on the damp grass, then, scrambling to his feet, ran straight into the back door of the kitchen. For one moment Paolo thought about throwing the knife at him, but then dropped it and gave chase.

The masked man bolted from the kitchen, through the restaurant and down the hotel's narrow corridors, barging guests aside, as they abandoned the last of their drinks to see what all the commotion was. The corridors automatically guided him to reception, where Maria made a brave attempt to hold him up by raising a chair in front of him to block his way. Grabbing the other end, he pushed her into the wall and escaped through the front door as she slumped to the ground like a rag doll.

Maria was crying in pain and holding her stomach by the time Paolo appeared in reception. He had no choice but to give up the chase and check she was all right. 'Are you okay? Stay still, Maria, show me what hurts.'

'My stomach,' she said. 'My stomach and my ribs, they hurt like crazy. What happened?'

Giuseppe and Nancy arrived seconds later, followed by several guests.

'It's okay, folks. Please don't be alarmed,' said Nancy, flapping her hands at them. 'We seem to have had a nasty incident but it's all over now. Please go back to the dining room and allow us to sort things out here. Thanks for your help.' She shut the connecting door from the reception to the rest of the hotel and joined the others as they helped Maria to her feet.

'Are you all right, Maria? Did he hurt you?' asked Nancy.

'I am okay, Mrs King, I think,' said the receptionist, still tearful. 'I picked up that chair to try to stop him with it, but he, he just knock me over and run away.'

'Sit down,' said Paolo. 'Have a drink of water, and get your breath back.'

Giuseppe grabbed a carafe of water from behind the reception desk and poured a glass.

Nancy stood for a moment biting her nails, taking stock of what had happened. It was at times like this that she missed having Jack around. Paolo and Giuseppe had been wonderful in chasing the intruder off, but if Jack had been here, well, by now the guy would have been wishing he'd picked any other hotel in Italy to burgle.

'Shall I call the police, or will you call Signor King?' asked Paolo.

'Ring the Polizia or the carabinieri,' answered Nancy. 'Jack has bigger things to worry about; I don't want to bother him with something like this.'

Paolo made the call and talked for so long that Nancy thought he'd discussed the case with every member of staff at the station. Maria gradually recovered and insisted there was nothing wrong with her other than some bruising to her tummy. She took consolation from the fact that it would be a terrific story to tell on television when she got to run for Miss Italy. Nancy thanked all of them for their efforts and promised that she wouldn't forget their support when it came to pay-packet time.

Giuseppe offered to run Maria home in his car and as they left Nancy wondered whether she could detect the first flicker of something more than just friendship between the two. Paolo volunteered to stay the night when he found out that the police couldn't send anyone until the following morning, but Nancy wouldn't hear of it. Nevertheless, he did a final check around the hotel before he left on his scooter, its rusted exhaust making such a noise that it set off dogs barking at a farmhouse almost half a mile away.

Nancy went upstairs and got ready for bed. She scrubbed her teeth and put paste out for Jack, forgetting for a second that he wasn't there. Then she went in Zack's room and scooped up her sleeping toddler in her arms. She carried him into her darkened bedroom and laid him down gently in the cool bed. She was doing it partly to make sure he was safe, but also, if she were honest, because she needed the comfort of him next to her.

When it started to rain heavily Nancy remembered the beautiful Independence Day cake that was still out in the garden, getting ruined. It would have to go to waste. There was no way she was getting out of bed until the room was filled with daylight and the hotel was once more alive with the sound of voices she trusted.

Downstairs, a key turned quietly in the front-door lock. Recent arrival Terry McLeod was trying as hard as possible to make sure that he didn't wake anyone.

PART FIVE

Thursday, 5 July

45

Hotel Grand Plaza, Rome

It was still the dead of night when Jack woke, dripping with sweat and struggling to breathe. The latest nightmare was the most personal and most intense he'd ever experienced.

He'd fallen asleep around midnight and thought he might get a decent rest. How wrong he had been.

Soon his sleep had tricked him back into the basement, where the white-coated ME was moving as mysteriously as usual, but everything else seemed somehow more intense. The blood was running faster from the pipes on the black walls, spilling on to the floor, and there in the puddles forming around his feet were strange shapes, like Rorschach's ink blots. In them, the faces of BRK's victims had appeared, one by one, and slowly morphed into each other, until finally Jack was left staring at the face of Cristina Barbuggiani. She was trying to mouth something to him but he couldn't hear her. For a second, her young fingers stretched out from the blood and implored him to grab her and save her. Then, in the instant that he touched her, her flesh melted and the hand became skeletonized and snapped off.

Jack wiped the sweat from his face and tried to remember what else he'd dreamt. He recalled a mixture of male and female voices shouting: 'IT'S *YOUR FAULT*!' He had hung on to the gurney for fear that his legs would give way beneath him as his head filled with voices.

'What they say is right. You're a failure, King, a burnout.'

'Think how many girls have died, because you've been unable to save them.'

'Think! Is it five, ten, fifteen, twenty or more?'

Jack had clung to the body on the steel gurney as the ME raised the bone saw. He had to save this one, there must be *no more* killing.

The blade came closer to the body on the gurney, its teeth seeking more innocent flesh and bone. Jack put his hand out towards the ME, trying to force the blade back, but as he did so, he stumbled. Falling into the pool of blood, he got a clear view of the face of the victim on the steel trolley.

It was that of his wife.

46

San Quirico D'Orcia, Tuscany

Terry McLeod sat on his own at a table for four, his breakfast plate piled high with ham, cheese, croissants, jam and butter. To one side of him was a large map entitled *Terre di Siena*, and on the other side was a copy of *La Nazione*. He didn't speak any Italian, but it was a quirk of his that, wherever he went, he always took a national newspaper home with him. He was a magpie, always had been, always would be, and he liked nothing better than international souvenirs.

Paullina, the waitress, arrived with his double cappuccino, something that she'd never been asked for before. She'd taken it to mean a single cappuccino with a double dose of coffee and the guest had laughed and said he was fine with that.

'Which visiting are you planning today?' she asked, noticing his map as she cleaned away a juice glass and cereal bowl. 'Maybe Siena or Pienza?'

'You know,' said McLeod, his mouth open as he chewed a croissant. 'I'm really not sure. I'm still a bit jet-lagged from all the travelling. Maybe I'll go here.' He jabbed a finger at a nearby town. 'What's it called?'

Paullina bent over the map and McLeod savoured the sensation of having her that close to him.

'Chianciano Terme,' she said, in a voice so sweet that he would have paid a premium-rate call charge just to listen to it.

'Or, you know what,' he added, 'I may just go to Montepulciano. Some folks at dinner last night said it was real nice.'

Paullina nodded. 'It is. It is very famous for its views and its churches. It is high up the hill, but worth the climb.'

'Sounds like my kind of place, I love your Italian churches and all that Da Vinci stuff,' said McLeod, wiping crumbs from his mouth. 'You just sold it to me, err . . . I'm sorry, what's your name?'

'Paullina,' she said. 'I am Paullina Caffagi.'

'Terry McLeod, very pleased to meet you.' He stuck out his hand and she shook it hesitantly. 'Been here a couple of days now and not seen you. Do you only do part-time?'

'*Scusi*, I don't understand.'

'Part-time – just mornings, just breakfasts?'

'Aaah yes, I only work at the breakfasts.'

'Then maybe, if you're free, you could come with me, act as my guide,' McLeod suggested hopefully.

'Oh no, I don't think I could do that,' said Paullina, wondering exactly what sights he was really interested in seeing.

'Why not? I'll pay you. Whatever you get paid to

work breakfasts, I'll pay you to show me around Montepulciano.'

Paullina thought about it for a second. Although he was a bit of a jerk, he seemed harmless enough, and the extra money would really come in handy. 'Then all right, I will be pleased to be showing you Montepulciano.'

'Great!' said McLeod. 'When's good for you?'

'Tomorrow? I will be finished here and could go by twelve o'clock. Is that okay?'

'That's fine,' said McLeod. 'Could you fix a cab, a taxi for us? I'm not big on public transport.'

Paullina smiled. 'I will have one waiting.'

McLeod's interest in Paullina disappeared as soon as Nancy King entered the dining room. The older woman needed only to throw half a glance Paullina's way to send her scuttling off to resume her duties.

His luck was in. She had come into the restaurant to mix with the guests, ask them how they were enjoying their stay, that sort of thing. McLeod played his spoon across the froth on the cappuccino and listened to the small talk. She did all the tables; moving from an old couple at the back to some honeymooners, then a pair of walkers and finally himself.

'Good morning,' she said brightly. 'I'm Nancy King, my husband and I own La Casa Strada, and we hope you're enjoying your stay with us.'

'Terence T. McLeod,' he said, getting to his feet

as he shook hands. 'And I'm having a terrific time, Mrs King. You sure have a great little hotel here and great staff.' He nodded towards Paullina as he sat back down.

'That's very kind of you to say so. Thank you, Mr McLeod,' she said. 'We certainly aim to please.'

'I hope you don't mind, but I've asked your waitress over there if she'd show me Montepulciano. I've offered to pay, of course. And if there's a surcharge or some kind of fee to you at the hotel, then that's also okay. I just want a good guide.'

The unusual request threw Nancy and she weighed it up for a moment before agreeing. 'No. No, I don't mind at all. We don't encourage the staff to mix with the guests out of the hotel, but providing this is purely a business arrangement, then I don't have any objections at all.'

'Great, thanks.'

Nancy smiled and started to walk away, to have a quiet word with Paullina while the matter was still fresh in her mind. 'Have a nice day, Mr McLeod.'

'And you,' said McLeod, adding, 'Oh, by the way, did you catch him?'

Nancy spun round. 'I'm sorry?'

'The man last night. Did you catch him? Everyone in the restaurant was talking about it. Some hooded guy running through the place.'

Nancy gathered her wits. 'No, no, we didn't. But let me reassure you, it wasn't anything serious. Nothing was taken and we've called the police. Please don't be worried by it. I can assure you everyone and everything here is perfectly safe.'

'I'm sure it is,' said McLeod. 'Was it your husband who chased him off? I think I read somewhere that he's an ex-cop, ex-fed or something?'

Nancy wished the conversation would end. The fright last night had left her irritable, and while she supposed that it was only natural that the guests would ask questions about what had happened, this guy was bugging her. 'No, Mr McLeod. It wasn't my husband. It was my chef and his kitchen boy. He was a lucky man. I hate to think what they'd have done with him if they'd caught him.'

'I guess battered burglar would have been on the menu?' quipped McLeod, feebly.

'And that would be just for starters,' said Nancy King.

She smiled again and this time did manage to walk away from his table. Terry McLeod was delighted. If former FBI man Jack King hadn't been here last night, on Independence Day of all days, and he wasn't here this morning to comfort his wife after her ordeal, then just where the hell was he?

47

Rome

Jack had been unable to shake off the horrors of his latest nightmare until he'd spoken to Nancy on the phone. He'd waited until just after seven, the time when he was sure the bedside alarm would have woken her. He had been soothed by listening to his wife's sleepy voice and imagined how warm she would have felt if he had been lying in bed with her. Nancy hadn't mentioned the burglar, although it had still been very much on her mind.

After the call, Jack felt reassured and energized enough to take a short jog around the centre of Rome, followed by a hot shower and a healthy breakfast on the terrace. By the time he climbed into the chauffeur-driven car to take him to police HQ the streets were almost gridlocked with traffic. The journey took twice as long as it should have done and Jack got out feeling hot enough to need another shower.

He tipped the driver Massimo had sent him, even though the guy insisted that there was no need, and made his way to the meeting room. Massimo had other appointments that day and it had been arranged that Jack would sit with Orsetta, Benito and Roberto to get an update on their enquiries and swap any new thoughts they might have had. The starting time for the meeting was noon and Jack was still finding it hard to become accustomed to the fact that people weren't at their desks by eight a.m. or earlier, as he was used to in New York. The Italians seemed to have the work–life balance thing better sussed than the Americans. They worked to live rather than lived to work. Free time, family time, me time – those were the three things they looked forward to most.

Jack sat in the plain, dull room on his own and was going over a checklist of the subjects he wanted to cover when Orsetta walked in.

'*Buon giorno*,' she said. 'You are a little early, no?'

'Not by US standards,' he answered. 'The meeting's not until twelve, right?'

'That's right,' said Orsetta, 'I thought I might already find you here, so I came along ahead of the rest.'

'Thought or hoped?' he asked, unable to resist flirting a little.

'I guess both,' she said coolly. 'But it's something professional rather than personal that I have in mind.' Nevertheless, she couldn't stop her eyes sparkling playfully.

'Then shoot,' he said.

They both settled into black plastic chairs across the corner of a long table that faced whiteboards and video screens. She was dressed demurely in matching dark brown jacket and trousers, accompanied by a green striped blouse, her hair tied back in a green 'scrunchy'.

'Okay,' she said, finally deciding how she was going to open the discussion. 'Some years back, I went to England and attended some courses at Scotland Yard and at a place in the country called Brams Hall . . .'

'Bramshill,' interrupted Jack. 'It's called Bramshill, not Hall, and it's the location of the National Police Staff College run by the Association of Chief Police Officers. I guess you were there as part of your profiling training?'

'Yes, that's right,' said Orsetta, a little irritated at being corrected.

'It was ACPO that launched offender profiling in the UK. They had to nurture it through the regional forces for years. The Bramshill course is probably the best in the world – outside Quantico, of course.'

'Of course,' said Orsetta. 'Well, when I was there, at *Bramshill*,' she continued, 'apart from the training, I learned a very important English saying.'

'Which is what?' asked Jack, intrigued as to what point she might eventually get round to making.

Orsetta spoke slowly, making sure the strange English expression came out right. 'We are all avoiding talking about the elephant in the room.'

'We're all what?' said Jack, wearing a smile as broad as his shoulders.

'We're avoiding talking about the biggest, most

obvious thing. We're pretending it's not there,' explained Orsetta.

'Well, I'm sorry,' said Jack, 'but you've lost me. To be truthful though, most of those Brit sayings are lost on me. There's many a slip twixt cup and lip, pride before a fall, shutting the barn door after the horse has bolted, crying over spilt milk – they talk in damn riddles half the time.' He could see from the look on her face that she was in no mood for levity. 'Apologies. You had a serious point; we're avoiding the obvious, the big thing that's staring us in the face. So what's that? What's the big thing?'

She chewed her lip, and then spat out what was on her mind. 'You, Jack, you're the big thing. You are the elephant.'

'Come again?'

'I've heard you and Massimo talking about how BRK is taunting the police, and how even the FBI reports refer to it. But what if it's more personal than that? What if it's Jack King that BRK is taunting?'

Jack shot her a dismissive look. 'Not worth putting in the frame. I don't see it. Why on earth should he fixate on me?' He paused for a second, searching for possibilities. 'Nope, I really don't see it. Over the years, there were seven senior investigating officers heading that enquiry, I don't think I did anything different from any of them.' He let out a sigh. 'I certainly didn't get any closer to catching him. Have you got something specific in your mind?'

Orsetta hadn't, it was only a feeling, but she'd

learned not to ignore her instincts when they kept nagging away as this one was doing. 'I don't know. I can't get away from thinking that you're the only thing linking BRK, Italy and the USA. Maybe you've somehow come to represent the police, or some government authority for him, and he has to destroy you to get revenge for something that was done to him. Perhaps you've come to symbolize an injustice against him, or someone he loved.' The explanation had come out much weaker than she'd intended, but she didn't know how to put it any better, and now she could see that Jack was looking at her as if she were some police academy first-termer who was hopelessly out of her depth. 'Look,' she added quickly, 'he killed when you were in the States, now he's killing while you're in Italy. Is that just a coincidence?'

Jack's sharp stare of disapproval disappeared. Simplicity was something that always appealed to him, and like all detectives, he didn't believe in pure coincidences. As a seasoned profiler, he knew there had to be a good reason to discount anything. 'BRK was killing long before I was drafted into the case. I only worked his files for about five years and PRO-FILER, the FBI computer system, links murders to him a good twelve years before that. The Kearney case, for example, well, that's now exactly twenty years old, and . . .' Jack stalled, as pieces of the case paperwork flashed through his mind. 'In fact, unless I'm wrong, it's exactly twenty years ago since Sarah's body was found. Now, that's far more likely to be the trigger for these latest activities; you might have inadvertently hit on something.'

Orsetta put her hand on his arm. 'Jack, this isn't adding up. If BRK was aroused just by the thought of the upcoming anniversary of his first victim, that might be a reason for him going back to her grave, but you're ignoring the fact that he sent that victim's skull in a package specifically addressed to you at the FBI, and the possibility that he killed in Livorno.'

Jack shrugged. It was something he'd already thought about. 'I was the last person heading the enquiry. I was in all the papers and on television; the front man always gets the attention, especially when it involves psychopaths.' He flinched. 'Even me quitting the case was in the papers, so I guess I was simply a soft target for his scorn.'

Orsetta's face soured. 'So, if you rule yourself out, then what's the connection to Italy?'

Jack thought he had the answer. 'Italy may be his new hunting ground, but that doesn't mean he can't fly home to mark an anniversary. When these whackos get all wired up they tend to be erratic, offending in sprees, until their energies have been spent. I'm much more inclined to believe that, than think BRK has some personal beef with me.'

Jack pulled away from her hand and sat back in his chair. He was thinking about what she had just said. Somehow she'd touched a nerve. The Italian connection really was an odd thing. And then, a thought struck him.

'You've got me wondering though. Why Italy? If it really is BRK, then why kill in Italy? There's nothing in his profile that links him with the country, and you're right, I am the only geographic link.'

Orsetta couldn't resist flashing him a 'told-you-so' look.

'Let's say we are dealing with BRK, and let's say the excitement of the anniversary has made him want to start killing again,' said Jack, starting to see a pattern. 'It would be very much in BRK's profile to organize his return to action, to set up a decoy, to have us spread our resources not just nationally but internationally and be massively distracted so he can indulge his sick little fantasies.'

Orsetta could sense Jack reliving the hatred, and the pain, of hunting his old foe. Subconsciously, he started twirling the gold wedding ring on his finger, and continued, 'So, following your line of thought, BRK kills in Italy, knowing that the Italian police will turn to me. That's a fair bet; our move to Tuscany was in all the papers back home, so he could well have read about that. He'd know that a dismembered body on a coastline, plus a note claiming to be from him, would be bound to get you guys calling at my door.' Jack visibly warmed to the theory. 'That would explain why he went to such lengths to mention twice in the note that we were dealing with BRK. Then, while everyone is focused on Italy, he turns his attention back to his old flame Sarah Kearney, as part of what he's really got in mind.'

Orsetta was unsure of his train of thought. 'Where are you going with this, Jack? Are you saying that you think he is no longer in Italy and he's planning to start killing again in the States?'

That was exactly what he was thinking. 'Either he's planning to kill there, or he has already killed. Italy's a red herring, built around me. You were right about me being the elephant in the room. Now it's only a matter of time before another body turns up, probably in the States. And you can bet that if BRK is killing again, then this time he'll be on a spree that is going to be worse than anything we've ever encountered before.'

48

San Quirico D'Orcia, Tuscany

Nancy King's morning was thrown into disarray when a landscaper unexpectedly turned up to survey the area of subsidence in the rear gardens. Vincenzo Capello was an old friend of her hotel manager Carlo, and the two hugged and kissed so affectionately in reception they could have been mistaken for gay lovers. It had been so long since Carlo had promised that his friend Vincenzo would fix the gaping hole that had opened up at the foot of their terraced garden, that she'd almost completely forgotten about him.

Vincenzo was living testimony to the much heralded benefits of a healthy Italian diet of fresh foods, olive oil and strong red wine. Nancy had been told he was nearer seventy than sixty, but looking at him now, she didn't think he looked a day older than fifty. Carlo said, '*Ciao!*' and went off to chase up his staff, leaving Nancy to show a still grinning Vincenzo to the trouble spot.

'Carlo, he tell me that you have a big hole in your garden. He says all the staff are afraid of a-falling in it.' Vincenzo's eyes twinkled and his permanent smile showed a full set of strong, white teeth.

'Not quite,' said Nancy, leading him from the reception. 'But it is a big fall of soil and I'd hate it to get worse. The end of the garden terrace, behind where we grow vegetables for the kitchen, has given way and some kind of tunnel has opened up beneath it. What I'm most worried about is whether the ground above it might also be unsafe.'

Vincenzo didn't appear to hear her. His eyes were fixed on the bathroom sign. It seemed that the one thing that might not be holding up as well as his looks was his bladder. '*Un momento brevissimo*,' he pleaded and ducked inside. Nancy waited patiently, her eagle eyes spotting some chipped paintwork that would have to be touched up once the summer season was over and all the guests had gone. Mr Capello duly reappeared, shaking water from his just washed hands. 'You like Italy?' he asked.

Italians visiting La Casa Strada always asked that, and Nancy loved the fact that they wanted her to share their passion for the country. 'I *adore* Italy,' she said with gusto. 'We've been here a couple of years now and I feel more and more at home every day.'

Vincenzo's face lit up. '*Meraviglioso*, wonderful,' he said.

'Let me show you the damage,' said Nancy.

As they walked outside, she slowed down and looked around. It was something she did every time she stepped outside La Casa Strada. To her, every view around the hotel was a visual feast, a delicacy marinating in time itself, growing deliciously better every day she spent there. Today the sunlight in the private garden behind the kitchen was as soft and golden as pure honey.

'It's just down that slope there,' said Nancy, pointing across the garden. 'You can see where my husband has moved some old fencing across to stop anyone going down.'

Vincenzo nodded and walked slowly over, his eyes drinking in the view across the lush valley towards Mount Amiata in the south and Siena in the north. Nancy watched him disappear down the banking, and then, amid the birdsong in the orange trees she heard a strange sound, a sort of harsh clunk and click, a metallic kind of noise, the type that simply didn't belong in a garden. She took a couple of paces around a tree and was startled to find herself face to face with her highly inquisitive fellow American, Terry McLeod.

'Excuse me,' she said abruptly, 'it's private back here. Would you mind returning to the guest gardens?'

'Oh hell, I'm sorry,' said McLeod jovially. 'You've got such a wonderful place; I was just walking around taking some photographs. I'm real sorry.'

Nancy noticed the expensive-looking camera strung on a thick Nikon strap around his neck, his finger still on the shutter button. 'That's okay. Just please remember in future.' There was something about McLeod she didn't like, something that she just couldn't work out.

'New camera, I just can't leave it alone,' said the

American. He lifted it from his neck to show her and in the same moment clunk-clicked off a head and shoulders shot of Nancy. This irritated the hell out of her. 'You never think of asking permission, do you?' she snapped, her face colouring.

'Hey, sorry again,' said McLeod, disingenuously. He sauntered off without saying goodbye, swinging the camera on its strap.

For one moment Nancy's mind went into flash-back. The heavy black camera looked strangely familiar. Why?

And then she remembered. It looked identical to the square, black object she'd seen the previous night. The object in the hand of the burglar in her bedroom.

49

Angelita Fernandez put down the desk phone and grimaced as she turned to Howie Baumguard. The big guy really looked as though he could do with a break. And this wasn't going to be it. 'I just talked to Gene Saunders out at Myrtle. Seems our man Stan is a no-show.'

'He ever done that before?' asked Howie, lost in some work on his computer.

'Nope. Doesn't seem that way. His boss at UMail2 Anywhere says he's a good kid. Always bang on time. Never swings a day off without asking, or at least calling in with a reason rather than an excuse.'

'Sounds like Jack's right,' said Howie, typing with two fingers. 'Poor kid.'

Fernandez tried to picture what the delivery boy looked like and settled on young, thin and scrawny, still trying to make his way in life. 'You really think Stan got wasted before BRK did a runner from Myrtle?'

'It's sure starting to look that way,' said Howie.

Fernandez picked up a pencil and twirled it like a baton through the fingers of one hand. It was a trick she'd picked up in high school and somehow it helped her concentrate. 'I'll check on the bones downstairs. Dental should have some results now on Kearney. You think it's a match?'

'I'm banking on it,' said Howie. He'd asked for the dental check to make doubly sure that the skull they'd found was really Sarah Kearney's and not someone else's. He didn't want the embarrassment of finding out later that they had all been jerked around yet another time by BRK. He stopped typing and turned to Fernandez. 'You know much about necrophilia?'

'You're kidding, right?' she said, shooting him a disapproving stare. 'I've dated some deadbeats in my time, ex-husband top of the list, but not literally.'

'Necrophiles,' said Howie, paraphrasing an FBI entry on his screen, 'get their rocks off having sex with dead bodies.'

'Go away. I would never have guessed that. Now I see why you got the big stripes.'

'Shut up and listen, I might just need your help here.'

She twirled her pencil again and thought he was kind of cute when he pretended to be annoyed.

'The word is Greek in origin, comes from *nekros* meaning corpse and *philia*, which as we all know means love.'

'I kind of like those two words when they're not in the same sentence,' said Fernandez.

Howie shot her another shut-the-fuck-up glance.

'The psych notes say necrophiles have poor self-esteem, have a need for power over or revenge against something or someone that makes them feel inadequate, and have been deprived of certain key emotional contact.'

'Hang on though,' said Fernandez, getting serious for a moment. 'What little I know about these creeps, which again I stress is not through any personal dating, is that they don't usually kill. They like their meat cooked already. Ain't that right? As you so eloquently said yourself, they "get their rocks off" by messing around with dead bodies, not by making people dead for them to mess around with.'

'Subtle difference, but yeah, you got a point,' admitted Howie, searching the on-screen files for more info. 'But let's agree that having sex with a dead body isn't normal. Now, from that intellectual standpoint, it ain't too big a leap of faith to think that an abnormal guy, who likes stiffing it to a stiff, might just start making stiffs for himself if his regular stiff supply has run dry.'

'You got a natural gift with words, anyone ever tell you that?' said Fernandez sarcastically.

'I'm constantly fighting the urge to write poetry,' countered Howie, scrolling to a new page.

'Why does BRK qualify as a necrophile?' asked Fernandez.

Howie started to run through a list. 'He keeps the bodies after death. Look at how long he kept the Barbuggiani girl after he killed her. He takes trophies from them. He goes back to graves, digs up their corpses and hacks off their heads. Sounds like a necrophile to me.'

'So this guy could be a serial killer and a necrophile. A kind of hybrid?'

'That's what I'm thinking,' said Howie 'A double-trouble psycho. Maybe he started killing for a non-sexual reason.'

'Revenge, accident, opportunity?' suggested Fernandez.

'Something like that. Then when he was faced with a dead body, he suddenly got turned on by it.'

'You got any case studies in there that I can read up on?' she asked.

Howie hit a search function. 'Yeah, here you go. Man, there's one hell of a list coming up: Carl Tanzler, Richard Chase, Winston Moseley, our old pals Ed Gein, Jeffrey Dahmer and Ted Bundy – those last three seem to be pretty much in every classification there is.'

'Lazy research,' said Fernandez, scribbling down their names. 'If everything that was written about Bundy was true, he'd have had to have lived three lifetimes.'

'This is interesting,' said Howie, ignoring her pet rant about Bundy. 'There's a bullet-point summary. It says necrophiles are usually fearful of rejection by women they sexually desire. Can you imagine what a necrophile would do in the kind of situation where he feels rejected?'

Fernandez was in step with his thoughts. 'You mean he'd kill her to keep her?'

'Exactly!'

Fernandez mused on it. 'Maybe BRK got badly jilted once, and he just couldn't bear the idea of anyone else walking out on him.'

'Once bitten twice shy,' said Howie.

'He couldn't face the idea of being on his own? Maybe he was just shit-scared of the whole thought of being lonely. A kind of lonelyphobia?'

'I think that's it,' said Howie. 'Death is the way he ensures that they never jilt him, that they stay with him, devoted to him, for ever.'

'Hmm,' said Fernandez. 'I'll remember that next time I give some Brad Pitt lookalike my number in a bar.'

50

Marine Park, Brooklyn, New York

It has been more than fifty hours since any food or liquid has passed the parched and blistered lips of Ludmila Zagalsky.

As she slips in and out of delirium, her mind is constantly tormented by the knowledge that she is involved in a unique act of self-cannibalism. As well as the awful stinging in her eyes, a new agony has surfaced, a raw and wretched stabbing pain in her kidneys. Lu doesn't know enough anatomy to be able to even name the organ that's hurting, let alone diagnose that she's rapidly heading towards permanent renal damage. But she knows one thing for sure; something important inside her is screaming for water and without it she is going to die.

Once upon a time, back in the real world where people weren't kidnapped, stripped naked and tortured to death, she'd been eating pizza with an old boyfriend; they'd watched *Scream*, or was it *Scream 2* or *3*? Anyway, they'd jokingly discussed what would be the worst way to be killed – the bullet, the blade, drowning or maybe fire. Her friend had said he'd hate to be burned alive at the stake, like they used to do in France with chicks such as Joan of Arc. Lu had confessed she couldn't swim, had never been in the sea or a swimming pool in her life and was shit-scared of drowning. As they'd finished off the deep pan and thought about making out, neither of them had considered that probably the worst way to die was to be deliberately starved to death.

Right now, Lu reckons drowning might not be such a bad way to go after all. A girl she used to work a corner of the Beach with once told her that she should drink about half a gallon of water every day to stay healthy. Half a gallon a day! She'd nearly wet herself laughing. The kid had said she'd been balling some kind of health freak, a gym monster who had muscles like the Incredible Hulk, and he'd told her that more than eighty per cent of blood is made up of water so you've got to keep topping up the fluid level. It had sounded like bullshit. Until now. For the first time in her life, she understood every word of it.

In the last hour or so, she's noticed that her mouth isn't only painfully dry, her tongue has started to taste bitter and almost poisonous. Were the gym monster around, he could have explained that her electrolyte balance is badly screwed, or, to be technical, critically destabilized. Her body cells are under fatal attack and her blood plasma is already seriously damaged.

Ludmila Zagalsky doesn't believe in God. She's never been in a church or, for that matter, anywhere holy in her entire twenty-five years. Her mother didn't even bother to have her birth registered, let alone have her baptized. But this very second she is praying. She is telling the God of her own special Darkness, whatever religion he is, that she is sorry for everything bad that she has ever done in her stinking, miserable, worthless life. She's telling him that she forgives her stepfather for all those things that he did to her; that she hopes he's fine and happy and healthy and that she didn't mean it when she told him that she wanted him to rot in hell while devil dogs chewed his bollocks off. She's asking for forgiveness for blaming her parents for her anger and for hating her mother for the beatings that she got. And she's confessing to all the sins she's committed and all the sinful thoughts she's ever had. And in return, she's asking God for only one thing.

Not to save her, but just to let her die quickly.

51

Rome

Roberto returned to the Incident Room with four coffees and a mouthful of bad news.

He put the tray of drinks down on a table and politely waited until a conversation between Jack and Benito finished.

'I am sorry,' he said, 'but while I was making coffees, I got a call from my contact in Milano.'

'About the courier?' asked Orsetta.

'Yes,' confirmed Roberto. 'They are now sure there is no such courier company as Volante Milano. It does not exist.'

Jack lifted a coffee from the tray and accepted he was hooked again on caffeine. 'So how did BRK get the package here, if not through a courier?'

Orsetta was thinking the unthinkable. 'In person? You think he delivered it in person?'

Benito nodded. 'Something like that.'

'Please,' interrupted Roberto. 'My contact had an idea what might have happened. Right now, there are many students looking to earn some extra money. It seems in Milano they stand as advertisements outside airports and railway stations, offering to do anything.'

'Anything? What do you mean?' asked Orsetta.

'I am sorry, maybe I don't explain properly,' said Roberto. 'They hold up the card, saying they will carry things anywhere for you. They stand near the parcel offices and offer to take things anywhere on a train, even on planes. The courier companies they do not like this, they find this very bad.'

'I bet they do,' said Jack. 'So what you're saying is that BRK may have given the package to a student at the railway station, and had it delivered here?'

'*Sì*, yes, that is what I am trying to say,' said Roberto, relieved finally to be understood.

'He's taking a bit of a risk, isn't he?' said Orsetta. 'I wouldn't trust a student to deliver something valuable for me.'

'How do these student couriers get paid?' asked Benito.

'It is cash, I think,' said Roberto.

Benito played with his goatee beard, thinking hard. 'BRK will have bought a return ticket for the courier, maybe rail, maybe air. He'll have paid cash, so we'll have problems tracing it. He may have given the courier some money upfront and then promised to pay him much more when he returned.'

'Doesn't work for me,' said Jack.

Orsetta was growing frustrated. She ran her fingers through her hair. 'This is just messing up my mind.'

'That's it!' Jack snapped his fingers. 'That's exactly what he's trying to do. Confuse us. Have us chasing shadows. There is no Volante Milano. Yet he went to enormous trouble to make it look as though he was there in Milan and used the company. He did this to make us think he had been there so that we would divert our resources to searching in Milan.'

'So he was never in Milan?' asked Orsetta, still struggling to make complete sense of it all.

'No, not at all,' explained Jack. 'I think you'll find that the Volante courier label was made on his own computer, and that the cardboard box and bubble wrap packaging will match the box from UMail2Anywhere sent to the FBI.'

'And the black felt-pen too,' said Orsetta.

'That too,' added Jack.

'He's pulling us all over the place,' conceded Benito.

'He's trying to,' said Jack. 'The courier story Roberto told us is probably old news and common knowledge. I've heard about students being used as couriers, it's been going on for a few years in the States. Like Roberto said, kids even get free holidays by babysitting boxes on flights all over the world. I think BRK will have wanted us to think our package was delivered by a real courier company in Milan, hence the label. If we got through that test, then I reckon he was sure we'd come across the widespread use of Milanese students as couriers and would have wasted even more time chasing that dead end.'

'Which means he really may have delivered the package in person,' said Orsetta, believing that the killer would no doubt get an enormous kick out of such an act.

Jack didn't think it likely. 'Remember that this guy is not a risk-taker, so I'd bet against it. No, I suspect Roberto's friend is partly right, but I think BRK used a student courier in Rome not in Milan.'

Benito volunteered another piece of the puzzle. 'Because in Rome he could pay the student on return, with nothing upfront, and be sure the package wouldn't be tampered with.'

'Which means,' said Jack, 'that our man flew to the States from Rome, not Milan, and that he probably left on the evening of the twenty-fifth of June or sometime during the twenty-sixth.'

'Maybe later,' said Benito. 'If he was confident that we'd be chasing around in Milan, he could wait in Rome until the twenty-eighth or twenty-ninth and catch a transatlantic flight that would have him arriving in the USA and getting to the cemetery in Georgetown on June the thirtieth. We'll check all Rome flight details as well.'

They paused for breath and looked at each other. Each and every one of them knew that, for the first time, they'd picked up the real scent of BRK's trail.

'One final thing,' said Jack. 'I don't want to rain on our parade, but let's check for recent student deaths in Rome as well. You know how our guy likes to tidy up as he goes along.'

52

Pan Arabia News Channel, New York

Crime editor Tariq el Daher was beginning to wonder whether he had made the biggest mistake of what he had once been told was a highly promising career. Just over a year had passed since he'd left his job at Reuters and joined the controversial Dubai-based station Pan Arabia to beef up their newly launched English language network.

At first, major technical problems had seriously delayed the station's long-awaited debut transmission and hugely undermined their credibility as a news outfit. But those difficulties had faded into insignificance compared with the vitriolic criticism unleashed upon them by competing Western media groups once they did get on air. Sitting in his New York office, scanning the digital airways to check the content of competing channels, Tariq consoled himself by recalling that neither he nor his bosses had been under any illusion that they were in for an easy ride.

As a Muslim, he didn't just understand the facts and figures of minority life – he lived them. Of New York's twenty million people, fewer than two per cent followed the doctrines of Islam and fewer than two per cent were Buddhists, Hindus or Sikhs. But behind those figures were the earthquake tremors of a massive change that wasn't yet visible. While New York is home to a quarter of all America's Jews, it has also quietly become the chosen land for a quarter of all America's Muslims.

Ask Tariq whether he loved Islam more than America and the devout 35-year-old would dismiss your question as naïve and ask you if you loved your child more than your wife or husband. His love for both Islam and America was equally passionate but subtly different and, because he didn't view them as mutually exclusive, when the chance came to join the New York bureau of one of the Middle East's largest and fastest growing news channels, he saw it as his dream job.

But lately, just lately, he'd started to worry about whether he'd made the right choice. As a staffer at Reuters he had been welcomed into any press gang in any hotel bar in the world. Similarly, his contacts book boasted some of the most important political, legal and social names in the country. But these days his calls went unanswered. His requests for access got turned down. And the press pack in the hotel bars always seemed to be turning in for the night whenever he arrived.

Right now Tariq el Daher was beginning to fear his dream job had turned into a dire nightmare. He looked at the first draft of the Prospects List his deputy had prepared for tomorrow and was disappointed at how thin it was. A couple of murders, both drive-by shootings in Queens, were only mildly interesting. A suicide by a Muslim woman who'd been secretly seeing a well-known professional gambler – that looked a bit spicier. But it was still thin.

He wanted coffee but his PA had disappeared from her desk again. The woman would have to go. She had been hired only for a month, from a temping agency, and was never at her desk when he needed her. Tariq couldn't be bothered making it himself so he tapped open the Inbox on his computer. Back in his Reuters days he used to fear firing up his machine. He'd easily have to clear more than a hundred e-mails a day. These days, he was lucky to find ten, and two would always be from his wife. Today was no different. He worked down the short list and killed junk mail offering him great deals on everything from stock market info to cut-price Viagra. The last message caught his eye.

It was marked simply 'Exclusive' and seemingly had been sent by a company called 'Insidexclusive'. He clicked it open. The mail was blank except for the web hyperlink www.Insidexclusive.com. And the instruction 'Enter the Password 898989'. He ran the cursor over it and pressed it. A box popped up saying 'Enter password before ten p.m.' Tariq glanced across at the office clock. There was plenty of time. He typed it in. The box disappeared and the screen started filling with the vertical colour bars that you sometimes see at the start of videotape. Then the bars disappeared and a black-and-grey mist filled the frame. Gradually, an image started to emerge, out-of-focus and blurred, as though the camera were moving rapidly sideways while simultaneously trying to focus. Eventually, he could make out something that looked like a newspaper, maybe a copy of *USA Today*, lying on the floor. Tariq got ready to kill the tape, dismissing it as another viral e-mail, sent by some trash advertiser pushing their useless products. Then he noticed that the camera lingered on the front of the newspaper. Tariq could even see the date. It was three days old, the second of July. He sat back and gave the video a chance; maybe this was *USA Today* trying out some weird cutting-edge marketing campaign. The camera slowly zoomed out and the paper seemed to disappear into blackness. Then the edge of a table came into shot. Tariq bolted forward in his seat. The newspaper shot suddenly made sense; it was there to show him that what he was watching was real and was current. The zoom stopped and the picture became razor sharp. Tariq could clearly make out the prostrate form of a naked young white woman chained to some kind of table.

'Sweet God alive!' he swore out loud.

The picture on his screen cut to an overhead shot.

He could see the young girl's battered face in horrifying close-up. She kept rocking her head from side to side with distressed monotony. Tariq had seen enough war-zone pictures, enough video evidence of tortured people to know what was real and what wasn't. He had no doubt about its authenticity. The girl was in an advanced state of trauma, and the rocking was a sure sign that she was close to breaking point.

Suddenly, the camera started to zoom in again. This time it headed towards the right side of the table.

On the floor, three white pieces of paper slowly became visible.

Tariq bent towards the monitor and squinted hard. He could see some big, blurred shapes or letters on each of them. The zoom stopped and the picture became sharp.

Tariq was shocked and confused. Three words blazed off the screen back at him: 'HA! HA! HA!'

53

FBI Field Office, New York

Howie Baumguard finished his call with the Director of the FBI and speed-dialled Jack King's cell number. His eyes never left the news bulletin on the TV screen.

In Rome, Jack was already asleep. The third rude peel of ring tone woke him. 'Hello,' he said groggily.

'Jack, it's Howie, I'm real sorry to wake you, I guess you were sleeping –'

Jack flicked on a bedside light. 'Yeah, oddly enough you guessed right. Sleep is that freaky thing that oddballs like me do every night for as long as we possibly can.'

Howie gunned up the sound a little on the TV as he spoke. 'I'm sorry, buddy, I'm not dicking around, I had to call you. We've got a real shit storm blowing up.'

Jack dropped his smart-ass act. 'What's wrong? Are you okay?'

'I'm fine, no worries, but we've got a situation and it looks like it's related to our favourite sociopath, old BR-fucking-K himself.'

The mention of the Black River Killer was enough

to get Jack to sit up. 'How do you mean? Go slowly with me, buddy; I'm not fully awake yet.'

'Well, this sure as hell is going to wake you up. You know Pan Arabia, the Arab channel set up in competition to Al Jazeera, the guys who do the special line in Bin Laden home videos?'

Jack rubbed sleep from his eyes. 'Yeah, I was part of one of the early validation teams that checked them out.'

'Well, they've got themselves one hell of a fucking exclusive this morning. They just friggin' well ran some video footage and a story about a woman being held hostage and being tortured to death.'

Jack struggled to catch it all. 'I don't get it, Howie; you're going to have to go slower, man. They've got pictures of an Arab woman hostage and you think it's somehow connected to BRK?'

'Fuck!' said Howie. 'I'm sorry. Let me start again. They're running an exclusive story on their English news channel, not their normal Arab output, video footage and a voiceover from their chief crime guy, Tariq el Daher. The report they've cobbled together shows a young white woman chained up in some kind of dark room. She looks in a hell of a fucking way. They're rerunning it now if you can find it on your TV over there.'

'I'll look when we're done,' said Jack, straining his eyes open. 'I'm still spaced-out at the moment.'

'Jack, you should see this girl, she looks really beat-up and distressed. Our friend Tariq showed a copy to some dumb-ass detective on Homicide down at the NYPD and got quotes enough to stand up a line that there's a nationwide hunt to find this kid before she gets croaked.'

'How do you know the footage is for real?' asked Jack, his brain in gear at last.

'I'm pretty sure it is,' said Howie. 'There's a copy of *USA Today* on the floor in the video and it's dated July the second, and here's the clincher, Jack, there were three other pieces of paper in the video, spelling out the words "HA! HA! HA!"'

Jack's head started to pound. 'Was it written the same way BRK did in his note here in Italy?'

'The very same way,' said Howie. 'All big capitals.'

'Holy fuck!' The worst of Jack's fears were coming true. The Italian connection was indeed a red herring, just as he'd told Orsetta he suspected. And, as he'd also guessed, BRK had been planning a new spree of America-based violence that was turning out to be unthinkably horrendous. 'Howie, do you really think this girl is being held right now by BRK somewhere in America? You reckon we've just been pissing in the wind over here in Italy?'

Howie could feel Jack's pain and humiliation. 'That seems to be the top and bottom of it. Italy's a false trail, laid just for us. I'm sure he had a lot of fun laying it, a creep like him would, but his real action is Stateside, always has been, always will be.'

Jack's mind focused on the videotape. He knew the film was going to turn out to be more than a one-off publicity stunt. BRK would be planning something far more sinister as a sequel. 'The way things are stacking up, BRK's going to kill this girl any time soon and then leak video footage of her murder to the Western world's most hated news channel.'

Howie shared the same fear. 'You got it. And you know these fuckers, Jack, they show beheadings of Western hostages and any manner of atrocity; they'll probably be praying to Allah, or Mohammed, or whoever the hell it is, that something happens right in the middle of the fucking ratings sweeps.'

Jack let out a long sigh. 'What are you going to do now, Howie? I guess your hot-shot new boss Joey Marsh is all over this and will be wanting a multi-agency briefing asap?'

'You got it. Marsh is so attached to my butt that I may have to have him surgically removed. We need you over here, Jack; can you get out of your obligations to the Italians?'

Jack took a beat to think about the consequences. 'Marsh okay with that?'

'Yeah, more than okay. He suggested it even before me. It's all going to kick off again, and this time this friggin' BRK screwball is begging for us to come get him. You never know, buddy, he might just be about to make his one big mistake.'

Jack weighed up the possibilities. Howie could be right. If BRK was behind the video footage, then he was taking risks, and he would do that only if he was very close to killing again. It was a unique moment; never before had they been able to so accurately predict when the serial murderer was about to strike next. 'I'll sort it out with Massimo. I'll come,' he said. 'I don't know when the next flight from Rome to JFK is, but I'll be on it. Meantime, get yourself all over this Tariq guy, clamp his balls in a vice and squeeze so hard that they come out of his ears. He's got to know that what happens next isn't about TV, it's about someone's life or death.'

PART SIX

Friday, 6 July

54

Rome

By the time Orsetta and Massimo arrived at their office, Jack was already en route to New York. The concierge at the hotel had managed to get him one of the few remaining seats on the 9.55 a.m. Lufthansa flight from Rome's Fiumicino airport. It wasn't going to be the best of journeys; Jack topped six foot and squeezing into Economy was one of his pet hates. To make matters worse, he had to change planes at Düsseldorf and make the last leg of the long haul also in 'cattle class'. Orsetta and Massimo learned all this from the various messages he left on their answerphones. Just before boarding, he'd called Nancy and told her where he was heading and not to worry if she didn't get calls at the times he'd promised. He'd been encouraged by how understanding she'd been. He also managed a brief chat with Massimo, during which he'd told him more about the breaking news on BRK and the reason why he had to leave so suddenly.

Orsetta sat in her boss's office leaning her elbows on his giant desk. They both cradled espressos and discussed their disappointment at Jack's departure.

Massimo resisted lighting a cigarette to go with his coffee, his new pledge to himself being not to smoke before lunchtime. He tapped the desk with his finger, as though he were banging ash from it. 'Orsetta, I am hoping that Jack is right and that the murder of Cristina Barbuggiani is just a cruel decoy, but it is not a risk we can afford to take. When Benito comes in, we must impress upon him that our own investigations must remain fully focused. I do not want everyone sitting back and thinking the ball is now in the Americans' side of the court. That might be a tragic mistake to make.'

Orsetta was ahead of him. 'I spoke yesterday to the murder squad in Livorno and they are a determined team. I know the officer in charge, Marco Rem Picci, and he is not the kind to allow anyone to relax and do nothing.'

'Good,' said Massimo, the tension of the case showing in his red-rimmed eyes. 'Almost every day now I have phone calls or e-mails from the Prime Minister's office, the Minister of the Interior, the head of the Polizia Scientifica, the Direzione Centrale Anticrimine della Polizia di Stato and even the damn Chief of Police wanting to know what progress we are making.' He threw his hands up to show his exasperation. 'Hopefully this development in America will take a little heat off us for a while.'

Orsetta finished her espresso and drank water to take the bitterness away. She wanted to press on with the case more than anyone else, this was the biggest investigation she'd ever been involved in, and as far as she was concerned, it was just starting, not winding down. 'I'd like to go ahead with the 3D reconstruction of the crime scene. Can you authorize payment and access?'

For some years, the Italian police had been nurturing the use of a sophisticated computer system that reproduced crime scenes with startling realism, re-creating everything from the path of a bullet to the movement of a corpse.

'Call RiTriDEC and tell them to go ahead. I will have the paperwork with them by early afternoon,' said Massimo, referring to the special laboratory in Rome known as the Ricostruzione Tridimensionale della Dinamica dell'Evento Criminale.

Orsetta was a big fan of the system. It worked by devouring all the crime scene data available, everything from traffic-camera video footage to the measurements a pathologist might make during an autopsy. Once everything was fed in, it would recreate crime scenes in 3D pictures on giant video screens in a special theatre. Experts like Orsetta were then able to examine the pictures, almost like art critics, studying every screen pixel for a clue that might lead them to their killer.

Massimo called her to the other side of his desk. 'Benito has patched through an FBI feed of the video footage that Jack spoke about. I have it now on the computer.'

Neither of them spoke as they watched Tariq el

Daher's report. Orsetta made notes and was the first to break the silence. 'Just because there's a copy of *USA Today* in that video it doesn't mean the location is in America. You can pick that paper up in a hundred places in Rome.'

'Or indeed on a plane landing in Rome,' added Massimo. 'Jack might be in the wrong place at the wrong time. I wish we could have discussed this with him.'

Orsetta nodded. She felt exactly the same way. As far as she was concerned, Jack King and the FBI were still ignoring the elephant in the room.

55

Montepulciano, Tuscany

Montepulciano stood out against an early-evening sky as beautiful and mystical as a fortified medieval settlement drawn in a kid's book of fairy tales. From its lofty perch on a limestone ridge, six hundred metres above sea level, it watched majestically over Italy's magic kingdom of Tuscany.

Nancy King had briefed Paullina, her waitress-come-guide-for-the-day, to make sure the photo-happy Mr Terry McLeod got to focus his lens on every corner of the town. And Paullina had been as good as the promise she pledged to her boss.

First, she made him walk the last part of the famous Corso, which starts at Porta al Prato and winds its way for more than eleven kilometres up to the top of the town and the huge open square of the Piazza Grande. They took a late lunch in the open air at Trattoria di Cagnano, where Paullina made the mistake of insisting that he try the local *vino de nobile*. McLeod enthusiastically complied. He drank most of the bottle, along with a brandy to polish off a hearty plate of pasta and a slice of torte large enough to wedge open one of the town hall's giant doors.

After lunch, she guided him along the sixteenth-century town walls designed by the Grand Duke Cosimo I de' Medici. He stopped once to take photographs, once to make phone calls and once to relieve himself of his surfeit of strong red wine.

Paullina showed him the church of Santa Maria delle Grazie and, just before they left, the Sanctuary of the Madonna of St Blaise on the outskirts of the town.

He was far less interested in church architecture than he'd led her to believe, and seemed more intent on finding out everything and anything about the lives of her employers.

As promised, Paullina telephoned Nancy just before they got in the taxi for the return journey home. She gave a full report of what they'd seen and what they'd done. After ending the call with Paullina, Nancy turned to Carlo. They were both standing inside the bedroom of supposed tourist Terence T. McLeod, Nancy having used the staff key to let them in. He was no more a tourist than she was, of that she was sure.

Nancy had agonized about whether she should break her guest's right to privacy by going through his room and his belongings while he was out. In the end, she'd subscribed to her father's old maxim that it was 'far better to say sorry than ask permission'. Surprisingly though, their search had turned up absolutely nothing to support her superficial dislike of him or her deep-rooted suspicion that he might have been the intruder in her bedroom.

'What do you think?' she asked Carlo.

The hotel manager shrugged. 'It was dark when it happened. And you say yourself that you never saw the man, because of his mask. We have found nothing that shows it was Signor McLeod.' He looked at her sympathetically; he was aware that she had been badly spooked by the incident. 'I can only think, Signora King, that you may have made a mistake. It seems our Signor McLeod is what he says he is. An American tourist. And in my experience, sometimes they can be much stranger and far more trouble than any burglar.'

56

Pan Arabia News Channel, New York

Tariq el Daher looked out over the hazy New York skyline while he tried to decide exactly how long he should keep the two FBI agents waiting. He checked his watch; it was a little after 11.30. Was twenty minutes enough to show them that he was in control and that things happened as and when he wanted them to? Or should he go for a full hour, to make sure that at least this government agency took Pan Arabia seriously in future and had the politeness to return its calls and treat it with the same respect they extended to the likes of Fox and CNN?

Tariq sent his PA to make him more coffee and asked her to tell the Feds that he was very busy and would do his best to fit them in as soon as possible. He drank the coffee while he finished reading the morning newspapers. He smiled to himself. To-morrow, they would be full of quotes from him, and probably a photograph or two as well. He hoped they used the one taken a few years back at a press dinner when he had been presented with the special award for investigative journalism.

Tariq fully anticipated that all the news media, be

it newspapers, TV or magazines, would steal screen shots of the girl from the video report he'd put together, so he'd already instructed Pan Arabia's lawyers to issue a legal copyright warning and circulate a range of digitally enhanced photographs that the press could use for free, providing of course they credited Pan Arabia. Yes, tomorrow all the hacks will be scavenging on his scoop, he was sure of that. He smiled once more, this time at the thought of them having to search for his long-forgotten phone number and wonder if *he'd* deign to speak to *them*. First though, he would have to put up with annoying meetings with the FBI and the NYPD. The tame cop he'd used to help stand up the story in the first place was now going crazy, claiming he'd been quoted out of context and threatening to bust Tariq's balls for getting him in so much trouble. Tariq wondered whether he'd also give him back the $500 he'd asked for in return for the interview. Somehow he thought not.

After forty minutes Tariq instructed his PA to show the agents through to the executive boardroom. Then he changed his mind. He decided instead that he'd see them, along with the company lawyer, in the smallest of all the ground-floor meeting rooms, the one usually reserved for junior reporters who were sent downstairs to get rid of potential time-wasters.

Ryan Jeffries from Legal met him in his office and they rode the elevator together. Fifty-year-old Jeffries had been round the block more times than a yellow cab and there wasn't anything about media law that he either didn't know, or couldn't find a way round.

'Good morning, officers,' said Tariq energetically as he pushed open the glass door to the cramped room. 'I'm Tariq el Daher and this is my Head of Legal Affairs, Ryan Jeffries. Sorry to have kept you waiting.'

Howie's first glance showed the obvious contempt that he had for both of them. 'Senior Supervisory Special Agent Howie Baumguard and Special Agent Angelita Fernandez.'

They all settled around a cheap wooden table that was so flimsy it almost buckled when Howie thudded his meaty arms down on it. Tariq sat back in his seat while Jeffries went in to bat. 'Mr el Daher and the channel have already made a statement to the New York Police Department, who we understand have operational control. We have delivered a copy of the material we uncovered and we will continue to assist the NYPD to the very best of our ability. Mr el Daher is, as you know, an extremely busy man and we do not think it necessary to waste his time with repetitive processes.'

Fernandez was curious to see how her boss was going to handle this. The bulging veins in his neck and the giant clenched fists hinted that he might be about to go Hulk green, shred his shirt and then pick up the lawyer and beat the smug bastard journalist to death with him.

'Okay,' said Howie, sounding surprisingly calm and

quiet. 'Agent Fernandez and I are real sorry to have troubled you. We'll be on our way now, if that's all right with you?'

Jeffries smiled and slapped his hands on the table to help him rise from his seat.

'Sit down, mister,' said Fernandez. 'He's jerking your string. It ain't going to play like that.'

Howie's face displayed a cruel smile. 'I'm afraid the lady's right. Of course, we could just soak up that bullshit you came out with and leave. But if we did, then I'd only have to come back this afternoon with a court order to seize every computer and video machine in the place and then lock up our extremely busy Mr el Daher in a room even smaller than this crappy matchbox you've got us in.'

'Ridiculous! On what grounds?' spluttered Jeffries.

'Withholding evidence. Perverting the course of justice, impeding police investigations. We'll find the right one eventually,' said Fernandez.

'Meantime,' added Howie, making a point of picking dirt from under a fingernail, 'every press guy in the world is going to love the story we'll be putting out, about how your station is endangering the life of a young American woman. Run that one past your CEO, board of directors and financial backers and see how supportive they are of you then.'

'That's presuming your footage is for real,' added Fernandez. 'Because if we find out that it isn't, then a fan load of toxic shit is going to be heading your way, and we'll be fingering the power switch.'

Tariq leant forward and put a hand on the lawyer's arm to silence him. 'What do you want, Mr Baumguard?' he asked in a voice that was so laid back it almost sounded bored.

'Let's start with some civility,' said Howie. 'And right after that, you can begin at the beginning and go through that whole repetitive process of telling us how you came to have the footage in your possession.'

'And hey, Mr Lawyerman,' said Fernandez, 'while he does that, maybe you could get us a couple of coffees and some doughnuts. We missed breakfast this morning.'

57

San Quirico D'Orcia, Tuscany

The sun was slowly setting in San Quirico, sponging a silky mix of vermilion and gold across the darkening blue sky.

In Terry McLeod's bathroom, the Vent-Axia panel above the toilet came off easily enough in his hands. McLeod lifted out the stuff he'd hidden inside the metal vent and carried it through to the bedroom. It contained some special photographs and some extra special equipment that he needed to keep very secret.

Paullina the waitress had been a good companion. And, when he'd given her a generous fifty-euro tip on top of the hundred euros fee he'd insisted on her taking for her 'work' as his guide, then she'd been more than helpful. Some of the things she'd told him about the Kings would soon prove extremely valuable. She'd spoken at length about how the Americans had not known a thing about catering when they'd moved into La Casa Strada, how Carlo and Paolo had effectively run the business for the first six months, but then Mrs King began slowly to take control and seemed really passionate about the cooking and treating the guests as though they were visiting friends. McLeod had listened patiently as she'd rambled on about the food and the menus, the work that she did there and her ambitions once she had finished her studies. Eventually, with only the gentlest of hints, he was able to guide the conversation to what really interested him, former FBI agent Jack King.

Paullina hadn't known everything that McLeod had hoped, but she'd known enough. She described in detail how depressed Jack had been when she'd first met him. How he would stay in the private family quarters of the hotel and seemed almost uninterested in the staff or the guests, never making any effort to meet them or chat with them if they bumped into him in the corridors or gardens. She mentioned that about two years earlier he used to go off on walks, usually on his own, sometimes pushing his son in a buggy, just doing laps of San Quirico. He went around so many times that shopkeepers and locals said he was *fuori di testa* – off his head. McLeod soaked it all up, the more bad things that were said about hero Jack King the better, as far as he was concerned. Paullina mentioned that at first Jack had really let himself go, that his weight had ballooned and Nancy had to get Paolo to come up with a special diet to help him shed the pounds. McLeod would have loved to have seen that. Lately though, she said he'd apparently slimmed down and instead of the long and lonely walks, he could be seen jogging two or three times a week and was now looking in *buona salute*.

McLeod had asked where Jack was these days and she'd hesitated before saying she thought he was a long way away, maybe on the other side of Italy. What really excited McLeod though was when Paullina revealed that she thought maybe Jack's absence had something to do with the Italian police. She recalled that a plainclothes policewoman from Rome had turned up to see him. It seems there had been some kind of row between Mrs King and the policewoman, and it had ended with the policewoman ordering Mrs King to get her husband to call her because it was 'an urgent police matter'.

The thought made McLeod smile as he looked at the photographs of Jack that he'd stolen from an album in Nancy King's bedroom. 'I've got a big surprise coming for you, Mr FBI man,' he said, putting them to one side. Then he slowly unpacked the special equipment that he'd hidden.

The equipment he now planned to use on Nancy King.

58

JFK Airport, New York

Jack's flight touched down at JFK terminal 4 bang on time. Howie was waiting out front with a car, a bearhug and some back-slapping that could have hospitalized a smaller person. They drove straight to the office, catching up on the way. 'You booked in anywhere?' he asked Jack as they finally got free of the snarled traffic around the airport.

'No, not yet. It was hard enough actually to get a flight out of Rome, so I didn't get round to it. Do you mind getting Janie or one of the other secretaries to fix a place?'

Howie scowled at him. 'No way. Not a chance, buddy, you're staying with us, for tonight, at least.' Howie's offer was partly out of politeness but mainly reflected his concern about how Jack might react to being back on the job and forced to spend a night on his own without anyone to talk to about it.

Jack slid the passenger seat back to stretch his legs. 'I don't want to put you and Carrie out.'

'You're not. Listen, I could do with a friend around the house right at the moment. And shit, man, I might not get to see you again until God knows when.'

'That's kind, thanks.' Jack took in the familiar buildings as the city started to roll up to the windshield. 'You know, this is the first time I've been back to New York since the breakdown. Hell, when Nancy and I caught our flights out to Italy, what, three years ago now, I would never have thought I'd be coming back here, and certainly not to work.'

Howie blared his horn at some idiot tourist trying to drive and read a map at the same time. 'Get a friggin' cab next time, you friggin' moron!' he shouted.

Jack laughed. 'Nothing's changed then?'

Howie laughed too. 'Nothing at all, buddy. As you can see, it's the New York you always loved.'

The drive was good for Jack. It helped acclimatize him and sharpen him up for what lay ahead. 'I caught the footage just before I took off,' he said. 'Grim stuff. You got anything new on it?'

'A little something,' said Howie. 'Fernandez and I went to see this jerk Tariq. He was a gold-plated asshole to start with but we scared him about a bit and then he coughed more than a cancer ward.'

'He briefed up?'

'Yeah, some smart Alec, but he was no problem. Seemed BRK posted Tariq a mail with a website hyperlink and a password, and that's how he got the footage they've been putting on air.'

'We're running webmaster traces?'

'Of course, but both you and I already know a twelve-year-old can build sites this simple. BRK will have used a false identity when he spoke to the hosting service. He's sure to have uplifted only the most innocuous of video during the testing phase. He will have waited and only made the real stuff available on the day he sent that electronic mail out to Pan Arabia. Tech boys think it's dongle encrypted.'

'Say what?' said Jack. 'Is that like catching your dick in your zipper?'

Howie laughed. 'It's a computer coding trick that makes the footage available only for a short period of time. The dongle is like a timer fuse on a bomb; it ticks away and then *boom!* It blows it up and you can't work it any more.'

'So it *is* like getting your dick caught in your zipper,' said Jack.

Howie's cell phone rang as they turned into Federal Plaza. 'Yeah, hello,' he managed as he spun the wheel.

'Boss, it's Fernandez. The boys in Myrtle have found a body. They think it's Stan Mossman, our delivery boy.'

59

It took Jack King ten minutes to shake everyone's hand and another twenty to hug, kiss and say hi to all his female ex-colleagues.

'Man, you really should go to the Men's room and get brushed up,' said Howie. 'I've seen dudes come back from stag weekends with less lipstick on their collars.'

'It's a small price to pay for popularity,' joked Jack, deciding to take his advice. 'I'll see you in the briefing room.'

The pow-wow was a big one.

It was chaired by FBI Field Office director Joe Marsh, a small, thin man in his early forties with hair greying at the temples and a natural smile that most politicians would pay half their campaign funds for. To his right was NYPD deputy commissioner of operations Steven Flintoff, a barrel-chested ox of a guy with short-cut ginger hair and his trademark rolled-up sleeves. Behavioural scientists Howie Baumguard and Angelita Fernandez came next around the circular table, followed by Elizabeth Laing, a Roseanne Barr lookalike employed as press information officer for the NYPD, and Julian Hopkins, the FBI's local press guy. They were still pouring each other coffee and water when Jack walked in and greeted them with a confident, 'Good morning everybody!'

A spontaneous ripple of applause erupted and Marsh rose to shake his hand. 'Good to see you back, Jack. Come and sit here right next to me.'

'Good to be back,' said Jack. 'Though I must say it actually feels like I've never been away. Same case, same room, just a few changed faces.'

'Angelita Fernandez,' said the profiler, leaning over the table to shake his hand. 'We kind of met by video conference.'

'We did indeed. Nice to meet you for real,' said Jack.

The rest of the room took it in turns to table-stretch and introduce themselves, then Marsh got down to business. 'For the sake of the press officers, Jack King is with us as a consultant. Ideally, we don't want his name mentioned at all, but let's be realistic, this ugly old mug of his is so well known that once he's been around a few days, you can be sure the papers will all be asking you what the hell he's doing back on the scene. No interviews with Jack, no comments from Jack, let's say he's over here just catching up with old friends. You got it?'

Laing and Hopkins both nodded.

'Good,' said Marsh. 'In a minute or two we're going to dial-in Malcolm Thompson on a line from Quantico and agree our strategy for the next few days. Jack, Malcolm is the new head of the National Center for the Analysis of Violent Crime. He's still at the ballbuster stage at the moment but he'll be fine when he's settled in.' Marsh slapped both hands lightly on the table. 'Okay, Howie, Angelita, before we call Mal, what's the latest?'

Howie kicked off. 'We've interviewed the journalist Tariq el Daher. After what we might call a reluctant beginning, he's come round to our way of thinking.' He nodded towards the NYPD's deputy commissioner of operations. 'Stevie's guys are fixing his office right now with full A and V recording and tracking equipment, phones, computers, the lot. This time we should be able to get into any new video feed from the perp practically the second it happens.'

'And he was fine with that?' checked Marsh.

'Absolutely. A total model of cooperation,' said Howie grinning in a way that everyone around the table understood.

'Is the material still out there in hyper-space?' asked Jack.

'No,' said Fernandez. 'Tariq called us about ten minutes ago and said his access code didn't work any more.'

Jack thought for a second about dongles and bomb fuses and zipper disasters. 'Is the code itself of any significance?' he asked. 'Does 898989 mean anything to anyone? Is it the Pan Arabia office number, have we tried it as a phone number, have we run the number itself through the Internet?'

'I Googled it,' said Fernandez.

'And?' asked Marsh.

'A hundred and sixteen thousand entries. I've been through about twenty.'

The whole room laughed.

'The domain name 898989 is already registered with someone. They're quite legit, no connection at all. It also gets you a gardening centre in England and a strange website called "Just Curious".' Fernandez paused for effect, then added, 'Sorry folks, that's also legit. I got excited as well because it has a motto on the front: "Strangers Helping Strangers".'

'What the hell is it?' asked Flintoff.

'You just ask a question anonymously and the whole world answers it and gives you advice,' explained Fernandez.

'Sounds great,' said Howie. 'Stick one on from us, and tell the whole world out there that we're just curious as hell to know where BRK is, someone should have seen him.' They all laughed again.

'Not a bad idea,' said Jack. 'Knowing what an egotistical son of a bitch BRK is, there's just a chance he might visit the site and respond. Unfortunately, I suspect a million other fruitcakes will as well.'

'What else?' said Marsh. 'We have to move things along.'

Howie picked up the ball again. 'The bad news for the day is that it looks like one of our possible witnesses, a guy who could ID our perp, got stiffed. The guys over in Myrtle had been following up on a delivery boy from UMail2Anywhere called Stanley Mossman. Best Fernandez tells you the rest; she just got off the phone to Myrtle.'

Fernandez took up the story. 'Stan the Man turned up in the trunk of his own car at the long-stay out at Myrtle International. I don't know all the details but from what Gene Saunders said, it looks like BRK arranged to meet him there and wasted him. The kid seems to have had his throat cut while standing around the back of his own vehicle, then the killer popped the trunk and bundled him in there.'

'Surveillance cameras, forensics?' asked Marsh.

Fernandez nodded. 'Yes, sir, all underway. The doc's doing the post-mortem tomorrow but he saw the body in situ. Says it's a single-bladed, short and razor-sharp knife. Cut was made from behind. Done real quick and hard.' She ran a finger across her throat and made the slashing sound *shweep!*

'It's a pro kill,' said Howie. 'He probably got the kid to put something in the trunk of his car, weaseled up behind him, then out comes some kind of flick blade and in a flash he takes out Stan's jugular.'

'Is it too much to hope that this was all captured on camera?' asked Marsh.

Fernandez smiled. 'I think you're a mind-reader, boss. The parking lot wasn't one of the regular approved ones; it was on an old building lot a couple of blocks behind Jetport Road. No cameras.'

'That's interesting,' said Jack. 'To pick a parking lot that doesn't have surveillance cameras you first have to visit the ones that do, and eliminate them. Let's get someone in Myrtle to call all the car rental places near the airport and have them save their surveillance footage from the last three weeks; there's an outside chance they may have caught him on tape.'

'Sounds great viewing for some wet-behind-the-ears detective in Horry County,' said Marsh.

Jack poured himself water, then added, 'Guess Myrtle have impounded the car?'

'Forensics have it in their playpen already,' said Fernandez. 'If there are any hairs, fibres or trace evidence of any kind, they'll find it.'

'There's just one drawback,' said Howie.

Jack finished his sentence for him, 'We don't have a friggin' suspect to match it to.'

60

They live in a small white cottage with a thatched roof beside a river with a waterwheel and their young children chase each other in a garden that has an old stone path meandering across a lawn full of daisies. Lu Zagalsky is hallucinating, and she's glad she is. She and Ramzan are married and have two beautiful young children, a boy and a girl who look exactly like them. They want for nothing and they live a perfect life in a perfect home in a perfect country where summer never ends, and no one ever strips you naked and leaves you to die like a dog. She's been dreaming a lot since being held in the basement, and few of her dreams have been as pleasant as this. Mainly they've been about pain, humiliation and death. Some have been so terrifying that she's now afraid of falling asleep.

For the past hour though, she's been fantasizing about Ramzan. In her life of a few days ago he was just a tall, good-looking waiter who'd caught her eye and turned her head. Today, she imagines him as her lover, her husband and the father of her children. The last thought hurts most, for she realizes now that she will never be a mother, her womb will never carry her children and she will never see smiles on the faces of her babies.

Lu opens her eyes and stares vacantly at the black plastic ceiling, with the shiny rodent eye of the camera peering back down at her. At times she is sure he is still in the house with her, watching her from somewhere on the other side of the door, moving the cameras to get a better look and no doubt jerking himself off as she inches her way towards death. She's met some sickos in her time, sadists and masochists, scopophiliacs and scatophiliacs, but this guy is a wacko way beyond her experiences.

How can you get your rocks off watching someone starve to death? What kind of warped mind finds that a turn-on?

It's been eighty-seven hours since Lu last had any sustenance, and even then it had only been a vanilla milkshake. The effects of starvation and dehydration are becoming more acute by the hour. As well as the onset of delirium and hallucinations, her body temperature is now sky high. Despite the lack of food she is vomiting a lot, dry-heaving doctors call it, because her stomach is completely empty and its lining is as dry as parchment paper. Each bout of retching brings spasms of crippling cramps and shooting pains through her abdomen and chest. She's almost completely stopped urinating, but when she does, it's like a burning trickle of acid that destroys the last shreds of her dignity.

Maybe someone will find you, Lu. Maybe they've caught him and right now they're on their way here and they're going to break down the front door. Any second now you'll hear them coming down those basement steps.

And then what?

Boom! That's what.

Didn't he say the whole place was wired and that it would explode into a fireball and burn everyone alive? Well, better to be burned to death than go like this. But then others will die as well, Lu. Innocent people will be killed trying to save you – is that what you want? Is that how desperate and unworthy you have become?

And so the thoughts torment her, never letting her rest, always crushing any sign of hope, always making her imagine the worst. And when they're done with her, then the guilt moves in.

You're getting what you deserve; this is God's way of punishing you for the sinful life you've led. Count them up, Ludmila, all the sins you've committed; the thefts, the lies, the adulteries, is there a single Commandment you've not broken? Murder was the only one that stood out, and right now she'd gladly kill the freak that was putting her through this living hell.

Lu's vision is now permanently blurred and her eyes are so painful that she can't close them. The head restraint has come loose from her straining against it and it is possible to move from side to side, but the strap has badly chafed her flesh. Most of her skin is completely numb. It has lost its natural oiliness and elasticity and is starting to shrivel. At times the numbness fades and her skin tingles. Only this isn't the pins-and-needles type of tingling that she'd experienced as a child. This is a high-voltage cattle-prod tingling, the type that stuns her so deeply she feels as if she's going to croak.

Lu wonders whether she is already so sick that even if the cavalry arrived right now, right this minute, she would still die from what he's done to her. She's fully aware that she's being killed by her own body; that it's been turned into a weapon to murder her.

It's justice, Ludmila, for the life that you've led. Sell your body to strangers and God will punish you appropriately – an eye for an eye and a tooth for a tooth; you should have remembered that. You really should have remembered that.

Lu tries to lick her lips but it's an effort agonizingly beyond her. Her tongue has swollen and cracked painfully. Her throat feels permanently blocked and it is hard even to swallow air. In the last few hours her broken nose has started bleeding again. Part of the cause of the haemorrhaging is the beating that he gave her, but the continual rise in her body temperature isn't helping matters, nor is the fact that the lining of her nose has completely dried up and cracked like plaster. The congealed blood almost blocks both nostrils and Lu feels as though she's breathing through a damaged straw.

She tries again to think positively. There is the cottage in the country, with the children playing by the river, and maybe there's a dog too, a long-haired golden dog jumping and barking for its ball to be thrown.

And then it happens.

The cattle prods are at her again, sizzling into her flesh, stabbing at her nerves. This time, they're stronger and more painful than ever.

Lu's entire body goes into convulsion.

The world turns black.

And she stops breathing.

Spider sits by the monitor, watching the series of spasms with the wide-eyed excitement of a sports fan on the edge of his seat. He leans towards the screen, his chin resting on interlocked fingers. It looks as if she's going to die much earlier than he'd wanted, but that's okay, he can adjust his plans.

He stretches out a hand and runs it gently over the screen and a crackle of static flows over his fingertips. He'd chosen her for a purpose, for a reason beyond lust or longing, but right at this moment he wants her, just as strongly as he'd wanted all the others. Give up the fight my sweet, sweet Sugar. Breathe out your final breath and go to the Better Place.

He watches the screen as her body shakes uncontrollably, her muscles snapping tight and then relaxing just as suddenly. The camera's wide shot shows her whole frame shuddering like a rag doll, bouncing up and down on the hard leather table in a fleshy muscular ripple from foot to head.

She's at death's door and he wants to be there to press his lips and flesh against her and feel that precious last spasm of life spurt from her body.

The shaking seems to become more violent and then Lu flops limply down on to the black leather of the bondage table.

The overhead camera shows her face in close-up. It is motionless.

Spider puts his hands tenderly on either side of the monitor, like a lover would hold a dying partner's face. He stares intently into Lu's eyes.

Glazed and glassy, like the marbles children play with. Look how the orbits of her eyes are all sunken. See how her cheeks are hollowing out so nicely, so beautifully. And her skin – isn't it gorgeous? So white, so beautifully pallid. Your mother would approve of her, Spider. Your mother would have picked this one too.

Spider strokes her face with his damaged hand and then presses his cheek against hers. He holds the monitor for almost half a minute, feeling close to her, connected to her last moments.

Beautiful, so amazingly beautiful.

The body hangs limp on the table. He longs to remove the shackles from her arms and legs. He aches to wash her, to powder her all over and to dress her properly. And then he feels saddened. Saddened that the plan he has for her, the scheme he's nurtured her for, is going to prevent him keeping her, and exploring her.

Time was always a problem. Putrefaction: his least favourite word.

Spider has kept diaries on what happened to the other Sugars and knows that within an hour from now those vivid blue eyes of hers will start to change as the blood vessels become lumpy and patchy and the red blood cells begin to clump together. Within two days, strange yellow, triangular spots will appear on her corneas and will then fade to brown and black. Spider has set the basement temperature at thirty-seven degrees, the same as body temperature, so he hopes to slow down the natural cooling process of her corpse but knows that this will prolong the state of rigor mortis to probably about forty-eight hours after her death. He also knows that there is nothing he can do to stop the gravitational slump of blood and other body fluids. They will flatten and settle against her back, shoulders and buttocks as she lies on the leather table and will leave ugly reddish-purple lividity marks that he will have to cover with concealment creams and powder.

Adjust the plan. Find a way to spend time with her.

Spider sits and fantasizes. He's been lonely for so long and he yearns to have someone new by his side. If he could, he'd stay with her night and day, holding her, talking to her, sharing intimate moments with her, sleeping with her and waking with her. It could be perfect. But that's not the plan.

And then something on the screen catches his attention.

Lu's left hand twitches.

Is it a cadaveric spasm, simply a dead muscle jerking as the body settles?

Or is the little bitch really still alive?

61

West Village, SoHo, New York

Jack never made it to bed.

After drinking a few beers and popping an Ambien, he fell into a sleep that was so deep and intense it could better be classified as a coma. Howie had thought about trying to shift him from the couch to the guest bedroom but then decided it was easier to shift the bedroom to him. He tucked a pillow under Jack's head, threw a light blanket over him and turned in himself.

Carrie was propped against pillows watching the end of *Law and Order* on TV, the last thing he wanted to see. He cleaned up in the bathroom and slipped into bed next to her, noticing how she seemed to look thinner every day.

Okay, so she'd got the diet thing cracked, which was something he couldn't do, but, man, all those creams and shit that she put on her face every night kind of defeated the whole point of losing the weight. The way Howie figured it, women lost weight and stayed trim to look more attractive for the guys in their lives. If that was right, then what the hell was the point of buttering your face with some snow-white poodle-crap cream and lying in bed in nightwear that wouldn't give a mac-flasher from Riker's Island a twitch in his pants? Unless of course, she's screwing someone else. The penny dropped like a grand piano from the roof of the Chrysler building. Howie grabbed the remote and turned the TV off.

'Hey, whatcha doing?' squawked Carrie. 'I was watching that.'

'Tell me straight, Caz. Who the fuck are you fucking?'

Only the white poodle crap cream hid the blood draining from her face.

Carrie waited a couple of heartbeats, wondering whether to lie her way out of it, or feel grateful that the big ugly secret was finally out there for her big ugly husband to see. 'I don't know what you mean,' she lied, trying to buy time.

Howie had never considered hitting a woman, until now. Now he could happily punch her lights out. Not so much because she'd been balling some other guy, though for some members of his family that would be reason enough, or even because he'd been too stupid up until now to figure it out. Nope, what really pissed him off was that he'd dropped a whole twenty pounds in weight and missed all those meals in what was plainly a pointless attempt to stay attractive for her and keep her in his bed.

Well, fuck her! He didn't want her in his fucking bed anyway. Howie's inner rage took over, and before he knew it, he was on his feet, giant hands grabbing and lifting his side of the bed.

Carrie tumbled on to the floor and crashed painfully into the wall.

'You cheating, cocksucking cow!' he said, then banged the bed down, like a weight-lifter with his last lift.

It hit the ground and made the noise of a small bomb as the wooden legs on his side splintered off.

Howie looked at the marital bed and saw it metaphorically. 'Well, it looks like it's all well and truly broken.'

PART SEVEN

Saturday, 7 July

62

West Village, SoHo, New York

As the last grey dregs of night filtered into the first warm reds of dawn Howie stretched out his aching bones on the couch opposite the one on which Jack was snoring. He and Carrie had screamed at each other in the bedroom, bawled at each other in the kitchen and even thrown things at each other in the back yard, until they finally ran out of fight-power a little after four a.m. The row had been enough to wake most of the neighbourhood, but Jack had slept all the way through the emotional earthquake. In the harsh light of morning, Howie felt as exhausted as he looked. His head hurt worse than any hangover he'd ever had and he felt more depressed, angry and humiliated than he'd done since someone at high school had stolen all his clothes and sports gear while he was in the showers.

By the time they rode to the office, Jack knew something was seriously wrong. 'So what happened to upset Carrie?' he asked, yawning as he fought off the fug from the sleeping pill. 'I noticed we both got the big freeze this morning.'

Howie let out a long pained grunt and turned down

the radio. 'She told me last night she's been fucking someone else. We spent most of the night rowing around you, but you slept through it.'

'Sorry, buddy. I hate sleeping pills, but every now and then I have to take one just to get a decent eight hours.'

'Sorry what? That you slept through it? Or that she's been balling someone?'

They both laughed. Jack started thinking about practicalities. 'I guess you've got round two coming up tonight, so I'll fix a Holiday Inn or somewhere else to shift to.'

'Might be an idea,' said Howie. 'In fact, maybe we can get a two-room discount; I'll probably need to check in as well.'

'It's that bad?'

'Maybe. The sad thing is, I really don't know if I want to fix things. Could be that we've had our time. Perhaps we're all burned out anyway.'

'You want my advice?'

'Go ahead.'

'Don't rush it. Maybe you're right, the best might be behind you, but you've got the kids to think about. It could turn out to be a wake-up call for both of you.'

'Man, right now the last thing I want is a wake-up call, I'd rather have eight hours of zedz,' joked Howie. A news jingle trickled out of the speakers and he turned up the radio. 'Let's see what the friggin' press know that we don't.'

From the sombre tone of the newscaster's voice Jack and Howie gathered that the first story was a tragic one, and they rightly feared that the subject matter might concern them. 'Some breaking news, just in. The controversial news channel Pan Arabia this morning showed more disturbing footage featuring a young woman who it claims is being held captive and is being slowly tortured to death somewhere in America. The video released half an hour ago on the English-speaking version of the Arab-owned news network, shows the woman, believed to be white and in her mid-twenties, tied naked to some form of restraining table. Pan Arabia's crime editor Tariq el Daher defended his channel's decision to broadcast more footage –'

'The fuckers must have disconnected our trace equipment,' said Howie, slamming his hand on the steering wheel.

Tariq's voice was calm and unemotional. 'Pan Arabia believes it is in the interest of both the American public and the victim involved to have broadcast the footage. Not only are we upholding the democratic principles of freedom of speech and the right to uncensored news, but we are broadcasting this material to ensure that the complacency of the FBI and the police services across America is brought to a rapid end. If this young woman dies, then her blood will be on their hands. We urge all law-enforcement officials everywhere to make her survival a priority. If, today, America puts the same money and resources into finding this woman as it does into fighting foreign wars, then by tonight she will be home safely with her loved ones.'

'Son of a bitch!' cursed Howie, banging the steering wheel again.

The newscaster came back to round the report off. 'The terrorist organization al-Qaeda has already released a statement saying that it has no knowledge or involvement with the kidnapping or the video footage being exclusively screened on Pan Arabia. It went to great lengths to stress that it has always condemned any torture of individuals.'

Howie turned the radio down. 'A veiled reference to Abu Ghraib?'

'Not so veiled,' said Jack.

Howie flicked on the indicator, checked his mirror and squealed the wheels as he spun the car around. 'Let's go see our friend Tariq. He might just be the perfect outlet for all my pent-up anger.'

63

Rome

Orsetta Portinari was furious. She'd rung Jack King's cell phone a dozen times and the pig hadn't even had the courtesy to return her calls. Screw him! Massimo said he hadn't heard a word from him either, but that was no comfort to her. Although in Orsetta's mind that proved that Jack was being unprofessional, rather than just blanking her out because she'd made a fool of herself by flirting with him. As far as she was concerned, Jack King might be attractive and clever, but at times he was also a pig-ignorant fool.

Orsetta slammed the door of her car; it made her feel better. His quick departure had enraged her. The Italian police had asked for his help, he had promised them his time and cooperation, and then all of a sudden he'd flown off to his precious America.

She felt betrayed. She felt rejected. More than anything though, she felt he was wrong to have gone.

Did he really think flying to New York was going to save this kidnapped woman? What evidence was there that she was even in America? As Orsetta had already said, anyone anywhere in the world could buy a copy of *USA Today*. Video footage of the paper was no proof, no proof whatsoever that the girl was American and was being held in America. The crime scene could easily be in Italy. Maybe that black hellhole was the very same room in which Cristina Barbuggiani had been killed. Maybe it was just a few miles from Cristina's home in Livorno. Maybe it was in Rome, right under the noses of everyone at their HQ. Orsetta thought Massimo was absolutely right. Screw the Americans. She'd carry on working the case as though they didn't exist, carry on working every bit as hard as possible because another innocent woman's life might well depend upon her efforts.

64

Special Agent Angelita Fernandez handed over the necrophilia research to the Task Force's newest recruit, Sebastian Hartson. Straight out of the Academy, he was so wet behind the ears Fernandez wanted to towel him dry. Incidentally, those ears stuck out like jug handles and weren't helped at all by the military-style haircut he'd ill-advisedly chosen. 'Grow it long, man, cover up those trophy handles,' she had told him.

Fernandez desperately wanted to join Jack and Howie in beating up 'Toxic Tariq' as she called him, but Howie told her that her mission of the morning was to chase up the other loose ends. Manny Lieberman was top of her list. The FBI had its own in-house forensic documents examiners but almost anyone who knew Manny, used Manny. He was eighty-two but his eyes were still as sharp as a fox on a midnight run to the hen house.

Fernandez knew there was no point ringing him. Whenever Manny was busy he ignored the phone; in fact he ignored everything. She grabbed her stuff, diverted her calls and made her way to his office off

343

Liberty Avenue near the Jewish Cemetery. The black lettering on the frosted window declared the business to be Lieberman & Son & Daughter. The '& Daughter' had been added two years earlier when Annie, his 'Princess', as he referred to her, had graduated and finally decided that she did want to work with the old man after all. As Manny would tell you, it had been a toss-up between him and taxidermy, and he had been forced to use all his charm, wealth and family connections in order to narrowly defeat a stuffed animal. What could he say? The Liebermans specialized in all forms of handwriting analysis, including detecting forged signatures, validating signatures, spotting alterations to wills, land titles, deeds and all manner of other business documents.

The walls of his tiny reception area were plastered with hundreds of forged cheques that he'd spotted and that the cops had given him as mementos of successful prosecutions. Beneath the bottom line of cheques, worth a total of about $2 million, Manny's son David answered phones and ran the admin. David was drop-dead gorgeous and gayer than Elton John. Such a waste, thought Fernandez, as she stared into his baby blues and waited for him to hang up.

David Lieberman cupped his hand over the phone and whispered to her, 'Go straight through, Agent Fernandez, my dad won't mind.'

'Thanks,' she said, wondering whether it would be possible to 'convert' him. What the hell, even if she couldn't she wouldn't mind trying.

Fernandez knocked on a cheap wooden door, pushed it open and walked into an even cheaper-looking room. Manny wasn't big on spending money on anything other than essentials and that was a category he reserved solely for the tools of his trade. Lately, his hearing had virtually gone and he didn't even look up from his work as Fernandez stood in the open doorway, waiting to be invited in.

The old man sat behind an uncluttered desk, with bright angle-poise lights and a variety of hugely expensive, long-handled magnifying lenses strewn across it like discarded lollipops. He wore an ancient dark blue jacket, white shirt and blue tie, pulled tight into the collar. 'Look professional, act professional' he'd always told his family.

'Morning, Mr L,' chirped Fernandez.

The head of thinning white hair half cocked towards her, one eye still focused on his M-glass and the paper beneath it.

'Morning, Agent Fernandez, come on in. Are you here to harass an old man?'

'Not at all,' she lied, moving into the heart of the room. 'In fact, I've come to make him very happy.' She dug into her purse and produced a paper bag containing a quarter of iced gem biscuits, a type only available at a local baker near her parents' home out on Staten Island.

Lieberman now gave her his full attention. 'Aaah, you're an angel fallen from the clouds of heaven,' he said as he took them off her. The iced gems were a running joke between them, going back to the first case they'd worked together, when Manny had helped Angelita bag a top burglar and a bent jeweller from Manhattan. The jeweller would sell high-quality diamonds to wealthy clients, and give the burglar the addresses where the 'ice' was. The burglar would steal the diamonds and the jeweller would buy them back from him for a fraction of their value. Afterwards the jeweller would resell the gems through shops he had in other states.

'You know, Angelita,' mused Manny, a five-carat sparkle in his eye, 'if only I were twenty-five years younger and free and single, then you and I —'

'Yeah,' laughed Fernandez. 'Then you and I'd be down the jail house 'cos you'd be busted, on account that I'd still be under-age and you'd still be a wicked old man.'

They both laughed. Fernandez took one of the tiny biscuits and crunched off the icing. 'You got anything for me, Mr L? Or do I have to come back again?'

Manny Lieberman sighed. He knew he was being 'worked' by the sassy agent, and he loved every minute of it. He put the document he had been examining into a file and demoted it to a desk drawer. He took out another file. Fernandez instantly recognized the carefully cut piece of cardboard with the black felt-tip writing as coming from the package containing Sarah Kearney's head sent to the FBI. Manny also slid out a photocopy of the BRK note from Italy and placed this alongside the cardboard.

'I know you officers have very short attention spans, so I'll try to be as brief as possible about this.' He folded his hands together. 'The same man wrote the same writing with the same pen. Your Italian package and your American package were addressed by the same hand.'

Fernandez's eyes widened as she took in the implications of his snappy summary. 'You're sure?'

Manny picked up some gold wire-rimmed glasses and popped them on. 'Aah, so now you want the not-so-brief version?'

'Afraid so.'

'Okay; then let's start with the science first. As you know, I am a little old-fashioned in my ways and methods, but they haven't let me down yet. I pin-scraped a tiny part of the ink from the writing on both samples that you gave me. I then subjected these scrapings to pyrolysis gas chromatography, which I have always favoured for analysis of paint and fibre samples. The final program produced in this process is virtually unique. Certainly reliable enough for me to say confidently in any court that the samples matched.'

'Fine,' said Fernandez, getting her evidential bearings. 'So that tells us that it was the same type of pen, maybe even the same pen, but it wouldn't be evidence that the same guy used it?'

'No, indeed it wouldn't. And that presumably is the main reason why you came to me.'

'Mr Lieberman, where else would I go – you're the best.'

'Flattery, my dear Agent Fernandez, will get you everything your heart desires.' Manny slid a piece of tracing paper out of the file envelope and paper-clipped it on to the photocopy of the BRK letter recovered in Italy. 'First I did top-of-the-letter analy-sis, and I've marked up this "trace" to show how the offender starts off his letters. Can you see?'

Fernandez had to stand behind him to get a proper look. The trace paper was covered with tiny marks. The first marks were made at the highest point of all the letters. 'I've got it,' she said.

'Okay. Next I marked out where his second peaks are. So, for example, on the letter B, my first mark is at the top of the B, then my second mark is where the top half-circle of the B hits the middle of the vertical letter line. You got that too?'

Fernandez looked at the trace paper closely. 'Yeah, Mr L, I'm still with you.'

Manny sat back. 'By marking out all the peaks and troughs of his letters with those small dots that you saw, I was able to join up the dots and get a kind of graph. Let me show you.' He returned to the trace paper and ran his finger along the pencil line, which looked to Fernandez very similar to the printout you might get from an ECG or a polygraph. 'Then, I was able to take this trace from the BRK letter and place it over the writing on the label of the box sent to your office here in New York.' Manny slid the trace over the cardboard sample and clipped it into position. 'You'll see now that although he wrote in capital letters, obviously to avoid handwriting detection, he has still given us enough to go on. The height of all the letters is identical, the mid-points are identical, the spacing between the letters is identical, the spacing between the words is identical and the spacing between the lines he's written is also identical. As I said, the same man wrote the same messages with the same pen.'

'Mr L, at times like this I wish I was fifty years older,' said Fernandez, planting a kiss on the top of his head.

Suddenly, all the hunches and gut instincts were justified. At last, they had positive proof, hopefully proof strong enough to one day put before a jury, that there hadn't been two killers at work. Just the one. The Black River Killer had indeed crossed continents and killed in Italy.

65

Jack and Howie had no time to waste on pleasantries. Howie shoved his FBI shield in the face of the security guards at Pan Arabia's reception and made it brutally clear that he and his colleague were going straight to el Daher's office, whether they liked it or not.

They rode the elevator, both visualizing how the coming scene would play out. The metal doors slid open, revealing a busy open-plan office with another reception area. Howie flashed his badge again. 'FBI. Where's Tariq el Daher's office?'

A young woman in her mid-twenties almost held her nerve and thought about stalling them, but caved in and said, 'At the bottom on the left. Shall I call his secretary and say –'

Jack and Howie were gone before she finished. They strode past journalists pounding computer keyboards and secretaries running off multi-coloured copies of scripts. Tariq el Daher was sitting watching TV with another man, when they pushed open the door to his glass-fronted office.

'I didn't know you had an appointment, Mr

Baumguard,' said the journalist, his eyes never leaving the screen.

'Do I need one?' said Howie, jabbing his finger on the set's off button. 'I thought yesterday that we had an understanding. Then I drive into work and listen to a pile of bullshit on the radio that upsets me so badly I have to come straight round here.'

Tariq looked at Howie. 'Be good enough to turn the television back on and I'll show you something of interest to you.'

Howie shot him a searching look, then switched on the set.

Jack sat down on a couch next to Tariq's companion and sprawled out his giant frame. 'Hi there,' he said, in a way that sounded more intimidating than courteous. The man, a professional type in his late fifties, looked back at him but said nothing.

Tariq hit a remote control and rewound some footage. 'This morning I received a telephone call from someone who rang our reception and asked to speak to me. Anonymous callers don't usually get put through, but he asked reception to tell me the numbers 898989. I took the call and he told me that the hyperlink I clicked yesterday would be reactivated in five minutes' time and would then be inoperable again within another five minutes. He added that unless I disconnected the police trace it would not work.'

'What did he sound like?' asked Jack.

Tariq frowned at him. 'And you are?'

Jack frowned back. 'I'm the guy asking you the question. What did he sound like?'

'His voice was disguised,' said Tariq. He waved a hand towards his glass-topped desk. 'I recorded it on my phone. I will have a copy made for you.'

'Gee, thanks,' said Howie. 'What'd he say?'

Tariq yawned, as though it was a big effort to answer their questions. 'That was it. He just said I had five minutes to access the site. I think we missed thirty seconds, maybe one minute of it. When you came in, I was reviewing the footage.'

'The same footage that you screened on this morning's eight o'clock bulletin?' asked Howie.

'Yes,' confirmed Tariq. 'But I presume if you only heard about it on the radio, then you haven't seen the material?'

'You presume right,' said Howie.

Tariq hit play on the remote and as the first picture came on screen he paused it. 'I will show you, but please understand we did not screen this version in its entirety. We selected only the least disturbing part of the tape and we showed it on air for only twenty seconds.'

'Very restrained,' said Jack sarcastically, 'how very responsible of you.'

Tariq put the remote down on his lap and frowned again at Jack. 'You're Jack King, aren't you? I remember seeing a photograph of you when I was at Reuters, what, four, five years ago now. Am I right?'

Jack stared him down. 'We don't have time for this. Just play the video.'

Tariq studied the man's face. He was sure he was right. He pressed play and the pictures started rolling.

Howie and Jack didn't flinch or react at all when they saw the awful scene of the girl's convulsions. They were unemotionally scanning every inch of the picture frame, searching for clues and any possible evidence that would tell them where she was, when the recording had been made and whether she might still be alive.

Jack's mind turned to the reasons why someone would record the scene through fixed cameras, rather than be there in the room with the victim. Why wouldn't he film it himself with a hand-held camera, so he could get up close and personal?

Maybe he would, if he had a choice. Which meant he wasn't in the building wherever the girl was kept.

Why wouldn't he be in the building? Because he was working during the day? Or, more likely, because he wanted to be away from the crime scene when she died, making it much harder therefore to connect him to the murder.

The tape ran for almost four minutes. After seeing the victim motionless for around thirty seconds, Howie called time out. 'Hold it. Stop it for a second. What do you think, Jack? Is she dead, or what?'

Jack scratched the back of his neck and was about to give his opinion when Tariq's companion spoke for the first time. 'If I may introduce myself, I am Dr

Ian Carter; I am a consultant to the television station and formerly a member of the World Health Organisation. I have seen the footage only three or four times, but from what I have observed I would say she has suffered a terrible convulsion and blacked out. I cannot conclude that she is dead. Sadly, nor can I tell you with any great confidence that she is still alive.'

'How long has she been like that?' interrupted Jack.

'It is possible that this footage was shot some time ago and the girl is already dead. Or it could be that this is very recent footage. If that is the case, then I can tell you that, in my expert opinion, even if she survived the convulsion she is critically close to death.'

'How long would you give her, doc?' asked Howie.

Carter took his time thinking about it. 'Forty-eight hours max.'

PART EIGHT

Sunday, 8 July

66

Holiday Inn, New York

It was the early hours of the morning when Howie had finally gone home for round two with Carrie while Jack checked in at the Holiday Inn on Lafayette Street.

Jack guessed the Bureau had a deal on the slate price because the room was tiny and stank of the unseen and unclean who'd been there before him. He flopped down on the bed and discovered it had springs crafted by cavemen. He rang reception and asked if there was a chance of a sandwich and a glass of milk. The guy laughed and said something in Spanish that Jack guessed meant 'no way'. He put the phone down and at first was pissed as hell, but then figured that missing a midnight snack might turn out to be a good thing. He remembered the girl in the video and felt guilty. Poor kid would kill just for the bottle of water in his room, let alone a bar of chocolate from the mini-bar, and there he was cursing about not being able to get room service.

Jack kicked off his shoes, checked his watch and called Nancy. Just approaching one a.m. in New York, meant it was seven a.m. in Tuscany and he timed things perfectly so he caught her seconds after her alarm went off. Nancy was a creature of habit. The clock was always set for the same time, even on holiday. She saw no point in lying in bed and always wanted to start the day as early as possible. They didn't speak for long, just long enough to say they loved each other, and for Jack to send Zack a hug and a kiss.

After hanging up, Jack lay back on the bed, still in his suit, and pictured his wife and child just about to start their day. The image was soothing enough to make him feel sleepy, but he popped an Ambien to make sure and washed it down with a slug of water. He'd meant to rest for a minute and then clean up in the bathroom, but he never made it. Within seconds of shutting his eyes, he was asleep.

And then the nightmare started.

Only this time, it was different.

This time he was in the same room as the girl in the video. She was having convulsions again, her body jumping all over that strange table she was tied to. Jack put his hand on her chest to calm her down. He checked her face and she was still breathing. He loosened her chains and turned her on her side so she wouldn't choke, then he got a blanket from some-where and covered her up. Soon the room was filling with paramedics, cops and scene-of-crime officers. The paramedics gently lifted the girl on to a stretcher, quickly attached a saline drip and carried her out to an ambulance.

Jack felt good; she was going to be all right. He'd saved her. He looked around the room as the forensics team started snapping pictures, bagging and tagging evidence. He saw something on the floor. Something utterly shocking.

Jack woke up.

A thought hit his subconscious like a bolt of lightning.

In the dream he'd just had, he was reaching for the newspaper on the floor, the copy of *USA Today*, the copy dated the second of July.

Suddenly, Jack had the answer to the questions he'd posed himself in Tariq el Daher's office.

Why wouldn't her attacker film it himself with a hand-held camera, so he could get up close and personal?

The paper had been left to prove to anyone watching the first video after Tariq got it on the fifth of July that it was recent material. But when Tariq received new footage on the seventh, there was no new paper.

Why?

The answer was simple. Because he hadn't been in that room since he left the paper in the video. Because from the second of July onwards, six days ago, he'd left the girl to starve to death and was remotely controlling the recording and delivery of the footage by Internet. Internet – the perfect tool of anonymous criminals.

But where was he now?

67

San Quirico D'Orcia, Tuscany

Dawn turned back the clock on San Quirico D'Orcia, making the village seem as unspoiled as the days its medieval founding fathers settled there.

Terry McLeod slipped unheard and unnoticed through the front door of La Casa Strada. None of the other guests was up and about and it would be a long time before Maria arrived, touched up her make-up and took her place behind the reception desk. McLeod had chosen rubber-soled shoes, so that his feet would not make a noise, even outside on the golden-coloured stone slabs that surrounded the hotel. He was dressed in loose green combat trousers, a brown T-shirt, a green jumper which he knew he would be removing as soon as the sun rose another foot in the sky and a brown cap to shield his eyes. On his back he carried a medium-sized green rucksack, packed with the 'tools of his trade' and some drinks and snacks that would sustain him while he patiently waited for the day's events to unfold.

The streets were deserted but still told their stories of how history and contemporary life had agreed to get on. Against the brightly painted walls of centuries-old homes, lines of washing hung, heavy with white bedsheets, coloured shirts and greying underwear. Next to them, outside the glass-fronted cafés and restaurants, tables and chairs stood stacked, waiting for the pavements to be cleaned. The odd dropped ice-cream cone had left multi-coloured stains on the smooth stone flags. Bicycles stood propped next to doorways or down alleyways, never locked by towns-folk to whom theft was as unthinkable as bad local food or wine. A few streets away church bells chimed every half-hour – it was 7.00 a.m.

McLeod knew exactly where he was going. Over the past few days he'd located the precise spot for today's event.

He headed south-east towards where Via Dante Alighieri meets the trunk of Via Cassia; then he came off the beaten tourist path and veered more southerly. Soon he was climbing a peak of scrubland that prob-ably only a few of the town's more adventurous kids were aware of. Here the grass was deep and had probably never been cut or even chewed on by local livestock. Big boulders of sandstone even darker than the colour of the town's ancient walls formed a perfect shelter from the sun and any prying eyes.

McLeod looked around and checked any possible routes to where he stood. He examined the ground around him and then settled down, his carefully chosen green and brown attire allowing him to dis-appear chameleon-like into the rocky terrain.

He undid the flap of his rucksack, took out a pair

of high-powered binoculars, wiped the lenses with a soft cloth and peered through them. He found La Casa Strada almost instantly. He refocused. A slight pan to his right gave him a perfect view of the private gardens which Nancy King had curtly asked him to leave. A fractional pan and tilt to his left showed him the bedroom window where he knew she slept, her shutters closed but the window behind them clearly open.

McLeod stood up and shifted behind one of the large sandstone rocks. With a little movement he could now see the roads around the hotel and the route she took to Pienza with her child. He was satisfied with the position. From this vantage point, he had the perfect shot.

The Tuscan sun lethargically trekked across the blue morning sky, seemingly buckling under the burden of carrying another blazing day on its back. Golden rays soon soaked the outside of La Casa Strada, turning the terracotta roof tiles the colour of a blood orange. Just after seven a.m. Nancy King opened her windows and took in the beauty of a newborn day.

Terry McLeod dropped the high-powered binoculars and slid over a Nikon D-80 fixed with a Nikkor 1200mm telescopic lens. He adjusted the small tripod and half-pressed the shutter button. The camera's multi-area auto-focus kicked in and he could clearly follow Nancy as she moved around the bedroom. She was still in her nightclothes but they were nothing that McLeod would call real sexy. He pressed the shutter and the Nikon filed its first frame. For a second, he thought she was wearing the top of her husband's PJs, but then he realized it was a striped nightshirt that no doubt cost a bomb. Nancy shook her hair at the window, breathing in the lavender-laced air.

Click, the Nikon struck again.

McLeod hoped she'd slip the top off and give him a shot of what he imagined was a great pair of tits, but instead she turned away from the window and bent down to pick something up.

She was now half in shadow and he couldn't make out what she was doing. Nancy ended his doubts by returning to the window with a child in her arms. Click, click!

McLeod guessed this was Zack, the three-year-old that Paullina had told him about. Nancy ruffled his hair at the window, kissed his cheek and pointed out things across the garden and towards the hillside.

Click, the camera caught every gesture.

Seeing the kid in close-up was good. Whenever there was a child on the scene, McLeod always managed to use them to his advantage. Yep, getting close to the youngster would really up the stakes.

68

Holiday Inn, New York

Jack was still asleep, his suit creased to hell, when his cell phone rang at seven a.m. He peered at the display through sleep-fogged eyes and just about recognized Howie's number.

'Hello,' he grunted.

'Hi man, get showered and dressed; I'll be outside your hotel in ten minutes,' said Howie excitedly. 'We've got a real lead. A guy from IAD has been putting the screws on some bent cop over in Brooklyn who's in neck-deep with this Russian pimp who runs a hooker who's friends with the girl in our video.'

The words whizzed past Jack so fast he was able to make out only the key phrases – a real lead – someone in Brooklyn – a hooker who's friends with the girl in our video. 'Okay. I'm up and about. See you in ten.'

Jack stripped and stumbled into the shower, still struggling to make sense of exactly what Howie had told him. It didn't matter. Someone somewhere knew the girl and that meant they had a chance of finding out where she was.

Jack had brought only one suit with him, the one

he'd foolishly slept in. The jacket now looked as though a tramp had borrowed it for an evening out at the Annual Meths Drinkers' Ball. He left it on the bed and put on a shirt without a tie and a pair of plain black pants.

When he got outside, Howie was flicking the finger at some driver who'd tooted him. Jack climbed into the passenger seat. 'Great to start the day with some good news. Where we going?'

'Breakfast in Brooklyn. We're hooking up with a guy called Pete McCaffrey.' Howie spun the power steering, floored the accelerator and squealed his way into a gap in the traffic. 'McCaffrey's one of the few Internal Affairs people who understands the Job. He isn't after cops who make mistakes and screw up from time to time, like we all do, he's got his arrows levelled on the real bad apples.'

'So help me here,' said Jack. 'What's the exact connection with our girl?'

'Pete and his partner, Gerry Thomas, got on the tail of a bent cop called George Deaver. Deaver had been getting laid for free by hookers over in the Beach area. He pulled the old scam of having his fun then flashing his badge and saying he wasn't going to pay.'

'Hardly major news,' said Jack.

'Sure, but it turns out that our friend Deaver has pissed off a Russian gangster called Oleg Smirtin. Now *he* is major news. Smirtin is one of the big boys in Little Odessa and it seems Deaver has been using Smirtin's girls for freebies.'

'Not a bright move,' Jack said. 'I suppose your pal McCaffrey got interested all of a sudden because of Smirtin's involvement?'

'Exactly. They think the Russki has a few cops on his payroll and they've pressured Deaver to be their wire man. Anyway, Deaver comes back to them and says the chick he was balling claims to be a friend of the girl in the video.'

'Give up a name?' asked Jack.

'Didn't get that far. Fernandez is already over in Brooklyn rounding everyone up. We should be able to see McCaffrey and Deaver together, and then the hooker. If needs be, we can then go visit Smirtin too.'

'Where's the meet? We still got the office in Cumberland Street?'

'Sure have,' said Howie. 'That's where we're heading and the deli round the corner still does the best breakfasts this side of my mom's kitchen.'

69

San Quirico D'Orcia, Tuscany

Terry McLeod had been sitting patiently in his 'hide' for an hour.

He understood that even at the best of times things never happened quickly in Italy, and in Tuscany on a Sunday, well, events were likely to move slower than an injured snail.

The longer the wait, the sweeter the shot, he told himself.

He sipped bottled water from his rucksack and used the military-issue binoculars to keep a watch on events at the hotel. The King woman looked so happy as she moved around inside the sanctuary of her home.

Make the most of it, he told himself, I'm about to turn your *happy* little life right upside down.

He sat back and waited for his chance.

Patience was a virtue of McLeod's; he'd wait all day if he had to.

70

Brooklyn, New York

The six-mile journey from Jack's hotel to Brooklyn should have taken fifteen to twenty minutes but traffic along Flatbush Avenue was snarled up and didn't improve much as they headed down Veronica and Erasmus.

Howie called in as they parked up and Fernandez sent out for their breakfast order – juice, coffee, muffins, pancakes and a mix of fruit. The fruit was an afterthought of Jack's; Howie was solely interested in the pancakes and muffins.

Fernandez was already holed up in a small room with Pete McCaffrey and Gerry Thomas, the two cops from Internal Affairs, and their new best friend, George Deaver. Jack knew who was who without even being introduced. McCaffrey sat on the edge of a big square wooden desk, wearing big square wooden clothes. He was craggy-faced, black tie pulled tight to the top of his plain white shirt, sipping water from a plastic cooler cup and trying to impress Fernandez in a way that only senior IA guys think they can do, which is with over-macho body language and stories of what they did before they got sucked into the hated world of IA. Thomas, a younger clone of his boss, with a slightly cheaper black suit and a much looser and cheaper tie, was hanging on McCaffrey's every word. George Deaver was the odd man out. He sat away from the others, glum-faced, arms folded like a guy with all the worries of the world on his shoulders, which was kind of appropriate considering he was a bent cop who'd been busted and was heading to court and maybe jail.

Howie introduced Jack and everyone shook hands, then McCaffrey introduced Deaver and the best he got was a nod of acknowledgement. The line had already been drawn and they couldn't help but let Deaver know it.

'Where's the girl?' asked Howie.

'Next office,' answered Fernandez. 'We've got her a soda, but should have probably got her a doctor. She looks as though she was totally tanked last night. There's someone watching the door, so she won't be doing any running.'

McCaffrey went over the background again and Jack listened politely, as though it was something he was hearing for the first time. Then Deaver filled them in on how he'd visited Smirtin and told him he was looking for his missing hooker.

'The kid on the tape is called Ludmila Zagalsky, though apparently everyone calls her Lu,' said Deaver, trying to sound like a helpful cop, rather than a bent one. 'She's twenty-five, a Russian, from Moscow we think. Smirtin said very little about her during our face-to-face in his kebab joint, even though I'd gone round there specifically to talk about her. He was more interested in whether I knew anyone over at the Department of Justice who could advise on some tobacco problems he had.'

'Smoking kills,' said Fernandez, 'least that's what the Surgeon General says, and that's the only advice that assholes like Smirtin should get.'

Deaver ignored her. 'Anyways, next day, that's the sixth, he rings me and says he knows where Lu is; says he's just seen her on frigging TV. Well, it turns out these A-rabs –'

'Yeah, we know that bit,' interrupted McCaffrey. 'Cut to the chat you had with her friend. These boys here are going to draw their pensions 'fore you get to the point.'

Deaver bit back his resentment and picked up the story. 'That evening I went round to see her friend Grazyna Macowicz –'

McCaffrey interrupted again. 'This is the whore we've got next door, the one he was screwing for a freebie.'

'Grazyna was shaking like a leaf,' said Deaver. 'She'd bottomed a bottle of vodka by the time I found her, and it was only five p.m. She said the kidnapped woman all the news channels were showing was her girlfriend.'

'She's a hundred per cent sure on that?' asked Howie, adding, 'This isn't some attention-grabbing time-wasting stunt by some lying little crackhead, is it?'

Fernandez took a deep breath. 'That's a bit steep, boss. I've spoken to her and I think she's a straight-up kid.'

Howie ignored her and carried on staring at Deaver, waiting for a reply.

The bent cop drummed his fingers on the arm of his chair and thought it over. 'I think she's genuine,' he said. 'The face-shot in that video is pretty clear. I've got one small photograph of Ludmila already; Grazyna's found a couple more to show us.' Deaver handed over the photo-booth picture of the two girls together. Howie looked at it first and then passed it to Jack.

The phone on the desk rang and someone asked Fernandez if it was okay to bring in breakfast. As the others cleared space on the desktop for the food, Jack and Howie peeled off into a corner.

Jack passed the photograph back. 'It certainly looks like the girl in the video,' he said.

'Yeah, I think so too,' Howie concurred. 'You reckon she's still in the neighbourhood?'

'No way of even guessing,' said Jack. 'More importantly, is there a chance she's still alive?'

The food came and Jack piled up two plates with muffins and pancakes, grabbed some fruit and two cardboard cups of coffee.

'Glad to see that all those years in the restaurant business taught you how to be a waiter,' joked Howie as they made their way into the other room to see Grazyna. Howie opened the door and the young woman sitting opposite them looked up; her shoulders hunched, her face white and gaunt.

'I'm Howie Baumguard, Miss. This human food trolley here is Jack King. He's brought you some breakfast.'

'Morning, Grazyna,' said Jack, gently. 'We're here to try to help find your friend.' Jack didn't ask if she wanted food, he just put it down on the table in front of her and uncapped her coffee. Experience had shown him that many people didn't want to be seen to have to accept anything from a cop, so it was better to give without even asking.

Howie sat down next to her. 'We're told that you're in no doubt that the girl in the video reports on the TV, the girl being held hostage somewhere, is your friend Ludmila Zagalsky. Is that right?'

Grazyna picked up the coffee. Her hand shook so badly that she had to put it down again, so she didn't scald herself. 'That's right,' she answered in a tiny voice. 'We're like sisters, I recognized her straight away.'

'When did you last see her, Grazyna? Can you remember?' asked Jack.

It was something Grazyna had thought a lot about. 'It was six nights ago, about one a.m., outside Primorski's restaurant down Beach Avenue.'

Howie and Jack exchanged quizzical looks. 'How come you're so sure?' asked Howie.

This time Grazyna hesitated. She chewed her lip and looked away from them. 'I've been seeing this waiter at Prim's, a guy called Ramzan. Lu was keen on him too, but I made a move on him when she wasn't around and I just couldn't bring myself to tell her about it. I'd arranged to meet him at the end of his shift and as I was coming up the street I saw Lu at the window, waving to him. I kind of stepped back into a doorway across the road and hid for a while.'

'Why did you do that?' asked Howie.

'Dunno,' said Grazyna. 'Guess I thought he might be cheating on me. So I hung around to see if he'd come out and kiss her or anything.'

'And did he?' asked Jack.

'No, he didn't. After a bit, she sort of waved at him again and then seemed to lose interest. Some guy drove up a few minutes later and used the ATM machine near the restaurant and she clocked him.'

Jack and Howie's instincts bristled like porcupines.

'I guess the machine wasn't working 'cos I saw Lu pointing down the street. Then she started working him, you know, flirting with him. Well, I thought, good for you, sister, you go get yourself some extra Benjamins. Sure enough, seconds later she rides off in this guy's car.'

'Which direction?' asked Howie.

Grazyna frowned for a moment. 'I'm not good at directions. Let me think.' She pointed her hands out from her body. 'He turned east. Yep, I'm sure of that. They headed off eastwards.'

Howie held his breath. 'You got the registration?'

Grazyna frowned. 'No. It was a yellow Hyundai; I saw the badge on the back.'

'Two doors or four?' asked Howie.

She looked up at the ceiling for inspiration. 'Four.'

Howie left the room and instructed Fernandez to start the search for a four-door Hyundai. He suggested that they look for white as well as yellow; the sodium street lights might have affected her colour judgement.

Jack's head was buzzing with excitement.

At last, some critical questions were getting answered. They now had a name for the victim – Ludmila Zagalsky; the place where she had been taken from – Beach Avenue; and perhaps a time of the possible abduction – one a.m. on 2 July.

The one crucial question that they couldn't answer was whether she was still alive.

71

Brighton Beach, Brooklyn, New York

The FBI and NYPD started checking car plates, surveillance footage from street and road cameras, and canvassing Hyundai dealers and second-hand car salesmen.

Fernandez stayed with Grazyna Macowicz while she tried to identify the man she had seen Lu leave with. A police artist worked on body shape, build and posture while a policewoman put together an E-fit of his facial components.

Meanwhile, Jack King stood on the pavement of Beach Avenue, his nose pressed to Primorski's window, imagining what Ludmila Zagalsky had been doing during her last moments of freedom almost a week earlier. It was important for him to know the mood she was in, the frame of mind that might have made her take a risk, or avoid one. First, he imagined the moment Lu saw Ramzan inside the restaurant. She waved at him, hoping he would come to the door and maybe invite her in, hoping her night would end in the arms of the big tall guy with good looks and a regular job. But for some reason he didn't come.

So what, fuck him! An average end to an average day.

He pictured Lu spinning around from the window and feeling rejected. But then what?

Jack turned away from Primorski's window, trying to feel her pang of loneliness, trying to work out what she would do next.

Some guy was rolling up to use the ATM right next to her. ATMs were always hot pick-up spots for good-time girls. It was the perfect distraction for Lu. Why not? He looked harmless enough. Opportunity knocked.

Rejected by one man, she was likely to want to reassert her self-confidence by taking money and power from another.

Was Grazyna right? Had the machine been out of order?

Jack made a note to have it checked. Even if he used a false account, which was inevitable really, it would still contain precise information about where he was at certain times, and Jack always hung on to the hope that one day this son of a bitch would make a simple mistake. He looked at the machine; there was nothing directing users to the next one if it wasn't working. Of course to BRK it wouldn't have mattered. Even if the ATM had been working he'd have just pretended it wasn't. The whole point was to get the girl in the car.

Did that mean he already knew where the other machines were? Had he checked out this area before? Maybe even been stalking Lu Zagalsky for a couple of days, just waiting for the right moment to inject himself into her life?

Jack was convinced it wasn't a random snatch. He carried on building the scene.

BRK would have tracked this girl all day, maybe for several days; this was his moment, the streets were empty and she was alone. He'd have just slid his car to the kerb and walked over to her. Once she'd turned away from the restaurant window he'd have moved in for the kill.

Moved in for the kill – the phrase stuck in his thoughts. For serial murderers like BRK, the hunt-and-kill instinct seemed as strong and primitively undeniable as most decent people's urges to meet and mate.

Jack looked up and down the shop walls for security cameras, hoping there might be at least one covering the ATM, but he was out of luck.

So, Lu, what did you do next? Jack slipped back into her time and space, the thoughts in her head that led her to make a fatal mistake.

The guy looks harmless enough; he's going to have a roll of bills in his hands. He's up late and after money, maybe he's looking to spend it on some fun. Hey, aren't I fun-shaped? Let's get some action going. A little chat, show him where the next ATM is, then wham-bam-thank-you, Mam, something extra in the purse before calling it quits for the night.

Jack walked slowly east down Beach Avenue. Opposite him, a patrol car crawled along, ready to take him anywhere he wanted.

As he paced, he called Howie and found out where

the next two nearest ATMs were. Somewhere between a DIY store that was closing down and a Russian-language video shop that was opening up, he stopped and fine-tuned his thoughts.

Where was she going to take him? Down an alley? Maybe bang him against a wall for a quick buck or blow him off next to a trash can? No, that didn't figure somehow. Jack leant against a shop wall while Lu's thoughts whispered in his mind.

Look at it like this, Jack: this sleazeball's about to withdraw a whole bundle of bucks, and even though he's acting all innocent he don't fool no one, he's sure as hell interested in spending some of them on yours truly. Look at the guy, he's an easy trick, he's in his late thirties, maybe forty-something, he's a professional-looking guy, he'll have a hotel, motel or rental nearby. Somewhere with richer pickings than the street.

Jack stood motionless on the pavement. To the torrent of shoppers and tourists flowing past him he looked as though he was in a trance, a man with his mind in an entirely different world.

Lu's thoughts were no longer of any use to him. The trap had been sprung, the hunter had his prey. From now on, Jack had to think like a killer.

Feel like a killer.

A flashgun went off in his head; images flickered by; the room he'd prepared, the restraints he'd readied, and most of all the way he felt – excited, exhilarated, unstoppable.

He gazed into the blur of passing traffic and pictured himself in BRK's place, driving along in the Hyundai, turning to Lu in the passenger seat.

I've got a house, not far from here, we can go back there.

Jack flinched. The flashgun popped again and a nervous twitch pulled at his right eye. Was he really ready to do this? He forced himself to concentrate. What kind of place did he take her to and where?

Not far from here, we don't have to go far . . .

Wherever he took her, it surely couldn't have been a long journey. The hunter would want to be alone with his prey as soon as possible. He'd be aching for the kill.

The twitch quickened, a tug on the skin like a hidden needle pulling thread through his flesh. Jack put a finger to his right temple and rubbed it.

Street girls aren't stupid. They'll go a few miles, but not more than a ten-, fifteen-minute drive, max.

The twitch slowed.

For what BRK had in mind, he needed to take her somewhere remote, the more isolated the better. But it would have to be respectable as well; somewhere residential that wouldn't spook her. No woman's going to take a dead-of-night trip into a barn or warehouse. And wherever he took her, he would have to get the car out of sight. It would have a garage, outbuildings, and a big room, somewhere.

A room he uses for other things.

Things such as the dismemberment and disposal of bodies.

It's a big, old house with a garage – and a basement beneath it.

The basement is where she's kept.

Jack felt sick to the pit of his stomach as he realized that at that very moment the young Russian woman was probably dying a slow and agonizing death in a basement less than fifteen minutes' drive from where he was standing.

His head was throbbing now; it was full of engine noise and the faulty flash of neons that buzzed but wouldn't light properly. And then the voices came again, the hopeless voices crying in pain and screaming for help. Jack put his hands to his temples.

It's too soon. Nancy was right. You're not ready for this.

He rubbed his face with his hands and told himself to forget the self-doubts and focus. He looked up and down Beach Avenue; fifteen minutes' drive from the spot he stood in would include all houses within a seven-mile radius.

'Shit!' he said out loud and felt his heart break into a sprint. Brooklyn was New York City's largest borough; almost a third of the entire city's population lived there. Ludmila Zagalsky was just one out of two and a half million people living within the area that had to be searched.

One in two and a half million – the odds against finding her alive were bad, very bad indeed.

72

San Quirico D'Orcia, Tuscany

The telephoto lens that McLeod unscrewed from the Nikon was the same one he'd used to take the photo of the headless skeleton in Georgetown. He capped both ends and packed it in its own cloth bag, which he then put into the rucksack along with the rest of his equipment. He'd earned a fortune from that snap at Sarah Kearney's grave and was eternally grateful for the anonymous tip-off that had sent him there ahead of the cops.

McLeod was a veteran hack, a freelance photo-journalist who made his money providing pictures and stories for the Crime Channel, Court TV, *Crime Illustrated* and all manner of other true-crime magazines and publications. He was well used to working alone, moving around secretly, acting on whispers here and tip-offs there. Mainly the tips came from cops, ambulance crews and a few villains themselves. Usually, 'the source' wanted some kind of kick-back at the end, but in the Kearney case there had been no demand for payment of any kind.

The fees he'd raked in from the Georgetown job had fired up his interest in the BRK case, and had got him thinking about what had happened to the cop who had quit the investigation after collapsing because of the strain of leading the murder hunt. McLeod had spent days researching the case, and had finally found the Kings' whereabouts on a website about Tuscan cookery. Rising star chef Paolo Balze had been the subject of the feature and, fortunately for McLeod, he had magnanimously thanked his proprietors Jack and Nancy King. Well, the old hack was planning a feature of his own, and it wasn't intended for the lifestyle section of some glossy magazine.

Jack King soaking up the good life in Tuscany, on a state pension, while his ex-colleagues have to deal with the desecration of a grave of one of the victims on whom he turned his back. This was great tabloid crime. Maybe a front-page splash in the *National Enquirer*, or a slide show of pics for Court TV. Only trouble was, King wasn't there.

At first McLeod feared that the story might be dead, but then he patiently set his mind to things. If he was lucky, maybe the Kings had split up; perhaps there was an even better human drama story to tell. *Cop that quit BRK case quits wife who stood by him!*

Sprinkle the story with some shots of the lonely wife looking after a sad toddler because Daddy's run out on them and he'd have editors eating out of his hand like pigeons.

Then within the last few days had come suggestions that the former Fed guy was somehow helping Italian cops with some job or other. This was also a good angle. *'Retired' FBI man on state pension can't help us, but he can help the Italians and help himself!*

The last headline needed work, but McLeod knew it was still a seller. In truth, anything about BRK was a seller.

With that thought in mind, he ended his long vigil and climbed out of his hide to return to La Casa Strada to question Nancy King about her husband's whereabouts. He was going to get the quotes he needed to clinch his story and nothing was going to stop him.

Whatever the King woman said, it didn't really matter. McLeod knew he now had enough to write the kind of exclusive that many people would die for.

73

Livorno, Tuscany

Orsetta Portinari had two questions on her mind as she arrived in Livorno: what were Cristina Barbuggiani's last movements on the ninth of June and what was the link between Jack King and her killer?

Marco Rem Pici from the local murder squad met her at the railway station, with a genuine smile and a kiss on each cheek that he had to stand on tiptoe to administer. He was a small man, even by Italian standards, but was always immaculately dressed in dark suits that complemented his short dark hair, gym-broadened shoulders and trim waist. He drove them to Cristina's apartment, a cheap place, high up a hillside, with a terrific view down on to the Medici port – providing you had a telescope. The ugly concrete building was a stark contrast to the ancient towers and fortresses that led to the historic town centre. They were shown to the third floor by the landlord, a fat, bald man in his sixties who thought white string vests and broken-zipped slacks were fashionable. He opened the heavy metal front door and without saying a word left them to their business. The business of murder.

Orsetta silently cursed Jack as she looked around. This was a trip that he should have been making with her, giving her his expert input on, instead of disappearing back to America. Visiting a victim's home was always like sticking a slide of their whole life under a microscope and uncovering the crucial secrets they thought no one would ever find out. It would have been a huge help to have had him around.

Orsetta took in the light marble flooring that ran throughout the place, a single yellow cotton settee and yellow beanbag crowded in front of an open fireplace filled with dried flowers in a terracotta vase. There were a few archaeology books on a shelf around the fireplace and a small television on a slab of marble in a corner of the room. And that was it. Yellow and white were the only colours on display. Calm but vibrant, simple, dry and uncluttered, thought Orsetta, starting to get a feel for the dead woman.

'You've been through all these?' she asked, waving a hand at the books.

'Book by book, page by boring page. There's nothing of interest to us,' said Marco.

Orsetta's heels clacked over the marble as she checked out the bathroom, then went through everything in the kitchen. A thin calendar hung on the wall near the sink. She lifted it off its drawing pin and thumbed through the months. Each one had a different recipe, tied to the seasonal use of food and wine, but Orsetta wasn't interested in the culinary tips.

Fixing her attention on June, she was disappointed at the absence of any jotted remarks on the ninth or tenth.

'Tell me again about who saw her last on the ninth,' she said, still peering at the calendar.

Marco let out a tired sigh. He'd gone over this info so many times he could recite it backwards. 'Two friends, Mario and Zara Mateo, called round at about seven p.m., and invited her out to dinner. She said no thanks and they went on their own. The restaurant says they stayed until gone midnight, got a bit drunk and caught a taxi home. Next timing we have is the following day. Cristina's mother wanted her to pick up some medicine and called her mobile, maybe six or seven times. By evening she was worried, so she and Cristina's father came round to the apartment and raised the alarm. Local police booked the call at 8.33 p.m.'

Orsetta nodded and went back to flicking through the calendar. There was almost nothing on it, just an entry in the last week of May: 'Diet and jogging start today!' She smiled and felt a stab of sadness at the same time. There wasn't a woman alive who hadn't made similar dates with herself. She returned the calendar to its pin and followed Marco to the single bedroom. It was barely big enough to accommodate a three-quarter-size bed, a cheap dressing table and a white plastic chair that looked as though it should be in a garden. Orsetta opened a built-in, sliding wardrobe made of slatted pine. It was empty. 'Clothes at the lab?' she asked, already knowing the answer.

'Aha,' said Marco. 'I've brought photographs and lists of everything that's been removed and not put back. I knew you'd want to see.'

Orsetta took a stack of small prints from him. The first shot showed what the photographer had initially seen when he'd opened the door. Jeans on the left of the rail, followed by trousers, then blouses, skirts and finally dresses. They were plain and functional; none of them looked expensive or particularly new. She shuffled through the photos and found the print she was looking for. Shoes. Orsetta's eyes widened.

'Are these the only pairs she had?' she asked, incredulously.

Marco peered over her shoulder. 'Yes, that looks about right.' One pair of high heels, two pairs of flat brown shoes, two pairs of flat black, and a pair of black boots. There was something wrong. Orsetta couldn't put her finger on it, but she just *knew* that there was something wrong.

She dropped the prints on top of the dressing table and quickly went through the three drawers.

Nothing.

She sat at the dressing table, waiting for her mind to identify what was disturbing her. 'Anything from these drawers still at the labs?'

Marco thought for a moment. 'No, I don't think so.'

Orsetta's eyes searched the room, flicking over every corner of it, desperate to uncover the clue that she knew lay somewhere close to her. 'What about a laundry basket?'

'Done,' said Marco, understanding where her thoughts were heading. 'Three pairs of panties, a couple of T-shirts, jeans, not much else. All free of any trace samples or DNA other than the victim's.'

'That's not what I'm thinking,' said Orsetta, returning to the bottom drawer. She tipped the contents out on to the bed and searched through a mixture of tights, stockings, panties, bras and socks. She was close to something, she could sense it. But what?

She quickly sorted the clothing into piles. She presumed the smarter underwear was for work or the few dates Cristina had, and the older, tattier stuff was for when she was hanging out at home on her own. That left two matching pairs of white Lotto running socks, the type found in a three-pack. Orsetta dipped into her jacket and produced a picture of Cristina to remind herself of the girl's size and shape.

'In the laundry pile, did you find a sports bra, or any white Lotto socks to match these?' She pointed to the pair she'd balled up.

Marco thought for a moment. 'No. No, we didn't.'

Orsetta felt a kick of excitement. She had a hunch.

She grabbed the photographs and scanned them again. 'No running shoes. The shot in the wardrobe shows no sports shoes,' she announced with a look of triumph. She could picture Cristina's last night. 'I think she was snatched while she was out jogging, probably not far from here. There are no trainers, no sports pants or sports bra among any of the belongings we've examined and I bet she was wearing the third pair of Lotto running socks.'

Marco got her drift. 'So, she turned down her friends' dinner invite around seven, then you think she went for a run straight after that?'

Orsetta weighed it up. 'Yes. She was on a fitness kick, so she said no to them in order to stick to a diet and probably went for the run almost straight away, before it started to get dark. So we can say she probably went out between seven and maybe nine, nine-thirty.'

The two police officers recognized the importance of the moment. They'd just discovered how, when and roughly where Cristina Barbuggiani had spent the last moments of her life before meeting her killer. It was a breakthrough that would allow them to filter their witness statements and start seriously focusing their enquiry on anyone seen within a short radius of Cristina's apartment on the night of the ninth.

Only one thing still preyed on Orsetta's mind as she left the landlord to lock up – Jack King. And if Jack himself wouldn't help her uncover the link between him and Cristina's killer, then maybe a visit to his wife would.

74

San Quirico D'Orcia, Tuscany

Terry McLeod took his equipment back to his hotel room and packed his suitcase. If his face-to-face with Nancy King went badly, then she'd no doubt have him thrown out of the hotel within the hour.

He checked the bathroom, wardrobes and bedside cabinets to make sure he hadn't left anything important behind, then locked his case and put it down by the door.

The veteran photo-journalist knew his main strength was his pictures rather than his editorials, so he took time to rehearse his questions before setting off again in search of Mrs King. He decided he would start by pretending he was doing a feature on hotels and restaurants for a new magazine and that, like the *Michelin Guide* inspectors, he had to keep his identity secret until after he'd tested the cooking and hotel facilities. He'd promise her a page, or maybe two, of free publicity, and then he'd say he just needed some background details on the family, stuff such as: when had they moved in, what had they needed to do to the place to make it into what it was today, how was life in Italy? All that non-controversial stuff. After that he'd get down to the nitty-gritty: where was her husband at the moment, what exactly was he helping the Italian police with, was he now officially back with the FBI or was he working on his own as a consultant? And, of course, how were things between the two of them?

McLeod checked that the micro-cassette in his pocket dictaphone was fully rewound and tucked it up his sleeve, so he could secretly record everything she said.

Sunday lunch had been incredibly busy and Nancy was enjoying a well earned rest in the cool shade of the patio, when she dozed off for five minutes. She woke with a start, and immediately looked around for Zack. When she'd shut her eyes, he'd been playing happily on his trike.

'Zack, where are you, sweetheart?' she called, as she trekked across the garden. She was in no mood for hide-and-seek. She'd played it a dozen times already and she'd promised Paolo she would review the Specials menu for tonight, while he and Gio made a quick trip into Pienza.

'Come on, sweetheart, Mommy's very busy. Let's go inside and get some chocolate.' Bribery usually worked. But this time Zack was obviously standing his ground and making her hunt some more. The handle on the kitchen door was too high for him to reach, so she knew that he had to be in the garden somewhere.

She searched among the apple, orange and peach trees, looking for evidence of his red sandals hiding behind some trunk or other. But she could see nothing. If he was lying down in the vegetable garden, she was going to be cross. He'd been told about that before. And if he was sitting in the herbs, stuffing them in his mouth again, then there really would be trouble.

Nancy strode over to the areas she'd told her son were out of bounds and shouted sternly, 'Zack! Come out right now.'

There was no answer.

'The game's over now, Zack; come on, please.'

Nancy's maternal instinct prickled. Her eyes darted around the gardens, across the pathways, among the trees.

No Zack.

And then she saw it.

At the edge of the terrace, where the ground had collapsed and where Vincenzo the landscaper had moved the temporary fencing to survey the subsidence, there was Zack's overturned trike.

75

FBI Field Office, Brooklyn, New York

Jack and Howie cleared an office of furniture and spread a variety of maps on the floor. They had everything from military maps to Brooklyn bus and cycle routes and there wasn't room enough or time enough to pin them to the walls. They both agreed that they had to take chances. There was no way they could canvas all of Brooklyn, so they had to send out teams to highly prioritized areas.

Jack's eyes ran down the Westside. Hunters Point – down where the ferries ran to Manhattan – this was a place that would have old isolated housing. Coming north down the East River – Williamsburg, near the Bridge area looked promising. Fulton Ferry and Brooklyn Heights – they were good too.

Howie was making similar choices: Prospect Park, out near the zoo – that offered ample opportunities. 'What about Greenwood Cemetery, close to the 278, lots of residential nearby – Perfect for getting rid of his leftovers too?'

'That's a good one,' said Jack, 'put it towards the top of the list.'

'And maybe Dyker Heights around 72nd Street,

it's residential but isolated out there,' added Howie, circling the areas with black markers.

Jack looked down at his map, focusing on Brighton Beach, zooming in on Beach Avenue where he'd just been. He now visualized the area as if he were in a helicopter flying over it. He could see the cars crawling down the shopping streets looking for somewhere to pull in and park. SUVs were heading up to the sands. A marching army of ant-like office workers moved out towards Manhattan. Day-trippers with sandwiches, soft drinks and excited kids migrated to Coney Island. And then, his earlier thoughts tumbled back to him: a street girl would never have agreed to drive a long distance with a stranger. The killer would not have wanted her in his car any longer than necessary. It couldn't be far from there.

Jack's eyes moved east on the map. A patch of isolated green caught his attention. He slid a fingertip along Belt Parkway; just four junctions away was the exit to Brooklyn Marine Park and the residential settlement of Gerritsen. Flatbush Avenue ran northwards from the other side of Marine Park, a straight road all the way down to Brooklyn Bridge. 'Come here and look at this,' he said.

Howie was still on his knees and stumped his way over to him.

'Look at Marine Park,' said Jack, jabbing a finger at the map. 'It's ideal. Flatbush and the Belt give fast exit routes. It's pretty isolated and JFK is just down the road. What's more, the Beach is less than ten minutes away and then you have the huge cover of Little Odessa in front of you. The guy is about as screened as you can get.'

Howie felt his mouth turn dry with excitement. 'Still a friggin' lot of homes to search, though.'

Jack stood up to stretch his legs. Blood pumped to his head and a burst of white-hot pain scorched through his temples.

'You okay?' said Howie, frowning up at him.

'Sure. Just stood up too quickly,' lied Jack. He looked down on the mess of maps and added, 'We've got to go for the more isolated houses, the ones with big garages, doubles not singles. He'll have picked a street that he can get away from quickly and that he can have good surveillance from, so he won't be in the heart of the estates, he'll be on an outer wing.'

'We'll pull together the sweep teams, right now. I'll brief them right after we're done.'

Jack was worried about that. Filling the area with squad cars or even Crown Vics could spook the perp. 'They're going to have to be careful. We know he's got cameras in the house, so he sure as hell is going to have them outside too. If he's in there, he'll probably see us coming.'

Howie climbed to his feet, his knees cracking. 'Do you think he owns the property or rents it?'

'Good point. This guy has to be forty-plus so let's do voting register and housing searches on people thirty-five or over. Get someone to sift mortgage and bank accounts too, focusing on that demographic.

He's certain to be using a false identity and showing himself younger or older than he actually is.'

'And renting?' asked Howie.

'Unlikely,' said Jack 'He'd never want to risk a landlord coming in and finding all his toys.'

Howie wasn't sure it was as simple as that. 'I just don't see him doing this kind of whacko stuff in his own crib. Like you always say, this guy is cautious. Surely he wants to make sure he's able to leave at a moment's notice and that, if the house gets busted, it cannot lead to him?'

Another explosion went off in Jack's head, but this time he poker-faced the pain. Concentrate, he told himself, get your shit together, there's time to rest up later, just get your head in gear.

Howie fiddled with some maps and it gave Jack the breather he needed. 'You're right. Of course you're right,' said Jack. 'Get a team on to the letting agencies. I'm willing to bet that he does own this house, but what he has done is put it in the hands of a letting agent and leased it back to himself under a false identity. In other words, he's both landlord and tenant.'

'He probably used a false name even when he approached the agent, purporting to be the owner,' said Howie.

'Exactly,' agreed Jack, feeling his eye twitch again. 'Letting the house back to himself is a really clever trick. The first thing it does is generate false paperwork. From false tenancy agreements and household bills you can set up bank accounts, apply for credit cards and start to build up a series of false identities for yourself.'

'I'm on to it,' said Howie, heading off for a phone.

'Another thing,' called Jack. 'You'll also probably find the tenancy has changed names a few times. Those name changes will roughly coincide with the dates of our victims' deaths. He'll shed an old identity, and adopt an entirely new one, after each of our known murders.'

'Back in a minute,' said Howie, leaving the room to brief Fernandez.

Jack was glad to be alone.

He felt himself break into an oily sweat. The strength in his legs seemed to run into a puddle around his feet and his vision blurred.

Breathe slow, breathe deep, he told himself, and then grabbed for a chair just before a tide of blackness and nausea washed over him.

76

San Quirico D'Orcia, Tuscany

Nancy ran to the edge of the terrace where Zack's trike lay abandoned and the garden fell away by more than twelve feet.

She could see nothing.

Panic set in.

Without even thinking about her own safety, she scrambled down the loose soil and into the deep crater. Surely to God he hadn't come down here on his own? And then she remembered how she'd once found him dancing on top of her dressing table after she'd left him in the bedroom for just a moment while she went to the toilet in the en-suite bathroom.

With three-year-olds, anything was possible.

'Zack! Zack, are you down here, honey?' she shouted.

Nancy peered into the darkness of the old workings that they'd discovered beneath the garden, the narrow opening to the cave-like area that she had hoped might contain an underground well or spa, the area she now hoped was shallow and bereft of anything that might endanger her son.

'Zack!' she shouted again.

Nancy squeezed her way into the narrow opening. She squinted and stared as hard as she could.

Finally, in the fetid darkness, she could see him. She could just distinguish the outline of her child's face.

He looked terrified.

She moved slowly towards him. 'It's all right, darling, Mommy's here,' she said. But, as she inched forward, the blood froze in her veins.

Zack's hands were bound in front of him. Around his neck was a noose.

77

Brooklyn, New York

By the time Howie returned, Jack had managed something of a recovery.

'You look white as a sheet, buddy, you okay?' asked Howie.

'Maybe a bit too warm in here, place lacks fresh air,' said Jack, keen to brush away the moment and get on with things. 'You got some keys for me?'

Howie fished in his jacket and threw over his car keys. 'Take it easy, eh?'

Jack nodded and headed out to the parking lot.

The clock was ticking.

They both knew they were in a critical race against time, in which the prize was a young woman's life.

Forty-eight hours max – that's what the doctor who'd seen the tapes had said that she had.

Just forty-eight hours.

Jack had no status in the Bureau any more, no shield and no gun; Howie would have to pull together the briefings and assemble the teams on his own. He would be updating Marsh, and they'd be making a call to the NYPD to bring their top brass up to speed. They in turn would assign officers from the

ESU, their equivalent of a SWAT team, and ultimately there'd be an FBI-led joint Strike Team. Jack had also suggested bringing in Josh Benson and Lou Chester, two instructors who ran Rodman's Neck, the force's specialist training base in the Bronx. Chester was about the best sniper in the world and Benson ran the most gruelling of urban-training scenarios; when it came to storming buildings and saving hostages he didn't just have the T-shirt, he *was* the T-shirt. Officers would be canvassing all the areas that Jack and Howie had pinpointed as likely to afford BRK the kind of cover he needed. Jack, meanwhile, was on his way to Marine Park. It was a vast area that lay between Mill Basin and Gerritsen Beach, straddling NYPD's 61st and 63rd Precincts, and was pretty low on the crime stats. The place had originally been a Dutch settlement and was home to the first tidal mill in America. Since then, the huge tract of marshland, parkland, bog, swamp and agricultural fields had been shaped beyond recognition. The area had also become home for many of New York's Italians and Jews, who lived in housing that had been mainly built sixty or seventy years ago.

Jack headed north up Gerritsen, cruising around the corners of Cyrus, Florence and Channel. At the bottom he turned right on to Fillmore and snaked his way around East 33rd and 34th. He lost his way a little and found himself out towards the Kings Plaza Shopping Mall. He cursed a couple of times and then doubled back and went up and down Hendrickson and Coleman from where he could see golf carts trundling over the velvet greens of Marine Park's vast golf course. Jack was frustrated. He got out of the car and looked around. Despite the warmth of the day a strong breeze blew in from somewhere out towards Jamaica Bay, and he hoped the fresh air would do him good, would prevent that nauseous feeling creeping up on him again.

The area was civilized and decent, respectable and well groomed. It wasn't rolling in money, but it certainly wasn't dog-rough poor either. In short, it was the kind of neighbourhood where people minded their own business and kept themselves to themselves. He's not here, thought Jack, it's too open, too many houses, and too many windows to be seen from.

Jack's mind swam with thoughts; images of the naked, dying girl, suspended in the blackness of some fearful room – a room surely not far from where he was?

He sat back in the car and made notes, then started to drive back the route he'd come. He was cruising past a whole street of people out manicuring their lawns and washing their cars, when his cell rang. It was Howie.

'Got a possible for you.'

'Go on,' said Jack, pulling over again and grabbing his notepad.

'Fernandez has been through the letting agencies.' Nultkins, a very old agency in Brooklyn, has been letting the same place for almost twenty years. The landlord is a single man, and the tenants' records show he has only ever let it out to other single men. It fits your profile to a T.'

Jack felt a shiver of excitement run through him. 'I've got a pen, shoot me the address.'

78

San Quirico D'Orcia, Tuscany

The rope suddenly pulls tight around Zack's neck, as though it has been thrown over something in the blackness and he is about to be hanged from it.

'Do as I say or I'll kill him,' says the voice of a man she can't see.

Nancy's eyes stay locked on her son's face.

She is starting to see better in the darkness, her vision adjusting to the lack of light. 'I'll do whatever you want, just please don't hurt my baby,' she pleads.

Zack's face is streaked with dirt because he's been crying and Nancy can see he is in pain and frightened beyond belief. She desperately wants to run to him and hold him tightly to her.

'Take two slow steps forward and then turn around so you're facing towards the daylight,' Spider tells her. 'Then put your hands together behind your back.'

Nancy takes one last look at Zack before obeying. She thinks how brave he is, not to be screaming. As she steps forward she's horrified to see that Zack's mouth is plastered with thick parcel tape and he's struggling to breathe.

'Don't hurt him, please. Please don't hurt my baby,' she begs again.

Spider doesn't answer. Pleas for help or mercy are things he never hears. He wraps the sticky parcel tape quickly around her wrists and hands, then slips a Stanley knife from his pocket, thumbs out the razor-sharp triangular blade and slices the tape off.

Is this the kind of thing Jack talked about? Is this how rape and murder start? My God, what will happen to my child?

Spider loops his arms around her and stretches tape across her mouth. She instinctively jerks her head away, and the tape ends up stuck half across her nose and half across her mouth. Spider rips the tape away and Nancy screams.

'Bad Sugar!' he shouts at her and slaps her face.

Nancy cries out but the tape comes again, smothering her scream. She can barely breathe, and desperately sucks in air through her nose.

Spider uses his knife to slice away the tape. Then he holds her by her bound hands and reaches down in the darkness for something.

Suddenly Nancy feels a stabbing pain in the top of her leg as Spider jams a hypodermic needle deep into the vein and leaves it dangling there. He looks at it as a hunter would proudly savour the sight of the spear that felled his prey.

Penetrate. Deep, deep!

He squeezes the last of the Lidocaine from the chamber and wonders whether the dose will be as effective as he wants.

Or whether it will be too strong, and will kill her.

79

Marine Park, Brooklyn, New York

Jack tried to look as touristy as possible. He grabbed the map book he had been using, put on his shades and got out of Howie's car. He walked down the side of the road opposite the target house that Fernandez had identified. It stood at a T-junction to a dead-end street. Jack walked straight past on the other side of the road, his face turned away, the shades and map helping him get to the cover of a house that he hoped would serve as an observation post for him. He turned up a narrow driveway to his right and knocked on the door. A small woman in her late sixties answered. She had curly white hair, gold glasses and looked as though she could play the role of grandma in any film you'd care to cast. 'Good morning,' he said.

'I'm not buying anything,' cackled the woman.

Jack smiled. 'I'm not selling anything, Ma'am. My name is Jack King and I need your help.' He reached into his pocket and took out Howie's business card. 'I'm a former FBI agent and I'm working with this man, trying to help him solve a very serious crime, and I need to come into your house to do it.'

'You're not coming in here,' said the old lady,

pushing the card back at him. 'You're one of those confidence tricksters. I know your type.'

Jack's cell phone rang in his pocket but he ignored it. 'Please. Please take the card,' he pleaded. 'I'm really not one of the bad guys. Take it, and go back inside your house, lock the door and call this man. He'll tell you why the FBI needs your help. I'll just wait here.'

The woman lifted her glasses and looked into Jack's face.

'Please, Ma'am,' he said again.

She grabbed the card, went inside and he heard her lock the door. It was painful for Jack to wait, and hard to resist the urge to spin round and check out the house almost directly behind his back, the house that might hold the dying girl. He'd noticed that all the properties around him were big enough to have basements. The area felt right. It was the kind of place a killer like BRK would choose.

The old lady's door opened and she reappeared. 'Come in,' she said, in a far more pleasant tone.

Jack stepped inside and let her close the door. The hall smelled of boiled potatoes and cheap meat.

'I'm just having some coffee, Mr King, would you like some?'

'I'd love some,' said Jack, relieved to be inside, 'but first I really have to ask you some questions and then I need you to take me upstairs to your bedroom.'

The old lady smiled. It had been a long time since Yoana Grinsberg had let a handsome stranger into her home and he'd been eager to go straight upstairs.

80

San Quirico D'Orcia, Tuscany

Terry McLeod was starting to get pissed off.

Apart from Maria, the dumb but pretty girl on reception, the whole place seemed empty. God damn it! If he really had been from a hotel and restaurant magazine, he'd be giving this place a minus five for service.

Lunch had finished some time back and McLeod found the dining room deserted. It had been fully cleared of all dirty crockery, cutlery and tablecloths.

He pressed on with his search, and came across a laundry cart full of dirty linen by the back stairs, so he guessed the couple of chambermaids they employed were busy on an upper floor, stripping bedding and collecting used towels.

He pushed open the flap-hinged service door to the kitchen. A teenage boy in an apron, red-faced from his labours, looked up from mopping the floor. '*Sì?*' he said.

'Hi there. I'm looking for Mrs King. Any idea where I might find her?'

Giuseppe stopped mopping and shrugged. Then, as an afterthought, he said, 'Signora King, she may be in the garden with her son.'

'Okay, thanks,' said McLeod. 'Can I go that way?' he added, pointing at the kitchen door that led into the private gardens.

Giuseppe moved protectively in front of it, holding the mop like a weapon. 'No, not that way, I'm sorry. That's private. Wait in reception and I will tell Mrs King you want her.'

McLeod glared at him. God damn it, minus ten was too generous for this place. If he had his way, he'd have the whole friggin' place shut down.

81

Spider manhandles his prey deeper into the darkness.

He'd spent days stalking the King woman and her child, following them at a safe distance, noticing and timing their movements, studying the way the free-spirited child wandered off from the over-busy mother who was constantly torn between attending to her business and carrying out her maternal duties.

Spider followed their car in the old Fiat motor-home he'd bought for the purposes of abducting, killing and then dismembering the young woman he'd targeted in Livorno. The motor-home meant he did not have to rent villas or check into hotels. It gave him untraceable freedom and the opportunity to spend time with his victims. The girl in Livorno had been killed in there. He smiled as he remembered how well that little escapade had gone. The surprising fun that had come with what was only ever going to be a functional kill. It had been early evening and he'd been parked up on a quiet country lane, doing a recce of the area when, through his rear-view mirror, he had seen her walking, red-faced from jogging, heading towards the back of the van. He was excited by how beautiful she looked.

Just your type. Dark hair, slight build, nice shape. Mother would approve.

He got out, taking a road atlas with him. He could see that there was no one around, no prying eyes to save her. He waved the road atlas and explained that he and his wife were lost, could she show him on the map where they were. He unlocked the back door of the motor-home to get some light, and handed her the atlas. As she traced a finger over the page, he grabbed her from behind, a well chloroformed handkerchief stopping her struggle as he bundled her into the van.

He'd planned to do the same with the King woman, but she was not so foolish. She was never alone. Except at night.

For the past few days, as Nancy and Zack had slept in their beds, Spider had been less than a hundred metres away from them, quietly preparing the underground area in their garden for what he was about to do. Here in the damp, stinking darkness he's hidden the tools of his trade: some specially customized electronics, several lengths of rope, thick coils of heavy-duty tape, a selection of razor-sharp knives, a sixteen-inch bone saw and a gun. The firearm came from Rome's Porta Portese. What the locals call *mercato delle pulci*. It has more than four thousand stalls, most of them trading illegally. It's not only Europe's biggest flea market, it's one of the continent's best-known one-stop shops for anything from counterfeit clothing to drugs and guns.

Spider shines his flashlight and can see that the Lidocaine is starting to act on King's wife. Her legs are beginning to buckle beneath her. Soon, the anaesthetic will rob her of the ability to move, let alone walk. He pushes her and the child on, deeper into the blackness of the catacomb, closer to their fate.

82

Marine Park, Brooklyn, New York

Jack stood impatiently in Yoana Grinsberg's small kitchen, while she insisted on boiling the kettle again.

'How can I help?' she said, excited by the idea of being involved with the FBI. Jack was praying she was going to give him the right answers to his questions and give them to him quickly. 'Do you know the man across the road? The guy in number fifteen?'

'Can't say I do. I've seen him from time to time. Never spoke to him once, though.'

'How long has he been living around here?' asked Jack, sensing he had to play a patient game with the old lady.

Yoana frowned so deeply that her face became completely corrugated with wrinkles. 'Fifteen, maybe twenty years. Fancy that. All that time and we've never so much as exchanged the time of day.'

The pieces were coming together. Jack fished a little further. 'Does he drive a yellow car, a four-door Japanese model, probably about three to four years old?'

Yoana shook her head. 'No, not him, that wouldn't be his car.'

'You sure?'

'I know my cars,' said Yoana, smiling as memories flooded back. 'Cars have fascinated me since I was a child. My husband once had a Buick. An Oldsmobile; beautiful it was. I think the stupid company has stopped making them these days.'

Jack's heart sank. Still, she was quite old and could be wrong. 'You really are sure?' he persisted.

'Positive,' said Yoana. 'The man across the road has a Hyundai, but that's South Korean not Japanese. And anyway it's white not yellow. I don't know of any Japanese cars around here. Mr Cohen had one . . .'

Jack cut her off. 'I'm sorry to stop you. But it might be our mistake. It is a Hyundai that we're looking for. Do you know exactly what type he has?'

Yoana didn't hesitate. 'Hyundai Accent SE. Nothing special, not even alloy wheels. I always thought that was a bit odd.'

'Why?' asked Jack gently. 'What was odd?'

'Well,' began Yoana hesitantly. 'Well, like I just said, I don't know his name, he never seems to be around and I've never met him, but he's always got personalized plates on his car. I used to think he was a car dealer of some sort, but then I noticed that sometimes he even changed the plates before he changed the cars.'

Jack felt a surge of excitement. His phone rang again, but he ignored it once more. Whoever it was, whatever they wanted, it couldn't be as important as this. 'Yoana, you don't know what plate he currently has, do you?'

She smiled. She liked helping the FBI, they asked such easy questions. 'Don't be silly. Sure I do. It's B – 898989.'

83

San Quirico D'Orcia, Tuscany

The entrance floor of the catacomb is covered in soft soil but, after you walk about twenty feet through the narrow gap, the surface underfoot changes into hard rock, cinder and compacted earth. Spider shines his flashlight up the walls. They are damp and green from an underwater stream that dribbles down from the hillside above them. He is searching for the point where the narrow route dog-legs left and opens up into a much wider, high-ceilinged chamber dominated by a raised marble tomb. The air gradually loses its last vestiges of freshness, as they move deeper into the sterile darkness where nothing grows. Spider feels perfectly at home amid the dank smell of infertile land. The smell of death.

He pushes the woman and child to the back of the catacomb and forces them to sit with their backs to the tomb, which contains the remains of a soldier and his family from Medici times.

Little Zack, his hands still bound in front of him, crawls over to his mother and puts his head on her knees, desperate for protection and reassurance. Nancy's wrists are still tied viciously tight behind her back, but her real pain comes from being unable to comfort or touch her son. She bends her body over the top of him and rubs her face against his back, like an animal nuzzling her injured young.

Spider clicks his laptop off standby. It hums into life and instantly locks in on the hotel's wi-fi hot spot, located almost directly above his head. He glides through Webmail and logs on to his own intranet system.

As the computer monitor fills with an overhead camera shot of Lu Zagalsky's body, he sees her face and shivers with anticipation. Not long now. Soon all that waiting will be deliciously rewarded. A tingle spreads from his neck, down the sweat forming on his spine.

He pulls Zack's young body away from his helpless mother, his eyes hardly ever leaving the image on the screen.

Spider senses death in the air.

Multiple death.

84

Marine Park, Brooklyn, New York

898989

The numberplate is the same as the code that BRK had given to Daher to access the video footage. Jack pumps his memory. What does it remind him of?

HA! HA! HA!

That's what it reminds him of. H is the eighth letter of the alphabet, but the ninth is not A. And then Jack has it.

Hi, Hi, Hi.

BRK was saying hello. Another of his fucking sick jokes.

Jack calls Howie with what he's just discovered and learns it will take another half an hour for the Strike Team to be fully mobilized and in position at Marine Park. He hopes the delay won't prove fatal.

Yoana Grinsberg talks all the time, as she guides him upstairs to her front bedroom, from where he hopes to be able to keep a watch on number 15. The room, full of old clothes and magazines, is far too warm. A bowl of stale pot pourri that should have been replaced months ago makes the place smell earthy. Jack notices double locks on the windows and guesses that the ultra-cautious Mrs Grinsberg hasn't opened them since her husband died years back. He pushes his face to the glass. Even if he unlocked one the view would be useless. A cluster of overgrown trees on both corners blocks the line of sight, there's no way he could get even a half-decent view of the target house.

'It's no good,' he says, heading out of the room and back down the stairs, 'but thanks anyway, Ma'am. Your cooperation has been appreciated.'

As she shuts the door, Jack thinks how he might have to use Howie's car to block the road if it turns out BRK is in the house, gets spooked and suddenly makes a run for it. While he's working out this end-game scenario, his cell phone rings again.

Nancy's cell number flashes on the display.

Jack's in trouble and he knows it. She's going to go crazy if it turns out that it's her calls he's been ignoring.

'Hello,' he says, frowning as he braces himself for the eruption.

'Hello, Jack,' says a male voice, drawing out the words slowly.

'Who is this?' He checks the caller display again.

Spider lets out a short laugh. 'Oh, I think you know who it is, don't you?'

A bomb of white-hot pain detonates in Jack's head. He struggles to think the unthinkable.

'Your wife's here with me. Would you like to talk to her?' Spider rips the sticky tape from Nancy's mouth, and she gasps loudly for breath. 'Jack!' she says weakly. 'Jack, he's got Zack and . . .'

Spider puts his hand across her lips. 'I'm sorry, Mr King, but your wife's not at her best at the moment. I've shot her full of drugs, so she finds it a little difficult to talk.' He traps the phone between his ear and shoulder, and replaces the tape around Nancy's mouth. 'You know, Jack, you really should take better care of your young family. Shouldn't you?'

Jack says nothing. His head is pounding and he feels sick. Don't upset him, one wrong word and they're both dead. Stay detached, be professional, not emotional.

'Answer my question!' demands Spider. 'I said: shouldn't you take better care of your family?'

Jack understands the game, and he knows he has no choice but to play along. 'Yes,' he says, feigning humility. 'I should have taken more care of them. My family's very precious to me. I'll do whatever you want, but you have to promise me you're not going to hurt them.'

'No promises,' says Spider, 'but it is good for me to hear that you and I share the same sense of family values.'

Jack squeezes his eyes shut and prays his mind will clear, that he will be able to stay sharp and cope with whatever is about to happen.

'I see you're in the road near my house in Brooklyn,' says Spider, looking at the laptop and its exterior camera views. 'Well done, you're a little earlier than

I expected. I had planned to lead you there myself, when the time was right. When the world had witnessed another murder that Jack King was powerless to stop.'

Jack's thrown. He glances across to the nearby house, searching for a camera.

'In the trees, King. The cameras are wired up in the trees and powered by my outdoor security lights.' Spider gazes at Nancy and Zack, then back to the image of Jack on his laptop. 'My plan was that in twenty-four hours' time that nice Arab news channel would be showing some new material; something of a double scoop. First I would have given them the final fatal instalment in the story of the wretched little Russian hooker that you and the fools in the FBI couldn't save. And then, Jack, then I had something even juicier in mind.' Spider laughs darkly and fixes his eyes on Jack's face, before adding, 'I thought the next exclusive footage could be the death of your lovely wife.'

Jack's self-restraint snaps. 'If you so much as harm . . .'

'Tut, tut, Jacky boy. Don't ruin all your good work, all your professional restraint, by being abusive. You must know that I'm going to kill her, otherwise there would have been no point in bringing you all the way to America, and me coming all the way here to Italy, would there?'

Jack's heart is beating double-quick time, as he realizes now that he has been the victim of BRK's carefully orchestrated plan to lure him away from his family and have him stand impotently by as they are slaughtered. But why?

Spider smiles as he watches Jack painfully putting the pieces together. 'You've been played like a sucker, King. The murder in Italy was merely a ruse to drag you out from your cowardly hiding place, and of course you came, like an obedient, scalded dog. Then poor, sweet Sugar needed to rise from her grave just so I could be certain that your dumb-ass buddies in the FBI would have no doubts that I was back at work. And finally, I added some live bait to bring you skulking back to the city you ran away from. So here we are, a little sooner than I anticipated, but almost exactly as I planned.'

'Why are you doing this?' asks Jack, fighting back another wave of nausea. 'I don't understand why my family is of any interest to you.'

'Aaah, Jack. If only you knew how long I have waited for you to ask that question.' Again the long pause fizzes out, before Spider continues, 'Does the name Richard Jones mean anything to you?'

Jack can't place it. His brain Googles 'Richard Jones'; maybe 'Dick Jones' or 'Dickie Jones'? Nothing comes back. 'I'm sorry. The name means nothing to me.'

'I didn't think it would,' says Spider. 'But it means everything to me. And I mean everything. Thirty years ago, Richard Jones was killed in a car accident. He was run over by a police cruiser turning out on a false 911. Can you imagine that? The cops killed him, chasing a crime that hadn't even happened.'

The name begins to ring a dim and discordant bell in Jack's aching memory.

'Richard Jones,' says Spider, his voice starting to break with emotion, 'was my father. He was killed just weeks after his wife, my mother, died from cancer. That murdering fucking cop left me an orphan, stranded me in this stinking life without any parents and forced me to live in a flea-pit orphanage. Have you worked it all out yet, Mr FBI man? That killer behind the steering wheel, that moron cop who never even had his knuckles rapped for murdering my father, was your old man. Do you understand now?'

Jack slowly starts to make sense of it all. Fragments of his family history flicker through his mind, but he can't form the full picture. Another bomb explodes in his brain. He covers his face with his hands and leans against Howie's car. The pain is unbearable and he is frightened of passing out.

'My father,' sobs Spider, 'was hit so hard by that police cruiser, that by the time his body stopped rolling across the highway, and the traffic had stopped running over him, his head was completely detached from his body. Can you imagine that? Can you?'

Jack is speechless, his mind frozen in shock, his nerves blistering from old pains, his senses over-whelmed and close to shut-down.

Spider wipes his eyes with the back of his hand and looks again at Nancy and Zack. She's now fully unconscious and the boy has pressed his body tight against her. Even though he's still gagged, Spider can see the child is whimpering like a frightened dog. He turns his attention back to the phone. 'I know you're stupid, King, so I'll fill in the rest for you. I saw your old man's retirement feature in the newspaper. At first I thought it was something about you. I'm sure you guessed that I read all your clippings and follow all the nonsense you spout about getting close to catching me, which by the way is horse shit. And then I looked again. And even though you're in the picture along with lots of other cops, I see it's about your father.'

Spider watches Jack on the monitor, pleased that he's visibly distressed. 'What you probably don't know, Jackie boy, is that the NYPD never publicly named the driver of the car that killed my father. So, imagine how I felt to read this piece, in which your old man goes on and on about the wonderful career he'd had, but how he'd trade all his commendations and promotions to have been able to have avoided just one traffic accident thirty years ago in Brooklyn, an accident that had killed a young pedestrian.'

Slowly, Jack remembers his father's retirement day and how his dad had mentioned that he felt guilty even though it had clearly been an accident. He had still wanted to say sorry publicly to wipe the slate clean.

'I'm sorry for your loss,' says Jack, with no hint of sincerity.

'Thank you,' says Spider, sarcastically. 'That means a lot to me, because I know you lost your own father in a similarly tragic accident. How long ago is it now? About five years, right?'

Jack's face shows the shock he just felt.

'Oh, how I'd love to be standing in front of you right now,' says Spider, leaning closer to the laptop. 'I really wish I could look you in the eyes and tell you exactly what it felt like to hear your old pa bump under *my* car's wheels, and hear his skull pop like a watermelon.'

Jack's head buzzes with static, his knees shake as the shock sinks in.

Spider holds the computer screen, determined to enjoy the power of the moment. He drums the fingers of his uninjured hand on the side of the screen. 'And Brenda, your mother, tell me, do you still think about her?'

Jack looks confused.

'Oh, come on, Mr Policeman. Did you really think she died in her sleep of a heart attack? P-leeeease.' Spider watches Jack clutch his head with both hands, overwhelmed by confusion and anguish. 'Afraid not. That was me again. You should never have left her alone in that big old house, now should you? Any caring son would have moved her in with you and your lovely wife here.' Spider pauses, so the full impact of his words can be felt. 'No matter. You have other worries now. Because shortly, I am going to kill your wife. And then I'll tell you what fate awaits your son.'

Rage roars inside Jack, and the anger triggers a surge of adrenaline through his body. His mind clears a little. Stay professional – keep him talking. As soon as he stops talking, he's going to start killing. Ask him something – anything!

'Why?' Jack says. The nausea dies back, he feels back in control. 'I don't understand why you want to hurt my wife and child.'

Spider rubs a bead of sweat from his face. 'Let me tell you something. Your father took everything from me. He left me orphaned, and probably made me what I am today. He ruined my past, present and future. Now I'm going to do that to your family.' Spider glances down at Zack and sees the child's head still buried beneath the protection of his mother's arm. 'I've killed your parents, now I'm going to kill your wife, and then you are going to die, trying to save your son. A fitting end for you. And this little boy here, well, his future is going to be filled with all the anguish, all the pain and loss that I suffered. He's going to wake every morning without any parents, and he's going to wonder why such a thing should ever have happened to him.'

Jack's temper snaps. 'You fucking monster!' His head is as clear as a bell now. He steps towards a remote camera fixed in the tree above him. 'I promise you, I will track you down to the ends of the fucking earth and I will kill you.'

Spider snorts out a shallow laugh. 'You fool, don't you realize, your earth ends today. You're out of time.'

A noise down the street distracts Jack and a second later the first of the NYPD cruisers slides around the corner.

'Does your wife love you, Jack? All those women, they all loved me. They loved me so much that they gave their very lives for me. What man could ever ask for anything more than that? And now yours is going to die for you.'

The first car screeches to a stop and Jack raises a halting hand as Howie's big frame emerges from the passenger side.

Spider's eyes flick back to the laptop monitor. 'I see your friends are here already. That's good; it means we can start the party. We're done talking now, and we can finish all this.'

Howie walks up to Jack, staying quiet and looking worried.

Jack covers the mouthpiece of his phone. 'It's him. He has Nancy and Zack, and he's going to kill them. Back off!'

Howie walks back to the others. Jack knows he'll notify the command vehicle and that everything will be put on hold until the situation becomes clearer and hopefully less risky.

'Inside my house you'll find the little hooker you've been looking for. And because you've been surprisingly clever in finding your way here, I'm going to reward you. I'm going to let *you* kill her. I'm going to let you put your hands around her throat and squeeze the last breath out of her body.'

'You're crazy,' says Jack. 'This isn't going to happen.'

'No, no, I'm not crazy, not at all. A trifle cruel perhaps, but certainly not mad. And it *is* going to happen, because if you don't kill her, then I'll mutilate your son as well as kill your wife. Maybe I'll let him see his mother die first, but then I'll cut him up a little, certainly enough to give him a personal, visible reminder of our time together. Perhaps you can imagine which parts of him I'm thinking of taking away?'

Jack's heart bangs in his chest. He smashes a clenched fist against the wing of Howie's car.

Spider smiles as he watches on the computer link. 'Temper, temper, Jacky boy. Now let's get on with this. You only have five minutes to carry out the kill. Take any longer and I'll start using my knife and saw on your wife and child. You'll be able to see it all on the Internet a little later in the day. Technology is amazing, isn't it? What a shame I don't have time to tell you all the tale of the Spider and his Web.'

Jack stumbles around the car, pure rage and hate firing his determination.

'Oh, and a few last rules. Leave your phone on; you know I'm going to want to talk to you. To make it a little more interesting, I should tell you there are booby traps in the house. I can trigger them from here, or you can trigger them, accidentally, from there. And finally, remember, if you don't make it to the girl and kill her, I'll blow you both up and then I'll finish my business here. Is that clear?'

'Yes. Yes, it's clear,' says Jack, spitting out the words.

'Good,' says Spider. 'My mother always told me to take a ten count before doing anything really big. So, here we go. Ten!'

Jack frantically tries to work out the situation.

'Nine.'

Ludmila may already be dead.

'Eight.'

If she isn't, BRK is hardly likely to let us both leave the house alive.

'Seven.'

It's possible that she isn't even in there, and this is another one of his sick stunts.

'Six.'

She may be in there, and the house may not be rigged with explosives; he might just be bluffing.

'Five.'

The house may be rigged with explosives and he may blow the whole damn thing up as soon as I step inside.

'Four.'

Will he really maim Zack? Is there any chance at all I can save my son from the agony and injuries that he says he'll inflict?

'Three.'

Whatever happens, he says he's going to kill Nancy.

'Two.'
My family is my world, my life, my everything.
'One.'
Please God don't let me fail them.
'Zero.'

85

'Howie! Howie! Give me your fuckin' gun!' shouts Jack.

The FBI man doesn't question what's happening, he unholsters his automatic and throws it to him.

Jack jams the pistol in his belt, sprints around the corner of the cul-de-sac and reaches the front of the house.

A big double garage at the end of the short drive faces him.

It's undoubtedly locked.

That leaves a solid wooden front door and a bay window that may both be rigged to explode.

It has to be the window.

The curtains are drawn.

Drawn curtains can hide a nasty surprise.

Jack spins around and checks the garden.

Ornamental rocks around a flowerbed. They will do.

He picks the largest and shot-putts it through the lower pane of the window. He stands back.

Nothing.

The window frame and the floor behind it must be safe.

Jack tears off his jacket, wraps it around his right forearm and uses it to batter out enough glass to squeeze his body through.

If he'd had time, he would have cleaned away the glass and put his jacket down on the jagged edges while he climbs in.

But there is no time.

He hauls himself up and feels shards of glass spike into his hands and knees as he clambers through.

He beats off the curtain as it wraps itself around him but it clings tight and sends him tumbling clumsily to the floor.

By Jack's reckoning he's already lost a minute of the five he's been given.

Two hundred and forty seconds left. That's all.

The room he's in is completely empty of furniture or carpeting. He runs across the wooden floor and pauses at the door.

It's locked.

And Jack is sure it's wired as well.

He stands back, releases the safety on Howie's gun and empties a shot into each of the hinge areas.

Nothing happens.

He levels the pistol at the lock and lets off another round.

There is a loud explosion.

The door bursts into flames and metal pieces of the lock fly at Jack like shrapnel.

Something rips into the side of his face, stinging and burning.

He feels his knees buckle and reaches out a hand.

Spider watches with amusement.

One minute and twenty seconds gone.

King may just reach the girl in time. Now won't that be interesting!

Spider shakes Nancy. 'Wake up and watch! You're about to see your failure-of-a-husband fail again.'

Nancy is groggy. Her eyes can barely focus on the computer's screen.

Jack, be careful. Please don't die. Please don't let us die.

Her thoughts are all muddled. She is dizzy and everything is blurred and spinning.

The anaesthetic swirls inside her, dragging her into a sickly fog of unconsciousness.

Zack, where's Zack? Where's my baby?

Jack steadies himself, then plunges through the flames.

Where?

Where next?

The lounge is empty.

He can see the room leads off into a kitchen and he starts to move that way.

This must surely lead to the garage and the stairs to the basement must be back there somewhere.

The kitchen has three doors.

One into the garden?

One into the garage?

And the third one? Into the basement?

Jack studies door three. He presumes it's locked. He quickly examines the door's round handle. It's brass and entirely unlike the others he's just seen.

It doesn't fit, Jack. Brass is the best conductor of electricity you can have. He's wired that handle to the mains. Touch that and you'll be cooked alive.

The door is thick pine; he knows he can't take it out with his shoulder.

Jack glances around the kitchen. The worktops are empty except for a knife block and a red plastic bowl for washing pots in.

The bowl!

He grabs it and fills it with water. Then, with Howie's gun tucked back into his belt, he stands well clear and throws the water over the handle of the door.

Somewhere behind the door he hears a crackle, then a 'phudd', which he hopes is the sound of an electrical appliance short-circuiting.

It's safe.

Isn't it?

If he's wrong, then Jack knows the water on the floor and around the door will help electrocute him.

It's a risk he has to take.

He pulls out Howie's Glock and blows away the brass handle and lock.

Four more shots take care of the heavy hinges.

Jack kicks at the slab of splintered pine and it gives

way, tumbling into the blackness that leads into the basement.

Jack steps over the threshold.

Into the darkness.

Spider checks his watch.

Two minutes gone.

'Look! Jacky boy is really trying. Sweet, isn't it?' He pulls Nancy's hair and pushes her face towards the computer screen.

Nancy stays unconscious. The anaesthetic has soaked into her brain and she's blacked out. Her body is limp and unaware of what's happening to her, her husband or her child.

'Wake up! Wake up and watch, you fucking bitch!' Spider slaps her. 'You fucking whorebitch, you're supposed to see this.' Anger erupts inside him. He wants to smash the computer into her miserable face. He wants to use the knife. He needs to carve her up and ease the pain that's awake and starting to crawl around inside him.

Kill her now, and the pain will go!

No!

Control yourself.

You know you have to control yourself. Mother will help you.

Mother is nearby.

You can kill the woman later.

Kill her slowly.

Kill her nicely.

But not now.

Right now, forget about her and the child and watch Jack King die.

The splintered door slides down the basement stairs like a runaway sledge. It smashes into something hidden in the darkness and slams to a stop.

Another door, guesses Jack. It's hit a second door at the bottom of the stairs that will be locked too.

And remember the girl is tied up. What are you going to free her with?

Jack quickly steps back into the kitchen and grabs a large carving knife from the wooden block on the worktop. He returns to the basement steps, his feet feeling their way down through the blackness.

The door in front of you will also be wired. Careful you don't touch it. Careful you don't touch the walls either, there may be a handrail that's rigged to a second electrical device inside the basement itself.

Jack takes another step down the creaking wooden steps.

And then another.

Suddenly, the ground goes from beneath him. The whole staircase collapses.

Jack's head smashes against something hard. A dull agony thumps through his back and chest. Nausea overwhelms him and he feels his mind going slack.

Fight it! Fight it! You have to stay conscious.

*

Spider laughs louder than he's done since he was a kid.

This is wonderful!

Pure slapstick!

The fool is like a clown in a circus, falling over things with perfect timing.

He glances at his watch.

Three minutes gone.

'I don't think Hubby is going to make it,' he says to Nancy, who is still unconscious.

'A shame you can't see this. Your man's final humiliation. It really is something to behold.'

Something even more delicious occurs to Spider.

He can make the child watch.

Yes, somehow that is even more fitting.

The child of Jack King forced to watch his own father's humiliation and death.

Thank you, Mother, you always make things work out for the best.

Spider reaches for the boy.

But he isn't there.

The child is gone.

Jack has no idea how far he's fallen. The only thing he's certain of is that he dropped both the knife and the gun as he crashed through the disappearing staircase.

Time. You're running out of time!

He drags himself to his feet.

He can see light.

He's facing the wrong way. He's looking back up

the stairs towards the kitchen. Jack turns around and waits a couple of seconds to steady himself and let his eyes adjust to the darkness in front of him.

Slowly the blackness becomes greyness and he can just about make out the basement door. He reaches down and feels the area around his feet.

His hand touches splintered wood.

Concentrate, Jack. Time is running out.

Jack wills all his feelings to the tip of his fingers.

Dirt, ground, wood, dust – metal.

Metal!

He has the knife.

He feels around for its blade.

Time, Jack. Time is running out!

Jack puts his hand down again.

No gun.

He can't find the gun.

He stops searching and pulls himself up and out of the broken stairway.

In front of him, only inches away, is the basement door.

And behind it, the life or death of Ludmila Zagalsky.

Jack takes a deep breath and fears that it might be the last one he ever draws.

If the door is wired, it's all over.

He crashes his shoulder against the wooden slab.

It doesn't move.

He dives deep into his reservoir of mental strength and powers his entire weight into his shoulder.

The door creaks.

Jack goes again.

He feels it move, but only fractionally.

'Aaargh!' screams Jack, as he drives all his weight and effort into the door.

The lock bursts and he falls headlong into the room. His hands and knees slide along the black plastic sheeting.

Jesus Christ! What is this? Where the fuck am I?

Jack stands up and sees the walls and ceiling are also lined with the black sheeting. It's as though he's suddenly tumbled into one of his own nightmares. And then he sees her. The naked, dying body of Ludmila Zagalsky, spreadeagled before him. The woman he's been instructed to kill.

Spider makes no effort to chase after the child. Instead, his finger hovers over the button on the remote detonator, itching to trigger the electronic charges and blow the house to kingdom come.

He watches as Jack checks the girl's chains and smiles as he sees him discover that they're attached to thick, metal hoops that are screwed into the basement's concrete floor.

Four minutes gone.

Spider turns the detonator over and over in his hand.

Wait, Spider. It will be all the more special if you control yourself and wait.

'That's my knife, King,' he says jokingly as the light

glints off the steel in Jack's hand. 'You really have no right to be borrowing things without my permission.'

Spider watches eagerly as Jack cuts through the leather restraints on Sugar's hands and legs.

He's not going to kill her; the fool is going to free her, just as expected.

He glances once more at Nancy and sees she's still unconscious.

'Wake up!' He'd like her conscious when he kills her. Maybe kills her at the same time he kills her husband.

Nancy's eyelids flicker. She has nice lips, he notices, nice and sweet to kiss as he sucks the last breath from her body.

He shuffles the remote in his hand. 'Wake up!' Spider pulls Nancy upright.

Her eyes open a fraction. Just enough for Spider to see that she's coming round, and for him to get his finger over the right button.

Terry McLeod isn't about to be told what to do by some kitchen boy with a mop. He walks back through the hotel and then stomps his way to the fenced-off area marked Private.

Respect – kids today have no respect.

He reaches over the small gate, flips the catch and pushes it open.

Mrs King, I have to admit, I've not been honest with you. I am not actually a tourist, in fact I'm an internationally acclaimed travel writer and photographer, and I'm here to do a feature on your fine establishment. Now, I would just like to ask you a few questions.

McLeod rehearses his lines and is confident she will be putty in his hands – providing he can find her. The kitchen boy said he was certain she was in the garden, so in the garden she must be. He searches the orchard and the pretty herb area boxed off with clipped privet hedging.

Nothing.

Then he searches the vegetable garden, carefully making his way through the onions, tomatoes, cucumbers and radishes. He comes to the patch where the ground falls away. It isn't new to him; he'd spotted it through his binoculars as he'd settled into his rocky hide on the distant hillside, and he'd seen it close up when she'd discovered him prowling her grounds. But what he sees now shocks him to his core.

Down on the soil below him is the King child.

His mouth is bound with parcel tape. His hands are tied in front of him. And around his neck is a length of rope.

Jack cuts the final restraint.

He knows he's reached the point of no return. Can he really do what's been demanded of him, and kill her? Will taking her life really save his son?

What choice is there?

The only thing that Jack is certain of is that his

own life and that of the poor girl lying limply in front of him are now dangling on a thread.

Knowing that his every move is being watched, Jack turns slowly around, looking for a camera. He sees one almost at head height, on a wall to the right of him.

He pulls out the phone, flicks off the hold button and traps it between his shoulder and ear. 'Jones, can you hear me?'

For a moment there's silence, and Jack wonders if it's because the killer is surprised by hearing his real name being used.

'I hear you, Jack,' says Spider, looking down at his watch.

Four minutes and fifty seconds.

'You've got ten seconds to kill the girl.'

'The game's changed. Let me hear my wife and child, and then I'll kill this girl any way you want. I don't care about her, just let my family go.'

Spider studies Jack on the monitor and sees desperation etched into every line on his face.

Could he really kill her? Maybe, just maybe. The love of a parent is so strong; it's possible that he'll do anything, even kill the woman he's been trying to save, just to have a chance of keeping his son alive.

'Listen closely,' says Spider. He yanks the tape from Nancy's mouth and holds the cell phone close to her as he grabs a handful of hair and pulls it out in one vicious tug.

Jack winces as he hears Nancy scream. He feels

another rush of adrenaline and anger inside him. 'Now my son. I want to hear my son.'

Even though he knows he's gone, Spider instinctively glances across the darkness of the catacomb. 'No deal, King. Get on with it. Or the next thing you'll hear down this phone is the sound of me killing your wife, then you'll hear your son, you'll hear him screaming under my knife.'

Jack drops the phone.

Do it now! he tells himself. He fumbles around on the black plastic-covered floor, seemingly taking an age to pick up the phone. Nothing, nothing in the world matters to him as much as the lives of his wife and child.

Jack stares into the camera, his eyes brimming with hate, his mind throbbing with fear and confusion.

He walks around to the far side of the bondage table so the camera can clearly see both him and the girl.

Do it! This is your only chance to keep them alive.

Spider leans closer to the monitor.

Jack uses his left hand to brush hair from Lu's neck and then he tilts her head back. 'God, please forgive me for this,' he says. Slowly, he draws the razor-sharp kitchen knife in a bloody cut, straight across her throat.

Spider's face is only inches from the monitor screen but he still can't believe what he sees. He gasps as the reality of what has happened sinks in.

Jack King has cut her throat.

The blood is flowing. It's all over him.

He's cut her throat.

McLeod scrambles into the crater beneath him and rushes to the child.

Mary Mother of God, who could do something like this?

'It's okay, son, don't worry. It's all going to be all right.'

The child's eyes are wide with panic. His face is crimson and McLeod can see his chest heaving as he struggles to breathe.

The sticky parcel tape has been looped several times around the boy's mouth and is plastered to his hair. There isn't going to be any painless way of removing this. McLeod turns Zack around and searches for the end of the tape. He finds an overlap near the back of the youngster's right ear. He scratches at it with his fingernails until a flap lifts.

'Sorry, little man, this is going to hurt a bit.'

McLeod grips the child tight with his left arm and begins to pull the tape free. The first loop comes off easily because it is virtually doubled over itself but the final circle of tape yanks clumps of fine blond hair out of the back of the child's head. Zack's whole body jerks with pain as the tape is torn away.

McLeod holds him by his shaking shoulders and looks straight at him. 'Be brave, little guy, just a bit more and it'll be off your face.'

The kid is wild-eyed with fright and McLeod knows the best thing to do now is to get it over with as quickly as possible.

He puts one hand against Zack's face and peels off the last of the wide, heavy-duty tape.

Zack starts crying and gasping for air as soon as the tape comes free of his mouth.

'M-m-m-mommy!' he sobs and McLeod holds him tight.

Gradually the child's crying begins to subside and McLeod wipes his face and comforts him. 'It's okay, son. I'm going to get this nasty tape off your hands, and then we'll find your mom.'

'P-please help Mommy,' pleads Zack.

'Where is she?' asks McLeod, getting a finger hold on the tape around the youngster's wrists. 'Where's your mom?'

Zack nods towards the thin, black slit in the hillside and his body shakes some more. 'Mommy's in there.'

McLeod drags the last of the tape from the boy's wrists. His skin is red and tender but the hands and wrists don't seem damaged.

'I'm going to help your mommy, Zack,' he says, 'but first, we're going to make you safe. Okay?'

Zack is too scared to respond, his eyes never leaving the gap in the hillside.

McLeod hoists him into his arms and hugs him. Then, still holding him close, he heads back up the soil banking. It's a slow and clumsy climb as the earth shifts and slides beneath his feet.

Breathless, he makes it to the top of the crater and stands Zack up. 'Run to the house, kid! Run and get help.'

McLeod taps Zack on the bottom, and then the child runs as fast as he can towards the safety of the hotel kitchen. McLeod slithers back down the banking once more, determined to find Nancy King.

Spider almost loses track of time as he stares at Jack cradling Lu's bloody head in his hands.

He still can't believe what he's just seen.

He hits a key on the laptop and the camera remotely zooms in on the heavy flow of blood, dripping through Jack's hands and pouring on to the table and floor.

He's cut her jugular. That much blood can only come from a main artery.

On the screen he can see Jack's body shaking as he tries to gulp back the sobs rising from deep within his chest.

Jack takes half a step back and Spider can now clearly see the blood all over Lu's neck and face. Jack slides his right hand under her armpits and his left hand behind her knees, lifts her up and holds her tight in his arms.

A disturbing thought hits Spider. His child. King has not asked about his child.

He glances down at the remote in his left hand.

Something's wrong. He can't have forgotten about his child and his wife.

On screen, Jack falls to his knees, Lu still held tight in his arms. It looks as though he's praying, holding her body and asking forgiveness for what he's done.

Suddenly, a beam of white light blazes across the floor and up into Spider's face.

'Armed police!' shouts a woman's voice. 'Stand up with your hands in the air. Do it, now! Or I'll shoot.'

Orsetta Portinari had ordered local police to keep a routine watching brief on La Casa Strada, just as she'd put similar surveillance on the crime scene in Livorno, the courier points at train stations in Milan and Rome and even the delivery-bay area at their own headquarters.

Her boss had demanded that the Italian investigation now be run entirely separately from the US one, and Orsetta was simply covering all bases and following up on her long-standing hunch that what connected BRK, Italy and America was Jack King himself. And as much as she hated the idea, the only way she could satisfy her curiosity with Jack out of the country, was through another unannounced meeting with his wife.

'Stand up, or I'll shoot!' she says a second time, acutely aware that although she's fully firearms trained, she's never fired a gun outside a range.

Spider slowly rises to his feet. 'All right. Okay. Don't shoot.'

The flashlight beam is bright but narrow. Orsetta

can see his face clearly, but can only make out the vague shape of his shoulders.

In the darkness, she misses a crucial movement.

Spider puts his right hand on the edge of the marble, not to help himself to his feet, as she thinks.

But to pick up his automatic machine pistol.

In one hazy action, he sprays gunfire towards her.

Orsetta moves instinctively, but she's way too slow.

Her right shoulder burns with pain. The impact of the bullet spins her round and drops her to the ground, spilling her own weapon as she falls.

Spider is sure he's hit her several times. She looks motionless but he isn't yet convinced that she's dead.

There's time enough to kill her. He'll finish her off, with a shot through the head. For now though, she's not important.

Spider checks the computer again.

Where's King?

Still praying. Well, Jacky boy, no God known to man is going to save you now.

Without further delay, Spider presses the red trigger button and a thunderous explosion rings out.

86

Jack tightens his grip on Lu and prepares to make his move.

The fingers and palm of his right hand are bleeding intensely from where he cut across them with the kitchen knife as he pretended to fumble for the phone with his back to the camera. Jack knew he had to cut deep for the flow to be fast enough to paint a line of blood across the girl's neck as he faked the motion of cutting her. By cradling Lu in his hands, he was able to smear the blood everywhere and make it look as if she'd been fatally wounded.

Now, on his knees, he knows time is running out every bit as quickly as the blood haemorrhaging from his hand. In one deft movement, he dips his shoulder, falls forward and rolls himself and Ludmila as far underneath the heavy wooden bondage table as he can manage.

They're barely beneath the chrome-legged slab of oak when the explosion rips the room apart.

Jack smothers Ludmila with his big body.

Timber, brick and dust blow everywhere.

Rubble tears into Jack's exposed head and back, belting him like iron baseball bats, smashing his neck, his legs and spine.

He holds Ludmila tight and this time he really does pray.

Spider's computer screen goes grey.

The dust and rubble obliterate his view.

He grabs the laptop and holds it at a different angle, trying to get some kind of picture.

Where are they? I must see their faces!

Spider tingles with the electricity of expectation.

Where are their bodies?

He'd fixed the cameras in the basement in re-inforced glass housings designed by film crews to withstand explosions and even train crashes.

He peers closely at the plasma screen.

Slowly, it fills with flames of vivid red and orange.

The fires of hell. May the flames consume King's stinking body.

Spider puts the computer down.

They're dead. King and the girl are dead.

Now I can finish off the policewoman and King's wife.

Spider looks over at Nancy, and then Orsetta. They're both lying down, curled up in near foetal positions.

Lambs to the slaughter.

He turns to pick up his pistol.

But he never makes it.

The first bullet hits him in the face.

His ears are still ringing with the sound of the

gunshot when the second and third shots tear holes in his stomach.

Spider falls backwards, his head cracking against the tombstone.

The fourth and fifth bullets splinter his ribcage and rip his heart to pulp.

Only when he is absolutely certain that the man is dead, does Terry McLeod drop the policewoman's Beretta.

Howie Baumguard and the ESU team were still holding back when the blast went off.

Howie had figured that BRK was running the show from remote cameras and he didn't dare give a 'strike command' that might endanger the lives of Jack and Lu Zagalsky.

But after the explosion, all bets were off.

The ESU team works, as usual, from a Radio Emergency Patrol truck, but even basic REPs are perfectly equipped for sieges and small building blasts. As Howie rushes towards the scene of the explosion, the small arms troops are at his side, and the rescue unit is already unbolting a variety of tools from the truck, such as fire extinguishers, metal cutters and the kind of inflatable airbags that can be used to lift heavy weights off bodies.

Lead officers with high-powered search beams on their weapons go in first. Behind them come their armed cover and then the Extrication Squad.

At the first sight of flames, the ranks part and the

guys with extinguishers lay down a blanket of foam.

Seconds later, when the gas boiler explodes, the heartbeats of the ESU team barely jump. It's something they'd been expecting.

Clouds of foam instantaneously smother the flames. There's no sign of panic. Howie Baumguard steps aside and calmly lets the experts do their work. He's seen the ESU magicians pull people out of mangled metal in multiple car crashes, bomb explosions and building collapses. They're the best. They've worked everywhere from the Oklahoma bombing to the hurricane in New Orleans. If anyone can get Jack and Lu out of this mess alive, it's them.

'Get some portable light in here!' someone shouts.

Through the flashlight, dust and plaster spins in the brick-coated red mist as expert eyes roam over the rubble.

Less than two yards from the door is a pyramid of timber and breeze block.

'More foam!' an officer shouts as a fire flares again near the doorway.

At the top of the basement stairs stands Bernie, the one specialist member of ESU that Howie doesn't want to see deployed.

Bernie is a bloodhound.

And Bernie's expertise is cadaver recovery.

Orsetta has taken two bullets in the muscle of her right shoulder and is bleeding badly. The fall knocked her unconscious. Now, as she comes round, she is too disorientated to move. In the movies, hero cops get shot and then simply carry on running as if they've suffered a bee sting. In real life, things are different. Most shootings blow you off your feet and you stay down until paramedics scrape you up and take you away. Orsetta struggles even to sit upright.

'Are you okay?' asks McLeod, both hands still around the pistol, now pointing at the ground.

Orsetta nods. For a moment she is unable even to find her voice.

'He's dead. I think he's dead.' McLeod waves his gun towards the body sprawled against the tomb.

Orsetta forces herself to stand up by sliding her back against the wall.

Finally she manages to talk, her voice croaky but calm. 'I'm a police officer . . . Please give me the gun.' Rather awkwardly, she pulls her ID card from her back pocket. 'Hand it to me very carefully,' she adds.

McLeod is an expert shot. He's killed deer, rabbits and all manner of birds, but he's never shot a human being before. Now his hands are shaking as badly as if he were mixing a cocktail. He takes hold of the pistol by its barrel and hands it to Orsetta. The policewoman checks it and then levels it at Spider's crumpled body.

She's taking no chances. One twitch from the motherfucking son of a bitch and she'll empty the rest of the magazine into him.

'Further back,' she says to McLeod, 'there is a

woman on the ground, please go and help her. I will watch him.'

'Sure, yeah, sure,' says McLeod nervously. He heads around the tomb and immediately recognizes the collapsed body as Nancy King.

Orsetta hears voices and footsteps behind her, coming from the entrance to the catacomb. She realizes that her hearing has been affected by the gunfire. She feels her head start to spin and her sense of balance slip away.

Through the fog she makes out that the voices are speaking Italian. We're safe, she tells herself.

The crackle of a police radio echoes through the catacombs and then beams from several flashlights illuminate the blackness. Someone tells her that everything is going to be all right. A hand reassuringly touches her and fingers gently prise the gun from her grasp. In the glare of a flashlight she sees McLeod start to remove tape from Nancy King's hands.

Then her mind goes slack and she allows herself to collapse.

It takes them twenty minutes to find Jack and Lu's bodies in the rubble of the building.

'Over here!' shouts ESU veteran Wayne Harvey. 'They're beneath this fall.' The blast has brought down parts of the ceiling and water is flooding in from ruptured pipes that have been ripped from the walls. The electricity is out and bright beams and helmet lights cross each other as people scramble towards Harvey. A dozen hands claw at the heap of bricks, wood and breeze blocks.

'I see someone!' he shouts, looking down on Lu Zagalsky's bloodied, naked and unconscious body.

The bondage table has taken most of the force of the blast, the slab of heavy oak not cracking and only the legs of the table finally buckling from the weight of the ceiling fall.

Howie Baumguard tears the table away and sees Jack's twisted torso lying protectively across the girl.

'Oxygen and stretchers!' shouts Harvey, taking off a glove to feel for a pulse on Lu's neck. He glances at his watch. 'She's alive, but only just. Get her covered up and outta here, quick as you can.'

'It's okay, buddy, we've got you,' says Howie, kneeling in the wreckage next to Jack, pawing away hunks of concrete as if they were unwanted cushions on his sofa. 'We'll have you out of this shit in no time.'

Jack is barely conscious and still too shocked and dazed to speak.

'Fuck, man! That's bad!' says Howie, suddenly spotting his friend's injured hand. 'Paramedic! We need someone over here, quick, fucking quick!'

'On my way!' replies a calm voice from somewhere off in the darkness. A beam of helmet light flashes in Howie's eyes, blinding him for a second, then the distinctive west coast voice of Pat O'Brien is next to him. 'I see him. Stand back and let me get in there.'

Howie steps aside and stumbles, his ankle twisting on the unseen jags of bricks and blocks.

'He's bleeding like fuckery,' he says, pointing. 'Look at his hand, his right hand.'

O'Brien aims the light down, takes one look and knows instantly what to do. He slips a rucksack off his shoulder, snaps on latex gloves and quickly blots the wound with an antiseptic pad so he can see the 'three S's': the size, shape and severity of the cut.

'Your buddy's right, you've got a main bleed here, my friend,' says O'Brien, turning Jack's hand in his own, wondering how much blood the guy might have lost. Another quick dip in the medi-sac produces a tourniquet, sterile spray and suture kit. The gash is still pumping and is filled with grit and dust. He sluices it with the sterile spray, picks out what fragments he can with his little finger and then dives in with the needle and thread. His ESU training didn't stretch to needlepoint, but if ever the Mother's Circle hold a battlefield category, O'Brien's odds-on favourite to win it.

Jack's eyes are fixed on the girl as they lift her on to a stretcher and attach a drip to her arm. He recalls the nightmare he'd had at the Holiday Inn, when he'd dreamt of saving her and how the room had been full with medics and cops, just like this. He digs deeper into the vaults of his memory and pulls out footage from the other nightmares, images of a black room, an autopsy scene, the water pipes and the blood on the floor. Like the shrink had said, for years his subconscious hadn't rested, it had still been puzzling over the crime scene, processing the psychological profiles, still trying to force him to forget about mundane distractions and return to the case.

'Get me a backboard over here and some lifters!' shouts O'Brien across the room.

'He okay?' asks Howie, hovering a few feet away.

'Should be,' says O'Brien.

'I'm fine,' manages Jack, his voice raw and full of dust.

O'Brien shines his light in Jack's eyes, pulls the lids wide and checks the state of dilation. 'Yeah, you're going to be okay. You've lost a bucket of blood, but then you're a big guy, so you've got some to spare.'

Jack lifts his undamaged hand and motions Howie to lean close to him. 'Look, I know this place is all fucked up, but get them to preserve what they can. Anything. Get Forensics in here as quickly as possible. This is it; this is the place where he cut up some of his victims. I've seen this hell-hole in my nightmares; make sure we get something out of it.' Howie looks around at the wreckage. It's as bad as a Beirut bombsite, but he knows CSU will find something; no offender can ever get rid of everything.

O'Brien pulls Howie to one side as his colleagues arrive and slip the backboard into place and start manoeuvring Jack on to it. 'He needs some shots. Tetanus, the full works,' he says to the lifting team. 'Keep an eye on the bleed, I've only tacked the deeper cuts across the fingers, they'll be able to open them up in the hospital and do a proper clean.'

The lifters nod, heave Jack up to waist height on

the creaking backboard and head for the door. Lu Zagalsky's now up top, covered by blankets and an ESU coat, being rushed to a waiting helicopter on the nearby golf course. Paramedics have managed to get an intravenous hydration drip into a vein and the word among the crew is that she's got a good chance of making it, though it's likely to be another twenty-four hours before medics know whether she'll be left with any permanent disabilities such as renal failure.

Jack's fully conscious by the time they get him outside. He squints at the sunlight and slowly sucks in the fresh air. He sees Howie emerging from the blackness and waves a hand again for him to come closer. 'Nancy, Zack, are they . . .' His voice chokes on him.

Howie finishes the sentence. 'They're okay, they're both absolutely fine.'

Jack swallows and feels the leaden fear sink to the pit of his stomach. 'And BRK?'

'Dead as the dodo. I don't know all the details, but some saintly soul shot him into oblivion.'

'A pity,' says Jack.

'Pity?' queries Howie, frowning.

'Yeah, a big pity. I wanted the pleasure of seeing him rot on Death Row for half a decade. Then I wanted front-row seats and a popcorn combo while I watched the fucker fry.'

Orsetta can barely stand unaided, but still manages to kick Spider's bullet-riddled corpse before paramedics shuttle her, Nancy and Zack into a helicopter waiting to airlift them to a hospital in Siena.

Once they're in the air, the medics clamp off Orsetta's shoulder bleed and give Nancy pure oxygen to help her get over the effects of the Lidocaine. Within a few minutes she's clear-headed enough to understand that Jack is alive. The Tuscan countryside rolls surreally beneath the low-flying copter and she spends the whole journey holding Zack tight to her, neither of them speaking. Her brain is still struggling to make sense of everything that has happened, but one thing she is certain of is that the biggest challenge ahead is going to be helping her son to put today's trauma behind him. The copter banks and she feels queasy as they come into land. She is desperate to hear her husband's voice and learn exactly what state he is in. And when she's sure he is okay, absolutely okay, then she's also desperate to remind him that today is Sunday the eighth of July. Their wedding anniversary.

But she knows all the teasing will have to wait. For now, she doesn't even have a phone. It still lies in the blood-soaked darkness of the catacombs next to the dead body of America's most feared serial killer.

EPILOGUE
Three months later

What does not destroy me, makes me stronger.
Friedrich Nietzsche

San Quirico D'Orcia, Tuscany

For the first time in the three and a half years that they've been here, La Casa Strada is free of tourists and strangers. That's not to say that all its rooms aren't fully occupied.

The celebration party was Nancy's idea. And everyone is agreed that it is a very fine one.

It is still warm enough to take drinks on the terrace overlooking the historic, undulating beauty of the Val D'Orcia, and several guests stand together finding peace and beauty in the views they're blessed with. Massimo, Orsetta, Benito and Roberto have travelled up from Rome, and they stand huddled in a group, babbling Italian at machine-gun speed as waitresses serve them the finest wines that Tuscany can offer. Terry McLeod has been invited back, and this time he hasn't needed to cheat or lie his way into the action.

Nancy glances at the one area that still gives her discomfort. As soon as the forensic teams had gone from her garden, she'd brought in Mr Capello, his team of landscapers and their equipment. She had the entrance to the catacombs sealed up with enough ready-mixed concrete to cover Manhattan, but the blocked-up catacombs still give her the shivers. Her eyes fall on her son Zack, riding his trike across the terrace, making sure he never leaves her sight. Since the incident he's been quieter than his parents had ever known and he still insists on sleeping in their bed every night. But he's on the mend and in bright sunshine, playing noisily, a smile returns to his face.

Her home is a crime scene no more. And she never wants to be reminded that it once was.

Nancy leaves Jack's arm for a moment to check in the kitchen on how long dinner is going to be. Paolo is preparing a special six-course feast, ending with Jack's favourite *Zabaoine*. The aroma of roasting pork drifts in the early autumnal air, sharpening the appetites of the waiting guests.

Howie has repeatedly declined the local wines, and instead has drunk everyone's quota of Bud. He's come alone, but lives in hope that he and Carrie might get back together in time for Christmas.

FBI Field Office Director Joe Marsh cleared his diary and crossed the Atlantic to be here. Jack awkwardly holds out his left hand as they greet each other in a corner on the sunlit terrace. His right hand is still heavily strapped and is going to need physiotherapy to repair the nerve damage caused by the knife wound.

'Still hurting?' asks Marsh as they get chatting.

'Some,' says Jack, slowly wriggling the end of his fingers. 'But not as much as my pride.'

464

Marsh looks at him quizzically. 'Meaning?'

'Well, to tell the truth, I'm still blaming myself for not reading BRK's strategy. If I had done, then I would have saved us all a lot of grief.' He looks up to make sure Nancy isn't nearby; he's been given strict instructions not to talk about the case. 'BRK staged the Kearney incident because he hadn't killed for a while and he feared that we had forgotten him. By picking the twentieth anniversary of when Sarah's body was found, he was fairly certain we'd put it down to him, but just to make sure, he wrote my name on the package containing her skull.' Jack pauses while Marsh takes a drink from a tray offered by a passing waitress. 'BRK gambled that the incident would reactivate the FBI investigation and put him back centre stage. Just as he gambled that if he killed in Livorno, it would be close enough for the Italians to come and try to persuade me to stop sitting around playing at hotels and get involved in the police case.' Jack nods towards the group of Italian detectives. 'Orsetta was right, I was the elephant in the room, I just couldn't see it.'

Marsh frowns. 'You were an elephant?'

Jack smiles. 'Yeah, I was the link between the US, Italy, Sarah Kearney, BRK and the Barbuggiani girl, only I couldn't see it. For years people had been telling me to stop taking the BRK case personally, so I guess I had.'

Marsh agrees and takes a sip of his white wine. 'Whereas, in hindsight, we know that this last affair *was* personal. BRK was intent on getting you back to New York, to kill you in his father's old house, and at the same time to attack your unprotected family.'

'Yeah, that's about it. He had us all chasing around in America, while the big show was about to go down in Italy.' Jack grimaces as he thinks how close the serial killer had come to adding to his death toll. 'And let's not forget that this sick fuck would have enjoyed planning all that. He would have fantasized for years about carrying out these killings, and I guess Sarah's anniversary gave him the nudge to try to push fantasy into reality.'

'Almost ready,' shouts Nancy, her eyes fixed disapprovingly on Jack and Marsh.

Carlo quietly makes his way over to his boss and whispers discreetly in her ear, in the way that only the best of maître d's can manage. She nods and instructs her waitresses to top up everyone's glasses.

'Ladies and gentlemen,' says Nancy, raising her voice to grab their attention, 'Jack and I want to say a special thank you to you all for coming here. I think you know that you all now have a unique place in our hearts. But before we raise our glasses and toast the wonderful fact that we are all alive and healthy, I want you to give a very warm welcome to our most special guest of all.' She waits a beat and then waves a hand back towards the hotel.

All heads turn.

Down the patio, walking gingerly with the aid of

crutches, comes Ludmila Zagalsky. Her face reveals the widest and happiest of smiles.

Half a step behind her walks a tall young Chechen man with a kindly smile and a steadying hand.

As the applause dies down, Joe Marsh checks that he can't be overheard and then puts his hand on his host's shoulder. 'Jack, I'll give this to you straight, I need you back on the team. We've got a case over in the States that we really could do with your help on.'

If you enjoyed **SPIDER**,

read on for a taster of Michael Morley's next novel,

NECROPOLIS

(Published by Penguin in early 2009)

The Bay of Naples

If nineteen-year-old Francesca De Lauro hadn't been so desperately shy she could have made a fortune as a centrefold. Tall and curvaceous, with hair as black as midnight, she had hypnotic blue-green eyes that were seldom bold enough to settle on another person for more than a second. On the rare occasions they did, she left an indelible memory.

They were fixed now on the man in front of her as he unzipped his trousers and looked hungrily towards her.

They were outside, in sweet-smelling summer woodland and Francesca's faultless skin was backlit by the golden flicker of a newly lit fire.

But this was no romantic encounter.

This was the worst moment of her life.

Slowly, but inevitably, the flames around her feet reached the metal stake that she'd been tied to. The fire surged vertically, a vicious roar of agonizing heat. Wind tugged at her hair and the rising flames flexed like the jaws of a giant orange dragon. Francesca twisted hopelessly, the white-hot lashes searing her paraffin-soaked skin.

He stood barely ten feet away, mesmerized by the slow murder, stroking himself pleasurably, his eyes fixed on the curtain of flames, through which he peeped at the beautiful, dying woman.

This would take time. A long time. He planned to enjoy every second.

Francesca had been tied with coils of wire around her feet, hands and neck. He'd learned from past mistakes. Rope burned, then they tried to get away. He didn't want any more messiness. No mistakes this time.

Bricks had been stacked in a waist-high, horse-shoe shape around her. A kiln to funnel heat up her body. His eyes never left the dying woman. He knew exactly what was about to happen. His timing would be perfect. The thick tape around Francesca's mouth melted away. She instinctively sucked in air and tried to scream with what was left of her lungs.

The gun in his right hand kicked his palm. The silencer coughed a single bullet through the crisp night air.

It tore into the darkness of Francesca's mouth and ripped out the back of her skull.

Her head hung limply on her chest, flames ate her hair, the smell of burning flesh carried in the cold night air. The smell would have made most people gag, but he sucked it in.

Amid the crackle of the fire he waited, listening intently, searching for the moment when he heard her skull crack and sizzle.

Popping chestnuts! How he just loved to peel away those crisp, burnt outer shells.

He'd removed all her jewellery and while he watched, he played with it in his pocket, turning the trophies over and over in his hand.

The blaze burned brightly enough to illuminate the pit that he stood in. It was almost twelve feet deep, twenty-feet wide and fifty feet long. It had originally been dug by the landowner as foundations for a house that never got built.

Dead dreams.

These days it was more commonly used to burn some of the overflowing rubbish that clogged the city's vermin-infested streets.

He stayed until blackness had faded seamlessly into the first grey of dawn, then he raised a gleaming stainless-steel spade and began softly singing a tune that had been with him since childhood.

When the stars make you drool joost-a like pasta fazool, that's amore;

He scraped Francesca's bones from the blackened wood, grey ash and red embers. Then slammed the blade of his spade across the snake of her spine.

When you dance down the street with a cloud at your feet, you're in love;

The metal sliced through shinbone and ankle bone –

When you walk in a dream but you know you're not dreamin', signore,

– through skull and hip joints –

'Scusa me, but you see, back in old Napoli, that's amore.

– through fingers, toes, wrists and knees, in fact every major joint that he could spot.

He searched the scorched ground, making sure he'd been his usual thorough self.

No messiness, no mistakes.

And then he chopped again. This time he used a small hand-axe on the troublesome hip, cleaving away at the sacrum, coccyx, ischium and pubis. Most small enough to bury, some small enough to keep – just a little souvenir or two, a moment's sentimentality!

He was dripping with sweat when he climbed out of the pit, carrying Francesca's young life in two dented steel buckets, her total existence reduced to ash and broken bones; ash that blew away in the wind as he walked to his car.

Would her beauty have stayed with her into her forties, fifties or sixties? Would her children have inherited those magical eyes? The ponderings amused him as he drove her to her resting place. The place that only he would visit. The sacred spot where he laid them all to rest.

He dug again, the blood-red sunrise painting his skin as he upended Francesca's remains into a shallow grave. He slapped the old steel buckets with his hand and cleared the last of the dust – the last of Francesca – that stuck to the sides. A couple of the smashed bones were still larger than he liked, so he stomped them into the earth.

The first blue hues of morning fought their way into the angry sky as he completed the burial. He bent his head, closed his eyes and slowly prayed:

'*Domine, Jesu Christie, Rex Gloria, libera animas omnium fidelium defunctorum de poenis inferni et de profundo lacu.*'

Before leaving, he urinated on the freshly dug grave; partly because he had to, partly because he liked to. As he zipped up, he wondered whether God would indeed heed his prayer to free the soul of the faithfully departed from infernal punishment and the horrors of the deep pit. But then again, he asked himself, *did he really give a fuck?*

Poggioreale Jail, Naples

Five Years Later

Half a decade ago, when Bruno Valsi was jailed, two of his arresting officers were shot in the knees in front of their wives and children. The message was clear. The Camorra would brutally punish anyone who crossed them.

Valsi, the twenty-seven-year-old son-in-law of Camorra Don, Fredo Finelli, had been found guilty of three charges of intimidating and assaulting witnesses. Although the police nailed him, years of work spent building a case against his father-in-law were ruined. All but one of the Finelli witnesses withdrew testimonies, or simply vanished.

All but one.

And one day – *one day soon* – Valsi would find her and make her pay.

Three guards marched Bruno Valsi into the discharge area for him to collect his personal effects and prepare to rejoin the outside world.

'*Andate tutti a fanculo.*' He gave them the finger as they watched him try to pull on a black, tailor-made Valentino suit. Prison life had made the trousers too big in the waist and the jacket far too narrow across the chest. Valsi had pumped iron twice a day, every day of the eighteen hundred and twenty-five that he had spent behind bars and the jacket now barely stretched across his rippling shoulders. Prison had made him fitter, meaner and more powerful than he had ever been. And jail hadn't only helped him gain muscle. He'd also added key underworld allegiances that he knew would soon help him build his own Family. Jacket over shoulder, he blinked at the sunlight as he emerged from one of the world's most notorious jails. To the far east rose the clearly visible slopes of Vesuvius and Mount Somma; while up close and all around him were the inner-city slums and the incongruously slick and shiny skyscrapers of the city's thriving commercial and business district. Hardly any of the ultra-modern structures had been built without kickbacks to the Finelli Family or other neighbouring Camorra clans. And once built, none of the businesses ran without paying the *taglio* – the share of the profit demanded by the clans.

Valsi took a long slow breath of the sharp morning air. A line of five black Mercedes saloons waited patiently down Poggioreale Road. He heard the prison gates creak shut behind him, giant bolts slamming and heavy keys turning. Almost in unison the doors of the waiting Mercs swung open and a legion of suited Camorristi stepped out. It wasn't only an act of personal respect; it was a public show of strength and defiance as well. To a man they were all heavily armed. Their weapons were on open display and no one, not the prison, not the police, nor even the army dared test their resolve.

Bruno Valsi soaked up the sight. He then coolly walked over to the one car that stood out, a new chauffer-driven Mercedes Maybach, the type of car that cost more in extras than most people earned in a year. Only when he was a few feet away did his proud and grateful father-in-law step out of the back and embrace and kiss him.

If Don Fredo had known what was on Valsi's mind, he'd have had him shot dead before the prison gates had even shut.

Carnegie Hall,
New York City

'Given the inclement weather, I want to leave you with some chilling thoughts,' Jack King told the audience, as he neared the end of his keynote speech at the International Serial Offender Conference in Carnegie Hall. 'People are like icebergs; we only ever see ten per cent of them. The really interesting – and sometimes deadly – ninety per cent lies mysteriously hidden in the dark waters of personal secrecy.'

Jack peered out from the stage in the Isaac Stern auditorium. Almost three thousand people, spread five tiers high, peered right back at him. 'Bergs are pieces of ice that have broken off from giant glaciers. Similarly, serial killers are people who have broken off from accepted civilized society. Some of these bergs are small fry, they're maybe only a metre high. Others are massive and murderous, reaching up to a hundred and sixty-eight metres, about fifty-five storeys high.'

The select audience was made up entirely of law enforcement officers, psychologists and psychiatrists who'd all paid $500 a ticket to hear Jack and four other expert speakers. Through the stage lights he could see some of them. They were scribbling, fidgeting, frowning and smiling. Some, he guessed, were recalling encounters with their own bergs.

'Serial killers, like those bergs, come in all shapes and sizes. Your job is to spot them early. Catch them after murder one, while they're still small fry. And remember, to do that, you have to concentrate damned hard on that ten per cent that's on view above the surface.'

Jack took a final look around, his gaze sticking for a second on the front row, where one man, thin and pale, stared up at him with black empty eyes that seemed to be hunting for his attention.

'In your investigations, please pay particular attention to these three things. *Thought, Feeling* and *Action*. Right now, right at this moment, you're all doing the same thing. You have a uniformed, shared *Action*. You're all just sitting and watching. That's your visible ten per cent. Your action is very much in full public view. But *Thought* and *Feeling* are complex masses that make up your private ninety per cent and that's what we can't see; that's what you're keeping hidden. A few of you may still be *feeling* shocked or sickened by some of the murder scene slides we looked at earlier, some of you may have been bored or fascinated by them. Whatever your emotions, you've all kept those *feelings* hidden. Similarly, as I come to a close, I know you are almost all *thinking* different things. I hope many of you are *thinking* that your time at this conference has been worthwhile. I'm sure some of you are worrying about how you're going to get home

480

through the snow tonight and I'm confident that they'll be several of you who are thinking, hoping, that your own dark secrets of infidelity, sexual deviation or petty theft from work will never be discovered. Well, don't bank on it, they might well be.'

A wave of embarrassed laughter rose and swelled through the audience. Jack let the tide settle, then finished his speech. 'Remember, everyone's an iceberg, and only ten per cent of each of us is on show. But, with careful examination, we can pretty much guess what the hidden ninety per cent holds. Thank you for your time. I wish you all a Merry Christmas and a very safe journey home.'

Applause rang out, and Jack mouthed several 'thank yous' left and right of stage. As he clapped back and started to head for the exit, his eyes caught again on the thin, pale-faced man staring up at him from the front row. The man with the blank, unblinking gaze. The only person in the auditorium not clapping.

Michael Morley

About Michael Morley

Born in Manchester in 1957, Michael Morley was orphaned at birth and never knew his mother and father. He grew up in care, foster and adoption homes. His first job was as a trainee journalist with the Bury Times Newspaper Group and his subsequent journalistic career has seen him work for Radio City in Liverpool, Piccadilly Radio and BBC Radio Manchester. In TV he was a programme maker and newsreader for Border TV in Carlisle and Central/Carlton TV in the Midlands. He was Editor and Executive Producer of many ITV network productions, including the investigative current affairs show *The Cook Report*. He won numerous international awards, including several Royal Television Awards for his documentaries and current affairs work.

Michael's first marriage produced two sons, Damian and Elliott, who both share their father's life-long addiction to Manchester City FC. He is now married to Donna, a former TV news director, with whom he has one child, Billy. He divides his time between the family home in Derbyshire – a converted farm, complete with ducks, Canadian geese and a growing population of rabbits – and a house in Naarden Vesting, in the Netherlands, where for the past half decade he's worked as a senior TV executive for an international production company.

Interview with Michael Morley

How did the book come about?

I wrote a factual crime book about a decade ago after making a documentary on psychological profiling and the seeds of a first novel have been growing ever since. It's heavily drawn on personal experience, particularly the scenery, the profiling and the characters. (The most personal experiences relate to the food though. Good food, and particularly Italian food, is a passion of mine.)

Can you give examples?

The killer in the novel has many traits that I believe were present in both Robert Berdella, an American serial killer, and Dennis Nilsen, a British serial murderer. I interviewed Berdella at Jefferson City Correctional Center in Kansas where he'd just cheated the death penalty. He was a highly intelligent and sadistic man who kidnapped and tortured to death a number of young people whom he tricked into coming back to his home. His coldness verged upon evil. Along with British psychological profiler Paul Britton, I interviewed Dennis Nilsen in HMP Albany, a maximum security prison on the Isle of Wight. Nilsen's fascination with death was a central psychological part of his murders and again there are echoes of that in the book.

Throughout the thriller you juxtapose the viewpoints of the profiler and the killer. Why did you do that?

I wanted to dramatically convey the feeling of hunter and hunted, so you get some very pacy intercuts between Jack King's profiling and the deeds of the serial killer he's hunting. As the thriller hits a series of twists and turns in the final third the intercuts become more frequent and more dramatic. I hope this conveys the pressure that real investigators feel when they know time is against them and that a critical mistake in the hunt for a serial killer can end up in more lost lives.

Interview with Michael Morley

You have a full-time job in television, how and when do you write?
In the dead of night. When else would you write a thriller? Seriously though, I seldom sleep for more than four hours a night, which is wonderful. It means that I have at least four hours to write. I used to lie in bed, tossing and turning, worrying about how to get extra Z's. Now I just switch on the light and lose myself in whatever story I'm writing. I'd be horrified to find I'd slept eight hours. It would be like finding I'd been burgled.

What about the scenery – New York and Tuscany?
I know both places really well. New York is my best place in the world for a memorable weekend. Tuscany is the best place in the world for a longer stay. I got married in Pienza and honeymooned in San Quirico in Val D'Orcia, the location of Jack and Nancy's hotel. It was a wonderful wedding, with locals turning out in the streets to throw rice and offer us drinks. A magical day with our closest of friends and family. We celebrated my wife's fortieth birthday in New York at a very famous restaurant. I had to pull favours to jump the waiting list but even that didn't stop our eight-year-old falling asleep at the table. It sort of summed New York up – great, but exhausting.

You spent time at the FBI's *Silence of the Lambs* Profiling Unit, didn't you?
They hate that kind of reference. I filmed at the Behavioral Science Unit at Quantico for a documentary I made called *Murder in Mind* and I had the honour to spend quite a lot of time with legendary profilers such as Bob Ressler, the man who first coined the phrase 'serial killer', and Roy Hazelwood, a quietly spoken genius of a man whose observational powers left me gasping. I also interviewed and spent time with people such as Mike Berry, Anne Davies and Don Dovaston, who along with Paul Britton did much to establish and promote offender profiling in the UK and Europe.

Interview with Michael Morley

What are real serial killers like?

Disturbingly human. I've spoken to more than a dozen murderers, ranging from gangland killers to child killers, and from hit-men to serial sex murderers, and all *appear* remarkably normal. Dennis Nilsen, for example, was very bright, articulate and polite. You have to reconcile it with the fact that he was also duplicitous and murderous. Robert Berdella was highly intelligent, ran several businesses before he was jailed (including being the head of the local Neighborhood Watch) and had a very quick (and dark) sense of humour.

Are most serial killers mad or evil?

That question still baffles courtrooms across the globe. I think neither. I think they're *broken*. They're people with damaged personalities who can't be fixed. The big questions are, what broke them and when? I'm not experienced enough to give you great clinical insight into what shapes a serial killer but from the studies and research that I've carried out, there is one factor that stands out more than most, *Love*. Time and time again you see that serial killers lack people in their lives that unreservedly love them, and that they unreservedly love in return. That's not an excuse for their crimes, it's just a fact. There are exceptions, of course, but in general you'll find that these people feel lonely, cut off, cast adrift and uncertain about their emotions.

Where does the fact end and the fiction begin?

Good question. You should see the novel purely as fiction. It draws from factual experiences but it's not supposed to be 100 per cent accurate. And there are reasons for that. Professional profilers will look at sections and say *that's not quite right*. Well, apart from the fact that I've never known two psychologists to agree on much, I'd simply say, *it's not supposed to be*. I spent 15 years of my life working every week with leading police officers and

Interview with Michael Morley

one thing that worried them more than anything was revealing detection techniques that are instructional to criminals. So, with respect to that, I uphold the premise that I'll always keep back or alter a little of the inside secrets that I've been privileged to see. If you keep that in mind, then you can judge for yourself what is true and what is a stretch or alteration of the truth.

Whose books influenced you the most?

Stephen King, Doctor Seuss and Steven Bochco. King for a lesson in how to unchain your imagination and not get frightened when it jumps the gate and runs off into some strange neighbourhood. Seuss for the joy of words, the simple pleasure of seeing sentences become secret songs that sing forever in your mind. Bochco for pace. Read *Death by Hollywood*, but first tie yourself to a fire hydrant because he's going to blow you off your feet and drag your butt at 70mph over rocks and broken glass.

What next for Jack King?

There are many adventures to come. The second Jack King adventure sees him in Naples, investigating a serial killer in the midst of the Camorra, a powerful crime organisation that makes the mafia look like Teletubbies. The action plays out against the Bay of Naples and in particular Vesuvius, the volcano that erupted in 79AD and wiped out the settlements of Pompeii and Herculaneum.

read more
www.penguin.co.uk

Psychological Profiling

The best psychological profilers are usually full-time experts and they play down their skills and are the most modest, well-balanced people I've ever met. They are true geniuses with astonishingly well-developed powers of observation and have very open minds. The worst of them are attention-seeking egomaniacs who attach themselves to high-profile cases purely for personal fame.

Psychological profiling, or offender profiling as it is sometimes called, is not crystal-ball gazing. A profiler can't just look at a crime scene and tell you who the killer is. But a good profiler can use tiny scraps of clues to build a profile – an outline of the characteristics of the offender – that will help investigators sieve all their information and focus all their resources in the right place.

Profiling starts from the understanding that everyone does things in their own particular way. Put simply, a lazy drunk will commit a crime, maybe a murder, in a lazy way. It will probably be unplanned, opportunistic, maybe accidental, possibly alcohol-induced and there'll be enough forensic clues to make three series of *CSI Miami*. A Project Engineer, on the other hand, will carry out a murder in a very organised manner, no doubt pre-selecting the victim, planning everything beforehand and having a very detailed clean-up plan. The crime scene will have few forensic clues. A profiler attending either of these death scenes would instantly be able to draw quite sweeping conclusions, and the forensic evidence (or lack of it) would also enable them to start to decipher the type of criminal responsible.

This is a really simplistic explanation, but nevertheless it's the root of offender profiling. The age, race and sex of the victim are big clues for a profiler – as of course are what has been done to the victim. Murders for sexual gratification indicate a different type of offender than murders for revenge. Attacks from behind indicate a different kind of relationship than attacks from the front. A good profiler takes all these things (and dozens more) into account as they shape the profile of the offender. That profile is always most useful when it can be compared to possible suspects. It's also valuable in helping to focus an investigation when there are no obvious suspects and law enforcement officers have to canvas a wide population. Psychological profiling is often coupled with statistical profiling and geographical profiling to give investigators the best insight into offenders. Many law enforcement officers remain sceptical about geographical profiling but there is increasing evidence that it has a strong value in pulling all the pieces of the jigsaw together.

Encounter with Dennis Nilsen

When I met serial killer Dennis Nilsen in a British prison it had been more than decade since he'd killed the last of at least 15 victims. He looked straight into my eyes, and told me, 'The bodies are all gone, but I still feel a spiritual communion with these people – they are a part of me.'

Psychologist Paul Britton and I interviewed Nilsen at the Maximum Security Albany Prison on the Isle of Wight back in September 1992. It was the first and only time TV cameras had gained access to interview a convicted serial killer in the UK. While in America even the worst offender has the basic right to speak to the press, in Britain that is not the case. The interview was every bit as illuminating as it was historic.

First, the cold, brutal facts: Dennis Andrew Nilsen was a serial killer who manually strangled to death at least 15 men. He masturbated over some of the corpses, washed them and dressed them, spoke to them, watched television with them, kept them under the floorboards of his London home and finally chopped them into small pieces, boiled their body parts in a pot on his stove, burned parts of them in his back garden and tried to flush some of their remains down the drains of his house.

I studied the details of Nilsen's case when I was preparing an internationally shown television documentary on psychological profiling called *Murder in Mind*, and I found myself fascinated, not so much by the monstrous things that he'd done but by *why* he might have done them.

Nilsen was no ordinary serial murderer (if indeed there is such a thing); he was a necrophile, and this breed of murderer is often the most difficult to catch (the very nature of their crimes means they tend to retain their victims' bodies for weeks or months and this gives police little to base their initial investigations on). Nilsen's employment record was also intriguing. It showed that he had been attracted to positions of authority; he'd been a cook in the army, an Executive Officer in the British Civil Service, a very active trade union rep, even a probationary police officer. On the surface, he seemed more dedicated to *helping* people than *killing* them.

For most of his professional life Dennis Nilsen also concealed the fact that he was homosexual. He was in the army for 12 years, from the age of 15 to 27, and used to force himself to laugh along at the jokes about *queers* and *puffs*. I wondered how someone who had exercised such restraint and dealt with such prejudice was unable to restrain his own failings and how he was internally driven to unleash such terrible violence. Were the two things connected? How could someone who was evidently intelligent, disciplined and committed to working for the public good suddenly do something so bad? And, did all those years of concealing his homosexuality help him when later in life he had to conceal much darker secrets?

My first stop in getting to know Nilsen was to meet Brian Masters, a British author who had visited him dozens (if not hundreds) of times in prison and written *Killing for Company*, the definitive book on Nilsen. Masters explained why, long after the publication of his book, he was still trekking across country to visit the killer regularly. 'I feel a responsibility to visit. I have no responsibility for his character or the way he is understood by the world. Whether the world likes him or loathes him is nothing to do with me. My only responsibility is to visit him because he was a great help to me. It would be, I think, morally reprehensible to say to him, "Well thanks very much for all your help and now you can rot."'

While applauding the principle of trust, I couldn't help but remember that Nilsen had no problems betraying the trust of the young men he'd brought home ...

Masters had grown to know Nilsen over a long period of time and had astutely developed the ability to see beyond the 'monster' tag that tabloid writers all too easily hung on him. But their relationship was often tested, especially when the murderer allowed his macabre sense of humour to surface. On one occasion, Masters discussed with him the prospect of collaborating in a film project about his life. Nilsen seemed agreeable, and then added that as a nice twist perhaps the end credits should not read 'Cast in order of Appearance', but rather 'Cast in order of Disappearance'.

Mad or bad? That was the final question I asked Masters, and his reply was as eloquent and incisive as I could have hoped: 'I would say that he was mad in the soul, that's the best way I can think of putting it. He's certainly not mad in the head. He's certainly able to plan, to devise things and to see them through to fruition. He's very articulate when he's talking; he's very funny and can make jokes.'

I personally spent many months corresponding with Dennis Nilsen and I spent two full days in his company. Like Masters, I found I was intrigued by him, much in the way that when you see a terrible road accident you can't help but look at the carnage. You know that what you see may shock or even sicken you, but nevertheless your curiosity gets the better of you.

Encounter with Dennis Nilsen

'Mad in the soul.' The phrase reverberated in my memory as I dug deeper into Nilsen's case history, consulted psychologists on both sides of the Atlantic and wrote to him in prison. After months of intense negotiation with the British Home Office, I received permission to record an interview with Nilsen at Albany.

During my research I had come across Paul Britton, an English psychologist who can legitimately claim to be the first profiler in the UK (his assistance in the hunt and conviction of Paul Bostock is the first and clearest example of psychological profiling being successfully used in policing in Britain).

Britton enthusiastically agreed to help carry out the Nilsen interview. He had been acting as an advisor to the Association of Chief Police Officers and harboured a desire to build a database of interviews with serial killers that would prove as useful as the one compiled by the FBI. I briefed him on everything I knew about Nilsen. I gave him prison letters sent to me by the killer, copious notes I'd made during my meeting with Brian Masters and all my research compiled from court reports and other sources. The psychologist was the perfect choice to ask the questions, while I filmed Nilsen and fed in any questions I thought necessary.

When we turned up at the maximum security prison we were accompanied by two high-ranking police officers (posing as members of my film crew) to make sure everything went as planned. After signing in we were shown through nine sets of barred doors to the jail's Segregation Block, where Nilsen was kept. He'd been badly assaulted while in London's infamous Wormwood Scrubs, his face slashed and scarred, and ever since then had been under special supervision.

Encounter with Dennis Nilsen

Des – as he told us he preferred to be known – appeared in a white T-shirt and faded blue jeans. He confidently shook hands and showed not a twitch of nervousness. 'Who is who? Who am I talking to?' he asked impatiently. I did the introductions and explained that during this visit we wanted to ask him questions as preparation for a full day's filming that we would do tomorrow. He was disappointed and for the next few minutes there was a sharp edge to his mood. That said, it soon became apparent that Nilsen's favourite subject was Nilsen. Without prompting he began to reminisce about his trial at London's most famous criminal court. 'When the shit hit the fan at the Old Bailey it was extraordinary – I was extraordinary, I always have been. I think I am a very rare animal indeed. I don't fit in with the herd.' The following day, we were to find out exactly how rare he was.

Dennis Nilsen told us that he killed his first victim after a night of heavy drinking at his local pub, The Cricklewood Arms. He had persuaded a young Irish man to come home with him and they had drunkenly fallen into bed together. Although no sex had happened, the next morning Nilsen said that when he woke up, he had felt a strong attachment to the stranger sleeping beside him. Nilsen said he had gently run his hands over the man's sleeping body, much as he had done to his brother and sister during his childhood. Then, he said, on the spur of the moment he picked up his tie and decided to strangle his bed mate. In short, he made a hash of it. The man woke up and started choking and thrashing around, so Nilsen had to pull the dying man from the bed, heaving on the end of the tie, using the ever-tightening material as a deadly ligature. They crashed around on the floor and banged into furniture and finally fell into a fatal silence. But Nilsen was still not sure the stranger was dead.

Encounter with Dennis Nilsen

Murder was new to him, he was amateur and unpractised. To ensure the man was dead, he filled a bucket with water and then held his victim's head beneath the water until he was satisfied that there were no air bubbles. He told us, 'After the killing there was this buzzing, buzzing in my mind. The image of him was buzzing all the time.' Nilsen insisted that the murder had been unplanned, purely spontaneous, that he had simply decided to act upon an opportunity to turn a fantasy into reality. Far from feeling shocked, disgusted or even guilty about the murder he'd just committed, he found he was fascinated and excited.

His next task was to move the body and dispose of it. Nilsen said he lifted the young man on to his shoulders and then, as he carried him to the bathroom, he caught sight of himself in a mirror: 'It was such a powerful sight; so powerful seeing myself carrying him like that.' If you picture the scene – one man carrying another – you'll realise that it is a visual image most often associated with someone being saved by a hero. In Nilsen's mind, he'd confusingly cast himself as both hero and villain.

Nilsen chain-smoked throughout the interview and played with his lighter as he added that after the murder he decided that he would bathe the body. 'I don't really know why I washed him. I think I wanted him at his best – for my fantasy. Funnily enough, at this point, I was him. In my mind I was him as well as me.' What Nilsen told us next was probably the most revealing of his early comments: 'I'd felt a compulsive necessity to reduce the person to a passive state. I didn't think at this point that the person was gone – I don't think he was ever there as a person to me.' Put simply, Nilsen saw all his potential victims as objects, and therefore he wasn't psychologically equipped to feel true guilt

or remorse. It was also interesting that he spoke of 'compulsion'; some police officers I know would have labelled it simply as a perverted and evil indulgence.

Nilsen explained how he had then dressed his victim in brand new underwear that he had stored in a bedroom drawer. 'I felt a frisson of excitement. I imagined him doing to me what I was doing to him. I wanted him to be me.' Four hours after the murder that internal excitement boiled over and he confessed to us that he then began to have anal sex with the corpse but it was a disappointing experience: 'I lost my erection because of the coldness of his flesh. It seemed wrong anyway, it spoiled the image of him.' At this point I found myself taking a long slow breath as my mind began to take in the raw data and make sense out of it. Part of me had identified Nilsen as polite and helpful, another part of me was dealing with the facts that he strangled people and had sex with their dead bodies.

Finally Nilsen came to the point when he decided he should dispose of the body. He told us that he had a simple plan – he would use an electric knife and cut it up into small pieces. He would then cook the body parts, flake off the flesh, and dispose of it bit by bit. As a former Army chef, he should have been well equipped to carry out this task, but apparently he made a mess of it. 'I bought an electric knife and a big cooking pot. I paid twelve pounds for the knife and it was useless. I eventually gave it away to a girl in the office.' I wasn't sure what sickened me most, the pictures in my head of the attempted dismemberment, or the fact that he had so willingly passed on the knife to an unsuspecting colleague.

Encounter with Dennis Nilsen

Over the two days that I spent with Nilsen I was in a constant state of shock and learning. Much of what I'd seen and heard from my visits to the FBI offices in Quantico made more sense as Nilsen spoke very openly (and I believe truthfully) about all his victims and his family, his childhood and his lovers. At the end, I shut down the camera and took the small microphone from off his white T-shirt. Nilsen's face was only a few inches from mine. I could smell cheap tobacco on the warmth of his breath, our eyes locked and he smiled. I'm sure he could read my thoughts. I'm certain that he knew I was wondering how few people had been this close to him and had lived to tell the tale.

I packed away the equipment and made small talk, and then I looked across the interview table and noticed that Nilsen now seemed genuinely pained to see us preparing to go. At first I dismissed this as simply that tomorrow he would miss doing something more interesting than the endlessly mundane routine of prison life. Then I realised it was something else, something far more important. He didn't want to be left; he didn't want to feel empty, used, rejected, ignored, all those sensations that had driven him to kill rather than let people walk out of his life.

The heavy metal door of the Segregation Block banged shut behind me and I felt a chill run the full length of my body.

Dennis Nilsen was convicted of the murder of six men and the attempted murder of another two. When he was sent down he was told he would be eligible for parole in 2008.